Jacky

Jacky

Edward Iversen

Order this book online at www.trafford.com

or email orders@trafford.com

Most Trafford titles are also available at major online book retailers.

Printed in the United States of America.

ISBN: 978-1-4269-5418-4 (sc)
ISBN: 978-1-4269-5419-1 (hc)
ISBN: 978-1-4269-5417-7 (e)

Library of Congress Control Number: 2011902023

Trafford rev. 03/08/2011

North America & international
toll-free: 1 888 232 4444 (USA & Canada)
phone: 250 383 6864 • fax: 812 355 4082

Synopsis

This is a story about some people that are brought together, some purposely and some by chance. They all become famous. They get together, work and play Three Star Admiral, still on active duty, Robert (Doc) Hunter. It is now 1951.

Twenty year old Eric meets Bill Turner, an ex-Spitfire pilot and a Reserve Two Star General. Bill is now in the motorcycle business. Eric purchases a bike and gets to know Bill.

Eric's buddy Arch is almost twenty years old, riding his bike down to Phoenix. He meets Dave Steele, a black motorcycle rider. Arch punches out a bigoted restaurant owner, points his bike south again and gets a job on a roofing crew in Phoenix. Arch is invited to a great party on a ranch owned by a fashion house in New York. He party's with a model. He then parties with his landlady, a Mexican beauty.

He heads back north, goes through a dry town, due to the fact that there had been no rain in a year. This town happens to be the watermelon capitol of the nation. No rain, no crop. The rain starts when Arch arrives. People have been praying for rain. They think he is a Messenger from God. The name sticks. The chain locks up on him and Arch and his bike land in a ditch. A Ferrari stops. The driver hits Arch on the head and takes his wallet.

Jacky and her buddy Jimbo witness this. Jimbo helps Arch and Jacky pursues the Ferrari on her 150 mph Black Lighting and captures the crook who is a bail jumper and car thief. Jacky receives an $18,000.00 reward which saves Jacky and Jimbo's motorcycle shop. This is where Arch first meets Jacky who is a decorated Reserve Commando Sergeant. She is unbeatable in hand to hand combat and is also a beautiful, well-built red head.

After a short stay at Jumer's Castle in Bettendorf, Iowa, by request of Iowa State Police, Arch meets with the hotel manager, Laura Mendoza, a sexy Spanish lady. After a brief interlude with Laura, he is on his way to Chicago.

After a free night's stay at the Drake Hotel, with dinner and breakfast, Arch heads to Eric's dad's machine shop. The next day Eric and Arch head to the Lemont Stone Quarry for a swim and observe some girls being attacked. They rescue Janice and Wendy from two Middle Eastern serial rapist killers. They say they have diplomatic immunity and are free from all laws. According to Eric and Arch, they have no immunity and must pay for their sins.

Bill recruits Eric and Arch for a special mission. They are brought to the Admiral's 90' Schooner. The Cora Lee sails to Beaver Island in northern Lake Michigan. They dive with Eric's Sea Sled, looking for some valuable sunken logs which are found, but they also find a sunken twin engine airplane which had bullet holes in the cabin top. The registration number matches a plane that had been missing, with a known whistle blower aboard. Back during WWII, three big officers and two enlisted men made millions of dollars by dealing with pirates, killing the crews and stealing the cargo and sinking the ships. This was done by putting pirates aboard chosen ships in the convoys. The missing ships were blamed on submarines.

Word of the wreckage being found was leaked to a Marine Major General, who was one of the traitors. A Navy Admiral, who was another traitor, showed up to Beaver Island with fifteen armed sailors, to confiscate a sealed case containing damning evidence against these officers. It was aboard the downed plane. The Marine Major General arrived later with twenty armed marines.

Art, the owner of the fishing business on Beaver Island was also an ex-Commando General. Art called Jacky who was in Sturgeon Bay only ninety miles away. Art sent a plane to pick up Jacky and her martial arts students. They disarmed the fifteen sailors and twenty marines. They handcuffed the two traitors and gave them to the FBI. They were then hanged by the neck, along with the third officer, that was found later.

After a great fish boil, the Cora Lee sailed off under the Mackinac Bridge. The crew had lunch and dinner in the Grand Hotel on Mackinac Island then sailed to Sturgeon Bay to deliver Jacky's crew. Jacky sings and dances with Frank Sinatra. Next it is home to Chicago and lunch at The Chicago Yacht Club. The guest speaker is the Clerk of Cook County, Richard J. Daley, who asks what anyone wishes. Jacky wants to see The

Art Institute and the museums. Daley assigns one of his Cook County Sheriff's Police as a tour guide and a county limousine.

While Jacky is sketching the skyline of Chicago from the north side of The Planetarium, three big bruisers grab her escort, duct tape his mouth and handcuff him with his hands behind a tree. These three rapists go to attack Jacky. They surround her and she said, "Don't worry boys I'm not going to run, this looks like fun." The rapists think she is going to like it. She did like it, but not the way they thought. She hated rapists. All three of them got kicked in the groin. Two of them had broken jaws and one had a broken wrist. They all wound up in the Cook County Jail infirmary. The police had been looking for these serial rapists for a few years. They each got 60 years in prison.

The schooner heads out of Monroe Harbor with three blonds singing "Amazing Grace". Jacky is now a blonde, and also has been found to have a great operatic voice. After a couple of interesting stops they finally get to Thousand Islands in Clayton, NY. Mario, the great chef on Cora Lee, shows the locals that Muskie can be smoked.

Jacky, Bill and Arch capture IRA culprits who have kidnapped the daughter of the Irish Ambassador.

Jacky is requested to come to Scotland Yard for a special mission. Four girls, three of them daughters of members of Parliament and one an industrialist's daughter, have been kidnapped. Jacky knows the kidnapper. Previously captured IRA members are convinced to give location of the IRA headquarters. Jacky and three guys go into Ireland and capture the leader and eight of the kidnappers and get them to eat some of the dope they were selling.

After the leader, McPhail, gets both of his big toes shot off by Jacky, he cooperates and tells where the girls are. Jacky and her three guys put the sixteen guys guarding the girls asleep with the powerful sleeping pills Jacky takes from her pocket. They release the four girls, plus forty-five other girls who were to be sold into Asian prostitution rings. Against all odds Jacky always devises a way to defeat her opponents.

They are heroes when they get back to London. Then they fly to Chicago and get a hero's welcome. Jacky marries Bill Turner in a wedding set up by Richard J. Daley in the Holy Name Cathedral where Jacky sings "Ava Maria" at her own wedding. There are twenty-five hundred people at the reception at the Merchandise Mart. All costs are picked up by the people of Chicago. She is considered an Angel in Chicago.

Each of the rescue crew receives a large bonus. They all head for different destinations. Bill and Jacky go for a month long honeymoon on a four engine Boeing Flying Boat chartered by someone named Howard.

This book is about five hundred pages, so this is as much of a description that can be given in a few pages.

For the consumer, this is too much information to be considered a synopsis, but a literary agent or a publisher needs to know what the book is about.

Forward

His name is Eric, which is probably one of the few truthful things in this story. The rest of it is a mixture of fact and twisted fact. Some of it is pure fiction and the rest of it is just a pretty good story. It should be interesting because a lot of it really happened and some of it did not happen. In many instances, I was there.

If you enjoy reading this book as much as I did writing it, then I feel that I have done something good in this world.

Then again if you vote for a politician because he told you what you really wanted to hear and not what he can do, you may be putting your trust in the wrong guy, but I say, "Trust me." The further you get into this story the more interesting it will get. It's about Eric Hansen, his buddy Arch and the great friends he becomes associated with. Eric and his friends and associates go through an unbelievable series of events. Some good some bad. They learn many interesting things and all become heroes in four different countries. To find out how, you have to read the book. It's fun and you won't be able to set it down once you get past those first thirty-five pages. Besides, Eric and his friends are the good guys.

Chapter 1

Eric Meets Bill Turner

Eric Hansen graduated from Westside high school. He was in the class of '48. Eric was glad to get out of high school and started working for his dad. For the last few years he had been working part-time as an apprentice machinist. It is now 1951 and Eric was becoming a pretty good apprentice and in a couple more years he would be a journeyman machinist. And then he would start making some decent money. Right now he was only making .95 cents an hour as an apprentice. So he didn't have a big pile of cash.

He saw an ad in the classified column of the Chicago Tribune. It said "1942 Army surplus Indian Scout motorcycle." It said "cheap", but gave no price.

This bike had a rugged 45 cubic inch displacement engine. It was a great bike to set up for flat track racing or stump jumping or hill climbing. Eric had done stump jumping and hill climbing but it was always on a borrowed bike. This was the bike that he wanted for field meets and hill climbing.

At the present time he did not have his own vehicle. So he used the shop delivery truck, a 1940 half ton pickup. He made a deal with dad that he would do all of the maintenance on the truck and the forklift if he could use the pick up whenever he needed it. His dad also told him that if he found someone who needed machine work he could make some side money since he only made $38 a week, minus taxes & expenses.

The advertisement for the Scout from Bill's Bikes on the 2400 block of W. Armitage Avenue was not too far from his dad's shop. It was Saturday so there was no work in the shop. He liked his 40 hour work week, which gave him time to do other things. He called Bill's Bikes and a lady answered. She said Bill Turner was not in but would be back in an hour. She said that, yes, the Scout was still there. He decided that it was best not to ask the price on the phone. He intended to see the bike first then bargain for the bottom dollar.

Although he had never heard of Bill's Bikes before, Eric climbed into the pickup and headed over there. He only had $95 in his pocket, so he had to negotiate a good price. It was probably like a fly by night used-car lot where they rip you off for a piece of junk and guarantee nothing. It was probably an alley shop and had dealt in repossessed and stolen bikes. He almost decided to forget it and go home.

Instead Eric kept going and made the turn off of Western Avenue onto Armitage Avenue. He almost rear-ended the car in front of him when he saw the most fantastic sign he had ever seen not on this corner or that corner, but right in the middle of the block! The sight was almost unbelievable! It was a neon sign of which the bottom was at least 20 feet off the ground. It was a three times life-size motorcycle hanging out from the side of the building. This was not a fly-by-night outfit .

The ad said "Cheap" but what would an outfit like this consider cheap? Well let's go find out. Eric walked into the show room the size of two storefronts. It was filled with bikes of all kinds; Harleys, Indians, BSA, Norton, BMWs, Ducati's, and a few more. One side of the shop had five or six beautiful custom bikes. Eric was so awestruck by all these bikes that he was almost afraid to ask about a war surplus Scout that was for sale cheap. He started to walk out when someone came up behind him and asked if he could help him.

Eric turned around and for the second time that day he was flabbergasted. Eric stood there with his mouth open when the man said, "No, I am not Rex Harrison," in a perfect English accent. "I may look like him and sound like him but I can assure you I am not him. If I was him, I would be on my yacht in the Caribbean or the Mediterranean. I'm really Bill Turner and if I'm related to Rex Harrison, I don't know about it. Even so I have never missed any of his movies I really should put a sign out saying "No I am not Rex Harrison". I won't do that. By the way what can I do for you?"

Again after seeing the fantastic show room and meeting who he thought was a movie star, Eric hesitated to say that he came about a war surplus Indian Scout, but he asked anyway.

Bill said, "I'm glad you came, let's go take a look at it." They went into the back room which was immense and a beautifully equipped shop. Bill walked over to one of his employees and said, "John, would you please go back to storage and retrieve the Indian." "Okay, Boss." He climbed up on a forklift truck and away he went. Ten minutes later he was back with a crate on the forks. "Here she is; I brought her with me when I came over to the US after the war. I was in the RAF and I used it for transport. I finally decided it should have a new home. What would you plan on doing with her?"

Eric said, "This Scout is a perfect bike for flat track racing with a modified engine, I also may be doing some hill climbing."

"That sounds great; I used to race tourist trophy races. That was the most fun I ever had other than flying a Spitfire during the war. I rode the Isle of Man race twice on a Norton Manx, a hell of a ride but it damn near killed me! Biggest motorcycle race in all of England," said Bill. Bill then asked if he had a place and equipment to do his modifications to the Scout. Eric told him that he worked in his dad's machine shop.

After that Eric said, "I wasn't expecting the Scout to be in that almost new shape. I am not sure that I have enough money to buy her, unless I can make payments?"

"Well" Bill said, "How much money do you have on you?"

"I only have $95 on me." said Eric.

Bills said, "That's exactly the price I was going to charge. But there is one thing."

"Uh oh," Eric thought to himself.

"The low gear in the transmission needs to be replaced and that cost is about $65."

Then Eric thinks that the price gets it up to $160 dollars.

"So now we have a $95 bike, then we take the $95 and deduct $65 and you owe me exactly $30 and the bike is yours. What do you think?" asked Bill.

Eric replies, "Well you sure drive a hard bargain."

"Okay so we got that settled; now you say that you work for your dad and he said you can use the shop facilities to make side money? If that's the case I have a deal for you," stated Bill.

"We buy, sell and repair motorcycles, and the major thing we do is modify and build custom bikes. When building custom bikes, we do a lot of welding and machine work here. We also have a lot of machine work done on the outside.

"Are you interested in making some parts for us?" asked Bill.

"Sure, but I would have to see what it is and determine whether or not it's something I can handle." said Eric.

Bill said, "Come up front in the show room, I saw you looking at a bike. The 1946 Harley 61 cubic inches overhead valve Knucklehead is for sale at $2,600.00. It's yours free and clear if you agree to do some machining for me at a fair rate. As of now I have been paying a shop rate of $10 an hour to my other suppliers. You can work off the $2,600.00 with your machining, if that's agreeable. I'll have the Knucklehead delivered to your dad's shop tomorrow morning. By the way it's got a side car transmission which means a reverse gear."

"It sounds like a great deal," said Eric, "but aren't you taking a big chance on me?"

"I take a lot of chances but I trust my judgment. Is it a deal?" They shook hands and Eric handed Bill $30 for the Scout. They loaded it up on the truck, and he waved goodbye and headed for his dad's shop. He was daydreaming on the way there, thinking of tomorrow and the 1946 Knucklehead.

He pulled up to the loading dock, went inside and opened the overhead door. He then climbed up onto a forklift and drove it out to the dock. He lifted the crate with his Scout in it off the truck and onto the shop floor and closed the shop, got in the truck and drove the 3 miles home. On the way home his brain started to re-engage. He could hardly believe what a day he had! He thought, I'll go home and sleep it off and then when I wake up in the morning I'll find out it was all a dream.

He woke up at 5:30 am, dressed in the dark and quietly snuck past his dad's bedroom so as not to wake him. He opened the fridge and grabbed a gallon of milk and poured himself a glassful. Then he pulled out a covered glass container, opened the container and took out four frickadellars (Danish pan fried meat balls). His dad, Art learned to make them from Swenson, a shipmate when he was in the Navy. They are about two and a half inches round but not spherical they are flat and fried nice and brown. The frickadellars were even better cold than hot. Between Eric and Art it was a challenge to see who got the most of them. He just took four; he didn't want to be greedy, because his dad loved them.

He quietly finished eating and snuck out of the house. The drive was on a down-slope to the street. He coasted down the drive so as not to wake his dad, put it in second gear and let out the clutch, the Ford started and he headed for the shop. Work started at 7:30 am and Art usually got to the shop at 7 am. It then dawned on him that this was Sunday and no one would be at the shop today.

It was now 6 o'clock in the morning as Eric entered the back door of the shop and walked over to the dock area where he left the crate last night. The crate was gone. Was it all a dream? Maybe it was. It all seemed too good to be true. It was pretty wild yesterday; it was too wild to be anything but a dream. At least it wasn't a nightmare! Then he heard it. An engine firing up and next he saw it coming out of the dark aisle between the machines and it came to a sliding stop right in front of Eric. It was his dad on the Scout.

His dad said, "Nice bike. Make a good hill climber or stump jumper. Bad first gear though."

"I know," said Eric, "I thought you would be home in bed since it's early Sunday morning."

"Well, Son, it's like this, you can't hide everything from your old man. Got a call last night, feller said that he would like to deliver something to the shop early this morning. He had to get out of town for a few days so this was his only chance to get it here. Wouldn't say what it was. Said you would be glad to see it. I also got a call from a guy in Arizona. He may become a new employee. He is on his way here now and should be here Thursday. He is riding his bike up here, a 1947 Indian Bonneville Chief. That right there puts him in good stead." Art said. "I was weaned on an Indian. I talked to him for quite a while; the more I talked with him the more I felt that I knew him. It turns out that he was a buddy of yours when you were a freshman in high school. His name is Archie Mueller, remember him?"

"Yeah, I remember him. We used to get in a lot of trouble together. I'll be glad to see him again. He should fit in here real well. Archie was doing senior math when he was a freshman. He was also promoted to drafting class which most students don't get till their junior year."

"Well," Art said, "you're right; it sounds like he will fit in real well."

Just at that time the front bell rang. Art went upstairs and through the office he looked out the window and he saw the most beautiful modified 1948 Ford van that he had ever seen. Multicolored with orange and red flames and supercharger intakes on top of the hood. On the side of the body just aft of the doors were beautifully recessed and not done by an amateur. In those recesses were perfectly fit 3 inch chrome exhaust stacks. They were also perfectly tuned.

The windows in the office were screened and opened to the sound and the van was parked below the window. Sounds like a 300 cubic inch high compression engine, just idling away with no mufflers. It sure did sound sweet.

Art went down to the foyer and opened the door he almost jumped out of his skin when he saw the man standing there. It was Bill Turner and he said "I'm not who you think I am, I'm Bill Turner from Bill's Bike's. It doesn't sound as if Eric explained anything to you or what transpired yesterday. Well, I'm Bill Turner and you must be Art, Eric's dad. And this is your machine shop."

"Right on all accounts. As you said on the phone you have something to deliver," said Art, "I'll say one thing; that is the most beautiful delivery truck that I have ever seen."

Just then Eric came out of the front door and just about flipped his lid when he saw the van. Then he saw Bill and said hello, but he had no idea what was going to happen next. Bill opened the back doors and slid out a ramp. He climbed into the van and a few minutes later, a Harley engine started and Bill rode out of the van on the most beautiful 1946 Harley they had ever seen. Bill explained that Eric had agreed to work off the $2,600.00 value of the bike doing some machine work on the side.

"Sounds great, but don't you guys have some sort of sales contract or an agreement?" asked Art.

Bill replied, "We have an agreement. We shook hands on it. By the way, here is the title all signed over."

Art said, "Bill this all sounds great but Eric will have to quote a price on whatever work he does for you."

"Art, I find that it's best to deal with people that you trust. And then do everything on time and material, at the normal shop rate. This way nobody gets hurt, and quoting is a waste of time. That's the way I work." said Bill. Then to Eric, "I have already applied for state plates in your name. You will get them in the mail. Make sure you get yourself covered with insurance, and Eric, you are set to ride. I'll give you a call next week when I get back from my trip, and we will talk about the machine work. Got to go. See you guys later."

Art looked at Eric and said, "Why I sure wish that I had a bunch of customers like that, and then being in business would be great." Art walked back in the shop and Eric took his new bike for a ride around the block. Art had told Eric that Archie planned on being in Chicago by Wednesday or Thursday. It will be great to see Archie again.

When Archie was 15 years old he moved out of Chicago. He went with his parents to Minneapolis. His dad worked as a sales executive for 3M. He told Archie that he would get him into 3M in the sales department. Archie told him that he appreciated the offer, but he would rather work with his hands. During his junior and senior years, he worked part-time for his uncle, who had a tool and machine shop in St. Paul. He worked as a junior machinist for a year after he got out of high school.

Chapter 2

Foleys Feed Bag and the Back Seat Strippers!

Arch was almost 20 and was built like a weight lifter, which he was. Arch was as strong as a bull, and looked like it; he was also a black belt in Karate. But he now had an itch to roam. It was late November and he decided he was going south. He heard that Phoenix was a nice place to be in the winter and a good time to leave was right after Thanksgiving. The weather on November 25th was in the 40s and 50s, but everyone wanted to say goodbye and have him over for dinner. So by the time he got going, it was November 27th and 25° with light snow flurries. Now they all said Archie you can't leave in this kind of weather. If I waited any longer it will be 10 below and blizzard conditions.

So Archie packed his saddlebags and climbed aboard his beautiful metallic green 1947 Indian Bonneville Chief and rode out of Minneapolis on Route 35 going directly south. He rode through the light snow with no big problems. Then about 200 miles south of Minneapolis, it started to warm up a little. It seemed a little better conditions, except it was still snowing. The snow coming down now was heavy wet snow.

Arch did not have a windshield on the bike (that was for pansies) so snow packed against his chest and his legs and then froze. It packed up below his headlight and on top of his front fender. It packed up so much in front of his headlight that heat from the light bored a tunnel through the snow. It was actually a beautiful sight. The road was wet but not slippery so he just rolled along. He passed most of the cars. The people he passed probably thought he was nuts, they were doing 50 to 60 mph and he would pass them doing 70 to 75.

What most of these people didn't realize was that their visibility was very limited. Archie was out in the open, and his visibility was excellent. Most motorcycle riders are fair weather riders and then there are some that ride in any weather. Archie is one of the latter. He was just on the outskirts of Des Moines when the traffic started to build up during the 6 pm rush hour. There was a three car pileup right in front of him. No chance in hell to stop. He went right off the road and into a ditch. Snow plows had come by earlier and thrown fresh snow that was piled high in the ditch. It was a soft landing, the bike was up right, but completely buried in the snow.

Two state police cars showed up inside of 10 minutes and a couple of tow trucks. The police saw Archie standing on the highway. They asked if he was hurt and where his car was. He explained that he was riding a motorcycle. The one cop thought he was nuts. The other cop just asked him what kind of bike. Archie said, "It was a 1947 Indian Chief."

"I ride a 74 Harley. Let's go find your Indian." said the motorcycle riding cop. It was buried deep in the snow with the rear fender showing. Then the cop said, "It looks like a nice paint job on your bike. The tow truck could pull you out but he would just put a chain on it and scratch the hell out of it. I've got a better idea. We have got shovels in the squad cars. We also have a mile of traffic backed up. I'll go talk to some of these people and tell them that they are going no place until we get your bike out of the ditch."

Five minutes later the officer came back with about 10 guys. They shoveled out each side of the bike. Then they almost carried the seven hundred pound bike out of the ditch. The police officer and Archie both thanked the men and they headed back to their cars. The officer then introduced himself as Rob and said, "Our job here is done here. We are going to head for the state police barracks to make out reports. It's just a couple miles up the road. Follow us and stop in at the barracks for a hot cup of coffee to warm up."

Which Archie did. The hot coffee in a nice warm room felt good. Rob asked him how long he had been riding. He said he started about 5 am. "It's about time you should stop for a rest. The snow will be ending about 8 am. We have a bunk room here and you are welcome to sack out and get a fresh start in the morning."

Arch said, "Thanks, I will be grateful for a good night's sleep." Archie got up at 7 am and took a shower in the bunk house restroom. He felt good as new and ready to ride. Rob and his buddies were just heading off duty. They were going to a truck stop a couple miles up the road for breakfast and told Archie to meet them there. He could gas up and have a good breakfast and then be on his way south.

After breakfast they all came outside to say so long to Arch. He said thanks and so long and pointed his Chief south and headed down Route 35. It had warmed up to 40° and the road was clear. It was a nice ride with no problem. He decided to ride about 150 miles to Route 36 which was about 25 miles north of Kansas City where he could make a fuel and lunch stop.

He got to Route 36 and found that it had a nice big truck stop there. Arch pulled in and headed to the gas pumps. When he got there he noticed a nice brand-new Gold and Grey 1949 Harley. It was the first time he had seen the new telescoping hydraulic forks, which were new in 1949. He parked his bike by a gas pump, and got off and walked over to take a look at the bike. While he was looking, a black guy came out of the restroom. He walked over to Archie and said, "Nice forks ain't they?"

"How do they ride?"

"Great," he said, I just bought the bike two weeks ago and I love it. You going north or south?"

Arch said, "I'm going south to Route 40 and then west over to Phoenix."

"I am David Steele and I am heading south to a little town called Carlisle about 30 miles east of Little Rock. So I'm going south to Route 40 and East to Carlisle."

Arch said, "You want to ride together? And by the way I'm Archie Mueller."

David said, "Great, it will be nice to have company."

They went into the restaurant and had something to eat. Archie told David that he was from Minneapolis and he had just decided to head south where it was warm. He had heard that Phoenix was not too bad a place to be in the winter. "I really don't want to stay in the south or go back to Minneapolis." said Arch.

David asks, "What kind of work you do, Archie?"

Arch answers, "I have mostly done tool and machine work, but I guess I'll look for some kind of construction work in Phoenix."

"Well, when you get tired of the sunny south why don't you head for Chicago? I am also in the tool and machine trade and there is plenty of work around Chicago. I work for International Harvester in Northlake which is one of the western suburbs of Chicago. I live in Cicero, which is another Chicago suburb, about 8 miles from work. Right now I'm a third year apprentice pattern maker, pay is pretty good. Two more years and I will be a journeyman pattern maker. That's when the pay gets really good. I've got a nice one-bed room apartment and just bought this brand new Harley," said David.

Arch said, "Sounds like you like Chicago. I was born and raised there and lived there till I was 14 years old. Then my dad got transferred to Minneapolis and I was there till a couple days ago."

David replies, "If you come to Chicago, look me up." He gave Arch his address and Arch put it in his wallet.

Arch said, "I'd give you mine, but I don't have one right now. I will give you my home address and phone number at my folk's place in Minneapolis though; they will probably know where I'm at. I'll contact you once I get settled. You said that you belong to the Black Eagles in Chicago. Are they anything like the Hell's Angels?"

"No, absolutely not. We raise a lot of hell, have field meets, and go to the races and do a lot of beer drinking, but absolutely no dope."

"Sounds like a pretty good club." Arch said.

"It is a good club and besides raising hell, we do some good things such as charity rides and have raised quite a bit of money. When we do these rides it is with a couple of dozen of other clubs. Some are black and some are white. It makes no difference when you are a biker," said David.

"That's the way it should be, Dave. You mind if I call you Dave? David sounds too formal."

Dave said, "Right and I'll call you Arch. Archie sounds like it's right out of a comic strip!"

Arch said, "Let's ride."

They went through Kansas City, got off of Route 35, jogged over and went south on Route 71 and gassed up in Carthage. They were just on the inside of the Arkansas border and they came to a cut off to the town of Springdale and decided that this was as a good place as any to pull off the road. They went through the town and found a bridge with a small river running under it.

They figured that this was better than looking for a motel room. They had both packed some blankets in their saddlebags and when they got up in the morning they could wash up in the river and then head for some breakfast. The guys got up, washed up, fired up their bikes, got back on

Route 71 and headed south. Twenty minutes later they spotted a sign that said "Foleys Feed Bag" and there were three Harleys parked outside. "It can't be entirely bad." said Arch. "Let's check and see if they are local." Dave looked at the plates, Michigan plates. Arch said, "Let's go find out if they have any decent food."

No sooner had they walked in the door when some big, ugly guy with a dirty apron on, came out from behind the counter.

He came right up to Arch and said, "I don't serve any niggers in my restaurant. He barely got to the word restaurant" out when Arch smashed him in the face with his big right fist. His nose was bleeding and maybe broken. Arch said, "You must be Foley. I just want to tell you that we came in here to eat and not to fight."

Foley said, as he is spitting blood, "He can eat outside, out back because no nigger is it going to eat in here."

"Foley, you don't learn too quick." and Arch landed one right in his gut, which almost doubled him over.

Foley said, "I got good friends on the local police force and if I call them, they will be right over and put you in the shit house."

Arch said, "Foley, you just don't understand. All we want is a nice breakfast. But you are trying very hard to get me to break your arm. But then you won't be able to make breakfast." Arch looked at the other three bikers and asked if they had a problem with Dave sitting down to eat. "No, no problem we are quite enjoying it." And then he got up and went behind the counter and ripped a phone off the wall.

He said, "Problem solved. Now you don't have to break his arm." And he went back and sat down.

Foley walked to his grill to make some eggs. Arch ordered over easy. Dave ordered scrambled, with a side order of ham. One of the bikers got Arch's attention and he was mouthing the word cayenne and pointing to Foley. Foley was loading Dave's scrambled eggs with cayenne pepper. When Foley set the plates down in front of Arch and Dave, Arch got up and vaulted over-the-counter. Now he grabbed Foley and dragged him around the counter and set him down in front of Dave's plate. The one with all the hot pepper, and Arch said, "Foley, you just don't want to learn. I am buying you breakfast. Now eat."

Foley tried to knock the plate off the counter, but this time Dave caught his arm and said, "You are lucky I stopped you or you would be eating off the floor." Dave asked the other bikers if they had seen anything hotter than Tabasco sauce.

"Here is one that these rednecks seem to like, it's got a skull and cross bones on it." Dave took the bottle and poured a good bit on top of the scrambled eggs. Dave said, "Now, Foley, we have these eggs seasoned just right for you." Foley exclaims, "You don't expect me to eat that do you?" Dave replies, "Foley, you made it and expected me to eat it. Now eat it or we will force feed you. Foley ate half the plate and was crying. When he reached for a glass of water they pulled it away and handed him a cup of steaming hot black coffee.

Arch said, "I think we have had enough of this place. Let's go someplace else and get something to eat."

The three bikers got up and said, "We might as well leave too. You guys did good. Foley got what he deserved. We are from Detroit, our club is the Falcons, and we ride quite often for charity and do some field meets. Our club rides with the Detroit Black Eagles. They are a pretty good bunch of guys."

Dave said, "I am in the Chicago Black Eagles. Maybe we will run into each other at one of these charity runs."

The leader of the biker group, Ken, said, "Wait a minute while I convince Foley why he shouldn't even think of having his buddies on the local police force hit on us as we go down the road. They should not bother us even if we go by them at 90 mph. I can explain to Foley that he really ought to learn how to treat people right."

"We have three guys from our club in Detroit and four guys from the Detroit Black Eagles. They are coming down to meet us in Fort Worth, Texas for a big motorcycle rodeo. I could tell them about a good place to stop for breakfast at Foleys Feed Bag. Or I could tell them that Foley sicced the local cops on us. So be smart and tell your buddies to back off or our buddies will trash you and your place. If we have no problem with the cops today I will recommend a stop at Foley's for breakfast. But remember one thing. Of these seven guys, four of them are black and I would not even think of calling them niggers. These guys are nice guys unless you press the nigger button. Because then you are a dead man. The black guy's money spends just as good as the white guys. So if you don't press that nigger button and you will live longer and make more money."

"Archie and Dave have no hard feelings toward you. They feel that you have suffered enough with the cayenne pepper and the hot sauce. So forget your bigotry and treat everybody as equals. You will be amazed how much better you will feel. You will be more respected, except for your redneck buddies. You will also be making more profit in your restaurant. Trust me. I've seen it work in Detroit and you can make it work here. You don't seem like such a bad guy Foley, but you need to change your attitude."

"I am really sorry about what happened. You have to live around here to know the people and how they react to race." said Foley.

"You have a nice restaurant here with a lot of empty tables. Your locals will never fill this place. You get a lot of tourist traffic past your restaurant. There is a reason they pass you up and go down the line to another restaurant. You need a sign that said "Equal Rights Restaurant". Some of the locals will back away, but you will make up for them with tourists ten times over." Ken hands Foley two $100 bills and said, "Fix your phone." Then he handed him a business card and gives him one last piece of advice. "Remember this conversation and you will do okay."

Foley took the card and looked at it as Ken was walking out. It said, "Worldwide Restaurant Consulting Association, we make restaurants profitable. Ken Jamieson, President."

Ken walked outside and walked up to the other guys and said, "All set crew. Foley's no problem. He's not too bad a guy after all." All five bikers climbed aboard their bikes and started out of the parking lot. They looked back and saw Foley standing on his front porch and waving goodbye. They stopped their bikes and turned around and waved back. Then they headed out.

The five bikers headed south on Route 71 toward Fort Smith which was near Route 40, the east-west route which they would all take. Dave would go east toward Little Rock, Ken and his buddies, Rich and Ernie would head west for 150 miles and pick up Route 35 S. to Fort Worth, Texas and Arch would head west for 1000 miles to Route 17 and go south for 125 miles to Phoenix.

All five of them, shortly before Route 40, decided to stop and eat at a big touristy type pancake house. They were directed to a large round table. Everybody picked up a menu. Ken asked if everybody liked good corned beef sandwiches. They all agreed that they liked them. Ken made the comment that when they are good they are great, but that's not more than 10% of the time. "I have tossed a good share of corned beef sandwiches that I ordered, and in some decent restaurants. Trust me here they are part of the 10%, they are great."

Dave asked, "You have eaten here before then?"

Ken said, "No, not actually."

"How do you not actually eat someplace?" asked Dave.

"Well, that takes a little bit of explaining. I happen to be the President of the Worldwide Restaurant Consulting Association. We have 250 field agents throughout this country and many parts of the world. We heard so much good about their corned beef that we sent people here three times. With the same answer." They all ordered the corned beef and Ken was right.

Arch said, "This sure beats Foley's." Ken came back with something that surprised Arch and Dave.

"Foley is not all that bad. His food is good but he has an attitude problem. If Foley was further north he would have no problem. I had a good talk with him and he is going to forget about the local rules about race. He is going to put out a sign to welcome all black white or brown.

"When I go back up north," said Dave, "I think I'll stop at Foley's."

"I think you will be surprised." said Ken, "Dave, here is my card. Call me when you get back and let me know how things are at Foley's." Ken then turned to Arch and said, "I gather that you are going to Phoenix. Are you familiar with that area?"

"No, never been south before," answered Arch.

"I have a place for you to go to. Good food and booze but most importantly is good information. When you get there ask for Lenny, the owner. If Lenny isn't there ask for Fred, the head bartender. Tell them that Ken Jamieson sent you. They owe me a favor. They will find you living accommodations and will help you find a job. They are both good guys and Fred is a biker and Indian man just like you."

Dave headed east when they leave the restaurant and the others head west on Route 41 toward Route 35 South. Ken, Rich and Ernie turned off and headed south, Arch just kept heading west into Oklahoma, then northern Texas, New Mexico and finally Arizona. He still has a long way to go approximately 1100 miles. A big Indian can do a nice cruise at 75 miles an hour, so it should be a nice two-day ride.

The weather was perfect for riding it was 5 pm when they parted. Arch rolled along at a steady cruise of 60 to 75 mph, depending on the speed limit. It was about 10 o'clock at night when he was going through the small town of Clinton, Oklahoma. There was no traffic when he went through town, but about halfway through, where everything was lit up with streetlights, this two-tone silver and pink 1948 Mercury convertible pulled alongside him. The car was neat but what was more curious was that there were two guys in the front seats and two gals in the back.

The gals looked like college students and they were both wearing jock sweaters from Texas University. They were all drinking beer and making obscene gestures at him, which he didn't mind. Then they started blowing kisses. So he blew some back and as they came under some bright lights, in a traffic signal area, the gals stood up on the back seat. Both of them took off their jock sweaters and they were buck naked and built like a brick shit houses.

Most strippers would love to have a set of jugs like these gals had. Then they made a bunch of obscene gestures that left nothing to your imagination. They knew just what to do with the beer bottles and they did it in tandem. Then they threw the used beer bottles at Arch. They missed and then the car accelerated past him. Last he saw, they must've been doing 90 to100 mph. Archie thought it would be the last he would see of them but that was not to be.

About 20 miles down the road on a curve, Arch saw a couple of cars parked on the berm of the road. When he got closer, he could see the silver and pink convertible which was plowed dead-center into a Cottonwood tree. As he got off his bike, he remembered that when he got out of high school he joined a volunteer fire department in Minneapolis, so he had a few years of training in first aid and he knew he had to try to help.

When he got to the car, there were two guys standing there. "Just two guys in the car and it looks like they are both dead." Arch checked and they were definitely dead. He asked where the two girls were, that were in the car.

"I don't know", one of them said. Arch told them that they had been in the back seat. "Must have been thrown out when the car hit a tree."

"So let's look for them. They can't be far," stated Arch, and looked in the back seat and pulled out the two jock sweaters.

One of the guys asked, "Why the sweaters?"

Arch said, "Because when we find them they will probably be cold."

They found the girls 20 feet behind the tree. They were not dead but they were sure muddy and mud was all they were wearing. They moaned and groaned and then sat up with a little help, the girls were lucky they landed in the mud. They probably landed in a perfect swan dive. Both of them on their faces, and their first-class boobs, which were covered with blood. The one guy said his name was Bob and the other guy is Joe.

"My name is Arch."

Bob said, "Arch, I am an Army officer, they give us a certain amount of training for this type of situation. Are you into any first aid, Arch?"

"Yeah, I was a volunteer Fireman for about a year," said Arch.

"Good," said Bob, "Let's see what we can do. Joe is a local guy so let's send him to call an ambulance. These gals don't look like they are seriously injured, but I think they are definitely in shock. I see why you brought the jock sweaters. The accident must have torn their clothes right off."

"Not exactly," said Arch, "I will explain later. Let's get the gals to some dry ground." They each picked up one of the gals and carried them over near the road and laid them down.

"We have to keep them warm or they may go deeper into shock," said Bob. By now a few cars had parked on the road and people wandered over to where the gals lay. Bob asked if anybody had blankets in their car.

One guy said, "I've got one, and will get it."

Another said, "I got one, but I don't want to get any blood on it."

Arch turned to him and said, "Go get the friggin blanket or get out of here! Get it now." He went and came back with a blanket, didn't mention blood. One gal was blonde and the other one a redhead. The redhead was now relaxed so Bob and Arch were checking out the blonde for more injuries. Down the road came a drunken broad in a full-length fur coat.

While Bob and Arch were busy with the blond the drunk leaned over the redhead and said, "I think this one is dead."

Bob turned back to the redhead. He looked up at the drunken broad. Then he looked at the man she was with and said, "Get this drunken bitch out of here!"

Arch said, "Leave the fur coat. It's just what we need for the blonde."

The drunk said, "I ain't leaving my mink coat for somebody to bleed all over."

The man said, "She is my wife and you are right about her. One, she is a bitch and two she is going to leave her $6000 mink coat here to do some good." He pulled the coat off of her and gave it to Bob. Bob asked where the coat should be sent. The man said, "Give it to the injured gal that it's going to keep warm." Then he said, "Come on, Bitch, let's go home. And now you can feel like you have done one good thing in your life by giving away your fur coat."

The ambulance finally came. A guy and a woman came over and checked out the girls. The woman came over to Bob and Arch and asked what happened to their clothes. Arch looked at her and smiled and said, "This is how we found them face down in the mud. How they lost their clothes, I don't think they would want that known once they sober up. The girls will be all right once they sober up and get a few stitches. The two guys are dead and the police and a tow truck should be here shortly."

"Somebody has got to stay here to talk to the police," Bob said, "I've got to get to my unit in Fort Sill and I think Arch has got to move on too. Joe is local he can talk to the police."

Arch asked the ambulance crew where they were taking the girls. They told him Amarilla General Hospital, the only hospital in town. It's on the north side. Ask at any gas station. They loaded up the girls and Arch said, "I'll see you at the hospital. Are you going with the lights on? If you are, I'll follow you."

"Okay we will go with the lights on." The ambulance pulled out.

Arch said goodbye to Bob and Joe and pulled out following the ambulance. The lights were flashing and they were running between 75 and 80 mph. When they got into some traffic, they slowed down since there was no real emergency. They got to the hospital and pulled up, then backed up to the emergency entrance. The driver got out and told Arch where there was a safe place to park his bike. He did that and then he went to the emergency room.

In the ER he asked a nurse about the two girls that were just brought in. She asked what their names were and he said that he didn't have a clue. He told her that he and another guy found them at an accident scene. He just wanted to stop and see what their condition was. The nurse said, "The doctor is with them right now. They need some cleaning up and some stitches. They need some ointment for a lot of scratches all over the front of their bodies. It seems like the two of them have perfectly matched abrasions. They are awake and the girls don't know what happened."

The nurse said that the Doc would like to see you. "He thinks that you may be able to shed some light on what happened. The police would like to know too because they have two dead bodies that were in the car and how did two naked girls wind up in the mud?"

"They were pretty high on alcohol but before I tell you what I know I'll have to talk to the girls first. I would like to talk to them in private," said Arch. So the doctor took Arch to their room. They are both pretty sober now and they are both in the same room. The Doc opened the door and walked in with Arch.

"This is the guy that pulled you two girls out of the mud. Actually he and an army officer saved your life. You were both going into shock when the ambulance picked you up," Doc said, "Okay I'll leave, and you three can talk."

They said that we were in a car that crashed into a tree and they found us in the mud. "I found you in the mud they didn't know you were there," said Arch.

"How did you know?" they asked.

Arch told them that he was behind them on his motorcycle and at one time alongside them. All of a sudden the redhead's face turned red as a beet.

She said, "I'm Peggy and this is Jean. Do you remember, Jean? He was on a motorcycle alongside the convertible?"

Jean said, "Yeah, I remember. I think we must've been pretty drunk. I'm starting to remember the night. Did we really do all those things that I think we did?"

Arch answered, "I don't know what you think you did, but probably that and a little more. I'm sure it would be a great act for a New Orleans strip club. The guy driving was totally wasted and so was his partner. They didn't feel anything."

Peggy said that she heard that they were both killed. "We are sorry they were killed but we really didn't know them that well. We just met them last night."

"If that was just a first date, what is second date like? I will say one thing and that is that if you were not completely naked when you hit that tree, you would both be in the morgue right now. If you had clothes on, you would have been sitting in the seat with no seat belt on and you would have gone flying through the windshield just like the two guys did. Instead you sat up on top of the seat waving your very nice set of boobs around. Being that was where you were sitting when the car hit a tree you both flew like birdies. One on each side of the tree. And like the Doc said the big thing that saved you from back or internal injuries was that nice soft mud. But more important than the mud was that nice soft cushioned landing, on your nice extra-large size boobs. I think the insurance companies should rate the size and call them safety knockers. I just thought I would stop by and see how you girls were doing. I got to go now, I'm off to Phoenix."

Chapter 3

Larsen's Mexican Restaurant.

Finally back on the road again, Arch was anxious to get out into the wind. It was a good feeling to have a great deal of power in your throttle hand. Sitting on top of a powerful engine, listening to its throaty roar and the wind in your face, it's not just a way of transportation it is a way of life.

Most people think that it is just a cheap and dangerous form of transportation, but it's not always true. A lot of bikes with modifications can cost more than the average car. Car people feel that they are comfortable in their car and the poor bikers are out there suffering in the elements. Riding in a car is a way to get from point A to point B and the passengers are always wondering how much further to go. On a bike when you go from point A to point B, it is an experience that you enjoy for the whole trip. Sometimes you have a problem with the weather, but it is something that you can't control, so you live with it. If you ask most riders if they had to make a trip from New York to LA, and they had a choice of a stretch limo or a new Harley, not many would take the limousine.

I thought that I would mention why many people have a misunderstanding about motorcycle riders. Sorry if I bent your ear a bit but when you are riding a long distance it gives you time to think about why and where you are going.

Arch decided that he had run into a lot of weird things so far on this trip. From this point on to the next there should be no problems, delays or anything unusual to hold him up. He would have three fuel stops and can eat at a stop when he gets hungry. He should be at Lenny's by 10 or 11 pm. By then he could surely use a beer. Arch is only 19 1/2 years old, but could easily pass for 24. He hoped that they were not too strict on carding in Arizona. He never had a problem in Minneapolis in the last few years.

He rode for about 3 1/2 hours until he came across 84 S. No fuel station. 20 more miles and he came to Santa Rosa; a small town a mile or so south of Route 40. He got gas and oil and then asked the gal, who was a clerk in the small grocery that was part of the station, if there was a decent restaurant in town. She said, "Only the best Mexican restaurant in the whole state of New Mexico. It's just two blocks south, the name of it is Larsen's Mexican Restaurant."

Larsen's Restaurant was surprisingly large. At least 20 tables and most of them empty. A beautiful Mexican girl in her early 20's came up to Arch and asked if she could help him. "I was hoping so, but it looks like you are closing," said Arch.

The hostess said, "We are closing, it's Sunday evening and we usually close at 6 on Sunday and it's almost 8 now."

Arch said, "Well, thanks anyway. I'll just head up the road."

"You going east or west?" she asks.

He said, "West."

She said, "Going west, you won't find any good food until you get to Moriarity, which is about 80 miles west of here."

"Well I guess I can survive for a couple more hours. Although I was looking forward to some good Mexican food," said Arch, "the gal at the grocery said that Larsen's is the best in the state."

"That's Cindy. She stretches things sometimes. Our food is good but I don't know if it's the best in the state. I guess I'll just have to let you find out for yourself. Just pick out a clean table. We have not cleaned up yet because we just finished with a banquet for the State Horse Breeders Association. Would you like a beer?" she asks.

"Sounds good. Have you got Bud or Miller's?" Arch asks.

"They drank up all the Bud but we still have Miller's and Jax," the hostess answered.

"I'll try a Jax."

She brought him a Jax and a cold pilsner glass and poured it half-full and set the glass and the bottle down. Then she took out her order pad, but changed her mind and put the pad back in the pocket of her apron. Then she picked the menu up off the table and said, "I've just decided that you are not a customer, but a guest."

He started to say that he was a paying customer, but she held up her hand and said, "As a fellow rider, you are a guest. That is your big Indian Chief out there, is it not?"

"Yes it is. She's got a Bonneville engine and she runs great," Arch said.

"She sounded great. That is a beautiful set of megaphone exhausts that you have on her. I would love to get a set of them for my husband Knute's Harley. Oh by the way I am Maria Larsen most people wonder about Larsen and Mexican food. My husband is a Dane but a great chef. Knute has a great passion for Mexican food. I met Knute at a cycle rodeo in Fort Worth five years ago. He took me to the best Mexican restaurants in Fort Worth. I'm from Mexico City but he explained to me everything there was about Mexican food and cooking. He knew the owners of every Mexican restaurant we went to. Most all of them tried to hire him, but he said no; he had other ideas. This restaurant was his other idea and it has worked out very well."

She said that she would be right back. She came back with a tray of beers and glasses. Behind her was a giant of a guy. She said, "Ain't that the biggest damned Dane you have ever seen!"

He said, "Maria, sometimes you talk too much." "But I still love her. Maria said that you rode an Indian Chief down from Minnesota and your name is Arch. I'm Knute and you have already met Maria. Maria and I have not had a chance to eat all day and I hear you have not eaten since this morning. You should be very hungry. We have plenty of food and we can sit down and eat family-style. Still before we eat I must hear those megaphones on your Indian."

"Okay, let me get the key out of my jacket," said Arch.

They went outside and the bike was under the restaurant's front lights. Maria and Knute both said the bike had a beautiful paint job.

Knute said, "I know that everybody is hungry, but I've got to hear those pipes."

Arch started the engine.

"Those are the most beautiful sounding pipes I've ever heard. I would love to get a set for my Harley," said Knute.

Arch said, "I don't know the name of the company that makes them but I do know that it is a small company in Chicago. They are custom made of swedged (hammered) and hardened brass. It has the tone of a musical instrument." Arch said that he got them in a trade; his pipes for the megaphones. "The guy was tired of getting tickets from the Minneapolis police. My dad knows the father of the guy I traded with. I'll try to find out who made them."

Maria said, "Come on, let's go eat. Sit down Arch we will go get the food." And they did exactly that. Enough food to feed a small army. There was it seemed, every kind of Mexican cuisine that you could imagine. But then there was something that did not seem to look Mexican.

"Those are a Danish delicacy. Frickadellars. Whenever we have a larger group of people here, someone always sticks his nose into the kitchen and said, "Hey, Knute, how about some Frickadellars." I complain and then I say okay. Actually I make as few hundred and keep them in the freezer. Somebody always wants some. They are not on the menu but I always have got some."

"Try some," said Maria.

Arch tried a bite and said, "These are great! Better than my dad makes. Too bad I ate all that good Mexican food, or I'd finish off the platter."

Maria said, "I think that we have had enough to eat. Let's go out in the garage and Knute can show you his pride and joy."

The three of them went out in the garage and Knute turned on the lights. Up on a raised ramp was a beautiful blue and silver Harley. On the other side of the Harley was another bike. It was a Vermillion red and shiny Guzzi. It was a single cylinder 500 cubic inch road racing bike. It had an outside flywheel that was all polished so as not to snag anything. The reason for the outside flywheel was to reduce the size of the cases, thus strengthening them enough to run as much as 14 to 1 compression ratio.

Maria said, "She's only running a stock 9 to1."

The Moto Guzzi had interested Archie enough.

Marie said, "The outside flywheel really gets people's attention."

They walked back to the Harley and on each side of the tank was a beautiful crest. Knute explained that it was the Royal Danish Crest. Then he explained how he was allowed to use the crest. He was an officer in the Danish cavalry. He belonged to the King's guard. As one of the King's guard, some of the unit competed in a steeplechase. "I was involved in a three horse pile up over a jump. I broke a few bones and had internal injuries. After six months in the hospital the doctor said that I would never ride again. They offered me a desk job but I declined and took retirement. They said that I would never ride again but if I did I could still use the Royal Danish Crest on my mount and this Harley is my mount."

"Since the doctor said I could not ride a four-legged horse, now I ride the "iron horse". As you will notice below the Danish Crest are two words: "Iron Horse". Now we take our time off and go riding. We would like to take a ride with you to Phoenix, but we already have too many things on our schedule. Our apartment is upstairs and we have an extra room. You are welcome to stay overnight. Then we can have a good Mexican breakfast and then we can see you off."

Arch said, "Sounds good to me."

Next morning they were all up at 8 am. Arch packed his gear into his saddle bags, and they all had a good breakfast. Arch mentioned that he'd met Ken Jamieson and that he had his business card and when he got to Phoenix; he would contact Ken and tell him about Larsen's Mexican Restaurant.

Knute said, "No need to do that, I have known Ken for quite a few years and he has eaten here more than once."

"I guess Ken knows everyone," stated Arch.

"He does," said Knute.

"Well, I guess I better saddle up and be on my way."

He thanked Knute and Maria for their hospitality and five minutes later he had the engine idling away.

Knute said, "Those megaphones are music to my ears!"

It was daylight now and it was the first time he got a real good look at Arch's fantastic exhaust pipes. The megaphones on each side were almost 3 foot long and about 5 inches in diameter at the end. Arch took off and cracked it on hard, as Knute and Maria stood in the road and listened to the mellow sound. It could be heard for at least a mile.

He headed out of Santa Rosa to Route 40 and then west to his next fuel stop which was Grant, New Mexico. Grant was about 70 miles west of Albuquerque and 70 miles from the Arizona border. After he passed through Albuquerque, he rolled through some Indian reservations. He fueled up in Grant and headed down the highway again. He crossed the Rio Grande in Albuquerque and in 30 miles he would be crossing the Continental Divide. So far, it's been an interesting trip, Arch thought, as he rolled on into Arizona.

It was early December and the weather was nice and comfortable. 50 miles after he crossed the Arizona border, he came to the Petrified Forest National Park. This was something he had heard about and had always wanted to see. It was beautiful to see. Arch rolled through the park and was amazed at the trees turned to stone. So he stopped at the visitor center to find out how this happened. It seems that it took millions of years. The normal organic cells in tree trunks were replaced by silica or other minerals. As simple as that. And now he knew just in case anyone should ask. That was enough education for today.

Now back on the road again headed for Flagstaff. At the junction of Route 40 and Route 17 he pulled in for his last fuel stop. While gassing up he noticed a fast food place. His stomach was growling so he pulled in there and got two hamburgers and a shake. It was 11:30 am when he finally left Santa Rosa and it was now 6:30 pm. It should be about 145 miles to Lenny's Place.

Considering that part of the 145 miles will be in city traffic, it will probably take 3 to 3 1/2 hours, so he should be at Lenny's no later than 10 pm. He rode south on Route 17 for about 110 miles, where there was a sign for Sun City. It was approximately 25 miles to Route 10. One half a mile before Route 10 is McDowell Road. He turned east on McDowell and went about 2 miles to Seventh Street and there, right on the corner of Seventh and McDowell was a big neon sign that said "Lenny's".

On one side of the building was a parking lot. He parked the bike, put his locks through the spokes and drive chain and walked around the front and through the large main doors. He had entered into the main dining room. It was pretty fancy restaurant and he felt out of place wearing a Levi jacket and miles of road dirt. Just then the door that Arch came through opened and in came a sort of a smallish guy about 5'9" or 5'10" and looked to be about 180 pounds. All the customers and waitresses seemed to know him and all said, "Hi, Lenny." He walked over to Arch and said, "I'm Lenny and you must be Arch."

"That's who I am. Ken Jamieson must have contacted you," said Arch.

"Ken called yesterday and said to expect you. So let's go back to the bar and I'll introduce you to Fred and then I've got to take a shower and change clothes. Just got back from a hare and hound race out in the desert. We had a hell of a time, I was the hare and I had about 16 bikes chasing me. We started at 5 pm and raced till dark. I ride a worked over Indian Scout that does not want to get caught. Next time we go out I'll still be the hare until I get caught. It's great fun. Let's go meet Fred," said Lenny.

They walked through the main restaurant and into a large room with a great big horseshoe bar. When they walked in, practically every one said hi to Lenny. A couple of them asked if they caught the hare yet. Lenny said not yet - maybe never. Lenny then turned to the bar and said, "Freddie, my boy, do we look like orphans or are you going to reach for a couple of nice cold Jax?" Fred brought the beers over and then Lenny introduced Arch to Fred. Lenny told Arch that Fred would show him a safe place to park his bike. "In the parking lot it's liable to get hit or knocked over by some drunk in a car. We have a place for it inside. It looks too pretty; kids will want to sit on it."

Fred took Arch out in back, to show him where to park his bike, and gets him a key to the garage, then they went out front to the parking lot. They walked over to Arch's bike. After looking at the monster megaphones, Fred said, "Start her up, Arch, I want to listen to the music." He rode it around to the back and parked it in the garage alongside of Fred and Lenny's bikes and they went back into the bar.

Lenny was back from taking his shower and changing clothes and said, "When I got out of the shower, I heard something that was music to my ears. Was that your Indian, Arch?"

"It was my bike and if I ever find out who made those pipes, I think I'll go into business selling them. It seems that everybody wants them."

Lenny said, "Arch I got somebody you have to meet." Just then a beautiful redhead walked into the bar. She was wearing a silky dress that looked like she was poured into, with some left over at the top. His eyes followed her all the way to the bar. His tongue was still hanging out when Lenny said, as she sat down next to him, "Down Boy, this is Brenda and she is mine! Who I wanted you to meet is Jim."

Arch turned and on the other side of Lenny was Jim. Lenny said, Arch, meet Jim Barr. Jim is one of our local contractors and he is always looking for good help. Jim said, "The help I need right now is roofers. You ever done any roofing, Arch?"

"No, but I learn quick."

"It's mostly flat commercial roofing. It's hard work but not too hard to learn and the pay is good."

"If the pay is good, hard work don't bother me."

Jim said, "I will give you a day to find lodging and you can start work the day after tomorrow. We work hard and we play hard too. I think you will like it here."

The next morning, Fred took Arch to Theresa's house. She is a friend of his and Lenny's and a widow lady with a 10 year old son. She worked for Lenny doing, as she said, a little bit of everything. Fred said that she did a lot of everything. She was scheduling his menus, ordering produce, meat, seafood, dairy, beer and liquor.

Lenny used to do this himself and then he hired her as a waitress, but after her husband died he found that she had far more capabilities than being a waitress. At first she just started helping order supplies for the restaurant, and then Lenny found that she was much better at it than he was. He also found that she was good at book work. Now she was doing all the ordering, book work and scheduling banquets for large parties and was doing a great job at it. She was basically running his company and he was making more money than when he was running it. Now, Lenny is not cheap, and he paid Theresa a good salary. He decided he would do something for her.

He knew that she traveled about 15 miles each way to work. There was a nice brick bungalow right up Seventh Street, about two blocks from Lenny's restaurant. It was a four bedroom single-family home and he offered it to her. At first she hesitated until he told her that there were no strings attached - it was a bonus because of her work. Finally he said, "Okay, I will rent it to you at a very low rate, or you could buy it for half the price that he paid for it." No, she liked the house and she would rent it and maybe buy it later after saving up enough money to pay the full price.

So Theresa and her son Juan moved into the house and now she was living in almost walking distance of the restaurant

Some months later Lenny asked her to do him a favor. This young man was coming down from Minneapolis and would need lodging and he wondered if she could rent him one of the extra rooms. She said that she would have to meet him before she could decide. Lenny then said Ken Jamieson vouched for him. She knew Ken very well and said if Ken said he's okay, then it's okay by me. So that's how Arch got a job and a place to stay.

Arch thought that Theresa was really great, and her son Juan and Arch hit it off like old buddies right from the start. He moved into his room which was clean and neat. The price Theresa quoted for the monthly room rental, Arch thought was much more than reasonable. Arch offered to pay more, but she refused.

She said that she did not require the rent to maintain her lifestyle. She said her salary and benefits from Lenny's keep her in fine shape. She said, "I only agreed to rent you a room without meeting you first because Lenny asked me to, and also you were vouched for by a good friend of mine."

"Who would this friend of yours be that knows me?" asked Arch.

"That friend of mine would be Ken Jamieson."

"I've only known Ken for a short period of time, but he seems like one hell of a sharp guy."

"He is a sharp guy and if he trusts you, that's good enough for me. So no need to pay up front. You can pay the rent after you get paid."

The next morning Arch got on his Indian and headed out to the location of the construction office, as given to him by Fred. When he got there, there were 20 large buildings under construction. They were condominium style, commercial buildings. The buildings must not all belong to the same company; because 10 of them were steel truss roof and ten were wood truss roofs. Arch knew the difference, but he would ask Jim why someone would prefer more expensive wood trusses than the more modern steel trusses. He found the construction office trailer and went right in. Jim was at his desk on the phone and waved and motioned for Arch to sit down. When he put down the phone he asked Arch what he thought of heights?

Arch said, "Never had a problem. I'm the guy that got sent up the mast on my dad's friend's schooner whenever there was a problem in the rigging. It was 80 feet up and sitting there in the bosun chair seemed real neat to me. So I would say, in answer to your question, heights don't bother me." Arch then asked why some of the buildings have wood trusses and the others have steel trusses?

"The trusses, Arch, as you may or may not know, are the structural frame work that supports the roof. They are constructed in a factory and then delivered to the construction site. The reason for the two different types of construction is a combination of economy and safety. Steel trusses are simpler to construct and quicker to build and are more economical as far as materials are concerned, so it seems that steel wins hands down."

Arch then asked, "If steel is so great, why do 10 of the buildings have wood trusses?"

"The reason is for safety and economy. First, no fireman ever wants to be on a steel truss roof if there is a fire below. Steel truss roofs collapse with no warning and go quickly. Wood gives plenty of warning and goes down slowly. Also, wood trusses may be repaired, where, if a steel roof starts to come down it has to be replaced. That is the difference between steel and wood trusses."

"It seems that you are not afraid of heights so I'll sign you on as a helper working on setting up the steel trusses. We have just gotten started on the first condominium type commercial building. These will be for privately owned small shops and factories. We have almost a year's work in finishing the roofs on all of these buildings"

Jim got on the phone and asked someone to come to his office. A few minutes later a short stocky guy that sounded like he'd just come off the boat from Ireland walked through the door. He looked at Arch and then at Jim, and said, "Is this the new flunky that you got for me? Looks like bottom of the barrel, don't you think Jim? I hope he's got medical insurance the way these new guys keep falling off."

"Arch, meet Bert. Bert, this is Arch, the guy I told you about that rode his bike down from Minneapolis. Bert is a number one steelworker and he will be holding your hand for a few days until he feels confident enough in you to let you work on your own. Don't worry about Bert; he greets all the new guys the same way. Once he even scared off a new guy, even before he started work."

Bert said, "I think we will get along just fine, and if you don't fall off too often and ruin my safety record, I'll take you over to Jack's after work and buy you a beer or two."

"Okay, Arch, you are on the clock so go with Bert and he will show you some of the things you will be doing."

Arch was surprised on how few men it took to put up the trusses. There were two guys on each side of the building who anchored the trusses and one guy on the ground hooking the sling to the crane. Bert showed him that the first truss on the end was secured diagonally and every direction. Then all the others were secured starting from number one and each one tied together by a steel tie otherwise they would fall over like dominoes. Work went pretty good and Arch had caught on fast.

True to his word, Bert and three other guys brought Arch over to Jack's place. Bert bought the first few rounds of beer. Bert and the other three were divorced or just single, so they had no reason to head home early. They sat drank and beer till midnight when Bert reminded the crew that they had to be back to work at 7 am.

Arch headed back to Theresa's house. He hesitated about going to her house at this hour which was now after 1 am but when he rolled down the block and got close he could see a light on in the front porch. Theresa was sitting there reading. He pulled up and parked the bike. She got up and walked out to the bike and handed Arch a key and said, "I forgot to give you a key this morning. I knew that if Bert liked you, it would be party time tonight. I fixed you couple of beef sandwiches. They are in the refrigerator; there is also milk in there, because I know you had enough beer. You are lucky you started work on Friday because you are off for the weekend."

"But Bert said to be at work at 7 am."

"When Bert drinks he forgets what day it is. If you show up tomorrow you will be there by yourself. By the way, Fred wanted you to stop by the bar this morning, sometime before 10 am." She said, "Goodnight, I'll see you in the morning."

Arch went to see Fred at Lenny's. Fred was on the customer side of the bar sitting on a bar stool. When Arch walked in Fred got up and said, "Arch, my boy, today is your lucky day. You have only been here two days and you have been invited to the best barbecue and pool party in town. It's a villa outside of town that is owned by a New York model. Her name is Cindy Harris and she invites some of her girlfriends down to spend some time partying and boy do they do party! She bought the villa four years ago and she comes down three or four times a year. I have known Cindy since she was a teenager when I used to live in New York. When she wanted to buy something down here she contacted me and I found this real neat villa for her. Since then I've been invited to every party and I've never missed one. Arch, don't know how you lucked out; you have been here two days and you get invited to a party that half the guys in Phoenix would give their left nut to get invited to. Just wear something casual and bring your swimsuit. I think I did hear you say okay, you would like to go."

Arch said, "After what you've told me I think I'd have to kill you if you were just pulling my leg."

"Okay, Arch, see you back here at noon. It's about a 45 minute ride." Arch went back to Theresa's and took a shower, changed clothes, got an extra shirt and shorts and put his gear into his saddle bags. He went back into the house and told Theresa that he had no idea what time he would be back. Said he was going to a barbecue somewhere near Paradise Valley at a friend of Fred's, a place owned by a gal named Cindy. Theresa said "You won't be back till tomorrow. You will definitely have fun at Cindy's!"

Chapter 4

A Great Party

Arch met Fred at Lenny's at noon. "Times a wasting, Arch, let's go." They fired up their Indians and headed out east on McDowell Road, then they headed north on Scottsdale Road and turned down a couple of different country roads. There were some horse ranches and some large expensive homes. Then they came to a hilly area that had a lot of trees. Fred pointed to a big fancy house on top of a hill, "That's Cindy's house."

They turned up a long lane and as they got closer to the house Arch noticed the palm trees. Fred stopped and Arch pulled alongside of him. Fred pointed out the main house, the horse barn, the house where the caretaker lives, the tennis courts and most important part, the pool and party area. They pulled up to a small parking lot in front of the house. This was no cheap used car lot. There were two top-of-the-line Mercedes, one Ferrari, a Maserati and a couple of Harleys. Arch parked next to a customized Ford pickup with twin stacks.

The guy in the truck got out and went over to Arch's bike and said, "Those are the most beautiful sounding pipes I have ever heard. I've got a Harley that could use a set like that." Arch told him what he knew about them. "My name is Mike Russell, I am Cindy's neighbor. I'll talk to you later." He went up to the front door, rang the bell, it opened and he walked in. Fred walked up to the door with Arch behind him the door opened and Fred said hi to someone named Jenny and he walked in as Fred moved aside; the view just about floored him. Then Fred said, "Sorry about that,

Arch, I forgot to introduce you to Jenny. Jenny this is Arch. Oh and one more thing nobody dresses too formal at 'Cindy's L. Rancho'."

Arch could hardly move. He was staring at the nicest set of uncovered tits he had ever seen on a beautiful blonde.

Arch's face was turning red. "Don't feel bad, Arch, Jenny loves to pull that on guys that are here for the first time, but she's harmless." Jenny whacked Fred on the side of the head with a fashion magazine. "Jenny is a good kid and she is Cindy's assistant. By the way she is the one that picked you out to come to the party. It's not that easy to get an invite. Lenny came to the first party four years ago. But Brenda shut that off. She told him that if he went to Cindy's party he could forget what he had at home. Now Brenda does not hate Cindy. They are good friends. She used to work for Cindy as a fashion model. Your boss, Jim has been trying to get an invite for the last three years. He finally got one; I put in a good word for him. I didn't have to do that for you. Jenny just picked you out. Jim is going to be jealous that it to him three years and only took you three days. Jim doesn't know that you are here. I want to see his face when he sees you."

Jenny comes back to Fred and Arch, who were still talking and said, "Come on, you guys, let's go meet the other people."

They went through the house and out on the deck and then down to Olympic size swimming pool and Jenny said, "There were six fashion models that work for Cindy, plus Cindy and me. You may wonder why the girls seem to enjoy being either naked or half naked with the men around. The reason is they have chosen these particular men to be here and in the fashion business, there are some of the girls who have to parade around in front of some men they hate, but it's their job. Here they can enjoy it because they are doing it for fun."

Jenny took them around the pool and introduced them to all the girls and some of the guys. All of the girls were topless, but some were also bottomless. In New York they get paid to show off their bodies and here they got to do it for fun.

Jenny said, "Fred, if you want to go find Evonne, she's over in the corner by the cocktail bar." He said, "Thanks, I'll just do that."

Jenny asked Arch, "You want to change into your swimming trunks and jump into that nice cool water?" "Sounds good to me." She showed him where he could change into his trunks and he took off his shirt. He left the changing room and met with Jenny. She took one look and said, "Wow, look at those muscles! You sure have a nice chest."

"Jenny, I can say the same for you. I've never seen a finer, sexier looking chest than the one I'm looking at right now."

"I am especially glad that you think so." They went to the pool and jumped in and swim around a bit. Then she dove under and came right up in front of him, she pressed her nice firm boobs against his chest and rubbed them around. Then she reached down and said, "I think something is arising."

Arch said, "Let's get out of this pool before I attack you!" She laughed and said, "Okay, there is plenty time for that. Right now Cindy is having the caterers bring in the barbecue and it is the best in Phoenix. The reason it is the best is because if it's not the best they won't be back. They like what they see. They want to be back."

All around the pool were custom-made deck chairs. They were twice as wide as a normal deck chair and made to comfortably seat two.

The caterers brought out the food on carts. There were pork ribs, beef ribs, pork chops, rib eye steaks, grilled fruit and vegetables. Arch was sitting on a deck chair with Jenny eating barbecue ribs. Jenny dropped some sauce on her breast and Arch grabbed a napkin and started to wipe off the sauce. "Not that way, Arch." And Jenny took the napkin away. She said, "Now lick it off." Being that Arch was a guest, he felt honor bound to do what he was told. He licked the left breast until it was clean, but she had accidentally spilled sauce on her right breast, so he went to work on the right. Arch said, "Look, there is some sauce on both nipples." After he fixed the nipple problem, Jenny said, "Arch, I think you've got a hard problem and I think I can fix it in my bedroom."

They went to Jenny's bedroom and by the time they got there they were both so hot that there was no time for foreplay. Arch was in her in a minute. They made love for about five minutes before they both came. They lay back for a few minutes and then she got up and said, "I'll go to the bar and get some beers." She went out to the bar and never bothered to put the bottom of her suit back on. Actually she never put it back on the rest of the night. She came back with the beers. They drank a beer and screwed again. Then they went for a swim and had some more food and jumped into the pool again and went back to Jenny's room and had more sex. By that time it was 4 am, they were so they flaked out they went right to sleep.

They woke up at 10 am and had some breakfast and by then it was almost noon and Fred said that they had better get going. "I've got the afternoon shift at the bar."

Arch told Jenny that he would like to see her again. She said they were flying back to New York tomorrow and she handed him her business card and said keep in touch. They fired up the Indians and took off down the road. They got back to Lenny's at about 1:15 pm.

Fred said, "I don't have to start till 2:30."

So Arch said, "Let's have a beer or two."

"Okay, Arch, now what do you think of Cindy's place?"

"It was great, Fred, and I think the gals are great, but I would have liked to meet Cindy."

"You can't meet Cindy. She said killed by a mugger. Now Jenny runs the business."

"The way the girls talked I thought she was there."

"It happened three years ago and they keep the party going as they did when she was still alive. Cindy knew that something like this could happen, so she set it up legally so Jenny could run the business. They all share in the profits and Cindy's El Rancho belongs to the company. Jenny is president of one most respected fashion houses in New York. She told you to keep in touch so why don't you?"

Chapter 5

Theresa is Great

Lenny walked into the bar and said, "How was the party, Guys?" Fred said it was just another boring party.

"Yeah, I am sure it was!" He turned Arch and said, "I'll bet you never seen him again once he found Evonne."

Fred said, "How he could know, he was partying with Jenny all night until 10 this morning."

Lenny said, "Arch, you really go first class! Jenny is some dish and a really a nice gal. She is also pretty smart."

Arch said, "I got to go." Arch headed home to Theresa's house. When he got there, Theresa was in the kitchen cooking up some meat and onions to make some quesadillas.

"Smells good, Theresa, what are you making?"

"Quesadillas, you staying for dinner?"

"Wouldn't miss it. You make the best I've ever tasted."

"You're not going any place tonight."

"No, I'm not going any place tonight, especially since you are making quesadillas."

"I told you that you wouldn't get home till today. It must have been a great party because you really look beat. Did one girl do that to you or did you take on the whole group of them?"

"One girl and she was great."

"Which one?"

"Jenny."

"I knew Cindy and met most of the girls; they were all pretty good kids. Here I am 33 and they average 24 to 28 and I called them kids. I think I'm in pretty good shape for an old lady."

"Theresa, you sure look good to me. You're built like a brick shit house!"

"Arch, I'll have you know that I was at the first party when Cindy was still around. From what I hear they still have some wild parties, but they don't compare to the first one. It was wild and fun. I know, because I was there. It was about three years after my husband was killed and I didn't socialize very much. Cindy was at the bar and she said, "Theresa you need to party and we've got a good one Saturday and Sunday." She sent a car for me, to and from, so I could party and not have to drive. I had so much fun that I stayed till Monday. When I first got there I was a little shy. Just walking in to the pool area and seeing all the gals topless and some bottomless too. And even some of the guy's, butt naked. At first I thought I made a mistake in coming, but Cindy came over to me and said, "Theresa I think you're a little embarrassed." She handed me a Grande Margarita. It went down nice and fast and warmed me up. She said once you get into it you will feel much better then she took off her bikini top, so I took mine off too. She looked at my boobs and said, "Theresa, anyone with a nice set of tits like that should not want to hide them. You have a nicer set than any one of my girls. I looked around and damn if she wasn't right."

Arch looked at Theresa and said, "I think Cindy was right." She took off her blouse and said, "Juan won't be home tonight or you wouldn't get a good look." And she took off her bra and Arch backed off and said, "Wow! I saw some great boobs yesterday, last night and this morning, but, Theresa, if I were a boob judge, I'd hang a blue-ribbon on each one of those beauties. Cindy sure as hell was right."

"After Cindy said I had great boobs, I felt much better and not embarrassed to show them off. After that she said, "Theresa, you also have a real nice ass and she took off the bottom of her bikini, so I did too. I felt good about it. We were bare ass naked and we walked right in front of all of the drooling men and over to the bar. I felt really good."

"Theresa, I would have loved to be there when you first decided to liberate yourself."

"Well, you're here now and let's see if you think Cindy was right about my ass." And then she dropped her shorts and she had nothing on underneath. Arch had taken off his shirt and now he took off his Levi's. She was naked and he still had on his jockey shorts. He stared at her and said, "Cindy was right about that too."

She had been hiding her beautiful body under some frumpy clothes. He reached out and grabbed hold of her arms and pulled her to him and put her nice firm breasts against his chest. She reached down into his shorts and grabbed hold of his now very hard dick. Then she leaned down and took it in her mouth and Arch felt like he was in Heaven. He then picked her up and carried her to his bed and laid her down. He backed off and just looked at her and said, "Theresa, you are the most beautiful piece of artwork I have ever seen."

Then he leaned over and kissed her on the mouth and her face and her neck she reciprocated. He kissed her breasts and then sucked on her nipples and she went wild. He got on top of her and she grabbed his throbbing tool and put it right into her hot pussy and he pushed it all the way in. Slowly because he was well endowed and did not want to hurt her. He found what she liked and then just made love.

After they came, Theresa lay back for a minute and said, "Let's have some dinner."

So they got up and ate some great quesadillas. Arch ate so much he could hardly move. Theresa asked if he wanted to play around some more. He looked at her, patted his belly and said, "Too much quesadilla." They both laughed and then she said, "Too much playing around yesterday." They went to bed and fell asleep. Theresa woke Arch at 6 am to get to work by 7 am and he was ready to go. She said, "Lover boy, you're insatiable, but you can't go to work with that telephone pole in your pants. I'll just have to fix it. So she dropped her robe, climbed into the sack and she fixed it."

Chapter 6

Time to Head North

He got dressed and ate a couple leftover slices of quesadilla, climbed on his Indian and went to work. When he got to the job site, he found Bert sitting in the office talking to Jim. Bert was nursing a weekend hangover and Jim was just sitting there with a big smile on his face probably thinking about his great weekend. When Arch walked in, Jim turned to Bert and said, "Go check out those new trusses that they unloaded this morning. Make sure of the count and then take a gage and check the mounting holes for size and location. We don't want to do that while they are up in the air." He turned to Arch and said, "It's no fun drilling out holes when you're 30 feet in the air.

Bert leaves, and Jim said, "Hell of a party Saturday. I hear you didn't get back until Sunday. You must have made out pretty good. I have been trying to get an invite to one of those parties for the last three years. You're here for three days and you get invited. You must have some pull."

"No, I don't know anybody Jim."

"Well, if you don't know anyone you sure do luck out. Where did you go after you came into the pool area?"

"I was with Jenny and we got along pretty good."

"You must have gotten along pretty good! No one had seen either of you from 3 pm till 10 am the next morning. I was with Melissa and she was one hell of a gal, we spent a lot of time in the pool and she said that she never liked to wear anything while swimming. We would have a margarita, jump in the pool and bang away in the water, come out and have another margarita and go back in the pool and do it again. We must have gone at about five or six times. That's why I'm moving slow today, but it sure was fun!"

"Jim, when I got here I wasn't expecting any great parties like that. But I'm not going to knock it. You just don't look a gift horse in the mouth. Well, I guess I better get out and get to work if I want to earn my pay."

"Speaking of work, Arch, I just thought I'd let you know, Bert said you're doing good. The business agent will be here Wednesday, so I will recommend that he gives you an iron worker's Union ticket as an apprentice, third-year."

"Thanks, Jim." Arch went out to work with Bert. They set all the trusses on the second building. Work on the buildings went pretty good in the next few months they set all the trusses on the first 10 buildings. Then they started putting the steel sheeting on top of the trusses. In the next month they finished with seven of the first 10 buildings. It got into June and it started to get really hot. From morning till late afternoon it was unbearable. Even for locals who should be used to it. The sun would get the steel sheets so hot that you could not touch the steel barehanded.

They did as a lot of other workers did in the sunny south; work from 5 am to 9 or 10 am, quit working, came back at 5 pm and work till 9 pm. It was still hot, but you could work in it. Now this was only the first part of June, it would get hotter by the third week in June they had 10 of the steel trussed covered. Then they started the next ten wood truss buildings. The wood is not as bad as the steel trusses to handle in the hot weather, but as it got into July, it kept getting hotter.

Arch could take the heat if he really wanted to, but this was not what he thought was what he wanted to do. He figured that he would help Jim get the wood trusses up and then it was time to head up north to the kind of whether he was used to.

It was Friday night, which for the last few months was playtime for the weekend with the sexiest gal he had ever met. Juan was gone on the weekends. He would visit with his grandmother in Scottsdale. She owned a very nice Mexican restaurant on the outskirts of town. She had a nice house right next door and a big swimming pool which Juan loved to swim in. Sometimes Arch would bring Juan to his grandmother's on his Indian. Juan loved to ride. Today Arch brought Juan to Scottsdale. Juan went in the house and changed into his swimming trunks and came out and said thanked Arch for the ride. Then he jumped into the pool.

Arch spent half an hour talking to Juan's grandmother. He could hardly believe that this 50+ woman was Theresa's mother. She looked more like her sister he mentioned this to her and she said that Theresa does have a sister - a younger sister.

"I was married to a red-headed Irishman at the time Theresa was born. That is why she's a redhead. Her sister has black hair like me and my present husband who is Mexican."

On the way back to Theresa's house he got to thinking that he was planning on leaving in the not too distant future. He was getting very close to Theresa, but he was not thinking of any kind of permanent commitment. He thought Theresa felt the same way, but he was not sure and did not want to hurt her. When he got back to the house, Theresa was cooking a pork roast and it smelled great and he told her so. He said she was a great cook and she said the reason for that is that you have to like to cook. He took a quick shower came back in the kitchen and got a beer out of refrigerator. They were both very quiet for a while and then Theresa said, "Arch, I've got something to tell you. I just got a call this afternoon from someone I've been waiting to hear from. Arch, I'm getting married in two months."

Theresa stood back and waited for Arch to say something.

"Theresa, that's great news! I hope he is a good man because you deserve the best."

"He is a good man and I have known him for years. He is a widower and has two kids about the same age as Juan. He is a mining engineer working on a job in South Africa. The job will be done in two months and he will come back here. He called and proposed to me this afternoon and I said yes. Being that I'm getting married in a couple of months, I am not sure that we should be playing around anymore."

"Maybe your right, Theresa, but I sure will miss it."

"I have known Hans for quite a few years. I even introduced his brother to my sister and they are now married. They are not more than 100 miles away in a little town called Santa Rosa."

He asked what her new name would be and she said, "Larsen."

Arch said, "He's a Dane. His name is Knute and your sister's name is Maria and together they own and run Larsen's Mexican Restaurant. Best Mexican food in New Mexico. He rides a Harley and she rides a Moto Guzzi."

She said, "Arch, you are amazing! That's exactly right! How could you know? I was the only one who knew they were married. Not even my mother knew. They were going to ride up here and surprise her. How can you know that?"

"I spent the night at their restaurant. Great food and nice people."

"I just thought of something - I'm not married yet, so how about a little something before dinner, that is if you're up to it? And maybe a little after dinner, that is if you can still get it up."

"Don't worry, Baby, I can get it up if you're still hot to try."

"I'll be hot to trot, but I may wear out that oversize sex tool of yours, Arch."

"I hope you try. If you wear it out at least I'll die happy." By 2 am they were both worn out and a fell asleep with smiles on their faces.

The next morning Arch told Theresa they would be finishing up on the wood trusses in about a month and that he planned on heading north after they were done. He said, "I was hesitant to tell you that I was going and I really wasn't sure that I would go. But now that you are planning to get married I feel much better about it. And if Hans is as nice a guy as Knute, you will have a great husband and he will have the sexiest wife in all of Arizona."

"Well, Arch, it looks like we have got a whole month of fun before you head north."

"Theresa, now that you are getting married I wouldn't want to chance getting you pregnant before you get married."

She said, "Can't happen, Arch, I almost died when I had Juan and the Doc said it was too dangerous, so he fixed it so I couldn't get pregnant again."

"It seems that today is a day of good news," said Arch. So every weekend it would be party time for Theresa and Arch, until he headed back north.

Arch went to work and climbed up the frame of the building where Bert was standing. He was watching the crane moving into place to lift the wood trusses for building number eight. In a couple more weeks they would have all the trusses up. He would talk to Jim after work about heading north after the trusses were finished. He had already told Bert about his plans and asked him not to mention it to Jim today; that he would talk to Jim tonight at Lenny's. Bert said he was sorry to see him go and that he was the best worker he's had in a long time.

That night after work, Arch went home to Theresa's house. Theresa had just gotten home from work. She had stopped at the store and picked up some groceries. She said that she was going to make shrimp fajitas, which was Juan's favorite dinner.

Arch said, "Theresa anything you cook is like from a five-star restaurant. He said I also agree with Juan, shrimp fajitas are great, especially when they're prepared by a great sexy cook."

She reached out and pulled Arch to her and gave him a big wet kiss. "Now go take a shower and come back down and have some fajitas." He came back down after a shower and clean clothes. She asked, "Where are you going all dressed up?"

"Going over to Lenny's to talk to Jim to let him know that I'm going back north."

"You say north, but where north? It could be Flagstaff or Alaska they are both north."

"I headed south and I didn't know I would wind up in Phoenix. Theresa, when I get where I'm going, I'll write to you and I would appreciate hearing from you, unless you feel that you shouldn't be writing to someone after you are married."

She said, "Arch, I will keep no secrets from my husband. What has happened now I feel no wrong and after I am married to Hans I will respect him and he should respect me for whatever I have done before. So Arch, let's eat and then you can go to Lenny's, take care of business with Jim, and then get back as soon as you can."

He said, "It's the beginning of the weekend, Theresa, I'll be back as soon as I can. I don't want to waste too much time sitting at the bar talking to Jim, when I could be with you. Theresa, I have one question to ask you. Do you think Hans will be able to keep up with you in bed?"

"Arch, I have known Hans before he was married to his late wife. This may make you feel bad but Hans is as good in bed as you are."

"No, it makes me feel good knowing that you won't be neglected."

When he got to the bar he said hi to Fred and ordered a draft beer, then Fred proceeded to tell Arch that Jim called and said he couldn't make it tonight. He said that he would see you here at noon tomorrow. Arch chugged his beer and slid off the stool. "How about another beer?"

"Sorry, Fred, got someplace to go."

When Arch came back to Theresa's, he walked in and didn't see her. Then he heard the shower running, he didn't want to scare her, so he called out. "I'll be right out, as soon as I wash my hair." He went right up to the bathroom and into the shower room. "Arch, you already had a shower. What are you doing back here so soon? You couldn't have been gone more than 30 minutes."

"I came right back because I thought I needed another shower." He got right into the shower with Theresa. He said, "I guess you're right, I really don't need a shower since I had one an hour ago. But tonight I thought that maybe I could be a good guy and help you take a shower."

"Why that's nice of you, Arch, and I sure do appreciate the help." Arch was behind Theresa, right hand washing right breast, left hand washing left breast.

She said, "Arch, you seem to be very proficient at helping a lady bathe, but what is it that you have between my legs? I think this is leading up to something." And it did. The next morning they didn't wake up till 11am and felt refreshed. After a very busy night, they got up and had coffee and a light breakfast.

Arch said, "I'm supposed to meet Jim at Lenny's at noon. So I better get going before you lead me astray." He pulled up into the parking lot at Lenny's, it was eleven forty five He went into the side door which went directly into the bar. Fred was setting on a tall stool jawing with a couple of customers.

He raised his hand and said, "Hi Arch; Jim will probably be here in 10 to 15 minutes."

Jim came in and ordered a beer and sat down next to Arch. Jim asked. "You wanted to see me about something?

"Yeah, Jim, I was planning on heading north as soon as we are finished with the wood trusses."

"Don't you like the work?"

"No, works okay, you guys are okay and the pay is okay, but I got here in winter. It was hot then and now it's getting into summer and it keeps getting hotter. I got to go north where it's cool."

Jim said, "Where is North, Arch? Have you got a job lined up? You don't even know anybody unless you go back to Minneapolis."

"You said that you don't want to do that. Fred Chimed in and said why don't you head to Chicago? You said you did machine work. They got a lot of machine shops in Chicago. Fred said I lived in Chicago a few years ago, and I still get a Chicago Tribune delivered here. I think I still have last Sunday's Tribune. That paper has the biggest help wanted section of any paper I've ever seen."

Fred went into the back room, when he came back he was carrying a big thick Sunday Tribune. They looked at their front page and one third of the page was a picture of Chicago's lakefront. The caption said a beautiful day, and beautiful girls at North Avenue beach, sunny and 80°.

The picture was in color, and the lake looked blue |green and cool. There were hundreds of people lying on blankets sunning themselves. Fred Arch and Jim was looking at the picture. They said the lake looked inviting, and so do all those gals lying on their back sunning themselves. Fred was really concentrating on the picture then he got up and went in the office and came back out with a magnifying glass.

He looked at the picture with the glass, he said, "I thought so," and he handed the glass to Arch. Then Arch handed it to Jim. They looked at each other and it was a consensus of opinion. Though one girl in the top corner of the picture was lying on her back and was topless with two very nice boobs. Then it was back to the magnifying glass. All three of them looked and were trying to decide what size her breast was. Just then Brenda walked in and said she was looking for Lenny. Fred called her over and asked her to tell them what size these beautiful boobs were. Brenda took the glass took one look and started laughing.

She said, "You three dopes are the boobs I have lived in New York and been a fashion model long enough to recognize what I see. You idiots have been drooling over genuine BF Goodrich rubber boobs. A Transvestite."

Brenda looked at the three of them who are sitting on their barstools, with a stupid look on their face. She said, "Are you guys queer or just dumb?"

They answer in unison, "JUST DUMB."

Brenda walked away laughing.

Jim said, "Well, I guess it's just bad lighting in here."

"Jim," Arch said, "Brenda didn't need a flashlight. So I guess that inside of 48 hours everybody in Phoenix is going to know about the three guys drooling over a Transvestite with rubber tits."

"Well," Arch said, "I'm getting out of here before that rumor gets all the way to Chicago. Speaking of Chicago, where is that help wanted section?"

By now they have had quite a few beers and a few shots of tequila and they were starting to get a little drunk and the paper was getting a little fuzzy. Arch was going through a different job classification. Construction jobs? "No way in hell." Factory assembly line? "Not for me, you become a robot." Sales jobs? Car sales? "Not for me." Inside sales? Women's undergarments? "I could do that, but I don't think they would hire me. Besides if they did hire me I'd probably work for nothing. Hey I think I found it Fred, another round of beers with tequila on the side."

Fred said, "Tell Sam the bartender."

Sam said, "I heard." Sam served the drinks and the three of them were pretty blitzed by now.

"Here it is, Junior Machinist, minimum two years' experience. Hansen Tool and Machine, 1800 W. Lake St. Hey, Fred, you said that you used to live in Chicago."

"Is Lake Street on the beach?"

"Yeah, right next to North Avenue Beach, except more and better broads, cheaper beer and booze, and higher wages," said Fred as he winked at Jim.

"Well, Guys, I'm off to Chicago next week."

"What are you smoking, Arch? You ain't got no job in Chicago and what makes you think you will get hired?"

"I am the best man for the job, that's why. There is a phone number. I'll call."

Arch tried to call, but got no answer. He said, "You think maybe they are out of business?"

"No, you Asshole," said Jim, "This is Saturday afternoon. Nobody in Chicago works on Saturday afternoons."

Arch said, "I'll call Monday." Well, Arch forgot to call Monday and he didn't think about it until Thursday afternoon. He called at about 4:30 pm and got no answer and it finally dawned on him that it was 6:30 pm in Chicago and the shop would be closed for the day. They finished the trusses at about 1 pm on Friday.

He got to Theresa's place about 1:30 pm and he called Chicago again. Art Hansen answered the phone and they must have talked for about 45 minutes, they had a lot to talk about once they found out that they knew each other. Then they talked about work and Art seemed pleased that Arch said he would leave Phoenix Monday and it was 1800 miles to Chicago. Barring any problems, at 450 to 500 miles a day he should be in Chicago by Thursday or Friday.

Sunday morning Arch said goodbye to everyone that he knew in Phoenix. He packed up his extra clothes, his leather jacket and some of the things he did not want to leave behind. Some of the things he wanted to keep, but did not have room for in his saddle bags.

He gave Theresa the postage money and asked her to mail a box to him in Chicago once he gets an address. He said, "I would love to receive a picture of your wedding, even better than that to be invited to your wedding. I would love to meet Hans he must be a great guy."

"He is a great guy and I would love for you to come to our wedding. Hans said that he would like to meet you. I told him all about you. Well not everything!"

Being that this was their last night together, they decided not to waste it just talking. Arch said, "I have one more thing to say, Theresa. I am already jealous of Hans, but I'm happy for you because I think he will make you happy."

"Thank you, Arch"

The next morning Arch got up and was ready for the long ride to Chicago. Most everything he owned was in the box. Other than that he had a small TV set in his room which he gave to Theresa. He also had a Zenith Trans-Oceanic portable radio, which he gave to Juan. Juan thought it was the greatest thing he had ever seen. He gassed up the night before, checked his oil and adjusted his rear drive chain. Arch knew that his primary chain was a little loose, but not bad, he thought. He would check it or replace it in Chicago.

Arch shook hands with Juan and picked him up and hugged him. He said, "Juan, I'll miss you old buddy." Then he turned to Theresa. "My good buddy's mama, you can't believe how much I'll miss you and I hope you will send me an invite to your wedding."

"I will, Arch," and she kissed him full on the mouth.

He said, "Theresa, that kiss will last me all the way to Chicago."

He jumped on the kick starter, fired up the Chief and took off down the road. He went west on McDowell to Route 17 then he went north to Flagstaff on Route 40 he went east. It was a smooth ride across Arizona and New Mexico and then he crossed the border into Texas. About 15 miles into Texas he hit a storm of June Bugs as he was cruising along at about 75 mph. They hurt like hell. He pulled up under an overpass, but he knew he could not stay there. He had to ride through them, so he rigged up a bandana and took off at about 30 mph and in about 10 minutes he was out of the bugs. He kicked it back up to 75 mph again and was rolling along at a good clip. Fifteen minutes later it felt like the bugs were back, but he found that it was not June Bugs, but what was trying to knock him off the bike was super large raindrops. He slowed down to about 30 miles an hour again and kept riding. He saw a neon sign up ahead, it said "Beer", so he pulled in because he was getting tired of being hit by the super-size raindrops.

Chapter 7

Arch is "God's Messenger"

He parked the bike, got off and walked into the bar. When he got inside he took off his wet Levi jacket and complained about the rain. There were about 10 guys in the bar and they all turned toward Arch.

The bartender looked at Arch and said, "You're complaining about rain? Do you know that this is the second biggest watermelon capital in the world? We need the rain to raise watermelons. This is the first rain we have had this year. We need it badly and you're complaining."

Arch said, "Sorry, I didn't know."

One of the guys at the bar said, "Quit knocking him, it may have been him that brought the rain." Somebody else said, "Joe may be right and if he leaves it may stop raining."

"I am Lou," one of the guys said and pulled up a stool. "I'd like to buy you a drink."

One after the other they kept buying him drinks. They would not let Arch pay for anything. This being the first rain of the year and nobody was superstitious but they did not want to take a chance. They felt that if Arch left to the rain might quit, so why take a chance? They kept buying Arch beer.

A couple of guys went over to the local restaurant and came back with a half a dozen pizzas, so everybody hung around and ate pizza and drank beer and Arch still could not spend any of his money. It kept raining and everybody kept drinking.

It was getting on to midnight and Arch said, "I think I really should be going."

Joe said, "Arch, it's raining too hard for you to ride and you're too drunk to ride anyway. If you try to leave on your bike, I, as a deputy police officer, would have to arrest you for drinking and driving."

"So, Arch," Ben the bartender said, "Why don't we wheel your bike around the back and put it in the shed behind the bar? We can lock the shed and your bike will be safe. I'm closing up at midnight and we have a guest room so you can come home with me and sack out and sleep off all that beer you drank."

Ben and Arch put the Indian into the shed, locked it up and headed to Ben's house through the driving rain. Arch crawled in the sack and promptly fell asleep. Ben explained the situation to his wife; that everyone in the bar had decided that Arch was a great rainmaker and said to let Arch sleep off his hang over, or at least till it stopped raining.

Arch slept till 3 pm the next day. It rained hard all night and he got up and said hello to Ben's wife and they introduced each other. She said, "Arch, you slept for about 15 hours. You must be hungry. How is your hangover?"

Arch said, "I feel great, but I guess I am a bit hungry."

"Ben told me to call him when you were awake. He will be here in about 10 minutes." Ben came home and it was still raining and looked like it would never stop. Ben's wife served an early dinner.

It was about 4:30 pm when Arch thanked Ben and his wife. He said, "I really should get going. I'm supposed to be in Chicago by Friday."

Ben's wife asked, "Arch, won't you get sick riding in the rain?"

He said, "No, I got a rain suit in my saddlebags. Besides, it's warm out and the rain seems to be slowing down."

Ben said, "You're right, Arch, it's slowing down. You know, Arch, everybody in that bar really felt that you brought this rain. If it stops now that's okay. Everyone feels that it saved the watermelon crop and you're the guy that did it."

"Ben, do you really think that I had anything to do with it?"

"I don't know, Arch, I just sell beer, but they do." And he walked out of the kitchen.

By the time they got to the bar and Arch rode his bike out of the shed, it had stopped raining and the sun was out. Ben said, "Let's go in and have one farewell drink."

"Okay, then, just one and I've got to get going."

They walked into the bar and it was full of people. Rudy was behind the bar serving drinks.

Rudy said, "It's been like this since noon. Everyone wants to say thanks and goodbye to Arch." Arch had Peppermint Schnapps with Ben and then he had one more with a group of men.

Arch finally said, "I've got to put some miles on before dark."

"What do you do after it gets dark? Do you look for motel?

"No."

"What do you do? Pull up and camp out?"

"No."

"Well then what do you do?"

"I just keep on riding."

"Won't you get sleepy?"

"There's a lot of ways to keep awake."

"Like what?"

"Sometimes sitting backwards on the seat and watching the traffic behind me. Then there is this standing on the seat trick. But the worst one is riding sidesaddle backwards and doing sit ups."

Somebody said, "Arch, you're full of shit."

Arch said, "That's absolutely right, but some of you believed me." And they all laughed.

Then Arch said, "On that note, I've got to get going. Thanks for everything."

Then somebody said, "Arch, we truly believe that you brought the rain, so thanks from all of us."

Arch rode out and turned east on Route 40 and rolled on and headed toward Arkansas. He knew that he needed a fuel stop and up ahead he saw a great big Texaco sign. As he got closer he saw that below the oil company sign was another sign. It said "You just went through Hoggsville. The second-biggest watermelon capital in the world."

He pulled into the Texaco station and filled up with fuel because motorcycle riders filled their own tanks back then. He went in to pay for his fuel and asked the attendant what all the celebrating in town was for.

"You haven't heard? We have not had rain for over a year. The watermelon crop would be dead in another week. People have been going to church every day and praying for rain. The faithful saying that you got to have Faith. They say God will send someone to bring the rain and by golly he did yesterday. A stranger came to Ben's bar and he brought the rain with him. They said he stayed till we had enough rain and then he just up and left on, what they said was his Indian friend of his. Sounds weird, but they say he brought the rain. They are right about that because he sure brought enough of it. I hope he comes back next year because I would like to say hello to him."

Arch looked him in the eye and said, "My name is Arch, so hello, and this is my Indian friend." He jumped on his bike and hit the kick starter and fired up his friend and took off down Route 40.

Bill, the attendant, looked up and watched Arch ride out. Then all of a sudden he saw it. He was looking at the back of Arch, a shadowy figure on an Indian motorcycle, when all of a sudden he was at the top of a rise. Bill could see it. A complete halo around the stranger. He knew then that he had been talking to a Messenger from God. He had been told that God works in mysterious ways. He sure does.

The halo was actually the flash of a sky rocket at half a mile up the road. The fact that Arch was on top of a rise and it was totally dark with the rocket exploding half a mile in front of him and Arch being in the middle between the rocket and Bill in the Texaco station when it went off, the light from the explosion bracketed Arch and his bike perfectly and created a beautiful halo. Arch was their Messenger from God.

He rode east on Route 40 and was making good time, just cruising along at about 75 mph. The big old Bonneville Chief engine was really perking. With the engine running smooth and the sound of the exhaust through the big megaphones; that was beautiful.

CHAPTER 8

BIG CHANGE AT FOLEY'S

The messenger felt that he was in heaven. If you are not a rider then you could not believe what a pleasure it is to be cruising along on a bike. He was going east on Route 40 and he was trying to decide if he should take Route 35 NE. into Kansas City, or go further east on Route 40 all the way to Route 71 in Arkansas. Then go north on Route 71 to Fayetteville. He headed for Route 71 After he would go through Fayetteville he would start looking for Foley's Feed Bag Restaurant. Up ahead he saw a sign and it said Foley's Feed Bag Restaurant, 'everybody welcome. The restaurant came into view from what Arch remembered when they were there six months ago it was run down, now it was painted white with green trim.

When he got closer he saw that it was nicely landscaped. There was also a large asphalt parking lot, it was a small and gravel 6 months ago. It also had a special parking area for motorcycles right near the front door. There was room for about 30 bikes, in front. Up against the building were about 30 lock boxes as you would find in a bus station or airport. There was only one difference there were keys but no coin slots. Then there was an arrow pointing to a door and a sign that said "If you would like to clean off the road dirt". Arch parked his bike alongside of about 15 or 20 other bikes and went into the washroom, which he figured would be a small sink and some paper towels.

He was completely surprised to find that it was very clean, and brightly lit. There were two separate showers and locker rooms for guys and gals.

Arch used the urinal and went to the sink to wash his hands. When he turned around he saw a guy standing behind him combing his wet hair. He said it sure feels good after riding some of these back roads around here. Arch looked at him and said, "When did this all happen?"

"What happen?"

"The shower room, the bike parking area and everything else around here."

Probably about four or five months ago. Ed said that bikers are his favorite customers. And nothing is too good for them. There is a suggestion box inside of the front door, and it is for bikers only. Anything he can do for their short stay at his restaurant he will do."

Arch figured that Ed must be a guy that Foley sold out to. Arch walked outside and over to the front stairs. He no sooner walked in to the front door and a big black guy in waiters garb walked up to Arch, he said "Are you Arch?"

At first he wasn't going to say yes. But this guy was 3 inches taller and outweighed Arch by 50 pounds so he just said, "Yeah, I'm Arch."

"Would you please follow me, Sir? Ed would like to see you, Arch."

How come this Ed knows me and what does he want? The big guy said his name was Jeff and he led Arch up some stairs and to a door that said "The Office". Jeff knocked and a voice said "Come in" and Jeff opened the door and they both walked in. Ed was behind a desk with his chair swiveled around and getting something out of a lower drawer of a file cabinet. He got what he wanted any turned around and stood up.

Arch said, "Foley."

"That's my last name. Call me Ed." He came around the desk and shook Arch's hand. Arch could not figure it. He thought Jeff was there to punch him out and then Ed turned to Jeff and said, "I want to formally introduce you to Arch. Arch is the guy that is responsible for the new and different Foley's restaurant. About six months ago, Arch punched me in the mouth and knocked out of couple of teeth. Then he punched me in the gut. He's got a mean punch. He could probably hold his own with you, Jeff."

"I doubt that boss. But let's not find out".

"Then after all that punching he made me eat a plate of scrambled eggs that was full of cayenne pepper and hot sauce. My mouth burned for a few hours".

Jeff then asked, "Why would he do that to such a nice guy like you?"

"Jeff, I wasn't always so nice. Arch and his friend came in for breakfast. Arch's friend, Dave, was black and I said his friend could not eat here and

I called him a Nigger. That's when Arch punched me in the mouth and then I said something else to his friend and I called him a Nigger again and then he punched me again. Then they ordered breakfast. Dave ordered scrambled and I loaded it would cayenne pepper, but Arch spotted that and came around the counter, dragged me out and sat me down next to Dave and covered the eggs with Diablo sauce and Dave made me eat it."

"Boss, I think you got what you deserved. You were sure some sort of bad ass and I think they fixed you good."

"They did, Jeff, and it changed my life. There was a guy named Ken Jamieson who was in here when all of this happened. He convinced me to change my ways. And I did. Arch, can you see the results? All because of you, Arch."

"Jeff, you can go back to doing what you were doing, I'll take care of Arch. Arch, you stopped in to eat so let's go out to the dining room." They walked into the dining room.

Arch said, "It looks packed looks like we will have to take a number."

"Not if we sit at the VIP table, where the level is raised two feet. We get some big wheels here now and then and sometimes they make speeches from there." They sat down at the VIP table. Jeff came over and asked if they cared for any wine?

Arch said, "No, I'll have a beer."

Ed said he would have the same. "Jeff is our wine steward, really knows his wine. Have you noticed that we have about half white and half black waiters and waitresses? We also have about the same ratio in customers."

Arch asked, "Do you ever have any racial problems?"

Ed said, "Rarely, but we don't solve them exactly the same way that you do, we can't afford to get sued. One night two big red necks sat at a table and they were with two gals. I guess they wanted to show off for their girlfriends. Jim the waiter comes over to their table and asked to take their order. I was on the floor at the time and heard what they said. The waiter asked them again. One of them stood up and looked at the waiter and said, "Get your nigger ass out of here. We ain't going to be served by no nigger waiter. That's right, no nigger waiter."

"So I went over there and told Jim that I would take care of these people and I said, 'I understand that your first order was that you did not want to be served by no nigger waiter.' 'That's right, no nigger waiters for us.' So I turned to the customers and said out loud. 'These people don't want to be served as they said, by no nigger waiters. Folks, when you come Foley's, is the customer always right?' And the people said 'Always'. 'As customers do you think these people should be served?' And they said 'No'. 'Jeff, show these people out the door and point the way to McDonald's.' One of the guys tried to resist, but Jeff had his fingers bent backward and he went out the door of his tip toes. 'Things have changed since you were here last year. I've changed and I feel much better for it.'"

"By the way, your friend Dave stopped by about three months ago, he was heading back to Chicago and he asked me to tell you to call him if you get to Chicago. He left his card with his phone number and address on it. I told Dave about what I wanted to do with this place and maybe open another restaurant. He said that he had an uncle that was president of a bank and mortgage company. He said he might be able to help. A week later a black man came to the restaurant and after he had dinner and paid his bill and left a nice tip, he asked to see me. I went out to his table and he asked me to sit down and I did. He introduced himself as Robert Johnson, Dave's uncle. He told me that after talking to Dave, they think they can take care of my financing problem easy enough. Looking this place over he didn't think there would be any problem for his bank to finance a new restaurant venture that I wished to engage in. But what he really came down here for was that his bank is heavily into the mortgage business and he used to live down here and he's seen the way they like to treat black people and he would like to help out where he could. He said that there are people that would like to buy their own homes, but when they go to a mortgage company or a bank; just the fact that they are black, they are quoted a higher interest rate than white people. Then a larger down payment is required. Johnson then said that he would like to help change some of that. He said Dave told him that I have some people working for me that would like to buy their own house. He left his card and a card of an honest lawyer in Fayetteville named Gary. Said he's an honest guy and not a bigot and can handle my problem too. Johnson left and a few days later a lawyer named Burton came into the restaurant to talk to some of my employees. Now six of my employees have new houses that before they never dreamed they could own and I bought another restaurant next to Lake of the Ozarks. Business is now great, my employees are happy and so am I. And I have a great many honest to God friends both black and white."

"Ed, you can't believe how much I worried about coming here. I almost didn't, but I sure am glad that I did."

After dinner the waitress came back to the table with a bill' Ed said, "Jenny remember this man's face, and his name is Arch. He is not allowed to pull out his wallet in this restaurant. You and your friends owe this man a great deal."

After a little more talk, Arch said, "Ed I think I had better get going. I'll Ride for another hour or two and then find a place to bed down."

"Arch I got a better idea; you can come home with me and meet my wife. Stay overnight and I'll wake you early because I have to be in the restaurant by 6 am. You can have a cup of wake-up coffee at the restaurant. Then you can stop at my new restaurant for breakfast."

Arch said, "You know Ed, I really would feel that I would be imposing."

"Arch, Linda, that's my wife, has heard so much about you that if she found out that I let you go without her getting to meet you she would do more damage to my face than you ever did. Besides when Dave came by, he stayed overnight. Dave and Linda stayed up till 2 am talking about anything and everything."

So Arch went home with him and they spent a couple of hours sitting around the kitchen table just talking and laughing. Then finally they all went to hit the sack, but Linda had one final thing to say. She said, "In all sincerity, Arch, the greatest thing that ever happened to Ed was you punching him in the mouth."

They all said goodnight and went to bed. Ed woke Arch at 5:30 am, but they had hit the sack at 10 pm, so they had a good night's sleep. They snuck out of the house and let Linda sleep.

Arch got on his bike and followed Ed to the restaurant. They went into the kitchen and poured some coffee and sat down at the employees table, they had fresh coffee and some fresh, hot donuts that were made by the head chef. He was a big 6 1/2 foot black guy named JD.

"Greatest chef I have ever seen. Can make something great out of practically nothing. He used to cook on a ship and said some day he is going back on a sailing ship. He said he will, just as soon as this guy Capt. Mike Burke gets his Windjammer that he has been talking about."

Arch walks over to JD and said, "Great donuts, JD, I hope you get your ship."

Then he turns to Ed and said, "Thanks for everything, Ed, and good luck on your restaurant."

"Thanks, Arch, it's all set up and operating and they will be waiting for you for breakfast at 9 am, so you better get rolling. Ed explained how to get to Foley Number Two, and then said, "Ask for Erin O'Brien."

Arch took off North on Route 71 until he got to Route 54 then he turned east. He rolled along at his usual speed of 75 miles an hour and at five minutes to 9 he saw the sign Foley Number Two. Below Foley, it said "Everybody Welcome at Foleys" and below that, "Biker's Rest Stop". On the bottom it said "Manager Erin O' Brian". He finally saw the restaurant and it looked exactly like Foley number one. There was a very large asphalt parking lot filled with cars and it had a motorcycle area with lock boxes and shower rooms. Arch walked in and was met by a big fat black guy. Arch asked to see Erin O'Brian.

"You're seeing him. All three hundred pounds of him. Arch, I'm Erin and my job for this morning is to treat you like royalty, because as Ed tells it, if it weren't for you, none of us black people would be working here. I've heard this story from Ed and from your buddy Dave Steele. Ed actually called Dave a Nigger twice and you popped him twice. Arch, when you came in the door looking for Erin O'Brian you were probably expecting an Irishman. I am from Barbados; Ed hired me because he liked my English accent. I also know my job. Ed said to give you first class treatment and a good breakfast of anything you would like."

Which Erin did. "He said to then send you on your way because you have places to go. There is one other thing. There is a rumor going around that a Messenger from God is riding a metallic green Indian."

Arch thanked everybody and headed out to his bike. When he got to the Indian, about ten of Erin's employees were standing next to the bike to wish him a safe trip. Arch shook every ones hand and climbed on to his big green Chief and was on his way. As Arch was riding down the road, he thought back to what a fantastic trip that it had been. From the time he left Minneapolis to where he was now and the great people he had met, the ones he had grown to love and some people that had helped him and some he had even helped. A great trip, Arch thought, but if he told anyone about his last six months experience they would say Arch you should write a book about it. Hell who would read it?

He was heading north east on Route 54 when he rolled through Jefferson City and was heading to Hannibal, Missouri. He went through Hannibal and about 10 miles north of the town on Route 61, Arch's bad decision in Phoenix came around to bite him in the ass.

Arch knew he should have adjusted, replaced or at least checked his primary chain. He was cruising along at a very comfortable 80 mph leaning forward and almost laying down. He had his butt way back on the big buddy seat. Then it happened, one or more of the links in the primary chain let go. It jammed and the rear wheel locked up solid. The stupid idiot that decided to put off proper maintenance of his almost perfect Indian was now being punished.

Chapter 9

Arch Spills and Meets Jacky

When you totally lock up a wheel on an Indian or a Harley, you have what is known as a very large problem. First, since you have a rigid frame as on a Harley or an Indian, there are basically no springs or shocks on the rear wheel. When the rider is sitting way back on the seat causing the weight to be over the back wheel, it just gives the wheel a lot of traction. When you get a lot of traction on a large tire with a wheel that is not going around, the big tire tries to stop and the rider is still going 75 or 80 mph. The rider instantly slides forward and across the gas tank. He comes to a stop when his crotch hits the yoke of the forks. That hurts. Now he is not in a great position for riding a motorcycle. He is now sitting on the gas tank his feet hanging loose past the center of the front wheel. His hands are still on the hand grip on the handlebars, but with this being awkward position that he is in, his hands on the grips are behind his back.

That's a hell of a way to steer a motorcycle going 75 miles an hour. Basically what Arch is doing is riding a unicycle dragging a big heavy rear wheel that is bouncing along behind it after the rider slides forward and the rider's weight is off the rear wheel. The tire slides on the pavement That is until it hits the tar strips and then it bounces on the pavement and will keep bouncing until the bike stops, or you get the bike on gravel at the side of road. Arch finally got the bike on the roadside gravel and the back wheel stopped bouncing and slid to a stop, but at about 30 mph the front wheel hit a hole and flipped the bike into a ditch.

Arch did not seem to be hurt but the bike was lying on top of one of his legs. He tried to get his leg out but in the position he was in, could not budge a 600 pound bike. Arch heard an engine; he looked up and saw a shiny red Ferrari stopped on the berm of the road the driver just sat there for a few minutes as if he was trying to decide something. Finally he got out of the car and came over to look at the situation.

Arch looked at him and said, "Can you lift one end of the bike so I can slide out of here?"

He said, "Okay, but let me get that piece of wood I see over by the fence to use it as a pry." He goes over to the fence and comes back with a broken piece of 2 x 4 about 18 inches long.

Arch asked what he was going to do with that short piece of wood and the Ferrari guy pointed to the back of the bike. Arch looked and the guy hit him over to head with the 2 x 4. If Arch was still awake he would now know how he was going to use the 2 x 4. Arch was unconscious. The Ferrari guy pulled a switchblade and cut off the leather loop on Arches belt which was attached to his wallet chain. He reached down and grabbed Arch's wallet and ran back to his fancy car and headed down the road.

About 100 yards south of Arch, two bikers were sitting at the side of the road on the east side of Route 61, they were about to turn on to Route 61 when Arch flew by and they saw the wild gyrations Arch was doing. It was hard to figure out what was happening. Then they saw him go off into the gravel and finally into the ditch.

Jimbo said, "Jacky, that Indian is in the ditch." Jacky had been off her bike tightening a loose screw on her tail light assembly. She picked up her tools and put them back in her saddlebags. They fired up their bikes and headed up Route 61 and they saw a red Ferrari stop by Arch's bike and the driver got out. He went over and picked something up and as Jimbo and Jacky got closer they saw the Ferrari guy hit the biker over the head. He then ripped something off the biker. It looked like a trucker's wallet with a chain on it then the guy jumped into his Ferrari and took off like a streak of shit down the road. Jimbo and Jacky cracked on the throttles and got to Arch real quick. Jimbo then asked Arch if he was hurt.

"No, but I think the son of a bitch stole my wallet." Jimbo, who was a big guy, picked up one end of the Indian and Jacky pulled Arch out from under the bike.

Arch introduced himself; Jimbo did likewise, and then said, "This beautiful gal here is Jacky. She will go and get your wallet and wrap this creep up for the cops. I'll stay here with you and your Indian. We will get the medics to check you out and Chuck will haul your bike to the shop. You seem okay, so if you stay here, I'll go to Lou's bar, just a half a mile ahead and I'll call the cops, Chuck, and the medics."

Jacky was already flying down the road at well over 140 miles an hour. Arch asked Jimbo how come he stayed here and sent this little gal down the road to catch a thief. Besides, Arch said, "He had a head start and he's driving a Ferrari and that model will do well over 120 mph."

Jimbo said, "Jacky is no ordinary gal and in a knock- down-drag out fight with her, you couldn't last two minutes. If this guy gets stopped and is stupid enough to get out and try to rumble with her, it would be the biggest mistake of his life. Jacky has a special feeling for motorcycle riders and anyone who would do what he did is on her shit list. You were asking how she should could catch that Ferrari? Did you see what she was riding?"

"Yes, I did, what was it?"

Jimbo said, "It's something you don't see around here very much. It's an English bike. A 61 Cu in. or a thousand cc Vincent Black Lightning. Hers will do about 150 mph. Yeah, she can and she will catch that creep!"

Now about 10 miles away on Route 61, Jacky caught up with the Ferrari. She pulled alongside of the car and motioned for him to pull over. He gave her the finger and cut the wheel hard left trying to drive her off the road, but that had been tried many times before and she saw it coming. She hit the oversized, powerful brakes on the Vincent and it just squatted and made a quick slowdown. The Ferrari shot ahead. She dropped back and then reached under her seat to a special mounting and pulled out a 1 inch diameter steel pipe about 14 inches long with a 3 inch lead knob on the end.

He was going about 95 to 100 mph when she came up behind him at 125 mph. She stayed far to the right side of the road till she was almost right behind him and she swung over and passed him on the left. As she went by, the side window on the Ferrari disintegrated. She put her steel pipe away as she was flying down the road at 140 mph.

She got about 5 miles ahead of him and when she went over a hill she made a quick U-turn and reached under her seat again and came out with a four-inch diameter steel ball. She turned down the road toward him but not directly at him. He was coming toward her now at 110 mph and she was going about 140 mph. With the closing speed of 250 mph, she let go of the four inch diameter steel ball. It went through the radiator and broke through the aluminum block and locked up the engine. The rear wheels were locked up at 110 mph. The car was twisting and sliding and totally out of control. It finally slowed but went into a ditch nose first.

Jacky slowed down and turned around and rode back to the Ferrari. Luckily he was not hurt. She wanted to do that herself. She took off her helmet and her leather jacket, went over to the car, pulled the door open and he came flying out with a switchblade in his right hand.

He said, "You Bitch, I'll gut you."

Jacky looked at him and smiled and said, "So you want to play."

He came at her swinging his knife and with one kick Jacky sent the knife flying, she caught it and closed it. "It seems that you like to hit riders over the head and steal their money. I'm a defenseless woman rider and there behind you is a nice two inch branch that you broke off of that little tree when you hit it with your car."

He turned around and saw the branch and picked it up. It felt good and he smiled. He said, "I'll beat that sexy face of yours so your mother won't recognize you."

She said, "Well, let's have at it." He came at her with his club. He swung, she dropped away and he swung again and missed. She smiled and said, "You're wasting my time." And kicked him hard, right in the crotch. He dropped his club and grabbed his crotch.

While he was bent over, Jacky picked up the broken branch and in one powerful swing across his face she made a bloody mess out of it. Then she said, "What were you going to do my face?"

Then she took another powerful swing in the opposite direction, which really messed up his face and she kicked him in the crotch again and he went out like a light. She went over and picked up his switchblade that she had thrown on the ground and then ripped open his shirt and saw a well-tanned and muscular but hairless chest. She said to herself, "He sure looks like a typical beach boy."

She opened his switch blade and proceeded to carve on his chest in large deep letters that will scar very well. She carved a message that he well deserved. "I AM A DIRTY BASTARD". Then she went back to her bike and got a combination lock and chain. Jacky wrapped the chain tightly around both ankles and then locked the chain to the car's bumper. The guy finally woke up and said, "What did you do to me?"

She said, "I did just exactly what you said you would do to me. When and if you go to the beach again and you take off your shirt, you will remember me."

Then she went to the front of the car over the dashboard and took the vehicle identification number and wrote it down in her pocket notebook. The car is probably stolen because anyone with enough money to buy a Ferrari doesn't go around stealing wallets.

She looked in the car for the wallet. It wasn't on the seat. The collision knocked it off the seat and it landed on the floor. Jacky picked up the wallet opened it up. Among other things, there was $600 in cash. She put it back in the wallet and inventoried everything in the wallet including the cash in her small notebook, just in case the wrong person handled it. But it turns out that this was not a problem, because a squad car pulled up at the scene and it was Jacky's friend Jimmy and his partner Rich from Hannibal PD.

"Hello, Jacky," said Jimmy, "We were on our way over to Chuck's Cycle to see about a biker who was assaulted and robbed of his wallet."

"Well, Jimmy, here is the wallet and an inventory is in my pocket." She handed him a piece of paper and said, "Here is the VIN number for the Ferrari. It's probably stolen. I figured that anybody that can afford one of these cars wouldn't be going around picking pockets."

"Where is the culprit?"

"Over there. The one hanging on the bumper. He fell asleep and I picked his pocket to find out who he is."

Jimmy called Rich over and he asked Rich to check out the VIN number and Rich checked out the driver's license and four more licenses plus 6 credit cards with different names.

Rich had gone back to his squad car for about 10 minutes and he came back and said, "Jackpot! The car and the credit cards are stolen, but the license is real and this joker has a $10,000 bounty on him! He skipped bail. It was $100,000 bond and the bondsman is paying $10,000. So, Jacky it looks like you hit it big. We will book him and then let the bondsman know who he owes the $10,000 to. So when we were heading to Chuck's Cycle, we called in and the medics were there. The rider is okay, so we can take this guy back and book him. I will give you back the wallet and money so you can give it back to the biker. We have enough witnesses so we don't need the wallet."

"Jimmy, what is this guy's real name? I've who got to know the name of a guy who is getting me $10,000!"

Jimmy said that his name is Dennis Ryan. She walked over to him and said, "Mr. Ryan, it has been good to know you. Profitable anyway."

Ryan looked over to Jimmy and said, "Look what she did to my face."

"After what you did to the biker, you deserve it. But you're lucky she wasn't really mad."

"Well, look what he did to my chest."

Jimmy said, "It looks to me like she spelled everything right."

"I'm going to sue her."

Jimmy said, "What are you going to sue her for?"

"For slander."

"You have to prove that you are not what she said you are. After what you did I would say you are one. Now as far as your face goes, it looks like self-defense and you lost and your chest was done with your own switchblade. Your only problem is that you don't want people to know that you are a dirty bastard. So don't go to the beach and don't take your shirt off in public. But you won't have to worry about that after we get you booked on assault of a biker, stolen car charge, stolen credit card and attacking a female biker with a switchblade."

"Well," Ryan said, "Look at what she did to me."

"Do you think the jury is going to believe this sexy looking 110 pound girl could do all that damage to a 240 pound bully like you?"

"Well, look what she did to my car."

"Correction, your stolen car."

"Well," Ryan said, "She must have shot it with a bazooka."

Jimmy asked Rich, "Have you seen any sign of a bazooka around?"

"No such thing boss."

He called Jacky over and asked, "Jacky, have you got a bazooka?"

"No, Jimmy, I don't need one."

He turned to Ryan and said, "I told you, no bazooka. It must've been your famous old Lightning and Cannonball trick."

Jacky said, "Jimmy, I don't know, but I think it could've been. Either way, Jimmy, tell Jake when he comes with the tow truck that I'd like to get my cannonball back."

Jacky then fired up her Vincent and said, "See you guys later. Don't forget to tell Jake to save my lock and chain too."

"What's the combination, Jacky?"

"You don't need one. I opened it half an hour ago."

She said, "Hey, Ryan, you were free for the last half an hour and you didn't know it. Rich let's get him booked and then we can go out and have a pizza."

"Well, what about me, I get hungry too."

"It would be a crime to take somebody with such an ugly face like that into a restaurant."

"Goodbye, all," and she shot down the road at well over 120 miles an hour.

Jimmy looked down the road and said, "Someday I may get her for speeding."

Rich said, "But you can't catch her."

"Rich, let's take our old buddy Ryan here to jail and get some pizza."

Ryan said again, "What about me?"

"It's Jail for you, Asshole."

Jacky made good time back to Chuck's Cycle Shop. She pulled up in front of the garage door where three guys were standing there looking at Arch's Indian which was up on a work stand. The primary case cover was off. They were all looking at the damage done to the chain and sprockets. One of them said, "The chain is shot, two sprockets and one shaft. The main shaft is okay. With parts and minimum labor cost I see nothing less than $500."

"Well," Arch said, "If that guy hadn't stolen my wallet, I could cover it. It would be tight but I could do it."

"Well, Arch, here is your wallet." And she threw it to him. "It's all there. I got him before he had a chance to open the wallet."

"That's great Jacky how the hell did you do it? That guy was at least twice your size."

Jimbo said, "But not half as good, nor one tenth as smart."

The phone rang and Chuck answered. He talked for a while and came back with a sheet of paper with some figures on it. "That was Jimmy from the Hannibal PD. Jimmy said your check from the bondsman is on the way. Also, the Ferrari was stolen. The Ferrari agency is sending you a check for $5000 and the three different credit card companies are sending $1000 each, Jacky. It looks like a total of $18,000 for your little jaunt down the road. Jimmy said that you really made a mess out of the bad guy. He is in the hospital now and he swears that he will never insult another beautiful lady for the rest of his life."

Jacky said to Chuck, "You wanted $23,000 for Chuck's Cycle Shop. Jimbo and I put down $9000 as a deposit with six months to raise the rest, which is fourteen thousand dollars, so Jimbo, as soon as I get those checks we will be the owners of Chuck's Cycle Shop. Jacky turns to Arch and said, "There have been a lot of rumors going around starting from Hoggsville that there has been a Messenger from God in this area. This messenger is riding a metallic green Indian and Arch, I really think you're it. You brought rain to Hoggsville, next you bring this corrupt Ferrari driver. The bounty that he has brought allows us to pay the rest of the money to Chuck and we will be the owners of Chuck's Cycle Shop."

Jimbo started to object because he said it was Jacky's money. She just said, "Partners, Jimbo. But I will concede to one thing and that is not Chuck's Shop or Jimbo and Jacky's. It's got to have a proper name like Jacky and Jimbo's."

They were all agreed on that. "There is one other thing. Since Arch was the messenger that brought the crook and the money, the money left over will also pay to repair a green Indian that carried the messenger here.

Also the Indians paint job is scratched up. We should repaint it a more fitting color for Gods Messenger. It should be a Golden Indian, a metallic gold. Arch agreed, so now he will ride a Golden. Indian. Jimbo said, "That's a great idea, Jacky. And being you're the one that comes up with all the good ideas, I vote for you as president of Jacky and Jimbo's cycles."

Arch said, "You people are amazing! If I ever go ass over tin cups on a bike again I would want to do it right here."

The check came in from the bondsman, the Ferrari agency and the credit card people. Chuck was paid off and Jacky and Jimbo were in business as partners. They talked to Harley about a franchise as a Harley dealer.

So they were happy, Chuck was happy, and Arch was happy and on his way to Chicago. After they fixed his bike, it purred like a big kitten. Right now he was headed for Davenport Iowa. From Hannibal it was only 350 miles to Chicago. A good day's ride. He was anxious to get there and see Eric and his dad but he decided that he would stay one night at a hotel and get cleaned up and rest up, then head to the shop in the morning.

He checked his map and saw that he could take Route 6 right up to DeWitt at Route 30 and take 30 east, right in to Chicago. He would hit Cicero where Dave lives. Just maybe he should give him a call. He should be home because it was Sunday, but then again, maybe he was out riding. He rode for an hour until 10 pm. He had a hell of a rough day and was tired. He pulled off the road and into a grove of trees and got his bedroll laid out; he was almost asleep before he hit the ground.

Chapter 10

Jumer's Castle

Arch woke at the crack of dawn at about 4 am and straightened out his gear, checked out his bike and was on the road by 4:30 am. It was a beautiful morning. The sun was not up, but it was thinking of it. He could see splays of nice red sunlight off to his right and finally, after another half an hour, the red ball of sun. He thought the same thought he had many times since leaving Minneapolis; it's great to be riding and even greater to be rolling along on his big Golden Chief. He loved his machine, almost the way a cowboy probably loves his horse. Arch was in heaven.

He rode along comfortably, feeling the wind and the sunshine and when he got to Muscatine, Iowa, he pulled in for fuel. There was a snack bar at the fuel station. He almost went over to have something to eat, but changed his mind. He said to himself, he should stop at a good place and get a breakfast like he had Foley's. He doubted very much that he would find anything close to that though.

He pulled out of the fuel station and headed east toward Davenport. After about 10 miles he saw a red light flashing. It was a police car and he pulled up close behind.

Arch was wondering what he did wrong; probably speeding. He was running his usual 75 mph. That was over the limit, but not by much. Arch stopped and got off his bike and the officer got out of his car. He was an Iowa State Police Lieutenant. He just walked up to him and said, "Are you Arch?

Arch said, "Yes."

The officer said, "Follow me." And he got in his car and took off toward Davenport. Arch fired up and followed the police car. I guess they decided not to take a chance with Arch getting away, because another police car pulled up behind. Arch thought that speeding must be a pretty serious offense in Iowa.

He followed the Lieutenant's car right through Davenport and into Bettendorf. Arch thought, this is a hell of a way to get to a state police barracks. Then they pulled into a wooded drive and pulled up to what looked like a castle. The Lieutenant showed Arch where to park his bike and an attendant opened a big sliding door and he rode the bike in. Arch got off the bike and the Lieutenant motioned for him to follow. The attendant closed the door.

Shit, Arch thought, they are going to impound my bike. They went around to the main entrance and walked up the stairs and through revolving doors. Inside Arch looked around and said to Lieutenant, "This does not look like a police station."

"It isn't, it's *Jumer's Castle.* A nice place to stay and very good food."

"Why am I here?"

"Arch, the reason you are here is that you have made a lot of good friends along the road you have traveled. Let's go to the reception desk."

She said, "Good morning, Gentlemen, how can I help you."

The Lieutenant said, "Miss, I'd like you to meet Arch."

She reached out a hand and said, "It's great to meet you, Arch. We have been waiting for you. Your suite is ready and any time you like, a bellman will take you up so you can clean up for breakfast. We have taken the liberty to put some casual clothes in your room. Being a biker myself, I know how your clothes pick up road dirt and bikers don't carry a suitcase full of clothes."

Arch said, "I don't know how this all came about, but I don't think I have sufficient funds to afford this first-class treatment."

She said, "Arch, do you have a last name?

"It's Mueller."

She said, "Mr. Mueller."

"Call me Arch."

"Okay, Arch, as long as you are in this castle, you do not have to take out your wallet."

The Lieutenant leaned over to Arch and said, "You have made more friends than you know. Everything here has been or will be paid for by your friends, Arch, and it's an honor to meet you."

"Why an honor? I'm nobody. Why me?"

"You might think you're nobody, but you are somebody great to all the people you have come in contact with and to them you're a hero. I've got to go, but before I do, I just want to tell you that your waiter at breakfast will hand you an envelope that will explain it all. Good luck, Arch. By the way I talked to the Illinois State police and they agreed that they will not bother a beautiful Golden Indian motorcycle along Route 30 unless you are doing over 100 miles an hour."

Arch went to his room and showered and changed into the casual clothes that were left for him and went down to the dining room. They were serving breakfast and it smelled real good. Arch walked up to the counter where the girl was taking names. As he walked up, she said, "We are very busy and you might have to wait 45 minutes and that he and could wait in the bar." Then she asked his name.

He said, "Arch."

She said, "I'm sorry, Mr. Mueller."

"The name is Arch."

"Okay, Arch, I'll have somebody show you to your table." She picked up the phone and within a minute a waiter showed up. The girl said, "James, this is Arch Mueller."

"Pleased to meet you, Mr. Mueller."

"He said his name is Arch. "

The waiter said, "Sorry, Arch, it will be Arch from now on. I'll take you to your table."

James led Arch to a table on the veranda overlooking a beautiful courtyard. Sitting at the table was a good-looking Spanish girl. She looked to be about 25. She stood up and said, "I'm Laura Mendoza. Manager of the hotel. When I heard you were coming, I decided that I wanted to meet you."

"It sure is nice to meet you, Mrs. Mendoza."

"It's Ms. Mendoza. Also, I prefer Laura. I hear they call you Arch."

"Enjoy your breakfast," said James, "anything you want."

"Have you eaten breakfast yet, Laura?"

"No, I haven't, I usually eat in my office."

"Why your office, when you could be on this nice Veranda?"

"There is not usually such charming company out here."

Arch said, "Then I would appreciate your company. It would be a much more enjoyable breakfast."

She said, "I also think I would enjoy it very much."

The waiter came back and asked, "Ms. Mendoza, are you joining Mr.

Arch for breakfast?

"Yes, James, I think I will."

"Mr. Arch."

"Just Arch okay?"

"Okay, Arch, I have been handed an envelope to give to you."

"Thank you, James."

He opened the envelope and inside was another envelope. He opened the small er envelope. Inside was a check for $500 and a small note. "Just a little something to help you get started in Chicago. Good luck, Arch, and come back and see us soon." Then the large, typewritten letters brought tears to his eyes and Laura's too. It started out with Ed Foley's letter. "Arch, my wife and I both love you. That may seem strange coming from someone that got his teeth knocked out by you, but you saved my life and actually saved our marriage. We were considering divorce before you showed up. I was a real bastard and that's what people called me. Now I have true friends. I hope you are one of them. Good luck and good God bless you. Linda sends her love too. Ed. PS I hear by the grapevine that you are God's Messenger. I believe it."

The next letter was written by Jacky. "Dear Arch, It's hard to say what Jimbo and I feel, but I'll try. Jimbo and I love motorcycles and we both like to work on them. When we heard Chuck wanted to retire and he said he would sell for $23,000. Jimbo and I agreed to go in as partners and between the two of us, we came up with the $8,000.00 down payment. Chuck's lawyer drew up a contract in which the remainder of $15,000.00 was to be paid in 90 days or we would lose the down payment. That was lawyer talk. I don't think Chuck would have held us to that, but it was in the contract. Once we saw that in the contract, Chuck said don't worry about it, it's lawyer talk, so we didn't worry about it, because Jimbo and I owned a 45 foot power boat on the Illinois River, free and clear. It's worth about $35,000.00 and we had a firm offer for $32,000.00. One day, someone was celebrating with fireworks and we had just painted the bilges and had left the engine hatches open to vent. Some boaters saw a skyrocket go right into the open hatch and the boat blew up and burned right to the water line. This happened just a few days before the sale, so we suddenly had a problem in making the 90 day deadline. You got hit on the head just four days before the deadline, you are a Godsend. Although we didn't know that when I first started to chase the creep, but it turned out your attacker was worth enough money to save our butt. Jimbo and I thank you from the bottom of our hearts. We are now in the motorcycle business. You Are God's Messenger. Jacky"

The last letter was from Ben, the bartender. He said Arch, "The town of Hoggsville owes you more than you can believe. Before you showed up here we needed rain so bad that everything that kept this town alive was dying or was about to die. The watermelon crop was at a point where it would be a good crop, or no crop at all. One more week without rain would have meant no crop. Whether you believe it or not, this whole town believes that you are the Messenger from God that they were praying for. Bill, the attendant at the Texaco station saw you ride away with a halo completely surrounding you and your bike. He knows you are God's Messenger and we believe it too. To show our appreciation for what you did for all of us, we decided to help make your trip to Chicago a little more pleasant. Ed Foley and his wife were the instigators of this plan and Ed did most of the legwork. Ed's got a lot of connections with the police department and restaurant associations, and with the help of his good friend Ken Jamieson the restaurant consultant, we all kicked in, but Foley and his wife set it all up. We all hope you will enjoy it and we wish you the best. Signed by the people who care. Ed and Linda Foley, Jacky Sax and Jimbo Scott, Ben and Betty Hogg and some of Ben's customers, Joe Smith, Bob Hansen, Art Berg, Sam Bell, Dick Curtis, Tom Olson, Jack Leonard, William Foster, David Lewis and a few more who were out working their watermelon crops. So, good luck, Arch. P.S. Also Bill Jones the Texaco attendant. P.S. Again. We also decided that you should have a good night stay in a first-class hotel in Chicago. You will like the Drake. Foley and Jamieson set it up, so all you have to do is tell them you are Arch the Messenger and they will take good care of you."

Laura read the letter too. She said, "This is really fantastic, Arch. If you keep going like this and doing so much for so many people without hardly trying, I really think that you may be God's Messenger. Arch, you should write a book."

"I've been told that before, I'll tell you what I told them. Who would read it?"

"A lot of people, Arch. But the real problem is, who would publish it? She said I know that's a problem, because I used to work for a publisher before I worked here. I was a senior editor. I've seen manuscripts that I have recommended get passed up, then only to be picked up by another publisher and become a bestseller. So I quit and became a hotel manager and Arch, I really think you have a lot more living to do before you write a book."

"Laura, when I get to Chicago, living is something that I plan on doing. If my buddy Eric hasn't changed, it's party time."

It was almost noon by the time they finished eating brunch.

"Arch, I understand that you are leaving in the morning. If you are interested, there are a few neat things to see around here. We could have all afternoon to go sightseeing. Then we could be back to Jumer's, have a great dinner and then go dancing in the ballroom."

He said, "Laura, I don't have any dress clothes to go dancing. When you travel on a motorcycle, that is something that you don't carry."

"No problem, Arch, it's all been taken care of. Your friends wanted you to have a good time. I talked to a woman, and a woman likes to plan. Her name is Linda, Ed Foley's wife. So when we get back from the afternoon tour, you can go up to your room, shower and shave and you will find a full set of dress clothes in your closet."

"That's great, but how did anyone know my size?"

"It's not the first time my people have done this. Remember when you checked in? The desk called for a bellman and three of them showed up. Two of them made an excuse and left. The third bellman picked up your duffel and took you to your room. He was your size; they had checked the clothes in your closet, so it should fit."

Twenty minutes later she picked him up at the front door in her Cadillac convertible. Arch got in and said, "I always said, if you've got to travel, travel in style or why travel at all."

She smiled at first, and then burst out laughing. She said, "Well, it looks like it's going to be a fun day."

First they went to the International Harvester Plant. "I know the people here really well. I treat them good at Jumer's and they treat me right when I come here too." She passed the visitor parking area and pulled in an excellent parking spot. It said "General Manager".

Arch said, "What if the General Manager wants to park?"

"No problem, he's in London. I had lunch with him last week. Besides if he does come back he knows my car and he will park somewhere else."

They went to the main office and she talked to a few people. Then a guy came over and handed them badges to wear. He said, "My name is Art and I'm going to take you on a tour of IHC." And so he did.

They walked out of the office and into what looked like a small restaurant. Coffee urns, pop dispensers and a lunch counter where you could order breakfast. Art asked if they would like something to eat or a snack. They both said no thanks, that they just had brunch at Jumer's. Art said, "I understand. I have had brunch there before."

He said to climb aboard as he pointed to an oversized golf cart. They drove out into the plant. It was immense. He said, "First we will see where the raw material comes in."

At a railroad siding he said that was where the raw steel came in. A giant overhead crane was lifting 1 to 2 inch thick steel plates, 10 feet wide and 24 feet long. It would pick up the big heavy plates and then move them off down the track at a high rate of speed. It would unload its cargo and within a few minutes it would be back for more. There was what looked like a 20 bay truck dock that had some trucks being unloaded with forklifts and with overhead cranes. There were steel bar stock, round stock, hex stock and angle iron. Then there was another section where suppliers delivered manufactured assemblies. Art said most people didn't find that part of the tour too interesting.

Arch said, "I find that seeing where it all starts as raw material is very interesting. The finished product that we will probably see in another part of the plant will be even more amazing when you know what the raw material looked like."

Then Art took them through the production plant. He showed them the big boring mills and giant lathes all in operation. Then in another section they saw a guy sitting on a seat going back and forth on a giant planer. Laura said, "And we pay good money to get a ride like that in an amusement park."

Then they went into the machinery area. This area interested Arch but it bored Laura. They then went into the stamping area. Art gave them each a couple of ear plugs and said to use them or they wouldn't hear too good for a couple of hours.

"How much longer is this tour?" asked Arch.

"We can cut it off any time, but I think you will want to see the finished product."

"That sounds good," said Laura, "Arch, I think we should head back to Jumer's because it's getting close to 4 pm."

They went to what looked like a show room. It was a large room with all kinds of bright red farm equipment. They spent about half an hour looking at all the different kinds of equipment.

Arch said, "Laura, I think you're getting a little bored. Maybe we should head back to Jumer's. We will have better things to do at the hotel." They thanked Art and bid him goodbye.

They headed out to the car and she threw him the keys. He said, "Hey, Laura, I don't want to bend up your pretty, new Cadillac."

"No problem, Arch, if you bend it up I'll get a new one tomorrow. A red one this time. It's leased, Arch, and they take care of all the repair or replacement. So drive on my man."

"Okay, Boss," said Arch.

They got back to hotel at about 5 pm and Laura said, "Arch, let's go shower and change clothes. I'll meet you in the bar at 6 pm." So they headed to their rooms.

Arch got to his room and looked in his closet. He found a full suit of clothes; shirt, tie and shoes. He showered and dressed and at 5:50 pm, he headed down to the bar and ordered a beer.

When Laura got to her room, she kicked off her shoes, took off her blouse and opened the closet door. Behind it was a full-length mirror. Laura looked at herself in the mirror wearing only her bra and panties, turned left and right, and thought, looks pretty good for 26. Then she took off her panties and said to herself, still looking good. Took off her bra and looked at her profile. She grabbed her breasts and said, "Arch is going to love these babies."

Laura showered and perfumed herself and she got dressed in the slinkiest, most sexy gown that she owned. She went downstairs and walked into the bar where Arch was sitting on a barstool.

He almost didn't recognize her at first, and when he did he practically fell off the stool. He just stood there and stared at her, along with about four other guys. He finally opened his mouth and said, "You sure do clean up real nice. I hardly recognized you. I won't make that mistake again because I won't be able to take my eyes off of you."

"Thanks, Arch, you're looking pretty good yourself." Arch had another beer and Laura had a Beefeater martini.

After they finished their drinks, Laura got up and said, "Let's go eat, Pete."

"My name ain't Pete, but I'll follow you anywhere."

He followed her into the dining room. She went directly to a secluded table that was all set up. They no sooner sat down when James the waiter showed up and Arch ordered drinks and an appetizer. Oysters on the half shell, which James said were excellent. Which they were. Dinner was also excellent. Arch had prime rib, rare and Laura had a seafood platter, which she said was great.

After dinner they ordered more drinks. Laura ordered a double Drambuie and Arch ordered a beer. She said "Ever try a Drambuie, Arch?"

"No, why?"

"It makes me horny."

"Then its Drambuie for me, James."

After they were through with their drinks, Arch said, "What about the check?"

"It's all taken care of."

"Well, at least I can tip James."

She said, "He won't accept it from you. He is more than generously taken care of."

The next stop was the bar in the ballroom and they both ordered double Drambuies.

"You're right, Laura, it really is a nice drink."

"Let's dance."

They got out on the floor and danced a couple of slow dances. Laura pushed herself tight against Arch's chest and he could tell she was braless. Her breasts were firm and her nipples were now erect, which he could feel through his shirt. Arch was also erect, but not his nipples.

"Arch, I love dancing with you, but I have some nice games we can play in my room and also a bottle of Drambuie."

"If Drambuie makes you horny, then lead the way partner." And they went to her room.

She said, "Make yourself comfortable, Arch. I'll be right back after I get comfortable."

Arch said, "I don't know how you can get much more comfortable than you are in that dress."

"I can, Arch, just keep your eyes open." She came back into the room, turned on the hi-fi and also turned on Arch. She was wearing the sheerest negligee he had ever seen.

"Now, Arch, if you would get a little more comfortable, we could dance." Off came the shirt and pants which didn't hide anything.

They danced for about 30 seconds when Arch said, "I may ride tonight but I'm not a jockey." So off came the jockey shorts.

Laura backed off a bit and said, "I like what I see Arch. It's made for kissing." Which is what she did and she swallowed as much as she could. She was driving Arch wild when she got up and took off the negligee and led Arch to the bedroom.

She laid back on the bed and Arch spread her legs and kissed her super-hot pussy. Then he put his throbbing tool right into her where he knew it belonged. They made love for about three hours with more Drambuie in between each bout of lovemaking.

Arch asked Laura, "You say that Drambuie makes you horny? Then it's a good thing the bottle is almost empty. I'm not sure I can last another round."

"I think you could Arch."

She got a hold of his dick and licked it hard as a rock again. They went at it one more time. Then he kissed her on the mouth and then kissed her erect nipples. Arch was erect again. She grabbed him, rolled him on his back and sucked on his hard dick and then climbed aboard. She said, "Finally, Arch." And she collapsed on him and they both went to sleep.

When they woke up the next morning, Laura kissed Arch and jumped out of bed and went in to take a shower. The next thing she knew, Arch was in the shower with her with a bar of soap in his hand. He soaped her up all over. He washed her breasts at least 10 times and every place else that felt good. She did the same for him. He now felt that he had the cleanest set of balls and pecker in the hotel. That felt so good that Arch now was as hard as he was any time last night. Laura looked at his hard dick and said, "Arch you can't run around the hotel with that sticking out. I'll have to fix it for you."

She leaned over in the shower. "Doggie fashion will get rid of your very hard problem." They went at it with gusto in the shower with the water coming down between them.

Finally both of them came two more times. Arch said, "My problem is solved."

"So is mine she said, I am going to stay away from Drambuie for a while." They dressed and went down for breakfast. Arch had steak and eggs, Laura had bacon and eggs and a fruit plate. After they ate they had coffee and Danish, then sat back and relaxed.

While sitting there Laura said, "Arch, I've got to tell you something."

"What's that?" he said.

"I'm not really the manager here. Right now I'm more or less the acting manager. You see, I really work for your buddy, Ken Jamieson. I spend a week or two evaluating the operation. At this time I am acting manager. When I get all the information I need, I leave and the manager comes back. I get together with Ken and we decide on how best to improve the operation. So that's what I do here."

"Laura, it sounds like you've got things under control and I have to get on my way to Chicago. It sure as hell has been great meeting you, I don't believe I have ever enjoyed myself more."

"You know, Arch, I can say the same thing. I sure as hell am going to miss you tonight."

Chapter 11

The Black Eagles

"Arch, let's stay in touch." She handed him her business card.

Arch wrote the name of the shop on the back of one of her cards and gave it back to her. "Well, I guess I better check out and be on my way."

"You don't have to check out, Arch. It's all taken care of."

"Well, I have to get my duffel and make a phone call."

"Make it from my office."

He got his duffel and went back to her office. He called the number in Cicero that Dave had left with Foley. It was Sunday morning so Dave was home. They talked for a few minutes and Arch told him where he was and that he was heading for Chicago. Dave gave him an address and told him to stop by. It was 9 am and he said he could be there in three or four hours. They hung up and he turned to Laura and said that he would get in touch as soon as he could.

She said, "Arch, just to make sure you don't forget." She handed him a small manila envelope. He opened it and found her business card and a 5 x 7 color picture of her standing on what looked like a Caribbean beach. In the background was a beautiful azure sea, but in the foreground was a picture of Laura, standing on the beach, topless and throwing a kiss to someone.

She said, "I thought that maybe this picture might remind you to call me."

Arch said, "It will and I'll stay in touch. But right now I'd better get my butt on the road." He fired up his big twin and it sounded beautiful and he felt great. He put it in gear and engaged the cradle clutch and he was off. He headed out of Bettendorf and north on 61 to DeWitt. He turned east on Route 30 and he would take that all the way to Chicago. He would make a stop in Cicero first to see Dave and then into Chicago. It was a short run from DeWitt to Clinton; about 20 miles. He crossed the Mississippi River at Clinton and rolled into Illinois.

It was only about 120 miles to Cicero. He should be able to make that in about two or three hours. Nothing ever seemed to work out as planned. Just like the Mississippi River. Ever since leaving Bettendorf he had been looking forward to crossing the great river. He thought it would be a fantastic scene, but when he got to the river, traffic was heavy. It was moving fast and bumper-to-bumper and the fact that motorcycles do not have any bumpers, the biker has to be very careful in heavy traffic. Some bikers feel car drivers think there is a bounty on bikes; they like to make them a target.

Because of the heavy traffic and the height of the guard rail, Arch did not see the river at all. After crossing the river he saw a sign that said "Scenic view of the Mississippi. Lock and dam number 13 five miles north". He said to himself, "I've come this far and have crossed the Mississippi, so I'll have to take a look." He took a ride 8 to 10 miles north on Route 84. The river widened out to about 3 miles wide, which is what he thought the Mississippi should look like. He spent another half an hour watching the pushers and the grain barges in lock number 13. Then he was satisfied that he had gotten to see an interesting part of the Mississippi River.

He headed back to Route 30 east. There were a lot of small towns along Route 30 and he rode through Rock Falls, Sabena, Big Rock and Sugar Grove at Route 47. He fueled up in Sugar Grove and had a hamburger and a Pepsi at a Dog and Suds. Then he got on Route 34 which took him right into Cicero. When he got to the junction of Route 34 and 31st St. and Central Avenue, he pulled into a gas station and called Dave. Dave told him that he was real close. He told him to go west on 31st St. to the first traffic light at Austin Avenue. North to the next light which was called Cermack. There was a restaurant on the corner; Dave would meet him in the restaurant.

Arch parked his bike right in front of the restaurant and went inside and found a booth in front of a window. Three teenagers came by to look at Arch's bike. They started getting a little too close for Arch and he was ready to go out there to make sure they didn't damage or steal anything off his bike.

Just then, Dave pulled up on his Harley. He parked right next to Arch's bike. Dave talked to the kids a few minutes and did a high five and gave one of the guys a couple of bucks. Dave walked into the restaurant and came up to Arch and said, "Arch, your bike is as safe as if it were in a bank vault." Arch looked out the window and one kid was sitting on Dave's bike and the other two on the curb.

"So how's it been going, Arch? I have been talking to Ken Jamieson. He said that you had a wild time down in Phoenix and even wilder time on the way back here. He said you became some sort of a hero in some town along the route. He said you have even become known as a Messenger from God. Ken said that it was too complicated and that you would have to explain it yourself."

They had some coffee and Danish and then Dave said, "Let's go over to my house. I've got a sister and a brother who are anxious to meet you."

Dave's house was only a few blocks away from the restaurant. It was a nice residential area. A nice brick bungalow. His sister opened the door and greeted them. Dave introduced Arch to Loretta. She was a good-looking 20 year old art teacher, who taught in Oak Park. She seemed to know all about Arch and said that he looked just like Dave had described him.

Then Dave's brother came in the front door. His brother's name was Richard Steele. After they did the introductions he said that he worked for his uncle Robert at the bank and mortgage company. He said that he was amazed at how many mortgages that Robert had gotten for people in Fayetteville. These were mortgages that black people in the Fayetteville area would never have gotten at a reasonable rate from their local banks and mortgage houses. He said, "It seems that we are doing some good down there."

Dave said, "Time's a-wasting, we were going over to the Black Eagles Club to see some of the guys and have a few beers. It's only about 10 or 12 miles from here. It's on 63rd St. in Englewood, as if that means anything to you. One thing I want to remind you about; go easy with the noise from your exhaust pipes. The cops are pretty tough on noise, so just take it easy and it should be no problem."

They got on their bikes and headed to Route 50, which is Cicero Avenue. Then south to 63rd St., which is on the south side of Midway

Airport. Then east on 63rd St. to Ashland Avenue. The club was just a few doors east of Ashland on the south side of the street. It was a storefront with black painted windows. A sign on the door said "Black Eagle Motorcycle Club". On the east side of the building was an empty lot, which was made into a motorcycle parking lot with a chain-link fence and a locked gate. Dave had a key and opened the gate and they pulled in and parked the bikes. They went inside and there was a long bar with about six guys having a beer. There were about eight restaurant type tables with roughly a dozen people sitting around drinking, some eating hamburgers and hotdogs. About half the people at the tables were women. Most of the people were black, but some were white.

"Nice place you got here Dave," said Arch.

"We like it, and some of the guys spend a lot of time here. There is more to it. Let me show you around."

They went into what looked like a nice, clean, well-equipped kitchen. "Everything here is on the honor system. Hamburgers, hot dogs and sandwiches have a set reasonable price. You make it, you clean up after yourself and you pay for your meal. You put cash or your IOU in the kitty here. Once a month IOUs are collected. It works out pretty good. We have pool tables that are usually busy as hell and two shuffle boards. The gals like the shuffle boards and are pretty good at it."

Then Dave said, "Let me show you my pride and joy. It's in the back on the lower level."

They went down some stairs to find a well-lit shop. It was about 40 feet wide and 80 feet long. Dave said, "This is the Black Eagles Motorcycle Shop."

There were eight bikes on stands in various stages of repair. "This is a profit-making, nonprofit venture. The money made here keeps the club going. We rate as nonprofit because we do a lot of charity work."

At one end of the shop were mills, lathes, saws and grinders. It was a full machine shop. The equipment was donated by Dave's employer, International Harvester Company. "We use these machines to do custom work. I have taught two guys enough to get jobs as junior machinists at IHC."

Arch said, "Your shop here is a nice set up and it looks like you do some good work for charity."

They went back up to the bar and ordered beers. A big muscular guy came over and Dave introduced Larry Thomas to Arch.

Larry said, "Is this the guy that saved your ass in Fayetteville? I had a couple buddies ride down to Little Rock a few weeks ago and on your advice they stopped at Foley's. They said it was great and that bikers get the red carpet treatment there.

Are you staying for dinner, Dave?"

Dave turned to Arch and said, "You hungry for some first-class grub? We have three members who are head chefs for some of the best restaurants in Chicago. One of them is cooking here tonight. My sister and her fiancé will be here. She never misses when Sergio the Chef is cooking. When Sergio is cooking the place is always crowded. There is no menu. Sergio just cooks what he feels like. You may have a choice of three or four different things. Tonight he making Polish, Chinese, Mexican and Danish dishes. I've had them all and they are all very good."

Loretta and her fiancé came in. Dave and Arch invited them to their table. Sergio came out from the kitchen and said hello to Loretta, Jim and Dave. He turned to Arch and said, "This must be Arch, the guy that saved your ass in Fayetteville."

Dave said, "I don't know how many times my ass had been saved. But this is the guy."

Sergio said, "Now that we got that settled, it's time to eat. We have four things on the menu. If you're hungry try them all. They can be served in courses."

Everyone agreed. Sergio announces that the first course is Polish and he brought out four bowls of steaming hot soup. Arch tasted the broth and said, "This is great. What is it?"

Sergio tells Arch, "It is sauerkraut soup. The broth and the meat of country ribs with sauerkraut is added."

Everybody ordered something else for the next course. Arch had two more bowls of soup.

On the third bowl, Sergio brought out another dish with two meatballs on it. Sergio said, "Arch try these, it's probably something else you have never tasted."

Arch took a bite and said, "These are really great, but I've had these before."

Sergio asked, "Where?"

Arch chuckled and said, "In a Mexican restaurant. A place called Larsen's Mexican Restaurant. They are Danish Frickadellars."

Sergio looked at Arch in disbelief and said, "The Chef's name is Knute Larsen and his wife is Maria. I worked with Knute in Fort Worth. He's a great chef! I heard that he opened a new restaurant. How is he doing?"

Arch tells Sergio that they have a Mexican restaurant in Santa Rosa, New Mexico. They serve great Mexican food and the people in the area consider it the best in New Mexico.

"Well," Arch said, "you have to go a long way to beat the food that was served here tonight. As much as I would enjoy hanging around and jaw with you all some more, I think I had better get going. I am supposed to show up at my new job tomorrow. I should also stop at the Drake Hotel tonight. Anybody know where it is at?"

Sergio said, "I worked about 1 mile south of the Drake, so I can tell you exactly how to get there. When you leave here, go east a few blocks to Halsted St. and go north on Halsted to 55th, which is Garfield Boulevard. Go east on 55th St. to Lake Shore Drive, then go north on Lake Shore Drive. After you cross the Chicago River, it's about one more mile. Make a left turn at North Avenue Beach to get off of Lake Shore Drive and go south on Michigan Avenue a few blocks and Walton is right there and so is the Drake Hotel."

Arch followed these directions and got to the Drake Hotel. He pulled up in front of the hotel and the doorman came over to him and said, "You must be Arch. We have been told to look for you. Your bike is not too hard to spot. Pull around the back and someone will be waiting for you."

He went around the back and a guy was there to direct him up a ramp and into a service elevator. He said, "My name is Pat and you must be Arch. Your bike is to get first-class treatment; we are going to give it a private room."

They went to the second floor and wheeled it down the corridor to a locked room. Pat produced a key and handed it to Arch. He opened the door and Arch said, "Is this for my bike?"

"The room used to be for the head of maintenance. It's still got a bed in it. This room is for your bike, but you have a high-class suite on one of the top floors. I'll take you to the front desk."

The head man said, "Mr. Arch, we here at the Drake have been authorized to give you first-class treatment. First off, we have a beautiful suite all set up for you for the next two days. Then our Chief Chef will prepare a most fantastic breakfast."

Suddenly there was a commotion down at the other end of the front desk. The clerk was telling a young man that he was very sorry, but there was nothing he could do. The man said, "But we had reservations. Our room was reserved for two days, three weeks ago and this is our honeymoon."

"That room was held until 7 pm and then we had to let it go. All other rooms are booked solid."

The man asked if there were any other hotels around with any rooms available. The clerk said, "Another couple was here 30 minutes ago and we had no rooms, so I called 12 different hotels in the area, but because of the time and the conventions, there was not one room available."

Arch turned to the head clerk and asked him if his suite is paid for two days. And his dinners and breakfasts, also for two days. The head clerk said that they were.

Arch walked over to the couple and asked where they were from and when did they get married. They said they were from Cincinnati and had a simple wedding Saturday morning. "Well it seems that you lost your room, but I think we can replace it with a nice, first-class suite."

"We appreciate that very much but we couldn't afford a suite."

"This one you can, because it is all paid for, for two days. Not only the suite but the dinners and breakfasts for two days also."

"But, Sir, who is paying for this?"

"I'd just consider it a wedding present from someone who is enjoying making amends for wrongs in the past. And if you ever get to Fayetteville, Arkansas. Stop at Foley's Restaurant and say hello to your benefactor Ed Foley."

Arch asked Dan, the head clerk, if there was anything wrong with what he just did. "No, you're alright, but you gave away your suite and your dinner."

"No problem Dan I can sleep with my bike, and as far as food goes, I just finished a great dinner at the Black Eagles Motorcycle Club. It was cooked by a great chef by the name of Sergio."

"In that case I know you had a great dinner. We have been trying to hire Sergio here at the Drake for the last four years."

"Dan, I plan on leaving tomorrow morning anyway, as I have a new job to get to."

"Well, I wish you good luck on your new job, but before you leave let me set you up for a great breakfast."

"Okay," said Arch, "but I have to leave by 10 am."

"Right, Arch, I'll see you in the dining room at 8 am, if that's okay."

Arch arrived in the dining room at 8 am and Dan was there to greet him. He asked if Arch would like to join the honeymoon couple for breakfast.

"That would be nice, but I've got to leave by 10 am."

Dan introduced Arch to Jack and his wife Betty. Jack said, "I can't believe that you did this for us, being that we are complete strangers."

"I have had many strangers help me in the past eight months. I didn't understand it then, but I do now. Some day you will find someone you can help."

After breakfast, Arch wished them good luck and headed to his room. He put his gear into his saddlebags and wheeled the big Indian to the elevator, down the loading dock and to the street. The address on the machine shop said 1800 W. Lake Street. He went south on Michigan Avenue to Grand Avenue and west toward Halsted and then south to Lake St. He was finally there. The sign by the front entrance said "Parking in the Rear". He went around the back and parked next to a pretty red 1946 Knucklehead Harley. Must be Eric's bike he thought.

Chapter 12

Arch Greets Eric.
Janice & Wendy Meet the Killers.

Arch walked in the front door and was greeted by Mary Lou, the company's all around office gal. He told her who he was and she brought him right into Art's office. Mary Lou got him a cup of coffee and then said she'd be right back with Art. A few minutes later Art and Eric walked in. Art introduced himself and Eric just backed up a bit and said, "Holy shit, Arch. Looks like you've been pumping iron."

"No," he said, "just working."

"Well, we have a lot of work around here and it looks like you can do all the heavy lifting," said Art, "glad to have you aboard, Arch. Eric, why don't you show Arch the shop. Then take the day off and show Arch some of Chicago. When you get back from wherever, bring Arch to the house. Arch, we have a spare room at the house and you are welcome to it for as long as it takes to get settled in."

Eric showed Arch around the shop and introduced him to the guys. Then he said, "Would you like to go swimming in a nice clean stone quarry?"

"That sounds better than good, but I think I better offload some of the things in my saddlebags first."

They went out back to the bikes and Eric took a look at the big gold Indian and said, "That is some neat Indian. I got his little sister, a Scout that will I show it to you later."

Arch took most of the stuff out of the bags and Eric watched Arch as he threw everything on the ground. He left some of the heavier stuff out and put the rest back in, except what looked like a strange looking case for a pistol. Eric asked why he needed all this stuff.

"Well, when you are going cross-country by yourself, you can never have too much emergency gear and hell, that rope save my ass once. And somebody else's another time. That Bowie is something that I've never had to use on anyone, but it is more impressive than carrying a gun. I'll show you what I mean. In a bigger town it is usually no problem, but in some of these one horse towns, teenagers tend to hang out in front of the only restaurant in town. There may be 6 or 8 of them. Sometimes they are good kids and sometimes they are not. When they are not, sometimes they want your wallet and your leather jacket and if they decide that they want your bike, then you will wind up face down floating down the river, or buried in a shallow grave. I never did like the thought of these things happening. So when I'm coming up to one of these small towns and I plan on stopping to eat, I take out my trusty Bowie knife, attach a sheath to my belt and put the Bowie knife in the sheath. That big old Bowie knife is impressive. Usually when they see the Bowie nobody wants to mess with me."

All of sudden, Arch reached down and swung his arm quick and sure. Four throwing knives were stuck in a telephone pole, no more than an inch apart. "That impresses the hell out of somebody that was about to do me harm. Usually there are about half a dozen guys or more and one of the guys that is carrying a knife in a sheath. He will always come up to me and say, "Let me see that knife man" in a very demanding way. The Bowie comes out of the sheath and into the pole. Then two more throwing knives right next to the Bowie. My good friend who wanted to see my knife is now walking to the pole. I shoot a knife right past his face and into the pole and say, "Reach for the knife and the next one will go through the back of your hand" and I go to the pole and pull out all the knives and put them back in their sheaths."

"I remember this one instance with a guy named Gary. "Gary," I say, as I'm walking back to my bike, "Come over here, let's talk." I pull out the Bowie and hand it to him, and say, "Now let me see yours." He hands me his knife I threw it at the pole it missed the spot by a few inches and I told him he needed a knife with more balance. So I said to take the knife and practice with it and read up on knives and get a good set of throwing knives and when you are good enough, you will never have to hurt anybody with a knife. Just scare them once and they will respect you.

He said, “Hey, Man, are you giving me this knife?” and I told him yeah, I am, but just do like I say and you’ll never have to hurt anybody with a knife. And then I asked him to watch my bike, while I went in to eat and he said, no problem and to tell Jimmy in the restaurant that Gary sent you and he would fix me up real good. I did just that and Jimmy made me the best Reuben sandwich I ever had and when I came out of the restaurant, I couldn’t believe my eyes. The guys had washed and polished my bike and it looked like new.”

“I have been throwing the knives for the last five or six years and I’ve gotten pretty good at it. I carry five knives on me at all times. Four in my boots and one in my belt buckle and then I have five more under the seat on my bike. I have never done anyone any serious injury. But, I have scared the hell out of a lot of bad guys. But, hell, Eric, that’s enough bull. Let’s go swimming.”

“Okay, Arch, let’s go back into the office and I’ll show you where it is on the map, so you won’t get lost.”

They did that and then bugged out. They jogged over to Western Avenue and then south to 111th St. and west on 111th St. all the way to Lemont Road. They decided that they would stop in Lemont and grab a bite to eat in a restaurant there, but as they were heading west on 111th St., they came up behind a big black Cadillac. It had Afghanistan Embassy plates on it. They were about to pass the Cadillac when they noticed a string of about 10 bicycles riders on the right side of the road. They decided not to pass the car until they passed the bicycles. As the Cadillac came upon the bicycles, the guy on the passenger side stuck a pole or something out of the window; it looked like a very heavy broomstick. He hit the back of each rider and they all fell into a ditch. Eric and Arch stopped to see if they could help the riders, but they were all okay.

Arch said, “Eric, let’s go get those bastards.”

They caught up with the embassy car just as it pulled into a restaurant parking lot. They parked the Cadillac and went into the restaurant. Eric pointed to a state police car parked in the lot with two officers sitting in the car, having their lunch. Eric and Arch pulled up alongside and got off their bikes. They explained to the officers what had happened with the bicycles and the officers told them to hang around as witnesses and that they would arrest them. Eric pointed at the Cadillac.

The driver shut off the engine on the squad car and said, “Forget it, Guys. We can’t do a damn thing. The people in that car have diplomatic immunity. We can’t touch them, no matter what they do. We have seen these two guys around here quite a few times and there have been complaints. Their favorite thing is to pick up gals, rape them, beat them up and lay them by the side of the road. We have picked them up a couple of times and tried to charge them, but they just give us the finger and they say "Diplomatic Immunity". Their lawyer shows up and they walk and we get chewed out. To tell you the truth, they get away with anything because their old man is some sort of a bigwig. We can't do a damn thing, but I wish some private citizen would tear the shit out of those sons of bitches. I could watch until the bastards almost bled to death. Then it would be a very slow trip to the hospital. But it will probably never happen."

Arch said, "You never can tell."

And then he said, "I'm Arch and this is Eric."

The driver said, "I'm Sam and my partner is Richie."

"We're going to get something to eat and then we may have a little talk with them. What do you think, Eric?"

"Sounds like a plan, Arch."

Sam said, "Now you guys be very careful in staying almost legal. If we hear a screaming diplomat in pain, we may have some engine problem. That could happen, Richie, couldn't it?"

"Sure could, Sam. You guys stay out of trouble, or at least don't get caught."

Eric and Arch went into the restaurant and located their prey and sat down where they could watch them. Arch and Eric ordered hamburgers and cokes. They finished eating and asked for the bill, but refilled their cokes to go, so they could sit and watch the creeps. The two guys got up and threw a couple 20s on the table. They walked by a booth where two college looking girls were sitting and just sat down. Each one next to a girl. One of them said something and the girl told him to get lost. Almost simultaneously, they reached over and grabbed each one of the girls' blouses and ripped them open. Then they grabbed their bras and ripped them right off with a very practiced motion. They had probably done this many times before. The girls screamed while the creeps fondled their boobs. Eric started to get up, but Arch stopped him and said, "Not yet, Eric."

The creeps ran out the door laughing and waving their girls bras.

Arch was watching them as they got into their Cadillac and pulled over to the far side of the lot and parked.

Arch said, "It's not over yet, Eric, them bastards will get theirs."

They sat sipping their cokes until the girls got up and were holding their blouses together as best they could. The girls got into a Chevy convertible and headed north on Lemont road toward 111 St. The Cadillac took off after them, caught up with them, pulled alongside and ran them right off into a ditch. Arch and Eric parked their bikes on the road next to the girl's car and asked the girls if they were okay? They said they were fine, but one of the girls said, "But my car sure ain't fine."

Eric said, "Don't worry, those creeps will pay."

Arch told the girls to wait by their car and if anyone stops, tell them help is on the way. If a state police car stops, ask if their names are Sam and Richie and tell them what happened and that Arch and Eric are taking care of it. Tell them not to make any reports as of yet. They will be solving the problem in the area and any help from the Rangers will be appreciated."

Eric said, "We will be back shortly."

Arch opened one of his saddlebags got his revolver and snapped it under his buddy seat. "You ready, Eric? Let's go get them."

They caught up to them in about 4 or 5 miles. Arch told Eric to stay back and he pulled alongside the car and motioned for them to pull over. Instead they wheeled over hard and tried to run Arch off the road. Arch cranked over to avoid them and then came back with a 12 inch steel pipe with a lead weight on it. First he crashed the driver's side window and then the driver's side windshield. Just as Arch backed off, a couple of shots came through the side window. Kind of expected, Arch said to himself. He dropped back alongside Eric and he reached under the seat and came up with the 38 revolver. "Going to shoot them, Arch?"

"No, that would be too easy."

He cranked it on and came up fairly close to the Cadillac. He fired off two quick rounds into the left rear tire and then backed off again. He and Eric watched a tire blowout and then fly apart. At 70 mph the car did not handle too well with a blown tire. They got it under control and pulled off the road. The bikes pulled up behind them. Eric on the right and Arch on the left. Arch gave Eric the pistol and said, "Just in case."

The driver opened the door and jumped out with a gun in his hand. Arch reached to his belt buckle and with a flick of the wrist the gun man had a knife in his forearm and Arch threw him to the ground and Eric said, "I've got the other one, Arch."

They got the two of them together and looked them over. Eric said, "They don't look like keepers to me. I think we should weight them down and throw them in the lake."

"No, no, you cannot do this. We have diplomatic immunity."

"Creep, we will consider your plea, when we hold court."

"No, you cannot do that. I must call our embassy."

Arch said, "Eric, will you get their radio out of their Caddy for them?"

Eric went over to the Cadillac, reached in and ripped out the radio and brought it to them. Arch said, "Now, let's discuss the problem at hand. You have a flat tire that needs changing. First, before we start doing all this work, let's get to know each other. I'm Arch and he is Eric. Now what are your names?"

"I do not have to tell you."

"Okay then I'll just call you Ugly Shit Face."

"My name is Jamaal and he is Saheed."

"Good, we got that squared away. Now we have to get to work to fix the Caddy. Eric, do you want to go back and pick up the girls? You can take my bike if you want. It's got a bigger seat than yours to carry three people."

"I'll take mine. I don't mind being a little crowded by two good looking gals."

"Eric, leave the gun with me. I may want to shoot these bastards, if they don't work fast enough changing the tires."

Jamaal said, "We will not be doing manual labor. We will call a service truck."

Arch said, "The only service truck you are going to see is an ambulance, so get the spare out of the trunk and get the jack."

Saheed said, "I have never done this before."

"Well, you better learn pretty fast or I may start shooting. If you don't have it changed by that time my partner gets back, I may just put you both in the Caddy, tie you up and set it on fire. Now let's see how fast you can learn and don't try anything funny or I'll put a bullet in your kneecap. And that is no fun. For you that is."

They must have gotten the message because the spare was now on the car. Even though Eric had been back with the girls for about 20 minutes. Arch asked if one of the girls could drive the Cadillac.

Janice said, "I'll do it."

Eric said he knew a nice secluded place in the forest reserve, by Argonne National Laboratory. They tied Jamaal and Saheed and threw them in the backseat. Eric used some of his good sailor knots so they were not about to get loose. Good thing Arch had the rope in his saddlebags. Jamaal was screaming and cussing at Eric and Arch, so Eric started looking for something to stuff in Jamaal's mouth and found a gym bag in the trunk. When Jamaal saw Eric with a gym bag, he screamed at Eric and said, "Put that bag back in the trunk. It is my private property."

Eric opened the bag and was shocked. He stood there staring. Janice and Wendy came over and looked in the bag. Janice and Wendy both went to the Caddy and with super girl strength, pulled the diplomatic bastards out on the ground. What set the girls off was what was found in a gym bag. First they found panties and bras mostly torn and some bloody. But what really set them off was a Ziploc bag. It contained an ear lobe with an ear ring and also two nipples, with rings and small gold chains. The nipples were stapled to heavy cardboard and then put in a Ziploc. They had come from the breasts of some poor girl who was now probably dead. The girls untied Jamaal's legs, but secured one leg at the ankle to a small sapling. Arch and Eric watched with fascination as Jamaal was cussing and tried to sit up. Janice kicked him right in the face. He screamed and laid back down. Then they tied his other ankle to another small, sturdy sapling making a perfect V to the crotch. The girls did the same to Saheed. He started screaming and Wendy kicked him in the face too.

Arch turned to Eric and said, "They seem to be a couple of nice girls, but they are really pissed off."

"You're right, Arch, what do you think of your first day in Chicago?"

"Well, it may be hard to believe, but it's been like this all the way from Phoenix. I happen to be a hero in towns from Arkansas to Hannibal, Missouri. The people there even consider me a Messenger from God and the way some things have worked out, I'm almost believing it myself. I'll tell you about it sometime."

Meanwhile the girls have got the two perverts all set up.

Eric went over to Arch's bike and got the big Bowie Knife out of the saddlebag. Jamaal and Saheed went wide-eyed when they saw Eric pull the big blade out of the sheath. This time Saheed said, "We have diplomatic immunity."

Eric said, "Yeah, but I bet you are not immune to two girls that are really pissed off."

Saheed said, "But someone will see you and my father will make sure that you go to jail."

"Listen, if no one ever finds your body, they have no evidence and the police hate you perverts already. And as you've noticed we have moved the Cadillac and our bikes behind the trees and away from the road."

Arch asked the girls if they were ready for interrogation to begin and Jamaal laughed and said, "What do these girls know of interrogation? In my country we are experts at it."

Eric said in a quiet conversational tone, "Janice has told me that Cindy is part American Indian Apache to be exact."

The way Eric tied them, they could not sit up and the girls decided to get their attention before the interrogation began. The girls stood between their legs and Janice said, "First, an old fashion pervert kick to the balls."

Wendy did the same, with the same groaning results. Janice said, "For our second act, it will be another kick in your sore balls."

She did it again and Jamaal screamed that this was illegal and they had diplomatic immunity.

"I have been told that Americans are not allowed to torture."

"Jamaal, I understand that torture is normal practice your country, but you are right here where torture is illegal. But this is not torture this is a scientific study. It is a pain clinic to see how much pain you can stand before you spill your guts."

So Arch said, "I think we should proceed."

Eric had found a portable tape recorder in the trunk and some of the tapes had the screaming of girls that they had abused. Eric found a fresh tape and put it in the recorder. Eric started, "What happened and where is the girl that you cut off her ear lobe?"

Jamaal said, "We don't have to answer that."

Janice kicked him right in the nuts. His eyes crossed and he almost passed out. "Same questions to you, Saheed."

Wendy got set to kick Saheed again, but he said, "Oh no, I talk. Jamaal did the earlobes; I do tits." After hearing that, Wendy gave him a kick so hard, that it would have made a Rose Bowl coach proud. Arch had an idea that the bastards were even worse than they thought they were. He went back and looked deep into the trunk and he found another gym bag. He brought it out for everyone to see and Saheed said, "That is my bag, as if he was proud of it."

Eric opened it and the same things were there, as the other bag, bloody girls' underwear, along with about 10 nipples neatly mounted in pairs. This bastard was even worse than Jamaal. Wendy was about to crush his nuts when Arch stopped her. "We need him for now. He seems to be willing to talk and if not you can make like an Apache. Right now, you girls can watch these two perverts while Eric and I go and get a couple of wooden picnic benches."

"Are we going to have a picnic?"

"Not us, just the perverts."

They were gone for about five minutes and came back with a picnic bench and then they were gone again for another five minutes and came back with a second picnic bench. Wendy asked Arch, "Why the benches?"

Arch said, "You will see shortly and you will be glad that you didn't give that final kick."

Saheed said that they used chloroform to get the girls, so they must have some in their trunk. Eric found a bottle in the second bag and Eric and Arch put the tables side-by-side. Then they blind folded Saheed, so that he couldn't see Jamaal and then they chloroformed Jamaal and stripped off his clothes except for his shorts. Eric tied him down, spread-eagle. Hands and feet at each corner of the table and then chloroformed Saheed and mounted him to table two. Then Eric secured their midsection so they could not move their bodies at all. Eric thought that it was nice of these creeps to have all this rope in their trunk. Now they stood the tables up balancing on the legs and the tabletop. Then they found some heavy branches and wedged them in behind the tables, so the tables could not fall over backwards. The tables had been turned so Jamaal and Saheed could see each other. Arch called the girls over and asked what they would like to do them. They both said, "They would like to cut their dicks off, or at least their balls."

Janice was standing nearby, holding the big Bowie knife and feeling the sharp edge. Eric said, "Gals, strip him down."

Janice took two quick slices and tore off Jamaal's shorts.

Jamaal came to and said, "In my country, a woman would be beheaded for doing this to a man."

"If I remember right, Jamaal, you ripped off their bras right in a crowded restaurant. So they have got their rights."

"In my country they have no rights."

Arch asked Saheed, "Is what Jamaal said true?"

Meanwhile Eric has turned on the tape recorder.

"Jamaal, are you saying that a man can do anything he wants to women in your country?"

"Some men are only allowed to do whatever they want to their wives and girlfriends."

"But you, Jamaal, are allowed to do whatever you like to any woman, right?"

"Yes, we are allowed, because of our station in life."

Arch asked Jamaal if he had raped women in his country.

"Yes, many times if it pleased me. And my brother - him even more than me."

"Were you ever punished for these rapes?"

"Never. Why do you ask such strange question? I am a man and she was nothing more than a woman."

"Jamaal, what happens to these women after you rape them?"

"Sometimes nothing if they keep quiet. But if anyone in the family finds out. Then someone in the family will kill the woman. It is an honor killing."

"Now what about the girls you and your brother have raped here."

"No one will ever know about them because of your strange laws you have in this country," said Jamaal.

"You have some neat souvenirs in the Ziploc in your gym bag," said Arch, "but they are not worth much in this country."

"We have many more of these, as you call souvenirs, back in our apartment. We do not live at the embassy because it is too restrictive."

"Jamaal, I have noticed that under each of your nipples that you have collected, there is a number. To me that sound like a great way to keep track of what you are doing."

"That was Saheed's idea. He keeps the ledger so when we return home, we can show our friends."

"Your brother must be a very smart man to do all this. So, Saheed, you know that you have diplomatic immunity. The police cannot do anything to you. They absolutely cannot search your apartment and that is good thinking to keep the ledger where it is safe from the police."

Saheed said, "That is true. It is safe in the apartment and also safe there from thieves. It is a secured building."

"It seems that your friends back home will be impressed, but how can you impress your friends if they don't know where your great souvenirs came from."

Jamaal said, "We have thought of that. As you have seen, the souvenirs are numbered and in the ledger with details. Without the details of each one it would be hard to remember exactly what we did. He even has Polaroid pictures of each girl. Both with, and without their nipples."

"Were they alive when you cut off their nipples? Oh, yes that is why we have the tape recorder. That will be much more interesting when our friends can hear, as well as see. Saheed knows how to make them scream."

"Jamaal, this should really impress your friends, but how can you impress your friends with souvenirs from unnamed girls and what you did with them."

He said, "I have the girls' names cataloged with times and dates and I also have the tapes numbered so our friends will not have any doubt as to what we have done."

Saheed said, "We will be famous back home."

"Saheed, how can you become famous just by killing a few insignificant girls?"

Jamaal said, "It was more than just a few. I would say about 28 girls, would you not, Saheed?"

"I would say more like 33, if you count the first ones that you did by yourself."

Eric said, "You guys really seem to have this figured out. It takes a smart person to get away with something like this, by the way, did you rape them first?"

"Of course, as the old American saying goes, waste not want not, we both did." And they both laughed.

Jamaal said, "We would be looking for the girls all over, that is why we did these girls in different parts of the country. And we're always carrying a shovel in the trunk."

Arch said, "Like I said before, you guys really have it all figured out with the diplomatic immunity and all. But if you want to amaze your friends back home, how are you going to get your souvenirs, ledgers and pictures back home?"

Saheed said, "That's the easy part. Everything will go back home in a diplomatic pouch carried by a diplomatic courier."

Eric asked Jamaal what they planned for Janice and Wendy.

"When we are free we will do to them the same as the other girls except they will die more slowly. Now as you know you must release us because of our diplomatic immunity and as you promised when we answered all of your questions, you said you would release us."

"Jamaal and Saheed, I have a secret. I lied. Sorry guys, but I'm really a no good liar and court is now adjourned and you are both found guilty as hell. When your father finds out what you both are, he will have to keep the shame a secret because he will have to disown you and you will never make it to paradise. Now, girls, I hope you remember that Jamaal said that they would make you die slowly. I think they wanted to make you suffer even more than the other girls that they raped and killed. Now anything that you girls decide to do to them is much less than they deserve."

Eric said that he had a suggestion, "Each of these fine gentlemen had a razor knife in his pocket. Everyone should know exactly what these perverts are. They are rapists, perverts and serial killers. This should be known before the newspapers make them out as innocent victims. Saheed said, "You must follow the law. We are being held against our will and we are citizens of another country."

Jamaal chimes in and said, " We have diplomatic immunity so you must follow your own laws."

Arch said, "Jamaal, do you believe in the saying "Do unto others as you would have them to do unto you"?"

Jamaal thought for a moment and said, "Yes, that is it."

"Jamaal, I like that saying too, but under certain circumstances we must change the wording. How about "Do unto those the same as they have done to others". Don't be a baby, Jamaal. It is time for you to suffer. At least as much as the suffering that you have caused those women you and your brother have killed."

At this time the tape recorder had been turned off.

"The only difference Jamaal, is that your pain will be administered by two pretty women that you intended to rape and kill. This is not vengeance. This is a necessary thing, to let other creeps like you know that immunity does not work here and that this is the final court."

Eric said, "You have confessed your evil deeds and your confessions have been recorded."

Saheed said, "Our father is a rich man and he will pay you well if you release us."

"If we release you, who will pay for your crimes?"

"There is no crime when you have immunity," said Jamaal.

"Okay, girls, you know what these creeps have done to dozens of girls just like you and you know what they planned to do to you."

Janice said, "Yes, we heard. People should know who and what these creeps are. It should be written indelibly and painfully. If it is written on paper, their associates may have it destroyed. We have their two razor sharp knives and Wendy and I have decided to issue some pain to these two creeps. We will make it known to the world what these animals are."

"It's your show," said Arch.

Janice started on Jamaal, Wendy followed on Saheed. Janice took a couple of small needles from her sewing kit in her purse and gave one to Wendy. Janice put the needle through the end of one of Jamaal's nipples and then took a razor knife and carved the whole nipple off. Jamaal was screaming like a banshee. Janice said, "Hurts, don't it." Then she stuck the nipple on his fore head and said, "The blood

will dry like glue and you and Saheed can lay there and look at each other's nipples for as long as you live." Wendy did the same as Janice on Saheed. He screamed even louder than Jamaal. As they girls finished the second nipple, both Jamaal and Saheed were screaming and crying.

Wendy said, "We should have recorded their screaming, as they did with their victims." Eric said, "I did record it."

"Now we will leave a message so that people will know about these killers," said Janice. Then she turned to Wendy asking if her razor knife was still sharp. Wendy said, "It is."

Jamaal and Saheed were still crying when Janice told them that they were going to carve a message in their chests with their own razor knives that they used on the girls they killed.

The message on Jamaal:	The message on Saheed:
I am Jamaal	I am Saheed
A rapist	A rapist
A pervert	A pervert
A killer of girls	A killer of girls

Eric told the girls to carve the message deep, because he was going to take some Polaroid pictures. He wanted the pictures of their carving to show up good. Eric took the pictures and they came out very good. After they all looked at the pictures, Eric showed them to Jamaal and Saheed, who by now had stopped screaming and crying.

Eric said, "All of these pictures, tapes and recordings will go to many newspapers, TV and radio news people. If we just sent them to the police, your people would get them quashed. I think that you will even be hated in your own country once they find out. Now you and your brother will be famous and hated for the evil persons you are."

"Well, Jamaal," said Janice, "As much as we both hate you and your brother, we have no more taste for blood, even though it is yours and your evil brother's."

"Then in that case you must release us and take us to a hospital to be treated."

"If we release you and are treated in a hospital, your diplomatic immunity will keep you from being punished as any other killer."

Both Jamaal and Saheed said in unison, "As it should be. In all our lives we have never been punished for anything and your laws should not force us to be punished now."

Arch looked into the eyes of Jamaal, and then into the eyes of Saheed and said in a loud, blustering voice, "I am a Messenger of God. You will not be going to paradise. You will burn in Hell!"

Jamaal and Saheed both screamed, "No! No!" and with a quick swipe, Arch slit their throats.

Eric had copied all the tapes, including the ones made by the pervert brothers. They left one set of tapes in the Cadillac. They also left a set of pictures of their carved up chests and the second set of eyes on their foreheads. They put all the original tapes and pictures in Arch's saddle bags, mounted the bikes and rode out of the preserve area. Arch asked the attendant in a gas station where the closest State Police barracks were. It was just a couple miles away, so they went there and asked if Sam and Richie were around. They were told that they just went on duty and were told where to find them. They found Sam and Richie, driving southwest on Archer Avenue, flagged them down and told them that the two creeps were more than just rapists.

Eric told them, "They were rapists, torturers and serial killers of girls. You will find the evidence in their car. Also there is an address of their apartment, which contains more evidence of their crimes. There is a ledger in which they kept the details of their crimes and the names of the girls. There is no problem with immunity. Janice said that a Messenger from God sent them to Hell."

Eric said, "Get to the apartment right away, because if the Embassy people get there first, they will clean it out. Can you get it sealed up right away?"

Sam said, "I can get a State Police crime scene lock on it and nobody can get in until I say it is clear." Eric gave Sam the address. Sam said that he would tell his Lieutenant that he was told by a citizen. That there is a major crime scene at Argonne National Labs. Sam said that he and Richie would check it out and confirm the crime scene."

Sam said, "Janice's car is at the state police compound. There will be no charge for towing or storage."

Arch and Eric brought the girls to their car and exchanged phone numbers and said they would be in touch. It was pretty late when they got home, so they hit the sack. The next morning while they were having breakfast, Art asked, "How was the swimming? Me and my friends used to swim there, that's when the only way you could get there was on a motorcycle. I hear that they have a big parking lot for cars now and charge admission to swim. And a parking fee. I often wondered why someone didn't do that sooner. It's a great place to swim. What did you think of it Arch?"

"Don't know, didn't swim."

"Why not?"

"Never got there."

Then Eric explained what happened and that they had tapes and pictures of it all, which they intended to make more copies and send them to a few different newspapers.

Art asked, "What about the police?"

Arch said, "The State Police have the same copies, plus the address of the apartment, which has much more incriminating evidence. These were two evil perverts, who had been getting away with their evil acts and thought they could do anything that they felt like doing. Even when they were charged at other times the charges were always dropped. Then they went back to raping, torturing, and killing innocent girls."

Eric said, "But this time the two girls, who were their intended victims, turned the tables on the perverts, who arrogantly spelled out what they planned on doing to these girls. Because of their immunity, they expected to be released. They felt that they had a right to molest these two girls, in any way that pleased them. The girls, after hearing what the creeps had done to the other girls, and how they felt it was their God-given right to molest any female they desired, felt that it was about time for these two bastards to feel some of the pain that was issued to the many innocent girls before them. They gave these creeps some pain, a lot of pain and the perverts cried like babies and begged to be released. They needed to be punished like this to keep the other creeps with diplomatic immunity from doing the same. If we released them, they would never be charged with a crime. As Arch said, he was a Messenger from God and told them they would not go to paradise and that they would roast in hell. They said, "No! No! This is not right. You cannot do this. We have immunity" That is when Arch's Bowie knife sent them to hell. Dad, if Arch did not do it, I would have."

Art said, "Eric, so would I, because they sure as hell deserved it and I might not have sent them to hell that quickly." Art then called his office and told them that he would not be in until the next day. "Arch and Eric, you may take the next couple days off and not be in until Monday."

Eric said, "Thanks, Dad. After today, I really don't feel like going to work for the next couple of days. What do you think Arch?"

"I feel the same way, but we have got to get these tapes and pictures to the newspapers."

Art said, "Let's take a look at the pictures and hear the tapes. I have a friend who can duplicate the pictures and the tapes. Then we should contact some newspapers. I think the Tribune, the Times, the Herald Examiner and maybe some more." Just then, the telephone rang. Art answered it and said, "It's for you, Eric." Eric picked it up. The voice on the other end said, "Hello, this is Sam Hogan of Illinois State Police. Do you remember me?" Eric said, "Yes." "Eric, do you remember what you gave me and my partner, Richie?" Eric said, "Yes, information on the crime scene and the address to an apartment."

"That's good, Eric, I just wanted to see if I was talking to a right person. Richie and I checked out Argonne Forest Preserve. I called my lieutenant who was already outside the apartment. Then we got our people to Argonne. We took many pictures of the perverts. The messages on their chest were very clear in the photographs. We opened up that Cadillac and found the tapes and pictures. Then we opened the trunk and we found the two gym bags, they were full of girl's bloody underwear. Then we found what you called "their souvenirs". The lousy bastards. They were evil scum. That was a nice touch, cutting off their nipples and sticking them their foreheads. I hope they were alive when the girls did that to them."

"Sam they were alive. Alive and screaming and begging for mercy. We just kept reminding the girls, how they showed their victims no mercy. This just made the girls cut deeper. I think they cut a half-inch deep when they spelled out rapists and killers, but they couldn't do the final, and I can't say that I know who did. But it was definitely self-defense. That is, defending any girl they would come in contact with, if they were ever left to live and run free. Sam, the copies of the tape and pictures will be sent to the papers this morning before the embassy people can put a stop to printing it."

"Eric, nobody is going to stop any of this. My lieutenant said that they have found enough evidence in the apartment to send those two bastards away for 1000 years. Immunity or not."

Art said he would take care of getting copies of the tapes and pictures and give them to his secretary to send everything to the newspapers. He told her to have them contact Sergeant Hogan at the Illinois State Police Department for any more information." Art said, "Why don't you two guys do something that would be more fun than yesterday?"

Arch said, "Great, let's go swimming at the quarry."

"Sounds great, Arch. What say we call Janice and Wendy?" They said that they were taking the rest of the week off. Eric called and talked to Wendy and they said that they would love to go swimming. They fired up their bikes and headed over to pick up the girls. When they pulled up to their apartment, the girls came right out.

Eric said, "Wow, you gals looked good yesterday, but you look even better today."

Arch said, "I second that. The gals both said, "Thanks, Guys. We feel better too."

They headed for the quarry that they were going to yesterday. Except today they had the company of two pretty girls. Janice rode with Arch and Wendy rode with Eric. The girls had a small nylon drawstring bag in which they claimed contained their swimsuits. Eric looked at the very small bag and then at both the gals, who were very well endowed. Then he looked back at the bag. Eric said, "Impossible." They all laughed.

Arch said, "Those suits sure won't hide much."

Janice said, "Is that bad?"

Eric said, "I promise I won't complain."

"You do and we will just have to rough it and swim without our mini suits."

You guys better keep it clean, because I have been known as a "Messenger from God". "

Janice said, "Okay, Boss, we will keep it clean." Then they all laughed and Eric said, "Let's get to the swimming hole."

They got to Lemont Road and Eric looked for the side road that led to the quarry. There was just a small sign that said "Stone Quarry". They went down the road for a couple of miles and they came to a railroad track. Eric was the only one who had been to the quarry before, and only once a couple of years ago. They asked Eric if he remembered how to get to the quarry? He said he thought so. They followed him over the tracks, into some woods and up steep hill. When he finally got to the top they looked across the beautiful green waters of the stone quarry. Wendy told Eric that she knew he would find it. "Yeah you were all ready to crucify me."

"Never," said Arch, "we all trusted your judgment. Now let's go swimming."

They rolled up on the east side of the quarry where there was a 30 foot bluff down to the water. There was a small house and a man sitting at a picnic bench drinking a beer. He said, "Hi, Folks. Nice day for swimming. And that will cost you two dollars apiece. And two dollars more if you want to use the changing room." He pointed to a small shed.

Eric said, "It looks real good. We will use the changing room." And he handed the guy a $10 bill. Arch asked if the water was deep enough to dive off the bluff. "Plenty deep, about 30 foot deep all around the bluff area."

The girls got their suits from the saddlebag and went to the changing room. Eric went to the bikes and got their suits. While they waited they talked to the man, whose name was Rudy. Eric said that he was surprised that there were so few people there. "It's Thursday and before noon. Give it another hour or two and the place will be busy as hell."

Just then the girls came out of the changing room. Rudy said, "For that view, I should give you your money back." Arch and Eric did a double take. Both of the girls made a few twirls and Janice said, "These are the latest fashion, called bikinis. They are named after the Bikini atoll, where an A-bomb was tested."

Arch said, "Wow, ain't modern science wonderful."

Eric was still drooling when he said, "You think those bikinis will stay on when you dive in?"

"They are very strong nylon, and guaranteed not to break or tear and they are very comfortable. It almost feels like you are wearing nothing."

Arch said, "It looks almost like that too, but you won't hear me complain."

Janice said, "I hope you don't complain when they get wet, because when they are wet they are transparent."

Eric said, "To that, I say again, let's go swimming."

They all dove into the water from the 30 foot bluff. They played around in the water for a while and then climbed up the ladder to the top of the bluff. The girls started laughing and just kept laughing. Eric asked what they were laughing about and Janice said, "Just watching you two guys, the way you can't take your eyes off of us. You are waiting for our suits to turn transparent. Guess what? It won't happen, but don't look so sad. You sure did like them when we came out of the changing room."

"We still do but we were looking forward to something that never happened."

"We could make it happen," said Wendy, "but let's go swimming instead." They swam across the quarry in back a few times. The girls were good swimmers and pretty fast. They said that both of them were on a high school swim team, but that was a few years ago. They got out of the water and up on the grass. Arch got a couple of beach towels out of his saddlebags. Rudy had pop and hotdogs and they each had two hot dogs and a coke, then laid back and relaxed. They did not intend to talk about yesterday, but Janice broke the ice when she asked what the police were doing about Jamaal and Saheed?

Eric said, "The police have all the evidence, their grisly souvenirs, the ledger, pictures and tape. If they were still alive they would never see the light of day again, immunity or not."

Arch said that he talked to Sergeant Sam Hogan this morning. "Sam said as far as anyone knows, they have no idea who was in the forest preserve and they are not interested to find out. The embassy people do not want to rock the boat. They just want it to die away. It is much too embarrassing for them. It will be in the evening papers and tomorrow's for sure. They can't stop it from being printed, so they plan to ignore it."

Eric said, "Okay, you guys, if you are going to keep talking about these creeps, I'm going to dive in and go to the bottom. I'll stay there until somebody comes to get me." Eric dove in and went to the bottom, picked up a heavy rock and sat on the bottom. Wendy dove in and swam down to Eric, straddled his lap and he nuzzled his face into her breasts. She grabbed her bathing suit top and pulled it up. Eric then sucked on her nipples. She wanted to stay down, but needed to go up and get air. Eric swam right to the top while holding his face in her breasts. When they got to the top she pulled her bra back down. As they swam to shore Wendy said, "Eric I think you're getting horny."

"How can you tell?" She reached over and put her hand in his trunks and grabbed hold of his rock hard pecker. "That's how. Nurses can always tell."

"Wendy I think you have led me astray."

They got back up on the grass and laid down on the beach towels. Arch and Janice had been swimming at the far end of the quarry and started swimming back. It was a race and Janice seemed to be winning until the last hundred feet, Arch turned it on and he beat her by two lengths. When they came up on the grass, Janice said, "You cheated, Arch."

"How so?"

"You didn't have one arm tied behind your back." Everybody decided they had enough swimming for the day and they were all getting hungry. The girls said that there was a pretty decent restaurant north of 55th St. on Kedzie. When they found the place, it was a Polish restaurant with a name that seemed very difficult to pronounce. Arch said, "Forget the name, as long as the food is good."

The girls ordered chicken and dumplings, which they said was the house specialty, do Arch and Eric said they would have the same until Arch spotted something familiar on the menu. He couldn't understand the words, Kapusta Zuppa, but they also described it in English. Country ribs in a tangy broth with sauerkraut on a bed of spaetzles. Arch knew what he wanted. "Sauerkraut soup, that's it."

Chapter 13

On Lake Michigan with the Sea Sled.

Arch had the sauerkraut soup and he was in Heaven. The others had their chicken and dumplings and they all agreed that it was great. They sat back and were stuffed. They had a few drinks and just talked. Eric asked Janice what she did at the hospital. She said she was a surgical nurse. Then Arch said, "That is probably why the blood did not bother you yesterday."

"No, that is not true, I feel for patients on the table, but I had no feelings for those evil bastards."

Wendy said that she felt exactly the same way and that she worked in the emergency room. "If those two creeps came into her emergency room and she knew what they had done, if she had her way she would have treated their wounds with salt and vinegar. "And now can we quit talking about these killers?" They all agreed.

Eric said, "It's Friday tomorrow. A good day to go boating. If you girls want to go that is. We can use my dad's boat. It's an 18 foot Lyman with a 40 HP Mercury. My dad and mom used to use it out on Lake Michigan almost every weekend until my mom died. He doesn't use it much anymore. Thinks of selling it, and then changes his mind."

Wendy said, "Sounds good to me. What do you think Janice?"

"I'm all for it. What do you want us to bring?"

Arch turned to Janice and said, "If you girls bring a picnic lunch, Eric and I will bring the beer and wine and whatever else we need. And don't forget your swimsuits. The Bikini ones."

Eric said, "We have a private changing room on the boat."

Wendy looked at Eric with a quizzical look on her face and said, "On an 18 foot boat?"

"Well, it's not exactly a room. What it is, is, all interested parties look the other way while you gals are changing."

Janice said, "Who would be the interested parties?" Both Eric and Arch raised their hands. Wendy said, "Now we know who to watch out for."

"Well," said Eric, "now that we got that settled. Do any of you water ski?"

Both gals said yes.

Arch said he never tried it.

"Well, we got water skiers and now one more question," said Eric, "does everybody like to eat fish? Particularly fresh smoked fish."

Janice said, "I love it and Wendy is a Swede too. Three of us like smoked fish, what about you, Arch?"

"Is the Pope Catholic? Of course I do. But where are you going to get fresh smoked fish?"

"We're going to spear it tomorrow. And then my dad will smoke it tomorrow night. He does a great job smoking fish."

"What kind of fish can you spear in Lake Michigan?"

"Carp, Arch. Nice firm cold water Carp. Most people think Carp is a trash fish. It's raised in cold quarries in Europe, then sold as a delicacy. Smoked Carp is good eating. You don't smoke or eat most of the belly meat because it is soft. Most people that catch Carp hook them in shallow warm lakes and rivers. They are not as good as what you get out of cold water like Lake Michigan. Eric asked the girls if they could be ready by 8:30 am. They would pick them up and head for Montrose Harbor to launch the boat.

Janice said they would be ready.

Wendy said, "Drop us off by the emergency room entrance at the hospital. There is an all-night delicatessen across the street where we can pick up some fixings for tomorrow. It's only a half a block from our apartment."

They dropped the girls off and headed home. Janice didn't say anything to Wendy, but she knew Wendy was plotting something. "Wendy, why are you going into emergency? We are off until Tuesday."

"I want to go in and see Shirley."

"Why do you want to see Shirley?"

"Because she works part-time at Second City and she is in charge of the costume department and they just had a play that was set in the1920s. It had a beach scene with 1920s style swimsuits."

Janice wised up and said, "Do you think she can get them?"

Wendy was almost sure Shirley could do it. "She's a practical joker at heart. The only thing is, she will want pictures of us in the suits."

"That's no problem," said Janice, "I've got my Polaroid at the apartment." So they went into the ER and found Shirley right away. When they explained everything to Shirley she cracked up laughing and said yes.

Shirley said she would get the suits to them after she gets off duty at 11 pm. She said that she would deliver them to their apartment by 11:30. Providing they had a Grande Margarita ready for her when she gets there. They stopped at the delicatessen and got some good Rosen's Rye bread, ham, cheese and some other lunch meats and a jar of kosher dills. They went home and started making sandwiches. The doorbell rang and it was Shirley. She had the costumes and insisted that they try them on. Once they had them on they did all kinds of poses, while Shirley just kept snapping pictures. Some of the poses would not set too well back in the 1920s though. After Shirley left they finished making the picnic lunch.

Next, they had to figure out how they were going to pull off the great swimsutit trick. They did a practice run. First they got all the gear they would need together, then they both stripped down to nothing, put on their bikinis. So far so good. Janice looked at Wendy and said, "Lady, you sure are one sexy looking broad in that Bikini."

"Hey, Janice, you ain't so bad yourself. You got a set of jugs that men die for."

"I'll leave them in the bra so we don't have any dead men around here."

Wendy said, "Okay, enough bull shit, let's proceed with our dirty deed."

They put on the 1920s suits and it covered up the Bikinis with no problem at all. Next they put slacks on and stuffed the 1920s swimsuit skirt down in the slacks and then long sleeved jackets. It was perfect. No one would be able to tell what they were wearing.

Janice said, "The temperature tomorrow is supposed to be about 80° and the guys may wonder why the slacks and jackets. We will just tell them just in case it's cold out on the lake. And if they will say no, it's going to be hot, we can just sluff it off. When we are on the boat and heading out we take off our slacks and jackets and reveal our new 1920s swimsuits and say, "These are the newest fashion super sexy swimsuits". After we hassle them for a while, we will get them to stop the boat and we can jump over to the side and hope to hell that we can swim in these ridiculous things. After a bit, we will start loosening up the buttons where they can't see and then we go under the boat and take them off. We will come up on the other side and throw the suits in the boat. Now that they think we are naked, they will tease the hell out of us and they will offer to pull us aboard. We will tell them that we can't come aboard naked while they are watching. They can pull us aboard both at the same time if they look the other way."

That is exactly what happened. After the gals were aboard, the guys turned around and found two sexy looking gals in bikinis. Arch took a look and said, "This is a hell of a lot better than the gals we started out with."

"Hey, what did you guys think you were going to pull out of the water?"

"I would say that whatever we thought, and what we actually got, I will admit was not a bad deal. I think that you are now one up on us," said Arch.

"Where are we heading, Eric?" asked Janice.

"We are going down below Miegs Field and maybe down to the 63rd St. breakwater. They headed south. The water had a very slight chop and the 18 foot Lyman rode through it very nicely. The Lyman was a boat made for Lake Michigan. It had a wood lap strake hull. Lap strake is when the planks overlap each other. This helps stabilize the boat in rough waters and it also makes a stronger hull. The 40 HP Mercury was the most powerful outboard that you could buy at that time, although the manufacturers had been talking about engines three times the horsepower.

As they were getting close to Navy Pier, they saw two round back lake fishing boats heading in towards the Chicago River. The fishing boats had their own docks along the river. There were many fish houses in Chicago, with fresh and smoked fish. Janice was watching the two fish boats as they were heading in from out on the lake. She asked, "Why were they completely covered?" Eric told her that they fished all year, even in the winter and Lake Michigan gets pretty rough out there starting in the fall. She looked out at the wide expanse of the lake and said, "I wouldn't want to be out there in the winter."

"It's their job, and judging by all the fish houses in Chicago they do pretty well."

Wendy noticed that one boat was moving much faster than the other boat.

Arch said, "The slower boat probably has a heavier load of fish."

"Not the case," said Eric, "the faster fishing boat belongs to a larger fish company and they have three boats. The slower boat belongs to a smaller company at Division and Elston."

"What has that got to do with the speed of the boat? They look like the same kind of a boat to me."

"They are the same boats, made by the same boat yard in Wisconsin."

Arch said, "Then they must have different kinds of engines."

"No they both have the same Kahlenburg engine."

"There must be a difference."

"There is a difference," said Eric, "the slower boat probably has only a two or three Cylinder engine. The faster boat has probably a six cylinder engine and they are expensive. You can buy a single Kahlenburg, which is adequate for that fishing boat, but not as fast. When you become financially in better shape, you can buy another cylinder or two and attach it to your existing engine. That's why the rich fisherman usually gets in first."

Arch asks, "Well, Eric, what's the plan now?"

"You see that piece of five eighth plywood that all our gear is stowed on top of? It's a sea sled, which I made last year. Never used it and ain't sure it works."

"You going to try it today?"

"Why not, otherwise I'll never know. In 1945, somewhere in this area northeast of Navy Pier, a consolidated PBY Catalina was anchored. A Navy 30 foot launch was running in the fog and the boat hit the bow of the plane and ripped out the anchor line and part of the planes bow. They found the anchor with a small part of the plane attached to it. The plane drifted out and they never found it. In fact, they never even looked. It was still wartime and they just wrote it off as a loss. I checked the weather conditions for the time when that happened, so I have an idea which way she drifted. So while I'm trying out the board, and if it works, I will take a few passes in the area that I suspect it might be. Does that sound okay?"

Everybody agreed and said, "Let's try."

Then Eric said, "After we make a few passes, we can water ski down to the 63rd St. breakwater." Eric took a canvas bag out of the small locker in the bow and opened it up. It contained what looked like a small motorized winch. He mounted it to a bracket that was screwed to the transom and then hooked an electrical cable to the battery. "This is the winch for the sea sled. I made this in the shop last winter. It has 600 feet of nylon line.

To function properly, when you are down about 30 feet, you need about 300 feet of line. This is a reversible gear motor. I've marked the switches in and out. Theoretically it worked beautifully. The Mercury has a trolling setting. You don't want to go too fast. I'll signal you on the surface for the right speed, then I'll go down. If you go to fast, I'll shoot to the surface. I think that the time underwater will be surprisingly long because you expend very little energy."

Arch said, "Sounds great, let's get this show on the road." Eric lined up on landmarks and explained directions to steer the boat. Arch said, "I'll help Eric get in the water and on the board. Can one of you gals handle the boat?"

Janice said, "Wendy you handle the boat. You are more familiar with boats that I am."

Arch said, "Until you get the feel for the right speed, keep checking the tension on the line. The nylon is strong. Just use your judgment. If you can play a tune on the line, slow the boat down."

Eric got into the water and climbed aboard the sea sled. The sled was 5/8 inch exterior plywood 3 ½ feet wide, 7 feet long and had a top that was rounded off. An oval cut out 2 ½ feet wide and 14 inches high was cut in the front end of the board. A half-inch pipe 34 inches long with and L shape. It was 10 inches high. The ends were anchored down loosely with clamps. The cut out oval area was locked solid. This oval would act like a diving plane, as you moved it forward or backwards. Move it forward you dive, move it back and you come up. There were foot loops on each side on the bottom and about three quarters of the way up were straps to put your arms through. You just laid on the board with your right arm through the loop and your hand on the diving plane lever.

The nylon line was hooked to the front of the sled. About 20 feet of the line was paid out and Wendy kicked the Mercury in gear at an idle. Eric had the control lever back slightly with the sled's nose out of the water. He found that he could control the bottom end of the sled with the angle of his feet. Wendy kept the boat moving at a steady three to four miles per hour. Arch kicked the winch motor in reverse and Eric slowly dropped back away from the boat. Eric was about 150 feet back when he stuck his left arm straight up and held it there. It was a pre-arranged signal. Arm straight up meant everything okay and proceed. Arms waving and something was wrong. Sop and winch in.

After the straight arm, Eric dived. He maneuvered left and right, up and down. The sled handled beautifully. Much better than expected. He rolled to the left side, then to the right side, on a knife edge, and back to level. He wanted to roll upside down, but decided he would wait until he had about 300 feet of line out. Everything was so effortless that he almost forgot to go up for air. He pulled the plane lever back and he headed for a smooth ride to the surface. He leveled out and could see the people on the boat. They were all clapping. Arch would tell him later that his first dive was over three minutes. He did the circular motion with his left arm, which meant ease out the winch and give more line. Now the plan was to go to 300 feet of line. Eric had the line color-coded so it was easy for Arch to tell when he got to 300 feet.

When Eric felt that the winch had stopped, he took a breath and pushed the lever forward and made his second dive. It all went very smoothly and Eric was super pleased with the amount of control that he had with the sled. Then he did a few maneuvers and finally totally upside down. He was amazed and so excited that he had to get to the boat and tell everybody how great it is. He popped up to the surface and could not remember the signal to reel in on the winch. He gave a few different signals and finally felt the winch pulling in. He used the okay signal and then he just laid on his board and relaxed, while they reeled him in. He got to the boat, got off the board and into the boat and said, "It was great! And so much better than expected!" After he explained all the things he did and how great it was they all wanted to ride the board.

Arch told Eric that on the first dive he was under for over three minutes, but on the second dive he was under almost four minutes. Eric said that it was so relaxing that he wasn't even thinking about air. They stopped and had some lunch and a beer or two and Eric asked who would like to go first. They all wanted to go, but agreed to let Wendy go first. She was in the water in an instant. She climbed aboard the sled and Arch let out the line. Janice took the helm. Eric told Wendy that they would not stop at 150 feet. He said that she would have more control at 300 or 400 feet; also much more fun. Wendy signaled back with her left arm straight up and dived. Arch was timing her. Wendy was trying out a great new toy. Going left, going right, up and down. Wendy had a private pilot's license and she felt that she was flying right now.

She did a roll to the left, a roll to the right, next a barrel roll and the inverted flight. She decided that this was more fun than an airplane when all of a sudden it dawned on her that she needed air. She leveled out down near the bottom, which was about 30 feet and pulled back on the stick and shot to the surface and went about 3 feet out of the water. But just before she broke the surface she started a tight roll and completed a full 360° in the air. She leveled out on the surface, then went back down again. She did a few more maneuvers underwater and came back up again. This time she signaled that she would come to the boat. Wendy got back aboard and was ecstatic. She said, "That was more fun than flying!"

Eric said, "That was a beautiful roll that you made. You must be a pilot."

"I am," she said, "but this is more fun!"

"I agree," said Eric, "Okay! Who's next?"

Arch said, "Let Janice go, she's frothing at the bit."

Janice said okay and jumped in the water. She climbed aboard the sled and was reeled out to 400 feet with Wendy at the helm. Then Arch asked Wendy if she had any idea how long she was down. She said, "Probably a couple of minutes?"

"No," Arch said, "you were under 5 minutes and 10 seconds, Wendy! You sure got one hell of a set of lungs."

"I know," said Eric.

"Not what you're thinking, Eric. But that too."

Wendy looked at Eric and said, "Why are you guys always thinking about boobs?"

Eric said, "It all started when I was a little kid about one hour old. I must've picked up the habit." After Janice made a few dives; she came in and climbed aboard the boat.

Arch said, "Why don't we just head down to the breakwater. I'll jump in and get on the sled on the way down. So Arch got on the sled and they start heading south toward the 63rd St. breakwater. Arch dove and surfaced about three times, then came back onboard the boat and said, "Eric, you're a genius! The ride on that sled is almost as much fun as riding a motorcycle, it's a blast!"

Eric wound up the Mercury and they were off to the breakwater. They got there inside of 20 minutes and shut down and just drifted. "Now this is what I wanted to show you. Watch that guy who is about to swing out a trolley anchor. Now pay attention as to how far it goes. The trolley is a method of fishing. The heavy trolley line goes out first with the lead anchor attached. It is about 1 pound of lead with a series heavy steel wires sticking out of it as anchors. There is a weighted trolley that rolls down the heavy main trolley line. It pulls a fishing line with a series of fish hooks on it or a small gill net. You don't want to get any closer to the breakwater than he can throw that anchor. Who wants to go first? "Why don't you go Eric?" said Wendy.

"Okay, I would just like to see if what I figured is right. The breakwater has been there since about 1880. Fishermen have been there since day one. So that is about 80 years of fishing and trolley lines have been around forever. Probably anchors have always been made the same way; lead with steel wires sticking out and the lead weighs about 1 pound. Just stop and figure if there were 20 people on the end of that jetty every day for one hundred and eighty days a year. That would be 3600 pounds of lead a year. After a few years of throwing out and losing anchors, there would be such a mound that no anchors could be retrieved. There must be well over 100 tons of lead out there and that's just at the end of the jetty. But that's all theory. Now I would like to see if it is true."

With Janice at the helm, Arch at the winch and Eric in the water, he said, "Just make a few passes across the end of the breakwater and I will check it out, then you guys can take a look."

Eric got all set up on the board and Janice brought the boat across the end of the jetty. Eric came up and said to move in about 50 feet. They went across the end of the jetty again and Eric came up and said, "You got to see this." Each one of them took a trip on the sled across the end of the jetty. They were all amazed. All around the end of the jetty, a few hundred feet out, there was a mound about 4 feet high and 30 feet wide. A lead mine that had been building for 80 years and keeps getting bigger.

Eric said, "We could start picking this stuff up, but I just got my notice for the draft."

"Yeah me too," said Arch, "okay, let's go get some fish to smoke."

"Let's head back north, a good place is by the breakwater near the aquarium."

Wendy was handling the boat, it was two o'clock and the sun was hot, but the wind picked up and created a nice little two foot chop. Wendy handled it very nicely. They each had a sandwich and a nice cold beer. They got to the area that Eric said was loaded with fish and Eric said, "You probably have heard people say that carp is a trash fish. It all depends on their environment and what they eat. Cold water Lake Michigan carp are excellent, that is if you know how to prepare them. That is true with most anything that you cook. Okay, I have a second cooler up forward that is filled with ice to keep the fish in."

Janice and Wendy brought their own flippers, masks and snorkels. Eric had extras for Arch. They dropped anchor fifty feet from the breakwater with the wind holding the boat off the rocks. They had a 150 to 200 foot swim to the breakwater. Eric got the ice chests ready. The one chest was filled with ice the other chest was now empty of food, so half the ice went into that chest. The girls declined the spear guns. He gave Arch a Cressi Spring powered gun. It had a spear attached to a 20 foot line. He warned Arch how dangerous the Cressi was and told him that for carp, it did not need to be loaded to full spring power.

Eric was going to use what was called the Hawaiian Sling. It was no more than a cross between a bow and arrow and a sling shot. It was a tube with a spear in it and a notch or groove in the backend of the spear. Attached to the backend of the tube was a heavy rubber band. You just engaged the rubber and push the spear back as tight as you could and squeeze down on a lock that fits into a groove on the spear. When you get close to your fish, you just point it and release the trigger and the spear slides out of the tube. The girls each carried a gunny sack to put fish in.

Everybody got in the water and headed to the breakwater, they got about 50 feet from it and they saw all the fish. There must have been a couple hundred carp next to the breakwater and in the rocks. Eric told Arch to only get the two to three pounders, that they were the best eating. Inside of half an hour, they had about twenty fish in the ice chests and headed for home.

"You girls are staying for dinner aren't you? Dad said if we brought fish, he would cook and smoke them," said Eric.

Wendy said, "After everything we did today, I sure don't want to miss the best part." Janice said, "Ditto."

They dropped the boat off at Eric's house. The girls asked if they could be dropped off at their apartment so they could get cleaned up and change clothes. Eric asked Arch to take the jeep and bring the girls to their apartment and he would stay and help his dad with the fish.

Art saw the fish and said, "Nice catch!" There were 22 fish. He said," I'll smoke 12 of these fish and we can cook 10 of them for dinner." Eric cleaned all of the fish and Art made up the marinade for smoking the fish and then made another marinade for cooking the fish. Eric got the fire going in the smoker. It was a decent size smoker and there would be no problem smoking 12 fish. The fish that were to be smoked were soaking in the marinade. Art and Eric filleted and skinned the fish to be cooked for dinner and then put the fish into the marinade. Art made his own special dill sauce to go over the fish at the table. Most people would bake carp, but Art used none of the belly meat and after marinating the fish, he broiled it with lemon and butter. While Art and Eric prepared the rest of the meal, Arch went to pick up the girls. When Arch got there, they were all ready and each carried a bottle of wine.

Both girls were wearing light summer dresses and they looked sexy as hell. Arch took one look and said, "Wow, you gals sure clean up great. It's a good thing that I showered and changed clothes or you would never get in this jeep with me."

Janice stared at Arch and said, "Okay, Arch, enough of your bullshit, take us to the fish. He looked backward and said, "Okay, Boss." And started up the jeep.

Arch pulled in the driveway and parked around the back. The smoker was going and already it smelled good. They went in through the back door and into the kitchen. The food was all set up on the kitchen table. Potatoes were baking in the oven. Art and Eric came downstairs all cleaned up. Art did a double take at the girls and said, "If you guys would have told me you were bringing fashion models, I would have worn a tux."

Wendy said, "You ain't so bad yourself, Mr. Hansen. If I had met you first, Eric wouldn't stand a chance."

"Well, 25 or 30 years ago that might be true, call me Art."

Art put the marinated fish into the oven on bake and told everyone to sit down. He said, "First course is Polish, it's a zuppe called Kapusta." Arch just smiled. Art pulled the fish out and put the lemon and butter on it and put it under the broiler. The fish came out flaky, juicy and browned on top. Everyone said the meal was great and the carp was delicious.

Janice said, "This fish sure changed my way of thinking. I was always told that only black people and Latinos ate carp."

"Okay," Art said, "Did you really like the fish?"

She said, "I loved it."

Then Art said, "Where do you think I learned to cook that fish? It wasn't from some white chef; it was from a Latin chef, a master chef from one of the top restaurants in Chicago. His name is Sergio Ramos."

Arch finally opened up and said, "This is the second time tonight that I have had something that, the first time I tasted, it was cooked by Sergio.

They all agreed that it was a great meal. Wendy said that she wouldn't hesitate to recommend this recipe to anyone.

"Well, I wouldn't have anything to cook if you guys didn't spear all those carp. Oh, by the way, you can come for dinner tomorrow night as well. We have carp on the menu again. Even if Arch and Eric are doing something else, you two gals can still come over for dinner, but then again, I don't think they will let you out of their sight."

"How did you first meet up with these two characters?"

Janice chimed in and said, "Remember what we told you before, these two characters saved our lives and that kind of gives you a pretty good impression of someone."

"What made them follow the two Arabs in the first place?"

"They saw them attack some other people. Eric spotted a State Police car and they went over and reported what they had seen. The police said these creeps had diplomatic immunity and they couldn't touch them. The creeps followed us into a restaurant and our heroes followed them. The creeps accosted us in the restaurant and then ran out."

"We didn't see Arch and Eric, but they were waiting for us in the parking lot, and when the two creeps followed us, our two guys followed them. The creeps forced our car into a ditch then Eric and Arch showed up. Eric stopped to make sure we were okay and Arch chased down the bad guys and put them in the ditch. You know everything that happened after that."

Chapter 14

Hill Climb

The next day, Arch and Eric went over to the shop to see if UP.S had delivered some roller bearings. These were parts that Eric was going to need Monday morning. They were part of a packaging machine that Eric was working on. While they were at the shop, Eric took Arch to the storeroom in the back. Eric hadn't mentioned his Indian Scout yet, which he had in the backroom. It was mounted up on a working stand. It was stripped down, the engine pulled out and up on the bench. Arch recognized it immediately. "Are you going to race her?"

Eric said, "Mostly hill climbing and maybe some dirt track. Arch, tomorrow is Sunday, so how about I take you over to bill's Bikes? I'll introduce you to Bill Turner, the guy I bought this machine from."

The next day, Arch and Eric rode over to Bill's Bikes. Eric clued Arch in about Bill Turner, the fact that he was not only British but a dead ringer for Rex Harrison. When they walked into the shop they were greeted by Bill. He seemed surprised and almost disappointed that he didn't have to explain who he wasn't. Eric told Bill that he had already explained to Arch about the Rex Harrison thing, which seemed to make Bill feel a little better. He said that he thought that he was losing his good looks.

Bill said, "Eric, give Arch a grand tour of the place, I have to load up some bikes. I'm going to a hill climb. It's just a club event, nothing big, but the hill ain't too bad. You guys want to go with? Have you done any hill climbing, Arch?"

"I did some in Minneapolis and some in Phoenix whenever I could borrow a bike."

"Well, I know Eric has, so I can load up a couple of extra bikes. You guys can leave your bikes here and we can go hill climbing for the afternoon. The hill is in the forest preserve which is on the property of the Argonne National Laboratory. They allow us to use the property as long as it is a sanctioned event. There will be two clubs riding today, the Blue Devils and the Black Eagles. Well, are you two blokes ready to ride today?"

Arch said, "Sounds good to me."

"Okay," Bill said, "we will load up two more 250s and then head south. Eric, get your Knucklehead and load it on board." Eric said, "Okay, Bill, but why the Knucklehead?"

"I'll tell you after we get on the road." Eric ran his bike right in off the loading dock. Bill walked over to the truck and said, "Eric, take your bike off, turn it around and then back it in and fit it into the holding rack. When we get to the field, you can ride down the ramp."

Bill was driving his truck that had an 18 foot box on it. It could easily carry 6 to 8 bikes. All the bikes were locked and padded, each in its own stanchion. They were now on the road going south on Route 83. It just dawned on Eric to ask Bill about the Knucklehead again. Bill said, "Eric, what is unusual about your Knucklehead?"

Eric scratched his head and then said, "Hell, Bill, I've been practicing with it so often that I've forgotten that 99.9% of bikes don't have reverse gear."

Arch said, "Eric, are you pulling my leg or do you really have a reverse gear?"

Bill said, "It really does have a reverse, also I've seen Eric ride it backward. I have never seen anyone do it any better or even come close. Have you guys ever heard of Damon Harrison, otherwise known as "Dirty Damon"? He used to be a great and formidable dirt track racer but he didn't get his nickname for nothing. He won a lot of races but he just could not stand to lose and he pulled a lot of dirty tricks to win. His one final dirty trick cost another rider six months in the hospital. For this final trick, the AMA pulled his racing license and number plate. Eric, today I'm going to set you up to race a real nice guy named Dirty Damon".

" Bill, I thought they pulled his license."

"They pulled his license to race. This is not an AMA sanctioned event, it's a club event. Basically, its outcome does not go into the books."

"You say that I'm to ride against him in a race. Why me?"

"Because only you can beat him."

Arch asked, "Whatever happened to the guy he put in the hospital?"

"Oh, he's still around."

"Does he still race?"

"No," said Bill, "because he can't pass the medical certification to get his

license."

"Why." asked Eric.

"Because he only has one leg."

Arch said, "It must be hell to have to quit riding, because somebody caused him to lose his leg."

"Well, I don't have my license for competition, but I will always have my number plate and with my artificial leg and I still ride."

"It's hard to believe that you have a prosthetic leg. I've never noticed," said Eric.

"It takes a lot of practice to walk normal, just like the practice it took you to learn to ride backwards and that's how you are going to beat Damon. Keep quiet about what you can do with your Knucklehead. We will wait until after the hill climbing to approach Damon."

They arrived at Argonne National Lab Forest Preserve. Bill pulled into a large field. There were many pickups with bikes in their beds and many cars and trucks pulling bike trailers. Then there were a few trucks like Bill's. Arch noticed one truck with "Black Eagles" printed on the side of it. Bill parked alongside of it and Arch said that he knew someone in the Black Eagles. Bill said that he knew some of them too. "Here comes one of them now." And a guy jumped up on the running board and said, "How you doing, Bill?"

Then he took a second look and said, "Well, don't say hello, you son of a bitch!"

It was Dave Steele. Arch got out of the truck and went over and shook Dave's hand and introduced Eric to Dave. Then he told Bill how he met Dave.

"Are you going to ride today, Bill?"

"Yeah, Dave, but not during the competition. I just want to make a few runs to get the feel of it again. What about you Dave?"

"No, I'm just watching today, Bill, I see that Damon is here, are you guys still at each other's throats?"

"No, Dave, we are even talking to each other. We may even have a race challenge today."

"Hill climb?"

"No, on the grass."

Arch and Eric started up the bikes and rode them down the ramp then parked them behind Bill's truck. There were two 500cc Indian Warriors all set up and geared for hill climbing. Arch said, "I ride an Indian, but I've never seen its little brothers."

Dave said, "This Warrior is a distant relative of your Chief. It's English designed and built vertical twin. It may be small, but it's no slouch. It will give your big Chief a run for the money. It looks like you and Eric will be riding these up the hill today."

"Sounds good to me and it looks like that hill's no slouch either."

"It's not bad, Arch, I've run it a few times. Have you climbed before?"

"A few times but not as steep as this one."

"It's not that bad, Arch, just remember one thing, strong power to get up your speed. Full power till your front wheel makes it to the top. Ease the power till your front wheel goes over, then more power. You just have to get the feel of it. If you hit power too much or too soon, you will go over backwards. Most hills are not like this one. This one has heavy grass on top which creates a short vertical bluff. The trick is to get your front wheel over. If you are too cautious and too slow you won't make it. You need the speed. If it looks like you are not going to make it, make a turn before you hit the vertical bluff and come back down. If you get all the way up but can't make it over, then the only thing you can do is bail out, or you can man-handle the bike so it comes down with the front wheel downhill. You may slide a little but with a lot of effort you can get it back on two wheels. Then you can come down the hill looking like a hero. Eric has done this hill a few times, but Bill is the master hill climber around here."

Dave continue, "Although Damon thinks he is better, but that's not the case. Bill will probably give you a lot of pointers before you go. Watch Bill when he makes his runs and see how he makes it look simple. Watch close as he goes over the top. He will be riding his 500cc Ducati. That bike has brute power. The 500 is strong enough, but Bill never rides anything that he hasn't worked over. Bill and Damon will ride first. They each get three runs. They have flipped a coin and Damon goes first, then they alternate until each has three runs."

Damon was riding his 1941 Harley WR, a 45 cubic inch side valve V Twin, which Harley introduced to compete with Indian's 45 cubic inch Scout. They were both great for flat track racing and hill climbing.

Damon fired up his Harley and let it warm up for a couple of minutes. He signaled to the timer that he was ready. He got the green light and he cranked it on. His big wide grass-snapper tire dug a trench 2 inches deep and 25 foot long. He flew up the hill and over the top. On his way back down he eased the bike over the edge too slow and the bike got hung up on the frame. He lost about 15 seconds breaking it loose. By the time he got back down, his time was 1 minute and 30 seconds through the trap.

Next came Bill. He and his Ducotti went up that hill like he was on a Sunday ride. He made a quick turn around and came flying over the edge. He was one third of the way down the hill before he touched ground. His total time was 1 minute and 12 seconds.

Damon did better on his next two runs and Bill did a little worse. Damon's total for 3 runs was 242 seconds. Bill's time was 228 seconds. 14 seconds difference for 3 runs. There were about eight other riders to try the hill and only one other rider made 3 full round trips. He was a Blue Devil rider. His time was 251 seconds. Anyone not making 3 full round trips did not get a count. Arch made the top once and turned around twice. Eric made it twice and turned around once.

Bill rode up on his Ducotti and said, "How did you boys like the hill?"

"It was great," said Arch, "except for that vertical bluff at the top."

"That's the part that separates the men from the boys. It gets scary as hell when you start going over backwards."

"It's good you gave us some clues on that."

While they were standing around talking, Damon came over. "Well it looks like you took that hill again, but I would have beaten you if I had as much ground clearance on my Harley as you do on your Ducotti. If I had the clearance I wouldn't have gotten hung up on the bluff."

"Damon, if, is one hell of a big word, it's just an excuse for not getting the job done. After doing that hill, my phony leg is too sore to do any more riding, but I'll bet you a hundred bucks, Eric here, can beat you on the flat."

"Make it a thousand and you can name the race."

"Okay," said Bill, "we will make it a short race for one thousand and I name the race. You will race the same bike as Eric."

Damon said, "Okay." Because he thought for sure that he could beat Eric in any race Bill could name.

Bill said, "Okay, the race is this; on the grass and across this field and around that lone pine tree and back. I'll time it with my stopwatch. You will both use the same bike to make it even. If your feet touch the ground you are out. One lap for one thousand."

"Okay by me," said Damon.

Bill said, "Okay, Eric, get your Knucklehead."

Damon was looking at Eric as he parked the bike at the starting line that Bill has scratched in the dirt. Damon thought that it was a stupid way to start a race, with your back wheel pointing toward the objective which is the lone pine tree across the field, but he figured, no problem, you just have to turn the bike before you make your run across the field. But Damon was about to get a surprise when Eric got on the Knucklehead, kicked it over and it fired up.

Bill and Damon watched as Eric let out the clutch and the bike took off backwards with Eric in perfect control. He went across the field, around the tree and back to the starting point. Eric pulled up and put down the kick stand and got off the bike. Bill pointed to the bike and said, "Your turn Damon."

Damon just reached into his pocket, took out his wallet and counted out ten one hundred dollar Bill's. He handed Bill the one thousand dollars and said, "Bill, I think I've been had. Good thing I can afford to lose some money now and then. I had no idea what kind of race you had planned. I should have known you wouldn't make it easy. I should have left the bet at one hundred, but I was sure that I could win any kind of race against Eric. It looks like I got sucked in. I should have known if it looks like a sure thing, then it definitely is not. I think I had an expensive lesson today. Eric, that was a real neat ride that you did in reverse. I would like to learn how to ride in reverse. Bill, are bikes with reverse available for sale?"

"I'll check it out and get back to you."

"Okay, thanks Bill, and now I had better get my bikes loaded and get out of here."

Bill said, "We better get loaded too."

Bill walked over to Eric and said, "You did the work, I did the sting so it's 50-50, and he handed Eric $500. They loaded up and started heading for home. After they got settled down and comfortable in the truck they started talking about everything that happened that day. Arch said, "Bill, at the time you told Eric to load up his Knucklehead, back at your shop, you already knew how you were going to con Damon and when you did, he took it pretty well. What kind a guy is Damon? "

"Well, if you have a lot of time, I could tell you all about Damon. I first met Damon when I had a motorcycle shop on the south side of

Chicago in Blue Island. Damon was one of the top dirt track racers at that time. He was real good. I know, because I raced against him. I used to work on his bike sometime when his own mechanic was too busy on other bikes. Damon decided that he wanted to buy a bike shop and he made an offer on my shop. It was a good offer. He offered money upfront. But he wanted me to sign a five-year contract to run the shop for him. He had already written up an eight page contract. I never did like to deal with people who believed in long contracts, so I had him checked out. Damon was very intelligent and well educated. He graduated from Northern Illinois University. Started with prelaw, but finished with an MBA. He had his own accounting firm in Chicago. He was totally unethical in business and enjoyed watching people suffer financially because of his underhanded dealings."

"He raced cycles on dirt tracks all the way through college and continued to race after college for a few years. Although he was an excellent rider, he committed every type of foul, that he thought he could get away with. A few riders were injured because of his fouls on the track and he became known as "Dirty Damon" and was a big draw at some of the tracks. I wasn't about to be signing any contracts with a guy like this so I turned him down. But, like I said, he was a big draw at some tracks. Other tracks didn't want him racing on their track it all. Most riders respect a novice plate, they know what that a novice rider is just in their race to get some experience. A novice is no threat to the other riders, but Damon had already lapped this one novice and he had plenty of room to pass him. Instead of just passing him, he drove him into two other bikes. Three bikes went down right in front of me. I wound up in the pileup and that's how I lost my leg. Two other riders were also injured. Damon went on to win the race but he was later disqualified when it was decided that he deliberately caused the accident. When the AMA put all the facts together, along with Damon's past record, they pulled his white expert number plate and banned him from racing."

"Well," Bill said, "that's about all you need to know about Damon, except that he is the leader of the Blue Devils Motorcycle Club. They like him because he has lots of money and spends it freely on parties. Also, Damon has no conscience, he scammed a lot of money from his trusting clients in his accounting firm. He can sweet talk people into anything, and out of their money. He was very close to being charged with fraud and going to prison, so he cleaned out his accounts of cash and hid them offshore. He owns a couple of porno shops and is a front for some gun dealing. He is not a nice guy, so if he makes any contact with you to make any kind of deal, watch out. He may want to get even. He won't get vicious, but he will pull a con job on you if given the chance."

"Well, Bill," said Eric, "if Damon wants a piece of me, he better get in line because it looks like the Army gets me first. I just got my draft notice and I've got to report in four weeks to the induction center."

Arch said, "And just so he won't feel lonesome, the government decided to send me one of those love letters too, except that I've got five weeks to report."

"So what do we do for the next few weeks before we go in?"

"We could just party, but we do that all the time anyway!"

Bill cut in and asked, "You guys like boats?"

"I plan on building or buying one when I get back from the Army. I used to sail with my dad." said Arch.

Bill said, "A friend of mine has a 90 foot schooner rigged motor sailer. She is more a good sailing ship than a motor sailer. Actually as long as there is any kind of wind, he hardly ever fires up the diesels. Doc is going to take a three week cruise up to the Sturgeon Bay and Door County areas. I'm going with him and he asked me if I could recruit a couple of good extra crew. He's a good guy to sail with and a damn good sailor."

The morning of Sunday, the 13th of July, was a beautiful sunny day. A perfect day to start a trip. Arch and Eric each had a well stuffed duffel bag. Bill said that he would pick them up at 6 am. He said not to bother to eat breakfast, that they would eat on board and that his chef was a fantastic cook. They took Jackson Boulevard to Lake Shore drive, then went south on the drive along the lakefront. As they drove along the lake, they could look out over Monroe Harbor. They turned east on Solidarity drive, which passed the Shedd Aquarium and led to Meigs Field, the airport. The Planetarium was at the end of Solidarity Drive. They stopped midway on Solidarity drive and on the left to the north was Monroe Harbor and to the right was Burnham Harbor and Miegs Field.

Bill got out and walked over to the north side of the road. Arch and Eric walked over where Bill was. Bill pointed out a beautiful white schooner on a can at the mouth of the harbor. 'That is the boat we will be on for the next three weeks. Doc is a great guy and a lot of fun. I have known him since 1940. I was an RAF Lieutenant and he was a US Naval Captain. His submarine picked me out of the North Sea after I ditched my Hawker Hurricane. She had too many holes in the fuel tank, thanks to a Messerschmitt BF 109. But before I went in I splashed him so we came out even. I got to know Doc pretty well and we have done a lot of sailing together. Like I said, a nice guy but when you are on his boat, he is the Lord and Master. By the way I don't think I mentioned it, but Doc is a three-star Admiral, so whatever he says, do it without question and you will get along real fine."

They turned down a narrow road that came out on the west side of Burnham Harbor. They pulled into a parking spot designated for a boat named "Lady Sue" and they went aboard a 50 foot power boat in a slip. Bill introduced Arch and Eric to the boat owner, Dick Mathews and then to Admiral Robert Hunter, otherwise known as Doc.

Eric asked, "Why are we in Burnham Harbor? I thought your boat was in Monroe Harbor."

"It is in Monroe Harbor and you will see it shortly, but first we will have breakfast aboard Dick's boat. He has a chef that is almost as good as mine."

"Don't let Carlos hear you say that, Doc, or he will not hesitate to toss you overboard!"

"Dick, I've got more sense than that. Especially when Carlos outweighs me by 50 pounds and that being the case, Carlos is the greatest chef afloat!"

"Okay, you guys, as Doc said, we eat breakfast, and while we eat, I'll tell you how he got his nickname. It was a stroke of luck when they spotted me in the water in the North Sea. It was dusk and in another 15 minutes it would be too dark to find me. They were surfaced and saw my plane go in. I saw the outline of a sub against the horizon, but I didn't know whether it was German or English. I didn't care! The water was that cold. It was neither, it was American. They brought me aboard and told me that I would be their guest for the next 2 to 4 weeks. Captain Hunter told me that they were on patrol under radio silence. He said that they were looking for a rogue German sub that had been sinking ships off the Irish coast."

"On the fourth week I was aboard, I was sick as hell. After a few more days and reading a lot of medical books, the captain and the pharmacist mate decided I had appendicitis. They also decided that if nothing was done until we reached port, that I would probably be dead. The pharmacist mate said that he couldn't do it, the cook was good with knives, but he also declined. They both said that they would assist but it was up to the captain to remove my appendix. He read all the medical books that they had onboard and then he said, "Let's do it."

So after a fair share of whiskey, Bill said I was feeling no pain, or so the saying goes. So I am told that they put me under with ether and the captain used the usual surgeon's tool kit, hacked away at me and removed my appendix. I survived as you can see, so he must have done a pretty good job. So after that he became known as Doc. Now, let's go eat."

They did just that and they all agreed that Carlos was a great chef and they told him so. Carlos thanked them all and said that Doc's chef, Chef Mario, was also a great chef. Doc got up from the table and said, "Let's get out of this firetrap and get the show on the road. Bill and I are going to drive over to Chicago Yacht Club in Monroe Harbor to have a couple of martinis and then we will take the service boat out to the Cora Lee. The Cora Lee is a 90 foot schooner and she is named after my late wife. She's a great boat. She will teach you something about sailing. Now you two gentlemen will have a different mode of transportation. Look down in the next slip to the south. You will notice there are two14 foot dinghies. Each with a set of oars."

He laid an aerial photo of the two harbors down on the table. "As you will notice, the dotted line is the course you will row these two dinghies. It is only about 3 ½ miles to the Cora Lee. It should only take you about 90 minutes if you row hard. I have done it in 55 minutes, but I will admit that it was a nice calm day. You have a little chop outside of the harbor today. Bill and I will see you off and start the timing. When you get to the Cora Lee, you can have a nice cold beer or a martini, then you can relax for a short while before we hoist sail and get underway. Did Bill tell you that Captain Bligh was one of my ancestors? Well, it ain't true, it may just seem like it."

Arch said, "Well, if that's the case, we had better get to rowing."

As they pulled out of the slip, Doc said, "First one to The Cora Lee gets to choose what's for lunch and we have got a fully stocked pantry and a $100 prize. Good luck, Guys."

And they started going south through the harbor, pulling the oars as if they were racing. Arch got into the mouth of the harbor first and turned east to go around the end of the airfield. As he got around the end he turned north toward Monroe Harbor. He was so intent on rowing hard that he didn't notice that Eric had passed him on the inside and was now about 10 boat lengths ahead of him. Eric was laughing and rowing for all he was worth. Arch had more muscle than Eric but Eric was more experienced at rowing. Now the race was on with Eric steadily ahead of Arch but Arch was now getting the feel of rowing his boat and being more muscular than Eric and with more powerful strokes he started to gain on Eric. Then all of a sudden, the weather started to change. Quickly, the wind was picking up and changing direction. It was now off the starboard bow and hitting at about 45°. Eric was familiar with this situation, but Arch was wallowing in the troughs of the waves and in danger of broaching, which could turn the boat over. Eric turned around and went back and showed Arch how to quarter the waves. They were rowing close together now and Arch was getting onto quartering the waves.

Eric said, "This may take longer, but we won't have to walk on the bottom, because it looks like it's getting even rougher. Don't worry, Arch, these little lap strake dinghies are pretty good sea boats."

A light rain started coming down and the visibility started getting obscured. Eric said, "Arch, let's stay together and keep each other in sight. I'm closer to the breakwater than you, so if we keep it in sight, we will come up at the mouth of the harbor."

The rain was now coming down much heavier but they could see the wall of the breakwater. The much heavier rain did knock the top off the waves and smoothed out the water. Now they could start rowing faster, but they had to keep the breakwater in sight, or they may row straight out into the lake. They decided to stay together and call it a tie race. Onboard the Cora Lee, Bill and Doc were sitting on the after deck sucking up some martinis. "Looks like we're getting some pretty heavy weather out there, Bill. I'm not so sure that it was a good idea to have those two guys row all the way from Burnham."

"Well, Doc you gave them an hour and a half to get here and it's only been 70 minutes so far. They have another 20 minutes to go."

"You said that you had made it once in 55 minutes."

"I lied! I have never made in less than two hours. Bill, I think that maybe we should lower the motor launch and go look for them. It's gotten pretty hairy out there for a couple of 14 foot dinghies."

"Let's give them their 90 minutes first. If I know those two guys, they will be here in the next 20 minutes, if they have to go by the way of Milwaukee!"

Fifteen minutes later Doc said, "Bill, I'm going to lower the launch and go look for them."

"Okay, if you're going to lower the launch, be damned careful that you don't set it down on top of those two yellow 14 foot dinghies." Bill laughed and Doc laughed even louder.

Doc said, "Good job, Boys! We were not the least bit worried about you. Right, Bill."

"Yeah, right! It never pays to argue with an Admiral."

"We will drop you a line. Secure it to the bow and come aboard. We will tie them off the stern and bring them aboard later."

They tied off and came onboard and went below to put on dry clothes and came back up and sat down with Doc and Bill. Mario, the chef, served hot rum punches that just hit the spot, and some grilled shrimp, ribs and little sausages. Then Doc said, "You guys did pretty good considering the weather, but you took all of 85 minutes. I think you could have done better."

Bill said, "Like your 55 minute row?" Bill laughed.

Doc confessed, "My best time was about two hours and as far as the contest goes, I think both of you won. So $100 apiece and you both can tell Mario what we eat for lunch. And what we eat tomorrow. Now you guys can look around the ship because it's 10:30 pm and I'm going to hit the sack. We hoist sail at 6 am. Breakfast at 5 am. Mario will ring the morning bell at 4:30 am to get you up and ready. No late sleepers on this boat. After we get underway, with all sails set and pulling, we will discuss some other reasons for this trip."

All four of them of had a little nightcap of double cognac. Mario joined them as well, but Mario had a triple tequila. He said he had learned to drink tequila from his Mexican compadres. He then told them about two more crew members that will be joining them, coming aboard at 4 am. "This will be Juan and Angel. They are both top-notch sailors. I don't think there is anyone in this world that can steer a truer course on a sailing ship than Angel."

Chapter 15

Out of Monroe Harbor with No Wind

Doc said, "I don't know how much experience any of you have had at the helm of a sailing ship, but I wanted to tell you that you don't just hold the wheel still and expect the ship to go straight. Nor do you steer by watching the compass. If you do you will go cross-eyed and your course will be so zigzag that it looks like you are trying to avoid a submarine. Everyone will have their trick at the helm and Angel will teach you how to steer a sailing ship. He will teach you to steer by a star and the roll of the ship. He will make sure you are not following an airplane's navigation or strobe-light. On a very dark and overcast night, you can usually find something on the horizon. If not, it's very close attention to the compass and the feel and roll of the ship. On a night like that, we definitely need a man on bow watch and absolutely no lights on deck. Not even a match unless it is covered. If a flashlight is needed on deck to do a job, never point the light aft. The helmsman can lose his night vision very quickly. So, good night then. See you all at 4:30 in the morning."

Arch and Eric hit the sack and immediately fell asleep. After what seemed like about ten minutes the 4:30 wake up gong went off. Arch and Eric slept in the same cabin, which was nicely appointed. "You had better get a move on Arch, remember what Bill said about the showers."

"No, Eric, what did he say?"

"He said Doc turns off the hot water at exactly 5:00 am and it's a quarter to 5 right now."

Arch jumped out of the sack and got into the shower and turned on the nice hot water. He started to say, "Eric, my boy, this is living, this nice hot shower feels... Hey, Holy Shit! Ice cold and it's just 10 minutes to 5 right now." Arch finished with a nice cold shower. They got dressed and went topside. Doc and Bill were sitting on the after deck drinking coffee. Doc said, "Good morning, Boys. Who got the wake up shower?"

"Arch did," said Eric.

"It wasn't even 5 am when it turned cold!"

"Sorry about that. Have some nice hot coffee to warm you up. I guess maybe my watch is off."

Bill laughed and said, "His watch is always off on the first day out and guess what, he navigates by his watch and it's never off more than 10 seconds. Your shower is the only one on this boat that he can shut off from his cabin."

"Well," Doc said, "guilty as charged! My full confession is in the mail. Now that that's out of the way, I think we should go down to the mid-ship cabin and have the breakfast you guys ordered. I think Mario said it was rib eye steak and eggs. Good choice. And Mario will make them however you order them, to perfection."

They ate breakfast and it was great. Eric said, "Sir or Captain, or is it Admiral?"

"Well, Eric, being that I am an Admiral, you could call me Admiral, but I really wouldn't care for that. I have commanded large aircraft carriers, so as an Admiral, this ship would be quite a come down. If you called me Captain, I would feel demoted. My name is Bob. If you called me Bob, then Juan and Angel would think it disrespectful. Call me Doc and everyone will be happy. You call your buddy here Bill and he is a General, or didn't you know that?"

Eric said, "No, we didn't know that he is a General."

"But I'm only a two-star General; Doc is a three-star Admiral."

Bill said to Doc, "Two-star – three-star, you think that's something, this guy has us all beat." He pointed to Arch. "He's known as "God's Messenger" in four states."

"Is that true, Arch?"

"That's what they say, Doc."

"Well," said Doc, "I guess we have to treat you with a little more respect. Do we call you Sir?"

"No, Doc, just call me Arch, but no more cold showers in the morning!"

"Okay, Arch, you got it."

Bill asked, "Doc, when are we going to get underway? You said 6:00 am and it's almost 6:00 right now."

"Well, Bill, the weather is kind of scuddy right now, but it is improving so I changed my mind, we leave at 8:00 am when the weather should be a little nicer. Changing my mind is a privilege of command. Given we have more time, I think it would be a good idea to educate everybody about the Cora Lee. I named her after my late wife. They say it's bad luck to change a boat's name, but when I bought her in 1946, my wife and I loved the boat but hated the name "Diablo", devil in English. So it was changed to Cora Lee. He rattled off her stats:

She was built in 1929
Designed by Cox and Stevens
Built by Wilcox Crittenden of Wiscasset, Maine
Planked with long leaf yellow pine 1 ¾" below W/L 1 ½" above
Deck – clear white pine 1 ½" x 2 ½" on edge
Draft 11'5" W/40,000 lb. outside lead ballast
Overall length 89 feet 6 inches
Beam 21 feet
Staysail Schooner Rigged
Main Mast 108 feet – Mizzen Mast 77 feet
Carries 5800 square feet of sail
Plus Queen Fisherman Quadra lateral Sail 25' x 35' – 875 sq. Ft.
Also King Fisherman Quadra lateral 35' x 43' – 1505 sq. ft.

The Fisherman's function is similar to a balloon Spinnaker on a single-masted boat, except a Spinnaker is 3 points and controlled at two points and a Fisherman is controlled at 4 points. It is handled by a halyard from each mast to the two peaks of the sail. It is a square sail. Now, the two bottom corners of the foot of the sail area attached to two sheets and the sail is controlled at all four points of the sail. The sail is cranked to the top of each mast with the halyards and handled at the bottom by the two sheets. When the top of the sail reaches the top of the mast, the winch handles are reversed, but instead of the sail coming down, it goes out and away, in front of the boat. As the halyard winches are eased out, so are the sheets and pretty soon the foot of the sail is above the top of the mast, way out front flying like a kite and pulling like a mule. On a quiet day, there is usually more wind the higher you go. When you look at it from the side, it looks like the sail is not attached to the boat. It is a sight to see. She is listed as a motor sailer because the original owner wanted twin screws for docking. She has twin 115 horse power Buda Diesels, with twin feathering props for less drag under sail. She is definitely not what most people consider as a motor sailer. She is a true sailboat with auxiliary engines."

Doc said, "Let's take a tour of the boat." They went down below into the aft cabin, Arch and Eric's cabin. There was a door on the rear or aft bulkhead (wall). They went through it and came out into an immaculate engine room. Bill said that he had never seen engines this clean and polished like this.

Doc said, "This is Angel's domain, nobody but Angel touches anything in this engine room, not even me." They went forward. He showed them the other cabins and the galley where Mario was busy, but stopped working and greeted everyone. He said he was preparing everything to make one of his favorite specialties for lunch.

Bill said, "I remember that specialty of Mario's. It's the best bouillabaisse I've ever tasted." He turned to Eric and Arch and said, "He must like you guys, he does not make his bouillabaisse for just anyone."

"Sounds good," said Arch. They went forward to the sail locker and the crew's quarters.

Doc said, "These are the original crew's quarters. We now used them for storage. We have enough cabins. Juan and Mario have a nice large cabin and Angel has his own private cabin. He is in charge when I'm not here. Okay, let's go topside and we will look over a few things up there, then we will get under way."

As they walked by the main mast, Doc pointed out the main sail halyard winch on the mast, the staysail winch and the winch for the fishermen sails. Then there were deck winches for the trimming sheets. Doc said there was more of the same at the mizzen mast. He said, "Let's go to the bow and we will take a look at our anchor tackle."

Doc said, "Bill, you explain what we have got for ground tackle."

Bill said, "First off we have two 150 pound kedge anchors, usually we just use one, but we can use two anchors if conditions warrant it. We have 400 feet of chain on each anchor which comes out of the chain locker below in the bow. The chain comes out of the hawse hole on the side of the hull. The chain runs through the anchor chain lock right here on deck. When you have enough chain out, you flip the lock lever over and that stops the chain. When you want to raise the anchor, you use the capstan winch here, mounted on deck. This capstan is motorized which saves a lot of labor. Then there are the two lunch hooks, one is a 75 pound kedge anchor and a 40 pound Danforth anchor. These are used to anchor for a short period of time and are secured to a ¾" nylon line."

Doc said, "Okay, that's enough about the ship, you will learn the rest while under way from Juan, Angel, Bill and myself. I forgot to mention, Mario, he is not only a great chef, but also a hell of a good sailor. Now everybody aft to the cockpit. Bill, will you go below and ask Mario if he can break away from his cooking. If he is too tied up, we can get under way without him, cause we sure don't want to ruin the bouillabaisse. Bill went below and came back up and said Mario can break away from the galley, since he had not started cooking the bouillabaisse yet. Doc said, "Good, I think that we will need Mario. We're going to fly the King Fisherman. Start the engines, Angel. "Aye, Aye, Sir." And he started the exhaust blowers in the engine room and after 5 minutes, he started both of the diesels.

Arch said to Eric, "Well, it looks like Bill was wrong on that one when he said Doc never starts a trip under power."

Eric said, "There sure ain't any wind out there. Look at all those sailboats out there, the ones that left an hour or two ago when there was some wind, they are dead in the water with their sails just hanging down." Eric then asked Doc if he was going out under power or waiting for the wind.

Doc said, "Eric, I never start a trip with the iron jib. Angel just started them to warm them up in case of an emergency, just in case of someone getting in front of us and we have to maneuver." And Angel shut the engines down.

Mario came up from below carrying a very large sail bag and Juan came from the rope locker with the Fisherman sheets. Doc said, "Arch, you are on the main winches and you take your orders from Bill. Eric, you are on the mizzen winches and you take your orders from Juan. Mario will be on the bow to watch for boats and to make sure the King Fisherman is staying clear of the rigging. Juan and Bill will take their sail trimming orders from Angel and Angel will take his orders from me. Eric and Arch, you two guys just work the winches just as Bill and Juan have explained it to you. These other guys have done this quite a few times before, but getting a King Fisherman to fly without collapsing can be quite tricky in light winds like this."

Eric said, "There is no wind."

"Angel will find it," Doc said.

"For the benefit of Eric and Arch, I'm going to explain exactly how everything is going to happen. And in the exact sequence. First, off come the sail covers and they are put away so that nobody trips over them when we get busy. Next, we take the sail stops off all sails and make sure the halyards are snapped into the peaks of the sails. Then remove the stops that tie the main boom to the boom crotch (what the main boom rests on when not sailing). Take up on the topping lift. (The line that lifts and holds the boom off the boom crotch), release the mizzen boom and the foot of all sails so they are free to float. Then we crank the main and mizzen winches to raise the main and mizzen sails, then raise the jib sail and staysails, with all sails hoisted and floating free. Finally, the King Fisherman is attached to the main and mizzen halyard by the two peaks just sticking out of the sail bag as it is cranked up by the two halyards. As still as it is, this light sail will catch some wind as it comes out of the bag. Before it is a third of the way out, the two lower sheets are snapped on to the two lower corners of the foot of the sail, the ends of the sheets are secured to a cleat so as not to lose them overboard."

As the King is nearing the top of the mast, it started to fill out and everything started to happen fast. As Mario sheeted in (pulls it in) the jib, it started to fill. He unhooked the anchor pendant and the boat was free. Angel steered the boat to fall off the wind. The Fisherman's peak was at the top of the mast. Now, by reversing the halyard winch crank, the halyard would let the Fisherman float free and up. Angel had the ship falling off to port. Mario sheeted in the mizzen sail and it started to fill out. Doc did the same with the main sail, it also filled out. The ship was now picking up some momentum.

Angel held her best heading to make it through the mouth of the harbor. Bill and Mario worked the starboard sheet around to the starboard side of the ship. Arch and Eric kept backing off on the winches until the foot of the sail was above the top of the main mast, then Bill and Juan started taking up on the Fisherman's sheets and it started pulling like a mule. Then Bill and Juan started trimming the main sail and mizzen sail. Mario did the same with the head sails and stay sails. Now the ship was picking up speed. Juan and Bill went back to trimming the Fisherman and it picked up more speed. Angel set his course for the best advantage of the wind after a final trimming of sails. Then Doc went down below and came back up with seven glasses and a bottle of cognac. He poured everybody a drink and said, "Great job, Boys."

They went by thirty or forty boats dead in the water and some of them quite large. Their sails were flapping in the dead still air. Cora Lee went by a 40 foot sloop dead in the water with Cora Lee's sails full and bye. Doc was standing at the rail with a drink in his hand when someone on the sloop asked where he got the wind. He answered, "No problem, we have "God's Messenger" aboard."

Bill said to Eric and Arch, "I told you that he likes to sail, didn't I?

Eric said, "That was unbelievable to sail out of a harbor with no wind."

Doc said, "There is wind; you just got to reach high enough for it." They sailed away from the harbor for about 20 miles and passed boats that were becalmed. They finally picked up a decent 12/15 knot west wind. All sails were full and pulling beautifully. The big King Fisherman was pulling its halyards and sheets so tight that they could be played like banjo strings. Eric asked Doc if the Fisherman was made of nylon, because it was so light. Doc said, "No, Eric, when those sails were made there was no such thing as nylon. The sails are made of Egyptian cotton."

Angel had set a true course of 10 degrees. Doc and Bill had decided to visit an old friend on Beaver Island. It was an Island 5 miles wide and 10 miles long, twenty five miles off of Charlevoix, Michigan, about 280 miles from Chicago. It would take 18 to 20 hours for Cora Lee to make Beaver Island Harbor. It was a beautiful sail, cloudless sky with a million stars. Both Eric and Arch had a trick at the wheel. They had both handled small day sailers before, but never anything this big. There was a half-moon out and when you looked behind the ship you could see the course that you made. Angel had let each of them steer for 30 minutes apiece. Both Arch and Eric had steered an amazingly erratic course. After each half hour, Angel steered for 30 minutes and it seemed totally effortless. He steered straight as a string. Angel put them both on the wheel again, each for another 30 minutes. This time he did not just tell them, but showed them how to steer by the stars.

Angel said, "Set your course by the compass, then quick look for a single star, and don't look at the compass again. Just follow the star for 5 minutes. When you have a good set on the star, then look down at your compass. You should be on your course, if not, do it over until you get it right. Eric got it pretty right the second time. It took Arch four times. Angel said, "Buenos, enough for tonight." He told them it takes a lot of practice to get good and if he knew Doc, they would get plenty of practice.

At about 11:00 pm, Bill came aft to take the helm. They checked the charts and decided to hold a course of 10 degrees for the next 3 hours. By then they would be above North Manitou Island and about 50 or 60 miles from Beaver Island Harbor. Angel would get about 3 hours sack time and then come back on the wheel. At that time, they would take a 45 degree heading and pass under South Fox Island and then turn north for the northwest side of Beaver Island.

Angel took the helm at 2 am, and with a nice steady speed of 13 knots, it brought them right off the western side of the island. At 4 am it started getting light and you could see Beaver Island off the starboard side. By now everyone was up and getting ready to drop anchor. Juan, Bill, Eric and Arch had hauled in and bagged the King Fisherman. When they changed course to 225 degrees, Angel brought the boat into the harbor, which he was familiar with.

He passed by the buoy's marking the gill nets and the small boat anchorage and headed her up into the wind. Doc released one of the 150 pound kedge anchors. The water in the harbor was about 35 to 40 feet deep, so Doc eased out about 200 feet of anchor chain and locked it in place. Meanwhile, the rest of the crew were freeing up the sheets and lowering the sails. They furled them on the boom and tied on the sail stops, then lowered the topping lift to rest the main boom on the boom crotch and the sail covers were put back on. They also furled the foresails and staysails. With the decks clear, everybody went down below for some hot coffee and a good long and relaxing breakfast. After everyone had their breakfast, Mario sat down and had his breakfast and a couple of cups of coffee and turned to Doc and said, "Doc, have you talked to Art Hobson on the radio yet this morning?"

He said, "I did, Mario, and the market is open."

Then Doc asked Arch and Eric if they Scuba dived. They both said that they did. Mario said, "Good, you guys can come with me to the store."

Mario fitted them with flippers and masks and got out 3 Scuba tanks. Arch and Eric carried the scuba tanks down the boarding stairs, loaded the three tanks and other gear into the 18 foot motor launch and all three of them boarded the launch and Mario fired up the engine. Eric said, "At least we don't have to row three miles in the rain."

Mario told them not to complain, it could have been worse. "I served under the Admiral in the Pacific on an aircraft carrier; there was never a better commander in the whole American Navy. Have you noticed his limp? He lost his whole right foot in a Kamikaze attack, had a medic wrap the stump, give him some morphine and he stayed on the bridge until the engagement was over. He refused to be moved to sick bay until all other injured were taken care of. He was fitted with prosthesis, but walked with a limp for a while after. Later at an award ceremony where Admiral Hunter was to receive a medal and his third star, as the people who were to receive awards were climbing the steps to the podium, Admiral Hunter did a slight stumble and a Marine Officer, a Captain no less, laughed, and then said there goes one of our stumbling fearless leaders. The Captain's mistake was that he was standing right next to some of the Admiral's crew. The fact that he was an officer made no difference to Admiral Hunter's crew. At least 5 of us beat the hell out of him. They hauled him away in an ambulance. After he was released from the hospital, he was determined to have some sailors court-martialed. I guess he was not too popular because even his so called Marine buddies refused to be witnesses for him. They all said they didn't see a thing, but they did say that they heard him malign the Admiral whom everyone knew was receiving this commendation for bravery. I know the Captain is now in charge of garbage detail somewhere in Alaska.

"Mario, what's this about going to the store? And why the scuba gear?"

"Do you like seafood?" asked Mario.

"Yeah," said Arch, "I see food and I eat it."

"Next question, have you guys ever had jumbo perch?"

They both said they have had perch, but nobody said they were jumbo perch. "Then they were not jumbo perch. There are two reasons we stopped at Beaver Island. One is to see an old buddy that Bill knew back in England in

WWII, Brigadier General Art Hobson, late of the Royal Commandos. The other reason is gastronomical, to spend about 3 days eating jumbo perch. I have about a half dozen ways of preparing jumbo perch and they are all good."

"Are we going to buy the fish at that fishing shack that you pointed out?"

Mario said, "Not exactly. We are going to a self-service market."

Eric said, "I still don't know what you are talking about."

Chapter 16

Make Sea Sled, Fish Boil

Mario then asked if either of them knew what a gill net was and neither of them knew. "A gill net is a long rectangular net. The bottom of the net is anchored to the bottom, the top to floats. The mesh grid is of a size to let the smaller fish go through and the larger fish get caught by their gills. That's why it's called a gill net. We go over the side with our burlap sacks and swim along the gill net, pick out the nicest jumbo perch and put them in the burlap sacks. About one dozen in each of three sacks, thirty six jumbos will make one hell of a good meal, and then we will do the same tomorrow."

They anchored the launch and the three of them put on their scuba gear and went over the side and down about 15 feet. Arch and Eric followed Mario and after a short swim, they saw the net, it was good timing. The net was loaded with fish. Mario had told them to pick the larger fish and only the ones that were lively. Between the three of them, they collected 40 nice fish and then swam back to the launch and climbed aboard. Mario fired up the engine and they went back to the Cora Lee. They each grabbed a sack of fish and carried them to the galley. "We should be eating some of the best fish you ever tasted at approximately 1 pm. That is if you two get them cleaned and filleted in short order," said Mario. Eric said that he had done quite a bit of filleting. Arch said he had never done it before, but he was willing to learn. "Actually, there is only room for one guy in this galley doing fish, so Eric you fillet this time and Arch, next time I'll teach you. This time you can be the gofer," said Mario.

"Okay by me," said Arch.

Mario reached in his pocket and pulled out a set of keys and pointed to one key. "This is the key to the liquor locker, underway, the liquor locker is off limits unless Doc says it's okay. Doc and I are the only ones that have a key. When we are at anchor, I can bend the rules. Arch, can you make a good Beefeater martini?"

"The best, Mario."

"Make it a double on the rocks, what about you two guys?"

Arch said he would have same as Mario with tequila and Eric said he would just have a coke.

"Good choice, especially while you are handling one of the super sharp filleting knives," said Mario.

By the time Arch was back with the drinks, Eric had about 15 of the fish filleted. Mario took a sip of his martini and said, "Eric, I think you are as good as I am with that filleting knife, and I'm good."

By the time they finished their drinks, Eric had all 40 of the fish filleted and he said he could go for a martini now. Mario said, "You heard him, Gofer. This man just did a great job and you can bring me one too and maybe one for yourself. Then give me back the keys."

They sat back and enjoyed their drinks. Arch looked up at the big pan on the table and said, "That's a hell of a lot of fish, Mario."

Eric said, "It sure is. I know. I filleted them." Then he asked Mario how he was going to cook them.

"Deep frying is the easiest, but pan frying in butter is the best. How do we do it guys, the easiest or the best?" They both said the best.

"The easiest is no problem, but to pan fry all those fish, I'm going to need some help. Any volunteers?"

Arch said, "Eric did the filleting, so I'll volunteer."

Eric said, "If you guys are going to prepare the fish, what can I do to help?" Mario asked Eric if he had ever made coleslaw. "Yes, but a pretty standard recipe."

"Okay, Eric, there is a large head of cabbage in the fridge. Shred it up and I'll tell you the way I do it. It's spicy coleslaw. I'll tell you the ingredients and you figure the amounts, but check with me before putting it together. This is what I put in coleslaw, mayonnaise, sour cream, hot sauce, dry mustard, horseradish, red wine and black pepper." Eric mixed the ingredients in a separate bowl with Mario watching. Eric came pretty close to the way Mario would have done it. They tasted the sauce before assembling and Mario said, "Sugar is missing."

Eric said, "Raw onion slices should be in with the cabbage too."

"Do it," said Mario, "sounds good."

Eric finished the coleslaw and it turned out great. Mario and Arch did the fish. Arch had the pleasure of carrying out the giant platter with about twenty two pounds of beautiful jumbo perch. There were seven people from Cora Lee's crew and there was Art Hobson (the fisherman) and his wife, so there were 9 people at the table. That was almost 2 1/2 pounds of fish apiece. Some ate more - some less. Everyone was stuffed and there was only one fish left on the platter. With very little coaxing, Arch finished it off. Art's wife, Linda, wanted the recipe for the coleslaw and Mario pointed to Eric. Between Eric and Mario, they gave her the recipe. After dinner, Bill said, "Eric and Arch, how about coming out to the cockpit? Doc and I would like to discuss something with you."

When they got to the cockpit, Doc and Art Hobson were already there. They all got a drink from the cockpit bar and they sat down. Doc started off by saying, "First off, we know that you two guys have received your draft notices. How would you like to tear up these draft notices?"

"No way, Doc," said Eric and Arch, "We're not draft dodgers."

"Didn't expect you to be. We have something more important for you to do. You will get credit for service time, yet, not be in the military service. If you agree, you will find that it is even more important than the military service. As you know, I am a three-star Admiral. I'm temporarily on leave from active duty. Bill is a Major General in the RAF on reserve status. Now Art Hobson is a Brigadier General retired. He was in command of one of the top commando brigades and he still has many connections in that area."

"This all sounds very interesting, but what does all this have to do with Arch and me?" asked Eric.

"Actually quite a bit, you two guys could be the nucleus of a group we want to put together. How would you guys like to go to England at Government expense, which includes eight weeks of commando training and then to Japan for 6 or 8 weeks of ninja training. By the time you get through, you will both be someone not to be trifled with. There will be two other people in this group. We will meet up with them in Sturgeon Bay next week, which will be on the 23rd, 10 days from now. Meanwhile, we will remain at anchor in the harbor for a few more days. Bill and I," said Doc, "will be doing some planning and organizing. Art said that he had some things that he knew that you would interested in."

Just then Art came up from down below. He said, "I hear you guys like motorcycles. If you do, then I've got something to show you."

Mario was standing at the gangway, "If you guys shake a leg, I'll give you a ride in the launch over to Art's fish dock."

Art said, "Thanks, Mario, I had forgotten that my wife had taken my boat and I would need a ride too."

Mario said, "Well, come on, you guys, let's get going. I've got to get back because I've got a galley to run."

Eric said, "What's for dinner?"

"Nice roast beef and baked potatoes and garlic gravy. But it will be well done if you guys are late. Dinner at 6:30 on the dot."

"Okay, Mario, we will be there."

When they got to the fish dock, Mario handed Arch a pressurized can with a horn on it. When you are ready to come back blow the horn three quick blasts and someone will come and get you.

"Okay, Mario, see you at 6:30." And Mario headed back to the Cora Lee.

Art motioned toward a Jeep and said, "Jump in and we will head to my shop."

They drove about 5 miles to a lakefront road. There were five nice looking cabins and a larger building a little further down. "These are my cabins which I built in my spare time. I rent them out in the summer. I've got three more to build. It takes me about two years per cabin to fully complete and that Quonset building down the road is my shop. Let's go down to the shop and I'll show you something that I think you will like."

When they got to the shop, they opened the door and Art turned on the lights, which were bright is hell. Arch took one look and just about did a flip. What he saw was a beautiful, highly polished red and gold 1949 Indian Chief and up on a work rack was an Indian Scout that was partially disassembled. Then Art walked over to another corner and he turned on a light which was directly over what looked like a large bike with a cover over it. He removed the cover and there was a black on black bike that looked like it was from another planet. Eric asked what it was and Arch answered, "It is a Vincent Black lightning. 150 mph plus out of the factory."

"Have you ever seen one before, Arch?"

"Just once, in Hannibal, Missouri. Ridden by a beautiful, sexy redhead. Whom I was told by everyone that knew her, that she could kick the shit out of five 200 pound guys at the same time without breaking a sweat. And on top of that a hell of a motorcycle mechanic."

"Arch, you know what you have just done?"

"No, Art, what?"

"You have just described one of my commandos. Her name is Jacky Sax."

"That's her," Arch said, "I'd love to see her again."

"You may just do that, Arch," said Art, "so how about a beer, Guys?"

"Sounds good to me," said Eric, "and Arch seconds it."

"Let's go back to the fish shack, I keep the cold beer there." They went to the fish shack and got a nice cold beer and sat down outside on the dock. Art said, "Right where you're sitting is where the ferry boat docks. She comes out here twice a week from Charlevoix."

Eric asked, "What about in the winter?"

"Once every two weeks, and that is, if the weather or ice permits. If we are iced in then our supplies are delivered once a month."

Arch asked, "Art, when and how do you get your fish off the gill nets?"

"Well, I have two employees. Matt and his 16-year-old son Carl. They take care of the fishing when Doc is in the harbor. I have a 35 foot fishing boat that they use. They took it out this morning and brought in the gill nets, the fish in the net are wound up on a spool and the fish are removed as the net comes in. Matt and Carl are out getting whitefish and lake trout right now and they should be in in a little while. We will be sure to have more than enough fish for tomorrow night. Have you ever been to a fish boil?"

They both said no. "Well, tomorrow night will be your first fish boil. And it will be the best!"

"Do you actually boil the fish?" asked Eric.

"Yes and no, it's actually all in the procedure and the timing."

When they were ready to go back to the Cora Lee, Eric gave three quick blasts on the air horn, but nothing happened. He did the three blasts again and this time he got one long blast from the ship. A few minutes later, the launch moved out from the side of the Cora Lee. Juan was at the helm. He pulled the launch up to the dock but didn't bother to tie up, but he reached back in the cockpit, and with one arm slung a few cases of Budweiser up on the dock. He said to Art, "The beer is for the fish boil. Doc said that he will bring some green chartreuse for after dinner."

Art said, "Sounds good to me, but what is green chartreuse?"

Juan said, "It is almost impossible to explain the taste, but if you like the taste of gasoline, that's a good start. Let's get going, Guys, we got to get everything shipshape before everybody goes ashore for the fish boil tomorrow. They got aboard the Cora Lee, went below and showered shaved and changed clothes and came back up on deck. Bill was sitting at the cockpit table nursing a double martini and watching the afternoon sun go down and he said, "I hear that you guys have never been to a Scandinavian fish boil."

Eric said, "Nope, never been to one."

"What about you Arch?"

"Me either, but it sounds real good."

"How did you guys like the jumbo perch last night?"

"They were great, Bill."

"Well, a good fish boil is even better and Art does a good one."

They were now ready for dinner. Both of them were ready at the same time and went upon deck. They could smell the aroma coming from the galley and they couldn't resist, so they had to go down and check it out. On reaching the galley, they found Mario lying on the floor with a pot on top of him. Arch lifted him off the floor and Eric asked Mario what happened. He said, "I went to the bin to get a pot full of potatoes. I was going to scrub them down and put them in the oven to bake when I slipped on a wet spot. I must have hit my head and it put me to sleep for a while. Now it is too late to bake these potatoes. The beef will be too well done."

Eric said, "Mario, you said you were going to make potatoes with garlic gravy. How about garlic mashed potatoes with diced onions that have been browned in garlic butter?"

"Sounds good Eric, have you ever made it?"

"My dad has made it and I've helped him and it always tasted pretty damn good ."

"Well, we have to peel some potatoes then," said Mario.

Arch said, "I can handle that."

"Okay, Arch peel them and cut them into one inch cubes and fill this pot."

Eric said, "I'll cut up the onions and mash the garlic and make the garlic butter."

Mario said, "Sounds like everything is under control. I'll bake the rolls and make the vegetables. Looks like you guys have saved my ass, I owe you."

Arch said, "In that case, how about a couple martinis?"

"Man after my own heart. We will make it three of them."

Eric said, "Mario, I like the way you run your galley."

They did their thing in the galley and served a great dinner with a beautiful rare roast beef. Art and his wife were there. When everybody had stuffed themselves till they could hardly move, they all said it was an outstanding dinner.

Art said, "After that dinner, I better do one hell of a good job on that fish boil tomorrow."

Doc said, "Art, they have all been good so far."

After dinner everybody sat around with a drink in hand. Eric asked Art about what Mario told him. "Mario tells me that you have been diving out in the lake looking for sunken logs. What's the story about that?"

Art said, "As far as we know, these are all logs that were lost just north of Beaver Island about 70 years ago. These logs were almost too heavy to float and some would not float. These were chained together with pine and cedar log booms. There were hundreds of logs chained together in each log boom and two or three of these booms towed by a steam tug. One morning a tug was towing two log booms in a heavy storm. They were passing by the northern end of the island when the chains started breaking up. After the first chains broke, the twisting of the logs caused the other chains to break also. When that happened the tug cut them loose. This was all seen from the shore by some people on the island. So it has been said. Some of the pine and cedar logs floated to Beaver Island and the other logs went down in what was probably 40 or 50 feet of water. I am told that they are worth quite a bit of money and I have been diving to see if I can find these logs with not so much luck. So far I have only found one log. It was an unusual log, very heavy. Diving like that, you just can't cover much area."

Eric asked if he had ever thought of using a sea sled. Art said he used one when he was in the commandos. "We borrowed one from the US UDT people "underwater demolition team", but it didn't work out."

"You seem to have all kind of equipment in your shop."

"Arch and I can have a sea sled that is perfect for what you want to do, before you start the fish boil. Then we can go look for logs on Wednesday."

"Well, if you think you can do it, go ahead. It sounds good to me. What kind of material and tools will you need to do your deed?"

Arch said, "We won't need much."

Art took a small tablet out of his shirt pocket and said, "Rattle off what you need and I'll have it set aside in the shop before morning."

Both Arch and Eric started calling out the things they would need. 5/8 plywood four by eight sheet. One half or three-quarter inch pipe 22 inches long, same size 15 inches long. 3/8 inch eyebolt or 3/8 threaded stock. One half or three-quarter inch Elbow 2 inch wide webbing or web belt 5 feet long. Quarter 20 and hex head screws and nuts 1 inch long screws saber saw and drills. Art said, "No problem. The shop will be open, but I won't be there in the morning. We have to go out and hang a gill net or two."

Arch and Eric got up the next morning and had breakfast with Mario. They had eggs and a big slab of ham. Mario called Juan and then Juan took Arch and Eric to the dock in the launch. Carl was waiting for them and he said that he would drive them to shop. They went into the shop and found everything that they needed, plus a lot more. There was a large vertical band saw, which they used to cut the plywood down to 36 inches wide and 7 foot long. They rounded the top of it and then drew an oval shape at the top end. Then they took the saber saw and cut the oval, leaving a one eighth inch gap all the way around, except at the top and the bottom of the oval they left 1 inch wide uncut tabs. Next came the control arm which was half inch pipe. The 32 inch piece was connected to a 12 inch piece by way of an elbow. The 32 inch pipe was screwed tight to the oval with pipe clamps. The ends that were overlapping the oval cutout, was also held with pipe clamps, but shimmed up enough to swivel freely. Next the uncut tabs were cut out. Now they had a movable diving plane. The 12 inch pipe was a control arm. The three eighth eye bolt was attached to the front end with two U clamps. The last thing was the web belts. The loops on the bottom were foot stirrups. Then there was the upper arm loops to keep the rider on the board. As simple as this design was, it was very effective which Eric and Arch had proven in Chicago. After it was finished they stood back and looked at their creation. Arch and Eric both knew that Art would not even be close to being convinced that the sled would work.

"You know something Eric? First impressions mean a lot ,so let's find some paint." They looked around the shop and found a cabinet that had all kinds of paint in it. Eric selected a can of semi-gloss, sea green blue.

Arch said, "It's a perfect color for a first-class sea sled. It's also quick drying, so we won't get stuck to the paint." Only one small 3 inch brush was found, so Arch volunteered to do the painting. They hung the sled upside down from the foot stirrups and when Arch finished painting, he backed off and said that Rembrandt could not have done a better job. Eric agreed and said, "Let's hike down to the fish shack. Maybe we can find a beer or two.

It was about a 2 mile hike to the fish shack and when they got there, Art had a couple of picnic tables set up and was washing and trimming vegetables and cleaning fish. It looked like he had enough to feed an army. "Hey, what are you guys doing here? I thought you were going to make a sea sled, or were you just bullshitting me?"

"No B.S., Art. It's already made and painted. It's ready to find your logs. There are only two things missing. A boat with a trolling motor and about three or four hundred feet of three sixteenth or a quarter inch nylon line. "

"We got that," said Art, "you think it will work?"

"It's worked before, Art. One other thing though, do you have any small marker buoys?"

"I've got three different sizes, so it looks like we are good to go."

Arch said, "The most important thing at hand is the fish boil."

"It is 11 am right now. The fish boil is set for 1 pm. I've got the veggies all cleaned up and ready to go into the pot."

"What have you got for the fish boil, Art?"

"Well, we have a bunch of small onions. I think they call them pearl onions. Then we have small unpeeled red potatoes and we have Brussels sprouts in butter. They are baby Brussels sprouts and they are tender. Last of all is the fish. We have nice fresh caught 3 to 4 pound whitefish and five to 7 pound lake trout. These fish will be filleted, so there are no bones. Then there will be bowls of melted butter to dip your fillets in and to drizzle on your veggies."

Eric asked Art, "What kind of pot do you cook everything in?"

Art called them over to the side of the building that was out of the wind. He showed them the kettles. They were 22 inches in diameter and 12 inches deep. There were propane burners under each kettle. "We will get the water hot, but won't start cooking until everyone is here. Now head back to the ship and get all gussied up and be back here by 1 pm."

Arch went into the fish shack and came out with the horn and gave three blasts and sat back to wait for Juan. In about 10 minutes, Juan pulled up to the dock with the launch. He took Arch and Eric back to the Cora Lee. They went aboard and down to their cabins and took a shower and changed clothes. They made it back up on deck by 12:50. It was almost

1 pm and the whole crew was gathered around the gangway. Juan was down in the launch with the engine running. Doc, Bill and Mario were standing on the deck having their last martini before going ashore. Bill said, "Mario, you make a damn good Beefeater martini, but it looks like we will just have beer at the fish boil."

"Just stick with me, Bill, I think we can do better." And he pulls out a bottle of green chartreuse out of a sports bag.

"Is everything all ship shape and locked down?" Doc asked Angel.

"All set, Doc."

"Well, then let's get this show on the road. I've got a hell of a taste for Art's fish boil." They all got aboard and the launch headed for the dock. When they pulled up to the dock, Matt was right there passing out beers. Doc said, "It looks like it's going to be a good party." They all walked around to the far side of the fish shack where Art was firing up the two kettles. Art's wife Linda was in the fish shack getting the drawn butter ready. Art hollered for everybody who has never been to a fish boil before to get back by the kettles. "Now this is the way a fish boil is done. The fish boiler is like a French fryer. Small red potatoes go in first, then the small onions go in next. The Brussels sprouts, which are in a net bag, go in last. The kettle had a basket to lift the food out. The potatoes go in one kettle and the onions and Brussels sprouts go in the other."

The plates and silverware were on the table along with a bowl of melted butter. Art checked the potatoes and said, "These are done." And lifted the basket out and dumped the potatoes in a large stainless steel bowl. He checked the onions and the Brussels sprouts and said, "The onions and the sprouts are done too." Then he dumped the onions in one bowl and the sprouts in another. Then he poured a cup full of melted butter on the Brussels sprouts and stirred them up. He poured about a half a pound of salt into each kettle and told everybody to get their veggies. Eric asked Art about all the salt in the water, "Won't the fish be salty?"

"No, Eric. The fish won't be salty. The salt just brings up the boiling point of the water and makes it hotter and cooks the fish faster, which is just what we want. The fish must be cooked hot and fast. Not hot enough and too slow ruins a fish boil." Art had a 4 foot square heavy table next to the fish boiling kettles. On it were two large trays of filleted fish. One tray had whitefish of medium-size and the other tray had lake trout. These were from larger fish and the fillets were cut into three pieces. On the same table was a piece of Cedar, one half inch by five inches, by three feet long. It was all sanded and nice and smooth. When someone asked what it was for Art said that it was the second most important part of the fish boil, the first being the salt.

Art said, "Okay, are you ready for a fish boil? I need two volunteers; one on each kettle. I volunteer Arch and Eric. Cold beer goes with the job. I'll tell you when to put the basket in the water and when I tell you to take it out of the water, do it very fast and dump the fish into the stainless steel bowl. Linda will pour the melted butter on them and put the fish into serving dishes. You ready, Arch?"

Art put the white fish in the basket that Arch had and then he put the lake trout in Eric's basket. Eric put the lake trout in the kettle and Art said, "Trout takes a little longer and that's why they go in first. Now, Arch, in with the whitefish." A couple of minutes after the whitefish were in Art turned up the flame on the burners and it flared up and the water started boiling over. He took the cedar plank and ran it across the kettles and scraped all the foam and sludge off the top of the water. As soon as he did that, he said, "Out, Arch." Then the same with Eric's lake trout.

When they started eating, Art asked, "How is the fish? Is it salty?" And they all said no. "You see," said Art, "the salt just raises the boiling point of the water and the long plank was to scrape off the oily sludge on top, so you don't drag the fish through it when you take it out of the kettle." They did the operation two more times in each kettle until all the fish was done. Everybody agreed that the fish was great and tasted as good as any lobsters they ever had. They kept saying that they couldn't eat another bite, but they just kept going until all the fish was gone.

Arch said, "I think I ate too much." Everybody agreed.

Art said, "The only way to cure that problem is to take a swim." Arch and Eric were in shorts and so was Angel, Juan, Mario and Bill. They just took off their shirts, emptied their pockets and jumped in. Doc wasn't wearing shorts, so Art said he had an extra swim suit in the fish shack. Matt and Carl had swimsuits.

Everybody was in the water raising hell and having a ball. Everything stopped when Linda came out of the fish shack in a sexy looking Bikini. She walked over to the outer corner of the dock, where there was a ladder leading up to a platform. Art said it was 30 feet above the water. He said he used it to check out the ferry boat from Charlevoix. She got up to the platform and did a beautiful swan dive. After that dive, Arch said it looked like fun and Eric followed Arch and then everybody else. Mario said that he didn't like anything higher than 3 feet and he just jumped in. Juan was a pretty good diver. He claimed that he dove off the cliffs in Acapulco, where they have the cliff diving show. Juan must have made a dozen different dives. Each one better than the last one. This time he was doing a beautiful swan dive, except on all the other dives, his shorts stayed on. When he lost his shorts, Angel found them and Juan hollered to Angel to throw them to him, but Angel and Mario were throwing them back and forth. After a while, Mario threw them up on the dock and Bill said, "Juan, come on, get your pants."

"I'm not going climb up on the dock with nothing on."

Linda said, "Juan, I will go in the fish shack and wait till you get your pants."

Juan said, "What about Carl's girlfriend, Sue?"

Sue, who had a good share of beer said, "I'm staying right here, but I won't look, even though I hear you're well endowed!" She repeated that she wouldn't look and cracked up laughing. Angel got up on the dock and picked up Juan's shorts and carried them up to the top of the platform. He made a motion to throw Juan's shorts down to Juan, but instead he hung them on a post above the platform and dove into the water.

Mario said, "Juan, don't worry, it will be dark in about four more hours!"

Doc was tempted to say "that's enough", when he saw Linda climb up to the platform and take Juan's shorts and sailed them out like a Frisbee. They almost landed on Juan's head. He put them back on and headed for the dock. He went right to fish shack and went in and came back out with a pair of Art's Cressi flippers. Everybody wondered what Juan was doing. He went over to Angel, who had just opened a beer and said, "Drink up, Man, it may be your last one."

"Hey, Juan it was just a joke!"

"I know, Man. I got a funnier one for you." And Juan picked Angel up and said, "How far can you swim underwater?" He threw him off the dock and dove in after him. Angel was swimming away, but Juan caught up with him and grabbed Angel around the waist and they both went underwater. It was quite a while before they popped up about 100 feet from the dock. They went under again and this time they come up closer to the dock with Juan waving Angel's swimming trunks. Juan walked to the beach and found a rock weighing about a pound and put the rock in Angel's trunks, rolled them in the ball and said, "Angel catch." Juan threw the trunks to Angel, but somehow he missed the target and they landed about 10 feet over his head.

Juan said, "Sorry, Man. Bad throw. I guess you'll have to dive for them. It's only about 20 feet deep there." After about a dozen dives and coming up empty, Juan said to Mario, "Your partner in crime is never going to find his trunks. You're a better diver than Angel, why don't you jump in and help him out?" Mario dove in and headed to the bottom. He was only down for about 90 seconds and came up with Angel's trunks. Everybody was back on the dock and the Admiral said, "Okay, you people, we have had one hell of a good feed, thanks to Art and his crew. Had some good entertainment too, thanks to Juan and Angel. And now I think they should shake hands and have a drink together."

Doc poured them each a shot of green Chartreuse and handed it to them. "Bottoms up, Guys." Angel had had green Chartreuse before and he sipped it slowly. Juan was not as wise and he tipped it up and poured it right down as you would with most 80 proof whiskey. Green Chartreuse is 110 proof and it tastes like gasoline. Juan gagged and coughed and tears came to his eyes. When he caught his breath and could talk again, he said that he thought he was poisoned. Angel said, "Good, huh??"

They all sat down at the tables and relaxed for a while and Doc offered everyone a shot of the green Chartreuse. They all took a pass after watching Juan gag on his first encounter with the green stuff and decided to stick to beer. Linda asked Sue to give her a hand and they went into the fish shack. They came out with plates and napkins and silverware. Linda said, "Dessert?" Everybody all agreed that they couldn't eat another bite of food. Linda and Sue went back in and came out with two large apple pies and two large cherry pies. They all looked at the four pies and said, "Well, maybe just one piece."

They all had a piece of pie. Some had two pieces because they had to taste both the cherry and the apple. Some had three because they couldn't make up their minds.

While they were sitting there eating and drinking, Doc said, "I've heard about the sunken log booms. You guys are going to dive out in the lake to look for them? Not much of a chance to find them, it's a big lake."

Arch said, "Art, found one log last year and they should be in only 40 to 50 feet of water."

Bill said, "Still, it's a big lake."

Art said, " Eric and Arch went over to my shop this morning and built a sea sled to tow behind the boat and they say it works pretty good."

Doc said, "Art, are you going to tow it with your Canadian freighter?"

"What's a Canadian freighter?" asked Arch.

"The one that I have is a canoe about 18 feet long with a 4 ½ foot beam. It has a square transom for an outboard motor. It takes some real heavy water. We can tow the sled behind it on a 300 to 400 foot quarter inch nylon line."

Bill said, "I'd like to see that. And you guys have tried it out before?"

"We tried it and it works great and it's real simple to make. We built this one in a few hours this morning. Not only does it work good but you can navigate with a grid on the surface."

Doc said, "We can meet you out on the lake tomorrow."

Eric and Arch explained how the sled worked and Bill was more intrigued. Eric said, "Bring another set of tanks out with you and you can try it out too."

Bill said, "I sure would like that."

Art said, "One thing I forgot to mention, and that is the water around here gets pretty cold at the 40 foot depth and I've only got one wetsuit."

Doc said, "No problem, we have more than a dozen wetsuits aboard the Cora Lee. All different sizes. What time, Art?"

"How about 9 am at our dock. Everybody can get suited up before we get in the boats."

The next morning they met at Art's dock. Art had gone to his shop and found the sea sled hanging upside down. He turned it over and leaned it against a cabinet. Its simplicity amazed him, but he wasn't sure it would work. Arch and Eric had assured him that it would. He was thinking, it may go up or down but what will happen if you are not alert and the water is cloudy and you scrape the bottom? Will it dig in and dump the rider or he just being pessimistic? Both these guys say it works fine but what about control sideways? Will it stay level? Or if it leans over one way, can you bring it back or will it keep rolling over and dump you upside down? Art thought back to what Eric was telling him about when they used the sled. He said they rolled it over upside down and she skated along the bottom and then turned it right side up. It's kind of hard to believe that this piece of plywood could do all that. Well he said to himself, time to try it out. So he loaded it into the back of the Jeep and headed for the dock. Earlier that morning, he had filled his two gas tanks on the Canadian freighter and he brought it around to his fish dock.

When Art got to the dock he saw that the guys were already there. There was Doc, Bill, Eric, Arch and Juan. Juan said that he would give his left nut to try that sea sled. Arch said, "Okay, Juan, put your nuts on the table." And he pulled out his pocket knife. Juan gave Arch a funny look and then backed away from the table. "Forget it Juan, I don't need an extra nut anyway."

Juan said, "Okay, I get to go on the sled?"

"Okay, Juan, you ride the sled."

Art unloaded the sled and they all looked at it and were amazed. Somebody said that it was unbelievable that they were going to ride this piece of plywood 30 to 40 feet below the surface. Everybody was wondering whether it would work or not. Finally Bill said, "If these two guys say it works, then there is no doubt it works."

They all went into the fish shack and put on their wetsuits. Everyone except Doc. Doc said, "This water is too damn cold for me." They were all set and the sled was in the freighter. The towline was aboard, three tanks were aboard and the sled. Then it dawned on Eric that they needed some marker buoys if they found anything. Art said he had some in his shop and he would go and get them. Doc said, "I know you guys are qualified divers, but has anybody asked Juan?"

Juan was just coming out of the fish shack and Bill asked him if he ever dived before. He said, "Yes, in Mexico last year. I worked on a boat that had scuba gear aboard."

Bill said, "Juan, just to be safe how about a little test."

Juan said, "Okay, what's the test?"

"Get your gear, flippers, mask and your tank. Bill took the harness strap on the tank and ran it through the mask and both flippers. He said, "Okay, Juan, I'm going to throw all of this stuff off the dock. It's only 20 feet deep. I want to see you dive down, find the gear, turn on the valve and take a breath of air, then put your mask and flippers on and then your tank. When you get your gear on, you can come up." Bill threw Juan's gear in and Juan followed after it. Bill said he used to teach a diving class in England and that was one of the tests for a primary class. About the time Bill finished talking, Juan was up with his gear and Bill said, "Good job, Juan. Just had to check it out."

Art pulled up with the Jeep and he put the buoys in the boat. He also brought a cartridge belt to hang the buoys on. Art said, "If everyone is all set, let's get this show on the road." They headed out of the harbor with the 18 foot Canadian freighter in the lead and the 19 foot launch following.

When they got outside of the harbor and into the open lake, there was a small chop. The freighter was meant for much heavier water. It had a 40 HP Mercury outboard and a 15 HP Evinrude trolling motor. The trolling motor would be used for towing the sea sled. Cora Lee's 19 foot launch was lapstraked. It had a 95 HP inboard engine. It was meant to be used as a work boat and not a speed boat. They rounded the north end of the island and Art cut back his speed because of the chop. Juan pulled the launch alongside of the freighter and they all discussed how they were planning to dive. Art checked his fathometer and said that it was ranging from 30 to 40 feet deep in this area and pretty steady at that depth for about half a mile. He said it should be a nice easy dive if the sled worked okay.

"Don't worry about the sled as long as your boat can pull it," said Eric, "I'll go first to check it out." They figured out a grid to use from Beaver Island. Art sighted a line between High Island and Hog Island. Next they sighted a line from Garden Island to High Island. Now that they knew where they were going, it was time to get into the water. First they put the marker buoys into the two clamps on the board. Then secured a 1/4 inch nylon line to the eyebolt and the other end of the line to the spool which was mounted to the transom of the boat. Eric put on his tank and Arch opened the valve. Eric put the mouthpiece in his mouth and tried breathing then spit it out. He said, "When I'm on the sled, I use less than half as much air as you usually do in normal diving. When on the sled the mouthpiece is only in my mouth one third of the time. It's very relaxing and the more you relax the less air you use. Another thing is that we are only diving to a depth of about 30 to 40 feet and not staying under too long, so we are not worried about decompressing. The last thing is our signals. One finger pointing to the sky is speed up, thumb down is slow down and waving is stop. At first we will let out about 100 feet of line, but feed it by hand to keep it out of the prop. If I wave with both arms, let out more line. One fist means no more line."

Then Eric went into the water, climbed aboard the sled and got his arms through the straps and feet in the stirrups. He gave them the finger and pointed to the sky and the boat started pulling the sled. They fed out one hundred feet of line. Eric was moving along on the surface as if he was on a surfboard. He kept going along that way because he had the control arm back with the plane set in the up position. When all 300 feet of line was out, he pushed the control arm forward with the plane down and made a nice smooth dive. Eric went down about 10 feet and rolled to the left and rolled to the right. He went up and down and he rolled the sled over completely upside down. He went along upside down for a while, totally inverted. He went up near the top and then back down to about 20 feet. With very little effort, he rolled it right side up and then went down to the bottom and saw that it was all sand. He decided that everything checked out great. As he got near the surface, he had an idea. When he was at about 10 feet in depth, he inverted the sled. He surfaced with the sled upside down and got everybody got all shook up and they figured the worst had happened. Then they saw Arch smiling and he said, "I think he gotcha!" All of a sudden the sled flipped over and Eric was on top and he gave the okay sign and then waved both arms to signal a stop. They reeled in the line and Eric got off and back into the boat. Everybody had a lot of questions to ask. He answered most of them and then said that they would have to try it for themselves. They all agreed that Art should go next, because it was his lake.

Art climbed aboard and went through the same procedures as Eric. He very cautiously pushed the control arm forward and she dove very smoothly, he pulled it back and he was on the surface again. Next time he pushed it forward, he dove all the way to the bottom. He was an expert diver so he had no problem to clear his ears as he went down. He thought that he had better find out if Juan was familiar with clearing his ears, otherwise he could rupture an eardrum. The rule is, if it starts hurting and you don't clear, you don't go deeper. Art was having a ball, he went up and down, rolled left, rolled right and then cautiously, totally inverted. He went along upside down for a few minutes and then with very little effort, he righted the sled. Art figured that he got his jollies. Now it's time for someone else's turn. Actually he could hardly wait to get back into the boat and tell everybody how great it was. Art went through the routine and got back into the boat. He was excited as hell when he got aboard. He said, "Where in the hell did you ever get this idea?"

"Just thought it up I guess," said Eric.

"Did you ever think of patenting it?"

"No, because it's too easy to make. You couldn't charge enough to pay for the patent."

Art explained all the things that he did with the sled, and told everybody how controllable it was. Bill was next. He jumped in the water, but didn't have a tank on. Everyone was hollering at him to come and get his tank, but Bill said, "I'm just going down for a short dive." He climbed aboard and said, "Let's go." And he did a short dive with only

100 feet of line out. He came back up and waited until 300 feet was out and then dove again and was back in one minute. Next time he dove, he was down for a full two minutes. He rode on the surface for a while and then dove again. This time he did not come back up for 3 ½ minutes. He signaled to come in.

Bill climbed aboard and said it was fantastic. "When I first saw that piece of plywood I had a lot of doubts. On the last Dive, it felt like the first time I flew a Spitfire. I really didn't want to come up and I didn't have to come up. It is so effortless and relaxing that you don't use much energy, like you would if you were swimming."

Doc and Juan were tied alongside and listening to Bill when he said, "Okay, who's going next? Arch, are you going?"

"I could go, but I've ridden the sled before and Juan is chomping at the bit."

Juan said, "I'm ready any time."

"Go," said Bill. And Juan jumped in the water and climbed onto the sled. Bill climbed into the launch with Doc and they pulled away from the freighter. Juan was on the surface and stayed there until a full 300 feet of line was out. He slowly submerged, then he tried the sled for maneuvering. Up and down, roll left, roll right, it was working beautifully. Then he tried what the other guys said it would do. He rolled it over and was flying upside down. He was 15 feet from the bottom when he saw it. There was a great pile of humongous logs with a chain laying on top of them. He knew what they were as soon as he saw them, so he released a marker buoy. Eric spotted the marker buoy first and then everybody saw it. The first thing they thought of is that Juan was in trouble, but all of a sudden he popped up on the surface. Arch shut the outboard down and they reeled Juan and the sled up to the freighter. The first thing Juan said was, "Logs. Giant logs!"

Everybody wanted to go down and see, but the weather was threatening and Art said tomorrow was supposed to be a better day. By now Doc and Bill were alongside. Doc said, "Art, you have been looking for these logs for a long time. While we get the gear in the boat, why don't you just take a dive down and take a look or you won't sleep tonight."

Bill said, "Art, take another marker buoy and put a second marker down." Art went down and within a few minutes, a second marker buoy was up and so was Art. They headed back, but before the boats separated and Doc said, "Art, this calls for a celebration! Go back and pick up Linda and come out to the Cora Lee for dinner."

Art took off by himself in the freighter, happy as a pig in shit. He pulled away from the launch and said, "See you about 6 pm."

When Art got back to his dock, the ferry boat was just pulling out. There were no passengers today coming or going. They just picked up Art's shipment of iced fish, which they pick up every Monday, Wednesday and Saturday. Then they make stops at High Island, Garden Island and Hog Island. There was one other island that Art couldn't remember the name of, but he did remember one thing about it; the whole island was a nudist colony. When they docked at this island, absolutely no one was allowed off the boat with clothes on. Bob, the Captain of the ferry, had once told Art about the time that he had about 20 girls aboard. They were all dancers from a show in Detroit. He said that they were all beautiful girls and they were real dolls, and they knew it. And built like brick shit houses. Captain Bob said that they had picked them up in Charlevoix and stopped at three different islands before they got to the nudie one. The girls mingled with the passengers and the crew. They were real friendly and everyone liked them. They said that they were taking a relaxing two week vacation on "Nudie Island" because when the show was going, they got very little time off. The gals invited people to come and see the show. They even gave out some free passes. I got one and I'm going to see the show.

He said the real show was when they docked at the nudie island and the 20 beautiful girls walked out of their staterooms carrying their small suitcases; naked as the day they were born. Naked and beautiful. Then, as if on cue they all turned at the same time and wave to the passengers and crew. Even the lady passengers waved, one of them was even a little old lady passenger who said to a crewman, "Now, wasn't that nice?"

He said, "Yes, Ma'am, it sure was." She turned and said she had never seen people wave so much. Everybody in the crew and the passengers came to see them off. They all waved for at least five minutes and when they started to leave, someone yelled "encore". They turned back to their audience and everybody clapped and waved again. They turned around and walked over to a bus and climbed on and away they went. Art said, "Well, Bob, being a ferry boat captain, sure has its good points! See you later."

Art tied the freighter and went into the fish shack. Linda was still there. Matt, Karl and Linda had just loaded 500 pounds of frozen, and 300 pounds of iced fish on the ferry boat. It was to go to the fish house in Charlevoix. Linda said that Matt and Karl had just gotten the fish out on the dock when the ferry tied up.

Linda said, "I'm beat, I don't even feel like cooking dinner. But I did make a cherry and an apple pie, to give to Doc and his crew before they leave."

"Everybody loved your pies. Let's go home and get cleaned up and all gussied up. I am going to take you out for dinner. We have been invited to a celebration dinner."

"Where? And what are we celebrating?"

"On the Cora Lee"

"Sounds good, but what are we celebrating?"

"We found the logs with Eric's sea sled. That sled is more fun than a barrel of monkeys! And we are going out again tomorrow. Maybe you would like to come along and try the sled?"

"I would like to, but I promised the lady in cabin number three that I would teach her something about stained-glass work. It's great that you found those logs! You have only been looking for them for five or six years. So let's go and party tonight."

"Okay, we will party, and maybe we will even take the Cadillac out of the boathouse." The Cadillac was a 1940, 18 foot Chris-craft runabout that Art had completely refinished. He had replaced a six-cylinder gray engine within 1941 Cadillac V-8. That was now the Sunday boat, or the Cadillac. Art took the five scuba tanks out of the freighter, which were to be refilled in the morning. He checked the dock lines on the freighter and finally headed up to the house. When he got there, Linda was just getting out of the shower. He stood there and said, "I was just admiring you."

She said, "Not too much admiration, Art, or we will never get to the Cora Lee!"

"Right you are." When they were finished dressing, Linda was wearing an evening gown and Art was wearing his Sunday suit. They then went down to the dock and he jumped in the boat and fired up the V-8 and away they went. The harbor was nice and smooth, so nobody got wet from spray. It was just about six when they arrived. Linda went up the gangway while Art was securing the lines on the Chris. As he started up the gangway she heard a whole bunch of wolf whistles coming from up on the deck. When Art got to the deck he saw everybody, including Linda, with martinis. Art said, "Linda, I think we should get out of here. These guys have been away from women too long!"

"No, Art, I think I'll stay. I kind of like those wolf whistles."

"Okay, then somebody get me a martini. Come to think of it, Linda, I forgot to mention it, you do look sexy in that gown."

Doc turned to Art and said, "That was the smartest and the most timely thing you said today."

Then Linda said, "So pay attention to Doc, Art. He knows how to treat a lady, especially a sexy one."

They sat down at the dining table on the after deck and Mario brought another round of Beefeater martinis and then he laid down some very appetizing, appetizers. Shrimp, sautéed in garlic butter, and deep fried calamari with deep fried mushrooms on the side. It was excellent. Linda said, "Art, we forgot something."

"What did we forget? It's a long way across the harbor to get something we forgot."

"No problem, Art, it's in the Cadillac. I put it there while you were taking a shower. In the forward cubbyhole."

"What did we forget?"

"When you look into the cubbyhole, you'll remember."

Art went down to his boat and came back up the gangway carrying two large pies in Linda's pie basket. He set them down on the table and said, "I would've remembered them, just as soon as my stomach reminded me."

Linda said, "That's enough of pie talk. What's this I hear about you famous divers finding a cache of logs?"

Bill said, "Linda, not only did we find a lot of logs, but also the greatest underwater flying machine."

Eric said, "Bill, one of the girls who tried it said the exact same thing. She was a pilot and said it was as good, if not better, than flying."

Mario came to the after deck and said, "Time to eat, Folks. Corned beef and cabbage. The best corned beef that you ever tasted. Also some good homemade cornbread." They went down to the midship dining room and sat down to one hell of a good meal. Mario was right, it was damn good corned beef. Everyone was stuffed but they finished Linda's pies anyway. After they were through eating, Doc said, "Art, what's the plan for tomorrow?"

"We basically went out today to try out the sea sled and to change the minds of some of the doubters. And frankly I have to admit, I was one of them."

Bill said, "I guess I was one too. I could not see how you could control a piece of plywood being dragged through the water, but it worked beautifully. Anybody else have any doubts?" Both Doc and Juan said that they had been doubters too.

Doc said, "I guess Linda and I have to take a ride tomorrow. Angel and Mario said that they would stay with the ship. Okay, Art, what time do we meet at your dock?"

"How about 9 am? I'll have all the tanks filled and in the freighter."

Doc asked Linda if she had a wetsuit. She said she did, but it had a big tear down one leg. Doc said, "Mario, show Linda where we keep the diving gear. Linda, go with Mario, I am sure you will find a suit that will fit you. While Linda and Mario are gone, let's figure out how we're going to dive tomorrow."

Art said, "While the diver is under, it would be handy if he could signal without coming up. We have a quarter-inch line towing the sled. I have some 3/16 nylon line that can be used as a signal line for faster or slower. I have a bunch of clips with rings that we use on the fish nets. This would keep the lines together. Just one clip every 20 feet. I'll have that rigged before we go out tomorrow. I think each person should get a chance to dive. We will cover a lot more territory if each person makes a 15 to 20 minute dive." They all agreed with Art and felt that they were all set for a good dive tomorrow. They were all sitting back relaxing, savoring their drinks and complaining that they ate too much. All eyes turned in one direction, as Linda walked up on the after deck. Linda said, "It was the only one that would fit."

Doc said, "I thought that you might find a good fit in that one and the pink suits you very well. It was left by an Italian actress. Sofia something or other. We were in the Mediterranean and were going to do some diving. She said that she would bring her own wetsuit, which she did. She said she used it in a James Bond movie. She was very well endowed and the suit fits you very well too. And you look really great in fluorescent pink!" Doc said with a big smile.

She did a couple of twirls and everybody clapped and she took a bow.

Bill said, "Good thing there is no reason to be secretive about the dive. Well, I think this is about the time we wrap this up if we plan on diving tomorrow."

Mario came up with a tray of cordial glasses, a bottle of cognac, a bottle of green chartreuse and Linda's gown on a hanger, in a plastic carrying case. As Art and Linda were getting ready to leave, Juan and Arch came over to her, each with a very bright spotlight. Theysaid, "Linda we want to light up your fluorescent wetsuit, so we can see you all the way back to the dock."

Both Art and Linda laughed and Art said, "She's kind of lit already! Go ahead and light her up some more!" Everyone watched as they got into the Chris-Craft. They saw Linda glowing, all the way across the harbor.

Doc said, "I bet that Sofia whoever, never looked any better than Linda does in that wetsuit."

Next morning everybody was up bright eyed and bushy tailed. They were all anxious as hell to see what the new day would bring. It sure as hell was interesting yesterday. Mario brought up a big thermos jug of coffee and Angel and Juan carried up a cooler with soft drinks and ham and beef sandwiches that Mario and Eric had made last night. They lowered everything into the launch.

Chapter 17

Linda finds Plane, Traitors Found in Service.

The whole crew of divers got into the launch and Juan pulled away from the ship, headed for Art's dock. Juan seemed to be anxious to get to diving again. They were halfway across the harbor when Doc said, "Juan, Art left something for you last night, after you left to hit the sack. He said that he is going to raise these logs and make some money from them. He said that since you found them, you deserve a bonus, so here is $500 from Art."

"No," said Juan, "I do not deserve this."

"Art will insist, Juan."

"Then I will split this with the two guys who made the sea sled."

Doc said, "I still owe Eric and Arch, which I totally forgot about, so with the $500 and $200, there's a total of $700 you get $300 and Eric and Arch each get $200. Does that sound fair, Juan?"

"Sounds good to me."

"Okay, Bill, remind me to pay off everybody when we get back to the Cora Lee."

When they got to the dock, Art and Linda were all set to go.

Bill asked Linda if she had her pink wetsuit with her. Then he told her that they could see some person dancing on the dock last night. They all had a cup of coffee from Mario's thermos and then fired up the engines and headed out to the north end of Beaver Island. They rounded the end and then headed north towards Garden Island. The two buoys were just about a mile north of Beaver Island. They anchored the launch and got into the freighter. Arch went down first, as he did not go down yesterday. When Arch came back up, he said that there was one hell of a lot of logs down there. Doc went down and stayed for about twenty five minutes. Each time somebody went down, they moved a little further north on the grid. Doc said that there were still logs down there. Then it was Linda's turn. Bill said, "Linda, that sexy suit of yours might attract a giant Muskie!"

Art said, Bill, you got it all wrong, giant Muskies are all female."

"Okay, Art, maybe a homo Muskie."

That got a big laugh and Linda jumped in the water. She climbed onto the sea sled and got out to the 300 foot end of the line and then very smoothly, she submerged. She was at 15 feet and went up and down, which went smoothly as well. Then she tried what Art had explained to her. She went upside down, then right side and left side. Now she was satisfied that the sled handled beautifully. She was at about 35 feet depth when they turned to go on the next leg of the grid. That's when she saw it. With quick thinking, she immediately dropped a marker buoy. She couldn't quite make it out, but it looked like a plane. She slowly pulled back on the control rod and went slowly to the surface. When she got to the surface, she reeled into the boat. She unlatched her harness and Bill lifted her tank. When she climbed aboard, everyone was asking why she dropped a marker buoy. She said, "I think I found an airplane."

Bill and Art both put on their tanks and they went over the side. The plane was right below them, in approximately 50 to 55 feet of water. They both came down almost on top of it. Bill recognized it immediately. It was a civilian version of the C. 45 the Beech H 18. Art was swimming around the plane. He was trying to look through the windows. The water was pretty clear, but it was too dark inside the plane to see anything. He swam over to Bill, who was trying to look under the plane. Bill saw that the wheels were retracted. It looked like the pilot was trying to belly land the plane on the water. They swam towards the tail and found the registration number. Bill wrote the number on his slate: NC 16784. When they swam over the top, Art saw something on the forward part of the cabin that he was interested in. He motioned for Bill to come forward and pointed out a series of holes in the cabin top. They had enough information. Bill pointed up and they went to the surface. Arch and Eric lifted off the tanks and Bill and Art climbed aboard. They told everyone that there was a twin-engine plane down on the bottom and that Bill got its registration number. Bill said, "It's a civilian plane, but someone shot it down, but it was not a military plane that shot it down. Doc, can you use your connections in Washington to check the registration number?"

"I can do that Bill, but I think we have to keep this a secret for now. We will want to know when the plane went missing and who was, or is, aboard. And who and why would anyone want to shoot it down."

Bill said, "It must have been a twin, with a faster speed than the Beech Craft H/ 18 that shot it down. The maximum cruising speed of the Beech Craft was about 220 miles an hour. It would have to be a plane with a side cargo door, where the shooter would stand and fire an automatic weapon. It was definitely not a military plane with a fixed machine gun. The holes are too random and not in line."

Doc said, "As soon as we get back on board the Cora Lee, I'll radio a friend in Washington. I won't give him many details. I'll use a landline for that."

Art asked if anybody thought we had a more reason for diving today and everybody thought that they should pack it in for today. Doc asked Art, "Does your friend in Charlevoix still do charter flying with his DeHavilland Beaver?"

"I'll give him a call when I get back, but I think he does. Did you plan on going to Charlevoix to make your call?"

Doc said that he would like to go in tomorrow morning. "I think this is too important to let it wait. Art, why don't you and Linda go home and make your phone call to the pilot. Get cleaned up and you and Linda come out to the Cora Lee for drinks and dinner again."

"Sounds like a good plan. We'll see you in a couple hours." Art and Linda headed for the fish dock and Doc and the rest of the crew headed for the Cora Lee. Bill said to everyone and nobody in general, "Do you think we did all right in the last couple of days?"

"I think we did great," said Eric, "but I really think we should quit while were ahead. If we keep diving, tomorrow we may find a submarine, then next day a destroyer, and then a battleship. I think we've found enough."

Doc said, "I think we should plan on spending one more day here. Then hoist anchor the day after tomorrow."

Bill said, "I believe we have had more excitement here than we expected."

Doc said, "I'll go to Charlevoix and call my friend, who is currently on the naval staff in Washington. When I knew him during the war, he was a Captain. Now he is a three-star Admiral. Come to think of it I was a Captain too. My friend, Admiral Leslie Ryan, has probably got as much pull as anybody in Washington. He can get the information we want and then he can get somebody from the Navy to very quietly raise the plane."

Art said he would radio his friend with the Beaver and when he found out what time he would be at the dock, he would bring his boat to the Cora Lee and would take anyone going to Charlevoix, back over to his dock. About 9 am, Art showed up with the Canadian freighter. Charlie, the pilot, had told him that he was just leaving Escanaba, which was only 90 miles from Beaver Island. About a 35 or 40 minute flight. Charlie would probably arrive about the time they would get to the dock. Doc asked Art if there would be any problem with Charlie's Beaver carrying five passengers, plus the pilot. Art said, "The Beaver would carry five passengers, the pilot and his Canadian freighter, if it would fit, so no problem."

They got into the freighter and headed for the dock. They had just tied up to the dock, when Charlie came into the mouth of the harbor. It looked like he was flying just about two feet off the water. He sat it down smoothly at a pretty good speed and kept the power on, until he was close to the dock, then shut her down easy like and taxied right up to the dock. Art jumped on a float, lifted a cover and pulled out a tie up line. Bill did the same on the stern. Linda showed up on the dock with a half-gallon thermos with hot coffee, cream, sugar and some Styrofoam cups. She said, "Charlie didn't come to pick you guys up, he came to pick me up and have a cup of my good coffee."

Art asked, "Is that right, Charlie?"

"Yes, that's right, Art. If Linda don't go, you don't go."

"I guess that settles that."

Bill said, "It sure would be nice if Congress could settle things that easy. But that will never happen, unless we elect the wives, along with the Congressmen." They all agreed to go to Kelsey's pub and Charlie said that he would go with them. He could have a couple drinks, but just two because he had a flight this afternoon. Arch asked Charlie about the battery. "It seemed like it almost didn't want to start back on Beaver Island. The batteries are way down. When I was in Escanaba, a friend had a boat with a dead battery and no one else was around, so we moved the boat to the plane. Then we jumped his boat with my batteries and ran them way down. It was down so far that it wouldn't start my engine."

"How did you get it started to get to Beaver Island?"

"I cranked it."

"What did you do? Stand on a float and pull the prop through?" Art said, "No, you couldn't turn it over that way. What the Beaver has is an inertia starter. You install a crank on the side of the fuselage, right in front of the cabin. It's a very highly geared manually driven motor. It has a heavy fly wheel and once you get it going fast enough, it is hard to stop. That's when you engage the clutch and it cranks the engine over."

They were all at Kelsey's Pub and Doc talked to Kelsey and went in the back room to call Washington. The rest of the crew sat down at a table and ordered drinks. Linda had one drink and said, "I hope you boys can get along without me, I'm going shopping."

"Be back in two hours and we can go to lunch," said Art, "Linda, if we are not here when you get back, we will be next door in Chen's Restaurant."

Linda said, "See you shortly." And she left.

Arch saw the dart board and said, "Anyone for darts?"

Bill said, "I'm for darts, but I'm probably just too damn good for you."

"I think you will have to prove that, Bill. Anybody else want to play?"

Both Art and Eric said they would play. Playing partners was settled by shooting for the bull's-eye. The closest and the farthest were partners. Bill and Arch were partners and were leading by one game. They were halfway through the last game, when Doc came out of the office. He said that he needed Art in the office. Linda had just walked in as Art headed for the office. Art said, "Linda, take my place."

She said, "Okay, Boss." She was up next and they were just playing a straight game. All numbers in sequence and out. Linda threw twelve darts and every dart hit the spot, not one miss. She went out and Arch was up. If he didn't go out this turn, they would lose and they did. So it wound up a tie score. Everyone agreed that they had enough of darts. Just at that time, Art and Doc came out of the office. Doc said, "Let's go, we have a lot to discuss."

All six of them went next door, to Chen's Restaurant and started to sit down. Doc told them to hold up on sitting down. Art had known Chen for a few years and asked him for a favor. Art knew that Chen had a room in the back, where Chen and some of his Chinese friends did some high-stakes gambling after closing hours. He slipped Chen a $100 bill and asked if the six of them could eat lunch in his back room. Chen said, "No problem, but you need not pay me this $100."

"Chen keep the money, we have something very important to discuss. And Chen, would you ask the waitress to knock before entering? We may be discussing something very important."

Doc said, "Chen we have one more favor to ask. I'm going to have to make an important phone call. I would like to use the phone in your office."

"There is no need for that, I had a private phone installed right in this room, so no one left to make a phone call in a middle of a hand."

Doc said, "We appreciate this very much. I will get the phone charges from the operator because it will be long-distance." And then he slipped Chen another hundred dollar bill and said, "Let's all order lunch. Then we can start the discussion after we are served." Everyone ordered lunch and after they ate, Doc had asked the waitress to bring three large pots of tea and not to disturb then until they called.

"That said, you may wonder why all the secrecy. Now, what I tell you is top-secret and what we say here must stay between us. What we have here is a top-secret criminal case. The people involved will not hesitate to kill anyone who gets in their way. They have killed many innocent people before. Many millions of dollars have been involved. The people are not only criminals, but they are traitors too. Their crimes happened during the war and in the commission of these crimes, they killed many American Navy and Merchant sailors. What happened was whole ship loads were hijacked, with the assistance of some people in pretty high places. These criminals were in the Navy, Marines and the Army, while Americans were fighting and dying for their country, there was certain scum with firsthand knowledge of ship cargoes, the routes and destinations. With this important information and a half a dozen of these pirates planted in the crew, these bastards would kill off the crew and then bring more pirates aboard. They would bring the ships to ports that had been paid off."

"Next they would offload the cargoes or food for sale in the black market. Some of the ships carried war material. Some other cargoes were even more valuable. Some with guns, drugs, ammunition and other military supplies. These went directly to the buyers in some third world countries ready for revolution. These military supplies paid off in millions and the kickbacks from the black marketers were also very great. After offloading the ships, they were taken out and sunk and written off as sunk, by German or Japanese submarines. Meanwhile, these traitors got very rich. There were about five people involved in this scheme. The officers involved were one Army, one Navy and one Marine. They varied from

Major to Colonel and one Navy Captain. Two of the five were enlisted personnel. Army corporals who were suddenly Sergeants First Class. These two were necessary, because one worked in a classified area that scheduled the type of cargo and the other one was privy to knowledge of routes and departures. Tim O'Brien, the one privy to the routes, was talked into this scheme by a $5000 bribe. He was told it was just one small hijacking and next time he would get paid more. He would get $7000 and then he could buy a new car when he got out of the army and a big down payment on a new house. They said they were only going to do two ships. It kept going until it was six ships. Tim had almost $50,000 in the bank and he wanted to quit. He told him that he would just refuse to do it. They told him to meet them at Dan's bar at eight o'clock..."

1945... All five of them met in the back booth at Dan's bar. They told him, "Tim, we've got a problem. We can still make a lot of money or we could quit. But if we quit supplying information as we have been doing, our contact with the hijackers will send information to the Department of the Navy. If that happens, we officers will stick together and we will hang you out to dry."

Tim stopped to think. There was Army Major Robert Maxwell, a Marine Bird Colonel David Griffith and a Navy Captain. These three officers could get away clean and leave him to face a court-martial. He would wind up with life in prison or a death sentence. Tim looked at Colonel Griffith and said, "You told me no one would get hurt. The hijackers just wanted the cargo and the crew would go free. You said the ship would be written off as a victim of a submarine, but no one has survived from any of the six ships." The Colonel said, "Use your head, Tim, we cannot afford to have any survivors. So now are we are going on as before. Or do we let the hijackers send this information to the Department of Navy? And then we let you hang."

Tim said, "Well, I guess I don't have a choice." They did 10 more ships that were loaded with even more valuable cargo than before. All three officers became rich. The two sergeants, each had a quarter of $1 million in the bank. By now it was getting too hot to continue, so the colonel and the captain came up with a plan. Colonel Griffith contacted the leader of the hijackers and planted the seed in Xinjang's mind. A $90 million hijack. He told Xinjang that this must be planned to the finest detail. Griffith says that there can be no mistakes. He said that he would bring all the vital information. It has already been planned. He said, "What I need is your complete approval. By that, I mean by you, and your two top lieutenants, Kim Mohammed and David Patel. We can meet at Nancy's bar in San Juan. I have chartered a 50 foot yacht, so we can get away from any prying ears and so we don't arouse *any suspicions, I have arranged for a few party girls. I will see you in exactly one week from today at noon, at Nancy's.*

Griffith had chartered the 50 foot yacht, the Island Queen, from the owner and Captain. He told Captain Richard Vazzano that this was a very important and secret business meeting and that they would need his yacht for two days. There are certain areas that he would not go to for fear of pirates and Griffith had no problem with that. He told the Captain that after the business was completed with his three associates, he wanted to be picked up by seaplane at 8 am the next morning. That they would be about 50 miles north of San Juan. "I will give you the exact coordinates after we board on Friday. My guests and myself will be at your dock at 1:30 pm. You had said that your charter fee for two days is $1200 U.S., so if you do not enter anything in your log and do not mention to anyone about this charter, I will pay you $6000 U.S. in cash. I will pay you $3000 now and $3000 when we board. As we spoke before, you said that you could arrange for three nice party girls. Tell them not to mention where they are going before we leave and I will pay them $800 apiece. They may talk all they want after they get back to San Juan."

At 10 am on Friday, Griffith showed up at the Island Queen's slip. The Captain was aboard early as Griffith asked him to be. He went aboard with two aluminum attaché cases and handed the Captain the $3000. He told the Captain that he would like to go to his private cabin and not be disturbed for an hour. He said that he must spend some time going over the contracts that he was going to propose to the people who are coming aboard. The captain showed him to his cabin. He had asked for this particular cabin. He had checked the boat builder's design and knew that this cabin was right next to the main fuel tank. When the Captain left, he lifted the mattress and box spring. When these were removed, there were four three quarter by six cedar planks. The two outside ones were screwed down but the two inside ones were kept in place by the other two that were screwed down. This was a stroke of luck, he needed no tools. He opened one of the cases; it contained 10 pounds of military grade explosives and a very sophisticated timing device, connected to a firing mechanism. He set the timer for 9 am the next day and closed up the case. Then he took a large tube out of the case. It was a very sticky mastic and he put a heavy layer of it on the back of the case. He threw the tube in the bilge and then placed the case against the hull and put the bunk back together.

The case with the explosives was in another smaller case that was inside the large aluminum case. The reason for this was that if the Captain saw him board with two cases and left with only one case, he could get suspicious, so Griffith left the one aluminum case on his bunk. In it were some technical magazines and blank contracts. Griffith figured that would satisfy his curiosity and he wouldn't go looking for any cases in the bilge. Griffith met his partners at Nancy's. They had one drink and decided to go to the boat. When they got to the boat, the Captain greeted them and said their other guests were on the after deck. When they got to the after deck they saw three very good looking topless girls in deck chairs sunning themselves. Xinjang said, "I'll take the redhead, Kim, you and David can choose between the other two." Inside of 20 minutes all three girls were not only topless, but bottomless too. Kim and David followed suit and were bare ass naked. Susan, the redhead, asked if anybody wanted a drink. Kim said, "I'm Muslim and Muslims don't drink, but I will bend the rules for some of the milder drinks, such as gin, vodka or tequila. But if it's whiskey, I am a Muslim."

Nicole, the blonde, said, "Kim, why just whiskey?" As she wiggled her butt around while sitting on Kim, she finally became impaled by Kim's large pecker. "Because I don't like it. But I do like this, Nicole, you got a nice tight pussy."

"No, Kim, you just have a big prick and I like that."

David was also getting it on with Karen.

Xinjang said, "You guys got no class. Then he grabbed Susan's hand and took her down below."

Griffith stayed up in the wheel house drinking beer with Captain Dick, who observed that his buddies seemed to be enjoying the ride. "They are no buddies of mine. They are business associates."

Griffith gave Dick the coordinates to meet the plane at 8 am in the morning. Dick said, "No problem, we will be here early, at about 7:45."

"Okay, let's shake them up and start our discussion." Griffith called down and told them that it was time for business. Xinjang shook the other two loose, and said, "All the gals up on the after deck. Griffith said that we would have drinks, cold chicken and lobster salad after business."

The four of them sat down in the main dining cabin. Griffith told Kim to knock off the drinking until after the meeting. Griffith told them that the meeting shouldn't take long. "I'm going to outline everything, then give you the case. In the case are the charts and schedules for each ship, along with each ship's cargo and the value of the cargo. Also included are the ship's time of departure, the number of crew on each ship and the number of hijackers aboard. The ship is Samuel Howlett. She has 26 in her crew; 10 of them are hijackers. They have each been promised $50,000 for their part in the hijacking. You can honor that or kill them. With all this information it should be a piece of cake, so when you sell the cargo it will make us all rich." He put all the charts and sheets of information back in the case and handed it to

Xinjang, and said, "Now let's go eat and drink. It's time to celebrate because $90 million is a lot of money!"

And celebrate, they did. After they ate, the three hijackers drank and screwed the night away, and most of the morning too. Griffith stayed up in the wheel house drinking beer with the Captain, but before the three hijackers got too drunk, he told Xinjang that they didn't need any witnesses. He said, "It's a shame to waste those three sexy girls, but what's got to be done, has got to be done, they are witnesses."

He shook hands with him and said, "Have fun tonight, I'll be leaving in the morning. The plane will pick me up at 8 in the morning."

Griffith went to see the Captain and asked him to make sure he was awake by 7:30 am. He said that it was imperative that he be on that plane at 8 am. Griffith didn't think he would be able to sleep that night, but in case he did fall asleep, the Captain would awaken him. If not he had his portable alarm clock. He did not get undressed. He just sat in a chair in his cabin. He really didn't want to fall asleep, he just wanted to make sure he got off the boat before it blew up, but at about 5 am, he fell asleep. Being he did not plan on going to sleep, he didn't think about setting the alarm. The Captain had been at the helm for a lot of hours and he fell asleep too. Luckily, the sound of the plane taxiing over to the boat woke the Captain. It was now 8:30 am. The Captain ran to Griffith's cabin and opened the door and said, "Sorry, Senior, it is 8:30. I fell asleep."

Griffith thought that it was lucky that he had set up the rubber raft last night. The plane had taxied within 50 yards of the boat. Griffith rushed up on deck and threw the rubber raft over the side. It was now 8:40 and he didn't know how accurate the timer was. He handed the line to Captain Dick. He went over the side and landed into the raft. He started paddling for all he was worth. Griffith reached the plane and climbed up into the rear hatch, which Gordon had opened up. He closed the hatch and said, "Let's get the hell out of here! That sucker is just about ready to blow!"

Captain Vincent Gordon was piloting the Navy PBY Catalina. By the time they got off the water and into the air, it was five minutes to nine. "If the timer is accurate, she should blow in about five minutes."

"You were cutting it pretty close, Dave."

"The Captain was supposed to wake me at 7:30, but he fell asleep and so did I. I didn't get moving till 8:30. Well at least I got here. She should be just about ready to blow. Circle around and make sure she goes down. There should be no survivors. I put the explosive within two feet of the main fuel tank and it should make one hell of a fireball."

It was five after nine. Griffith started to worry that he might have done something wrong. Then there was a flash and then the sound. Next came the second explosion of the fuel tank. It was a big blazing torch. The boat went down within five minutes, but the fuel from the 800 gallon tank had set the water on fire.

Griffith said, "No survivors. Let's go. I could use a nice double martini."

They flew into Key West Naval Air Station. Gordon landed next to the base and taxied over to, and then up the ramp. Then he taxied the Catalina over to the hangar area. They went over to the flight office and Gordon said, "I got to check in for my flight pay today. 100 bucks is 100 bucks."

"As if you need it, you rich bastard!" And they both laughed. Griffith said, "Come on, let's get our asses over to the officer's club. I'm getting real thirsty."

"Hell no, Dave, we can't drink in that shithole officer's club. Shit, Man, we can afford to go first class."

"That sounds good, but we have to go easy so we don't create suspicions."

They went to the Key West Ocean Breeze Resort and had a great lunch and a lot of drinks. Griffith said, "So how does it feel to be a multimillionaire?"

"Great, Man, now we got to make sure we keep it. What about our two Sergeants?" asked Gordon.

"I talked to them and we are in good shape. I told them there would be no more hijacking. And O'Brien said that was good and Meyer said that he would like to make a little more money. I explained to him that he had already made almost $500,000 and it was starting to get chancy. I told O'Brien and Meyer that we needed to get rid of the boss hijacker and a couple of his Lieutenants. I told them what we needed was a legitimate looking document for three ships, carrying very valuable cargo. All phony routes and departures and cargo. I told them that if they got these phony documents, I would do the rest. I told them that I would get rid of the hijackers and we would be home free. They both seem to be satisfied."

Gordon then asked Griffith if he were satisfied. He said, "Hell yes! We have each got a little over $2 million. That sure as hell warms the heart."

Gordon said, "We should both invest in real estate and stocks, starting in a small way and then steadily increasing. That way when we draw out heavily it will be due to the markets."

Now, after the three officers and the two enlisted men knew that making dirty money was over, they felt that they were free and clear and also pretty well set up financially. One thing that was in their favor was that none of the five were married, so they had no one that they had to explain anything to. They all went back to doing their jobs, as they should have been done in the first place. They did this right up to the end of the war. After the war, and just before the two Sergeants were discharged from the Army, Colonel Griffith contacted them and said he wanted to talk to them before they got out. Griffith had enough pull, that he set up their discharge on, or near the same date and in the same place, which was Newark, New Jersey. He named a bar in Newark, where he said they could talk. They both agreed to meet with him. Meyer and O'Brien got there at the same time. They walked in and the light was dim but they finally saw the Colonel in a booth in the back with a martini in his hand. He greeted them with a big smile and a handshake. He offered them a drink, Meyer said he'd take a beer and O'Brien had a coke. Griffith said, "I just wanted to get you two boys together to see how you were doing. You both look pretty good. You know a lot of guys did not come out of this war too well."

"A lot of them are dead thanks to our little group," Brian thought to himself. Griffith said, "Both of you should be pretty well off financially."

Meyer said, "I already got something going, a real nice bar and restaurant in my hometown. The guy wants to retire. He wanted 100 grand and I offered him 75 and he said okay. I gave him a check for 40 grand and told him I would borrow the rest of it from the government on the G.I. Bill. Besides, I don't need any problems with the IRS We had a good thing going. Five or six more ships and I would have been on easy street."

Griffith said, "Larry, you have to know when to quit, we did just that and we got away clear. What about you O'Brien?"

"I don't know, I haven't even thought about it too much. I may get married and buy a house."

Griffith said, "Good for you. So I guess you guys are doing alright. I got to get going, so good luck to both of you." When he got up to leave, they noticed that he was no longer a Bird Colonel. He was a Brigadier General.

Doc had his second conversation was Admiral Leslie Ryan. After this call he told his crew that he had a lot of new information. "Originally, I told you that five people were involved in this hijacking scheme, but there were three officers and two enlisted men involved. The first officer was a Major in 1943 and is now a Bird Colonel he is Army Colonel Robert Maxwell. The second was a Navy Captain in '43. He is now Rear Admiral Vincent Gordon. The third, and the leader of this group, was a Bird Colonel in '43. He is now Marine Major General David Griffith. Then there was the two Sergeants. Sergeant Larry Meyer, he wanted to keep the hijacking going so he could live a life of ease. The final one is Sergeant

Tim O'Brien, he is the whistleblower. He also is one of the occupants of the plane we found. Admiral Ryan said these men are really dangerous for more than one reason. First the documents in that case would at minimum put all of them away for life, but being this happened during wartime, they would be charged with treason and murder and anything else they could think of. They would be hanged. Also, these officers control a lot of men. Admirals and Generals can get a lot of innocent troops to do their dirty work. All they have to do is generate some lies about a top secret case that has to be retrieved before anyone else gets to it. But Admiral Ryan said right now he is the only one that knows this plane has been found. If I try to raise a group of people, word would probably get to the General or the Admiral and they would very quickly get troops, probably Marines, to confiscate the case as soon as the plane is lifted out of the water. I don't think General Griffith would send more than a squad of Marines because a lot of troops would cause too much publicity about the case. That is something he doesn't want.

Chapter 18

Plane Raised, General & Admiral Confess.

"Now," Doc said, "what the Admiral wants to know is, do we have enough manpower to hold off a squad of Marines? That is until our Admiral can get his Navy people here."

Art said, "If there would be a confrontation, there is one person I'd like to have here and she is not far away. Jacky Sax and her Korean buddy, Kung Fu Fighter. They are in Sturgeon Bay, not more than 100 miles away and she is always looking for a good fight. She can handle any three men at a time and not even break a sweat and if the Korean is as good as she said he is, Hell, that takes care of a squad right there."

Doc told everybody what Admiral Ryan said. That these three officers are criminals of the worst kind. They have killed their own people to make a profit and won't hesitate to do it again. These bastards know what is waiting for them if anyone gets in that case before they do. General Griffith will have his best squad of Marines to do his dirty work. His people have no idea what an evil person their leader is. His men will follow orders no matter what they are. They will be well armed and willing to fight and Griffith knows that there will be shooting and people will be killed and the case may be confiscated. Or even if he gets away with the case, too many questions will be asked. He knows there are other people who know about the hijackings. But it could not be proved."

Art called the hotel in Sturgeon Bay where Jacky was staying. Art asked for the manager at the front desk and asked for Jacky Sax and said that it was very important that he reach her. The manager said that Admiral Hunter may call. Art told him that he was calling for Admiral Hunter. The manager told Art that Ms. Sax could be reached at a martial arts Academy in Sturgeon Bay and he gave Art the phone number. Art called and asked for Jacky. She picked up the phone and said, "Hi, Art, want to go for a round or two? Or are you out of practice?"

He told her that they had an emergency situation here in Charlevoix and that her skills were needed. Then he asked if Peter Chen was with her. She said that yes, he was with her and Art explained the whole situation or at least as much as he could in a few minutes. She said she would be glad to help, and asked if they could use a little more help as well.

Art said that there were only four of them and he didn't think that the local police would consider fighting American Marines. "I have been training a group in Sturgeon Bay and all of them are ready to prove themselves."

Art asked if they would be capable of disarming about 20 Marines. Jacky laughed and said, "With surprise, each one of them could probably disarm at least two of them. You said that this would probably happen on your dock. In that case their weapons would all be in the water in 10 seconds. I said these guys are good and what would make it a big surprise is that these 12 are not very big and the Marines that this general would pick, will be big and strong. The Marines, with the physique of weight lifters, would not be concerned about these seemingly lightweights standing next to them on the dock. They would be small as compared to the Marines and unarmed. The Marines carry side arms and rifles and a Marine would consider them a joke and that they just wanted to talk."

Art and Bill went out to the site of the sunken plane. They anchored over the site, and then they took sightings with a Poloris, which is basically a compass rose with a rotating site. Art wrote down the sightings in his fishing timetable book and put it in his pocket and then pulled up the marker buoys and cut the buoys away from the anchors and threw them over the side and let them float away. They went around Beaver Island and headed south to the southern end, which was about 15 miles from where they were. A couple of miles south of Beaver Point Lighthouse, Art dropped his first buoy. He brought five buoys. These were bigger than the ones they had pulled up and two of them had red lights on them. Art placed them about a mile apart and then they headed back to the harbor and Art's dock. When they got there, the whole crew was waiting on the dock. What surprised Art and Bill was that Mario and Angel and Juan came in off of the Cora Lee. Then there was Doc, Linda and Arch, who was talking to a redhead, dressed in black. She turned around and Art had no sooner said "Jack", when she picked him up and swung him around. She said, "Art, you sly old dog, how come you only call me when you are in trouble?"

He said, "Well, Jacky, I couldn't think of anybody better to call."

"You are full of shit, but I still love you."

"And I love you too, Saxy, or should I say sexy. Speaking of that, let me introduce you to my wife, Linda."

She said, "Hi, Linda, you have a good man here. So don't kick him out if he snores."

"He does, but he is still a keeper."

"By the way, what are you doing nowadays, Jacky?" Art asked.

"I have a Vincent shop in Hannibal, Missouri and I do a lot of martial arts training. Speaking of martial arts, come on over and meet some of my people."

She first introduced Peter Chin. "He's number one." She said that she had been training people in Missouri, Kansas, Iowa, Nebraska, Illinois and Wisconsin, and she had about 100 of her students at a two-week martial arts meet in Sturgeon Bay. The 12 she had chosen, represent about five or six different states.

As soon as Charlie brought everybody back from Charlevoix, he flew right on to Sturgeon Bay to pick up Jacky and her crew. Then he flew right back to Sturgeon Bay to pick up the last eight of Jacky's crew. When Charlie dropped Jacky's crew off at Art's dock, Doc had Juan run him right back to the Cora Lee. He was back out at the dock in about half an hour, but now he was resplendent in summer whites of a three-star Admiral's dress uniform, with a chest full of ribbons and medals. Doc said, "If there is one thing I know about Marines, they do respect rank and I do out rank their leaders. I intend to pull rank to the utmost. Once we get the plane on the barge I intend to be on that barge until the tug brings it to Art's dock. If Admiral Gordon tries to get his Navy personnel aboard the barge, I won't let it happen. I've got two more stars than he has. No one in this man's Navy will argue with a three-star admiral."

Charlie landed the Beaver in the harbor and taxied up to the dock. The eight martial artists climbed up on the dock and Jacky introduced them to everybody. Charlie said that he saw activity at the south end of the island. "I flew over and saw a Navy ship with a crane on the stern. I circled around and saw that they had a diver in the water, so I thought it was all over with and Doc and his crew lost. Then, as I was heading back north to the harbor, I saw activity on the north end of the island. I saw a tug with a barge in tow. The barge had a crane on it and it also had a plane. There were about four or five guys on the barge with guns and one guy in a white suit waving at me and then there was what looked like a Navy launch. Looked like a 38 footer and there were about 15 sailors on the launch all carrying rifles. I think maybe there might be something wrong with my eyes, because I swear I saw another guy on the launch wearing the same white suit. Same as the guy on the barge. The guy on the launch was jumping up and down and screaming at the sailors. You know the guy in the white suit on the barge looked a lot like Doc."

Linda said, "Charlie, that man you saw on in the white suit was Doc. Here he comes."

Just then the tug with the barge entered the harbor. The tug brought the barge up to the dock and it was tied off. The tug Captain jumped down on the barge and over to the dock, climbed up and walked over to Doc, who was now off the barge. He said, "Admiral, I think the sailor boys really want this plane that we lifted out of the water and they seem to have a lot of guns to back them up."

Admiral Gordon walked up to Doc, and said, "I don't know who you are, but that plane is government property and I demand it be turned over to me and my men. He called over a Navy Chief and said, "Chief, I want you to go down on that barge and open the cockpit and see if you can find an aluminum attaché case and bring it to me."

Then Doc said, "Nobody, goes near that plane." By now, Jacky and her crew were mingled among the sailors. Admiral Gordon then said, "It sounds like we have to take it by force. Chief, take all these people off the dock and keep them there, so I can get done what we came here for."

The Chief said, "Okay, Men, lock and load."

Before the sailors could even think of pulling back the bolt on their carbines, they just flew out of their hands and most of them went into the water. They threw some of them to Arch, Eric and Art. All the sailors were now face down on the dock, with someone pinning them down. Doc said, "Now all you sailors listen to me. The only reason for this little activity was strictly to disarm you, so nobody get trigger happy and start shooting." Then he told Eric to go into the fish shack and look behind the door and bring him what he finds hanging on the hook. Eric came out with a pair of hand cuffs and Doc said, "Give them to Art." Art whipped the Admiral's arm behind him and almost pulled it out of the socket and Gordon then put his other arm behind him, so Art didn't rip that one out of its socket too. Gordon said, "You can't do this. I am a United States Navy Admiral."

Doc said, "Not any more. You're nothing more than an ugly, shit faced traitor and you will be tried and hung for treason." Then he said, "Okay, all you sailors, we are all on the same side except for your handcuffed Admiral. Now I will explain to you what is going on. Doc explained what the five traitors had done to get rich. These five cost the country millions of dollars and the lives of more than 350 American sailors. Now they are going to be tried for treason. Right now, knowing what his future is, he would probably like to commit suicide. Chief, take your ex-leader into the fish shack. Art, you got any duct tape?"

"Sure, Doc"

"Okay, gag him real good, because some Marines should be here shortly, and we don't want them to know the Admiral has been here. Juan and Mario, you two guys jump in the water and retrieve the sailors weapons."

They both said, "Aye, Aye, Sir." And stripped down to their skivvies and jumped in the water. In a short time, all the weapons were out of the water. Art and the Chief brought Gordon back to the fish cleaning room and Art said, "Normally, we clean out the fish gut tank every day, but I knew we were expecting a couple of guests, so we haven't cleaned it for about six days. It sure does stink, doesn't it, Chief?"

"It sure does, but not as much as this rotten ex-Admiral."

Gordon started to complain when the Chief held him, while Art gagged him with the duct tape. Then Art said to the Chief, as he handed him a length of 1/2 inch manila line, make like a sailor, Chief, and sling him under the arms. The Chief did this and Art pulled the overhead hoist into position. They put the rope into the hoist hook and started raising Gordon off the floor. Gordon started to struggle and the Chief kicked him in the nuts. The Chief said, "I always wanted to do that to that lousy bastard."

They raised him up and swung him over the pit, then down into the stinking fish guts. They lowered him, until he was up to his ass in fish guts, then they raised him up and let him hang there. He was a pitiful sight. He was trying to scream through the duct tape, but it didn't happen. The sailors all had their weapons back and Art said, "There is an air hose all the way in the back of the fish shack. Go and blow the water off your weapons and get back here because we have more to talk about, and because the Marines are on their way. They are being led by another traitorous officer, a Major General and he was the leader of these five traitors. He is the most dangerous. Also, take a look at the bastard, that was your leader. He will be hanging over the stinking fish guts until we catch his partner, then they will hang there together."

Doc said, "From the information that Art has received from his friends, the Marines plane has landed at Emmett Airport and by now should be on board their boat and on their way here. The Marines should be here by 2 pm."

Art said, "If we can get this all put together by 3 pm, we can have one hell of a Navy and Marine fish boil!"

Doc said, "Art is the combat guy, so we operate under Art's orders. Just so that there is no complaints about command. I would like you to know that Art is a combat hardened commando General. Art was a real general. Not like this rotten bastard, that is on his way now."

Art said, "This is the way it should go down. First let me ask if you were surprised by Jacky's martial arts class."

They all agreed that they were surprised. Then someone said ."You can't disagree . Where in a matter of seconds, your weapon is in the water. And you are face down on the dock. I think if that was for real we would all be dead."

Then Art said, "We don't want is anyone dead or injured. He asked were any of you injured, besides your pride. And that is all we want to do to the Marines, they are only following orders as you did."

"Ok this is the way we will do it. From my contact at the airport, there are 15 of them plus one leader. With you sailors here we out number them. Now what we don't want is any shooting .With you sailors here walking around the dock. We can lead them to believe that, the Navy has everything under control. We will tell General Griffith that Admiral Gordon is in the fish shack, checking out the case. He will probably then tell the squad, at ease. Once Griffith is inside ,Jacky and Peter Chan will cuff and gag him."

"When the Marines are parted from their weapons. Doc will come out on the dock. Has elected to stay undercover until Griffith was taken care of. If Griffith saw another Admiral he might get suspicious."

Doc came out on the dock, and explained the situation to the Marines. Doc sent a couple of the Marines down on the barge, to take a look at the bullet holes on the cabin top.

He said, "Those bullet holes were put in there, by the Marines fearless leader, General Griffith. And the man piloting the plane, that shot down this plane was Admiral Gordon. Doc explained how five men worked with hijackers, to make themselves rich. The reason they shot down this plane, is because inside of it is the whistle blower, of their whole evil scheme. And they made millions for themselves and cost the lives, of well over 300 Navy sailors. And we don't know how many merchant Marine. Your general was the leader of this evil group."

"One of the men inside this plane, was one of the group of five. He was a sergeant with a job that was necessary to their scheme. He tried to get out of their group, but Griffith told him that he was just a Sergeant. Three of them in the group were officers, and they would get away with it. But they would hang him out to dry. He continued, but he kept the records. And got each of the officers to sign orders, that would implicate them. The records that would condemn this group. Are in the plane, and that is what they wanted."

Griffith showed up with twenty Marines. Just as the sailors the Marines were disarmed. Griffith was told that Admiral Gordon was in the fish shack checking out the case. He went into the shack, was grabbed and hand cuffed by Jacky and Arch.

They showed to Griffith, Gordon hanging over the pit and Griffith threw up.

Then they asked him, "Would you confess in front of your men?"

He said "Go to hell."

Art and the Chief rigged Griffith up the same as Gordon and had him on the hook along with Gordon.

They raised him up, and he said "You can't do this I'm a United States Marine Major General ."

Then Art said, "I was only a brigadier general. But I was a real general and you ain't one anymore. And he ripped off Griffith's stars.

The Chief pressed the button and raised them up enough so Art could tie their feet together, and their waists. They were still cuffed. Needless to say they were not very comfortable. Art then ripped the gag off of Gordon. Then they lifted them up and swung them over the pit, lowered them until they were up to their chests in stinking fish guts.

"Art said just hang around guys, we will be back in a short time. We're just going to step out for a beer."

Art and the Chief came back out to the dock. Art said, "Have you explained everything to our Marines?"

"Yes I did, Art and Linda have contacted the FBI. They will be here by 8 PM. Charlie is flying them in from Petoskey, on the mainland .

"Why don't we just ask if anyone would like a beer?"

Doc said, "Maybe we should wash down our guest's. They are probably stinking up your fish guts."

Art said, "Chief why don't you grab a beer. And help me wash down our stinking guests. Nobody I'd like to hose down, more than those two bastards." Art said, "I'll give you the privilege."

When they got back to the cleaning room, Griffith was crying his eyes out.

Gordon said, "Shut up you son of a bitch, your greed has got us into this."

"Well you didn't complain, when the money was rolling in."

Then Gordon said, "We should have quit when we each had 1 million. But you wanted to go for 2 million."

Art walked into the cleaning room and said, "Hi guys how you doing? I hope you ain't farting in my nice clean fish guts."

"I am going to ask you some questions, some of which I already know the answer. I just want to see if you can be honest."

Griffith said, "Go to hell."

Art lowered them up to their armpits and said, "Next time to your eyeballs."

Then the Chief said, "Art let me lower them all the way down."

"No, Chief, if you lower them much more, their feet will go right into the grinder.

Then their leather shoes will ruin the blades, on my nice new gut chopper. So don't do that unless you take their shoes off first. Pull them out Chief and let's give them a bath."

"They already had a bath Art."

"Now they need a rinse."

"Okay Chief you're in charge of officer cleaning." Art took the control pendant and moved them out into the middle of the floor. Then the Chief started hosing them down with a 1 inch high pressure hose.

Art said, Now that you are nice and clean. "Maybe you would like to answer some questions. Or do we take your shoes off first."

Griffith started to say something, when Gordon said shut up you bastard. "What do you want to know?"

Art said, "It's cool in here, let's go out in the nice warm sun."

Griffith said, "Untie us you can't expect us to hobble out there like this."

Art said, "No problem guys." And he wheels over a large hand truck, and puts it under the hoist and lowers the two soggy officers down onto it. Then the Chief ties them to it so they don't fall over.

Art said, "Well this is your ride guys. Take it away Chief, and bring them out on the dock."

When they got out on the dock, Griffith tries to order some of the Marines to untie him. One of them said no way you shit head. Another one said, only if I could cut you up and feed you to the fish.

Then Griffith said "I'll have you all court-martialed."

Doc said, "There only two people here ,who are going to get court-martialed."

"Art untie them, but cuff them in front. Somebody get a couple of chairs, now you two sit down. We will have a little discussion. What you two have done together is documented, it's right down there in that plane."

The Chief said, "Let's open up the plane and get the documents."

"Sorry Chief we can't do that. We have to wait for FBI and the local police. They have to do it. If we open that plane, then open the case. We would have broken the chain of evidence, some sleazy lawyer may get their sentence reduced. So we have to wait."

Doc said, "Meanwhile as I was saying. There is a charge of murder which will be placed on Griffith and maybe Gordon, by San Juan police. The murder of three girls, the captain of the Yacht Island Queen, and two hijackers. We won't prosecute you for the hijackers."

But we have one survivor in custody, "He will be hung along with you. His name is Xinjang . He confessed to the hijackings and implicated you and Gordon. But he also said you chartered the boat, and blew it up, while you left by seaplane."

Art said, "They checked the bank records of the Captain. He deposited $3000.00 in cash with your name on it, as the charterer. Will you confess to what I have just said? Just confess this to your Marines."

Griffith said, "Go to hell."

Art tells the Chief, "To take off their shoes."

After the Chief takes off the first shoe, "Griffith said okay, I did what you said I did."

Then Doc said, "Art why don't you untie your prisoners. And shackle them around that tree over there. Where we can watch them while we eat."

After they shackle them to the tree, Griffith said, "I got a take a piss."

The Chief said, "Go ahead general it's okay piss in your pants. Let me know when you're done and I'll hose you down. Now you two can stand out here in the sun shackled in to this tree, and watch us enjoy ourselves, We will be drinking beer and eating, from what I hear, is the greatest fish boil on the lake."

A short time later Charley landed, and taxied over to the dock. He tied up the Beaver. Charlie and six FBI agents walked over to Doc. Who is now Adm. Hunter.

Doc told them, "There are your criminals, shackled to the tree. The plane is on the barge, it has not been opened up. The state coroner is on the way. So everything is under control. So grab a beer and let's go eat some fish with the Navy and the Marines."

After they had a hell of a good fish boil. They were all stuffed. The number one FBI guy Dan Leary got up. Rubbed his belly and said, "It looks like that's probably the coroner's plane that just landed in the harbor. He should be here in a short time. So come on all you overstuffed FBI guys, Oh, I forgot to mention hard working, get your asses up and let's get to work." Dan said, "Johnson go and get the toolbox we may have a tough time getting into the cockpit."

Dan said, "The coroner is really going to appreciate whoever thought of putting that big wet tarp over the top of the plane."

Doc said, "That was Linda's idea. And she has been hosing it down just about every hour."

Dan figured that plane's cabin would have been cooking in this hot sun, without it.

The coroner walked down the dock with his pilot. They were introduced, and offered a beer.

They both accepted and the pilot said , "A guys got to be an idiot to turn down a cold beer on a hot day like this."

Then Art said, "How about some good fish, to go with it?"

The pilot tells the Coroner, "That he never had the chance to try Art's fish. But I hear it's the greatest on the whole lake."

The coroner said, "In my business, my clients never complain if I'm not in a rush, so let's try some of that good eating fish."

Gordon started hollering again, "He said I really got to take a piss."

Griffith said, "Yeah me too, I got to take a piss too"

The Chief walked over to them, like he was going to uncuff them. "Tell you what gentlemen. I'm not going to uncuff you. So that you can reach down and get your dicks out, And I sure as hell ain't going to do it for you. So just go ahead and piss in your pants. And I'll take the blame for you."

Charlie opened up and said, "You better hose them down if they're going to ride in the back of my airplane."

Art said, "Charlie that's already in the plan. We sure did and want to stink up your airplane with piss and fish guts."

After everybody quit eating the Coroner said, "Let's do it" and they went down to the barge. Eric and Arch pulled off the big wet tarp. Even though it was bright and sunny the aluminum cabin top was cool. The evaporation from the wet tarp acted like a refrigeration process.

Dick Johnson of the FBI tried to open the cockpit. It was locked from the inside. The side cargo door opened without too much trouble. Dick looked inside and saw three bodies the pilot and two passengers. Meanwhile Tom Martin photographed and had been taking shots all around the plane and on top of the plane showing the bullet holes in the cabin top. Dick went into the plane and looked around with his lantern.

Then he saw it the elusive aluminum case. It was under one of the passenger seats. He wondered why it hadn't floated away. Then he saw it was cuffed by the case handle to the seat. Dick had a bolt cutter in his toolbox, and he cut the cuffs. Then he let Tom in to take more pictures. Next the coroner with his body bags went into the cabin, and came back out with three full bags.

Dick Johnson walked up to Griffith, and said, "That shooting was not done by a fixed machine gun. What did you use? It looks like some pretty good shooting."

A B.A.R. (Browning automatic rifle).

"You must have shot out of a side door. What kind of a plane?"

"Another C 45, a later model with twin 450 HP engines . This one has 330 HP engines."

Then Gordon said, "That's how we came up behind and flew over the top of them."

"That was good flying."

"Yes it was, said Gordon, I may be an admiral, but I still know how to fly."

They loaded up the bodies on the twin otter. Then the coroner told them he appreciated their efforts. And it was time he got back to work and he climbed aboard the Twin Otter. The pilot fired up and he and his taxied away from the dock and took off toward the mouth of the harbor.

Dick Johnson said, "There goes the last three people that you guys killed, as he saw the otter lifting off the water."

Gordon said ,"It's not that we wanted to. We had no choice."

" I understand your predicament. You had no choice but to sink 16 ships, and to cost the lives of more than 350 American sailors. No choice, no choice at all. I hope they hang you slowly by the balls. Once for each of the 16 ships. Have a good day and he walked away."

Doc asked the F. B.I. Agents if they had opened the case.

They said, "No Admiral, it won't be opened until we get back in Washington. We drilled a small hole in the case to see if it leaked any water. Negative to that. We took pictures ,and sealed the case with Evidence tape."

Doc Asked the Marines and sailors, "How they liked the fish boil." They all agreed that it was a great. The Chief said now that everybody is stuffed with food and beer there is only one thing I wish I had.

Doc said, "What's that?"

"A picture of our fearless leader handcuffed to a tree with his evil buddy."

Art heard him say what he wanted and he said, "Hang in there Chief." He went into the fish shack, and came out with a 35mm camera. Art walked over to the tree, they both tried to duck out of the way, but how far can you duck when you're anchored to a tree. Art said that he would have a couple of dozen of prints made and send some to the Chief, and some to the Marine Gunny Sergeant.

The Marines and Sailors got aboard their launches fired up the engines and headed out of the harbor. The F.B.I. agents said that they were all set, and should get back to Emmett Airport, then head for Washington .

Bill and Art had the same question to ask the agents, "It seems that we have captured the two top dogs of this evil group and one was in the plane. Somewhere out there is a Colonel Robert Maxwell."

"Admiral Hunter has received information that he has packed up and skipped out of Fort Sheridan in Illinois."

Chapter 19

Capture Colonel Maxwell.

We have been watching him for quite a while. He doesn't trust banks, particularly overseas banks. He likes cash. He has more than $1,700,000 in cash. It is mostly in $50 and $100. He drives a 1950 Buick and about a month ago he started working in his garage at night.

We went to see his girlfriend's boss, and we told him what we wanted him to do. It had something to do with national security. We wanted him to give her two, hard to get tickets, for and Opera in Chicago, at Orchestra Hall. They knew he loved opera and would not pass this up.

The boss told her that, "They appreciated her work, and one of his clients gave him the tickets, and he doesn't like Opera. So that's how she lucked out."

The FBI figured that he was modifying his Buick to smuggle his money across the border. The agents wanted to see how. Colonel Maxwell went to the opera and the FBI went to his garage .The FBI contacted the people who installed his security system. They bypassed the system. Before entering they checked and found electric eyes set up, four ways down near the floor, which they temporarily disabled.

They found that he shortened the Buick's deep trunk. He had cut out the original wall very plainly and it looked like he was going to reinstall the original wall but 16 inches back. Also he cut through the floor of the trunk in that 16 inch area he went down about 8 inches and welded in a new floor. It looked like it would hold four suitcases.

He wanted to take his money with him. Now they knew who and what to look for on either the Mexican or Canadian border. They reset the electric eyes and a security alarm, got out of the garage and went home. They had also installed an electronic bug inside the frame of the Buick.

Colonel Maxwell had a house at Fort Sheridan in officer's country. He stayed at Sheridan most of the time when on duty. On weekends and other times when he took the time off, he stayed at a house that he rented in Bannockburn. About 4 miles west of Sheridan. He kept his money hidden in the house. It was buried in the crawl space in a trench about 2 feet deep. He was worried about fire. It was in four small suitcases.

Maxwell decided that it was time to split and get out of the country. He had heard that a plane was found up near Beaver Island. He knew that Gordon and Griffith had shot down a C45, it was down in that area. The one with Tim O'Brien on board. Griffith said, "Not to worry, he will be there with a squad of Marines. And Gordon will be there with his Navy men. He said one of us will confiscate the case with Tim's documents as soon as the plane is raised."

When he heard that two senior officers had been captured and charged with treason, he knew it was time to leave. He had the perfect plan. His girlfriend Anna had been hinting for them to get married and she had a five-year-old kid. A perfect cover, a man, a wife and a kid.

The last thing he needs is a wife and kid but right now he needs her for cover.

He told her that after we are across the border, we can get married in St. Catherine. and then we can spend our honeymoon in Québec. His friend Dustan Racet will meet him in Québec. He will meet him with his 42 foot boat. For $30,000 Dustan and will deliver him to Halifax Nova Scotia. Later when things are quiet he can get a flight out of Halifax to Europe. As he was thinking to himself he is a millionaire and he doesn't need a wife and a kid. Dustin who is a smuggler will do anything for a buck. For another 10 grand he would be glad to drop Anna and her daughter off somewhere in the Gulf of St. Lawrence. Then all his problems would be solved.

He thought that maybe he would go to Rio de Janeiro instead of Europe. He heard that the girls in Rio are friendlier than they are in Europe. Especially if you don't have a wife and a daughter. But he does have a lot of money. He just has to make sure that Dustan doesn't start getting curious about his suitcases.

Colonel Maxwell and Anna are almost to the border. Then he explains to her that he cannot use his real name, to cross into Canada. He said years ago when he was a second lieutenant, he got into a drunken brawl with some other officers in a restaurant. The management called the police. I cold-cocked one of the police officers. I was convicted of assault which is a felony. I tried to get into Canada once and was refused. Now they have got my name and number.

So now when I cross, I am Jack Ross, a landscaper from Chicago. He told her that going through customs is no problem. He then said going into Canada from the US, the new US customs almost just wave you through, after asking a few questions. Now on the Canadian side, they sometimes wave you through and then sometimes they check you out pretty good ,but we should have no problems

Here we go through the US customs. They will just wave through. The customs officer walked up to Maxwell's car, and said good evening sir would you please pull your car over to the side in one of the parking stalls. Maxwell did as he was asked. Two more officers came over to the car. One who was a lieutenant asked a couple of questions. Then he asked Maxwell to step out of the car. When he got out the biggest of the officers grabbed Maxwell by the shoulders and swung him around and the third officer slapped the cuffs on behind his back.

The lieutenant then said greetings Colonel Maxwell. We have been waiting for you. They led him away. And put him in the back of a State Police car. A car that had caged windows. But before they put him in the car they took him inside and did a very thorough and undignified strip search. Also when they put him in the caged back seat, there were large steel rings on a chain that was attached to the floor. His cuffs went through the ring.

He could see his Buick from the side window. A matron was leading Anna and her daughter, into the customs building. The matron and another customs officer, said they had been waiting for Colonel Maxwell and that she was lucky to get away from him. He is being charged with murder and treason. Then if he isn't hanged, he will never see the light of day again. They told her that they will furnish transportation for her and her daughter back to Chicago.

Maxwell saw the custom officers open the trunk, and then with no effort at all they pulled out the phony bulkhead. Next came the four suitcases full of his ill-gotten money. Right now he would just like to commit suicide but they won't let him.

Chapter 20

Larry Meyers Goes to Midville

They are going to make him pay for his sins. The military wanted to court-martial the three of them. But that would mean three separate court-martials. There was much more chance, that something might go wrong. The Atty. Gen. said let it be known that if the ACLU sticks it's stinking nose, into this trial. Then every member of the ACLU and their friends, will be then investigated by the FBI, back to the day they were born. And if that's not enough every member's taxes will be severely audited back for 10 years.

The Atty. Gen. said this is not a threat, it is a promise and he just wants no interference by the ACLU. He then said that if they do interfere and he has to implement his promise, then there are a lot more people going to prison.

The director of the F.B.I. said there were five people involved in this hijack scheme. we have captured three and one, the whistleblower, is dead. That leaves one unaccounted for, his name is Sergeant Larry Meyer of the US Army. Meyer was discharged from the Army December 5, 1945.They tried to trace him down. It seems that he used someone else's name and Social Security number. The FBI found Larry Meyer and Larry Meyer had the right Social Security number. But the Larry Meyer they found was not the man.

There were no military files, or fingerprints at this time. And there was no way to establish, who belongs to what prints. In an office he worked in seven or eight years ago. There were no pictures of him, so nobody knew what he looked like. The FBI agents checked all of his friends that he had in his Army unit, he had very few friends. The few friends he did have told them that Larry was never short of money.

During the war, you could not buy a new car. He likes Chevys and he always had a fairly late model Chevy. He said that he had An uncle that had a Dealership in North Carolina. When he spent a lot of money, his grandmother left it to him in her will. He never seemed to run out of dead rich relatives.

But nobody had any pictures of him. In any company functions were pictures were taken he always seemed to be standing behind someone. Like he did not want his picture taken.

They've finally found a Sergeant Johnson who said, "We had been on a double date with him. We went to an amusement park and the gal that Larry was with wanted pictures taken, he flat out refused. He said it was against his religion, so we walked out of the Photo shop. We went on some rides and drank a lot of beer, after a lot more beer he was pretty drunk. We went back to the Photoshop, his gal dragged him in and he got his picture taken along with the rest of us."

"The gals got the pictures but I had taken one of the group, I had that picture thumb tacked to the wall behind my desk. A couple of days later the picture was still on my wall but Larry was cut out of the picture. I was now curious about a guy that was afraid of having his picture taken. I went back to the Photoshop and asked if he had the negatives from a few days ago. He said that he usually keeps them for a week and then chucks them. He made me a couple of prints. Johnson pulled out a drawer in his desk and picked up two nice clean prints."

Now we had the Larry Meyer, at two different angles. Johnson then said, " I just felt that it was important to get these prints. Was it really important?" Agent Woods said that these pictures are very important." What did he do that could make him so important?"

"He was never important, it's what he did that was important. I cannot tell you now, but it took a lot of leg work by a lot of agents and you have basically saved our Ass. I will take your name, along with some other people. As soon as anything can be released, I will let you know what you did for your country. The only one thing that I will tell you which you must never repeat, until I tell you that you can, that one thing is this. Larry Meyer is a traitor to his country, but now thanks to your pictures, we will find him."

Larry Gronick had lived in Clarksburg West Virginia ,which is about 116 miles north east of Charleston. When he was in the Army, he put his ill-gotten money in eight different banks. Now that he was discharged, he withdrew all the money from each of the banks. He had $35,000 in each bank under his own name he, had another $10,000 in a checking account. In a bank in his new hometown Midville, West Virginia. He drew cash in $20 and $50 and hundred dollar denominations. He put all the money in small suitcases.

Now he had a long trip across the country. He had $280,000 in two suitcases in the trunk of his car. He thought that his Chevy was nice attraction for an auto thief, so he went to an auto dealer and sold his nice clean Chevy, then bought a ratty looking 1939 Plymouth. He took it to a mechanic and had it all checked out by a qualified mechanic. Then had the brakes checked and put on a new set of tires.

Now he was set to drive to Midville, West Virginia. He didn't have to worry about anybody stealing his ratty looking car. When he got to Midville he deposited $35,000 in the Midville bank. Then in seven other banks in local towns around the area he deposited $ 35,000 in each bank. Now that he got the money out of his trunk. He sold his ratty looking Plymouth, and bought a late model Chevy convertible.

Now he needed a house. He went to a real estate office, and realtor showed him about five houses. He settled on a nice brick bungalow, on the edge of town. The owner wanted $9600, and Larry got him down the $9000. Gave him $1000 earnest money.

The realtor asked if he needed a mortgage. Larry said, "No I'll pay cash when we close." They closed in two days and Larry brought the cash when the sale was finished.

The realtor asked, "If there was anything else, he could do for Larry?"

He said, "Actually there is. On the north end of town, there is a bar and restaurant, with a for sale sign on it. Check that out for me." While I go shopping for some furniture.

Larry went to a furniture store. He bought a kitchen set, dining room set, a couch and chairs, a radio and a TV, which was just coming out on the market and finally a bedroom set. Which all came to $2,034.25. Larry told the salesman that he would give him a $30 tip, if it would be delivered tomorrow. He said no problem. Deliver it between 5 and 6 PM today, and you get a $50 tip. I'll deliver it myself.

Chapter 21

Three Traitors Hung, Larry Meyers Convicted.

Larry wrote out a check to the furniture company, in the amount of $2,034.25, best sale of the day. Then he handed Glenn the salesman a $50 bill, and said don't be late. They went back to the service desk, to fill out some paperwork. This was just the second time, that he had to use his new name. The first time was when he bought the Chevy convertible, and he almost signed Larry Myers. He had better get used to his new name. Which was Larry Higgins.

His real name was Larry Gronik. He lived in Clarksburg West Virginia. He was charged with aggravated assault, and rape, in Charleston. His lawyer got him out on a $5,000 bail. Using a bail bondsman, he skipped bail and he skipped Charleston. He went to California, with a new name, Larry Myers. Now after he was discharged he got new identification, and a new name, it was now Larry Higgins.

When the salesman and Larry, went to the service desk, they were served by a good looking, platinum blonde. After the paperwork was taken care of. Larry told her that he had just moved into town. And he sure would appreciate a good looking gal like her, showing him where a nice restaurant, could be found in this town. Glenn gave her the nod, and she said okay and she gave him her address. He picked her up at seven, and surprisingly she directed him to the restaurant, he intended to buy.

They went into the restaurant and had a nice dinner. And after dinner they had a couple drinks. When the waitress delivered the second round of drinks Larry asked if the owner was in. The waitress pointed out Mr. Harold Logan. He was sitting at the bar talking to the bartender. Larry told Trish, that he would be right back. Her name was Trish Bonner. He told her he had to talk some business, with the owner. Larry sat next to Mr. Logan, and introduced himself.

He told Mr. Logan that he was the one that Glenn from the realtor's office talked to him about the sale of the restaurant. Glenn tells me you are asking $75,000. If the title is free and clear, and it checks out by the title company. I will make you an offer right now I will give you a check right now for $5000 in earnest money, contingent to a title search. My offer is $80,000 if you agree to stay for 30 days as manager. And teach me something of the restaurant business. If that is agreeable I'll write you a check right now, it was agreeable, so he wrote the check and the rest is to be paid in cash on closing.

Larry went back to his table and sat down. She said, "You said that you would be only gone for a few minutes. You were gone for 20 minutes." Then Larry said, "I guess it takes more than just a few minutes to buy a restaurant. You are now looking at the new owner of this restaurant." "Glenn said that you just bought a house today and now a restaurant. You must plan on staying here."

Within one week Larry was the owner of a house and a restaurant. In the next 30 days he found out that managing the restaurant was a lot of work. So we sat down with John, the head bartender, who knew the restaurant business pretty good. He made a deal with John. Find someone good to replace himself and he would be the new manager. Also if he improves the profits he would benefit by a percentage over and above his salary. And in the next few months the profits did increase and so did John's income.

Everybody was happy. And Larry was happy as an absentee owner. He enjoyed bringing girlfriends to dinner, at the Midville Bistro and bar. And being treated like the owner, which he was. He enjoyed his new life for a few years, then things changed.

Back in Washington, where the three traitorous criminals were incarcerated, things were not going too smoothly for the three of them. Tim O'Brien's case has been opened and all the documents in the case, were copied and organized. There was a listing of all the 16 ships, that were hijacked. The dates destinations and the number of crew on each ship.

The total number of men, lost on the 16 ships, was 384 sailors killed by the hijackers. This was all set up by five American traitors for profit.

This information, was finally doled out to the news media. Inside of a few days, the facts and the faces, of these three perpetrators, was known throughout the world. Tim O'Brien was not mentioned, being that he had a conscience and was the whistleblower. It was told to the media that there was one more culprit, as of now name and description was unknown.

Back in Midville, people heard the news about the traitors, and the 16 ships lost to the hijackers. The people in Midville, as in towns all over the country, were incensed by the news. They conjured up all kinds of ways to torture these traitors. Some of them would talk to Larry about this latest news, and what he thought. He tried to avoid the subject, but sometimes he had to agree, that hanging them by the balls was the way to go. They all said that they would love to have a go at this bastard still on the loose.

Larry decided that he had better get out of town. But where could he go? At least they had no idea who he was, or what the real Larry looked like. He had his money here, his house and restaurant and some new friends. Even though they just seem to like his money. A few weeks went by, and there was not any more news, about the hijackings or the traitors.

Then something very rare happened, without any fanfare or complaints by the ACLU. The three traitors were found guilty and hanged the very next day. There were pictures in newspapers, magazines, news reels, and television all over the world. What was shown was a massive scaffold strictly built for a special hanging. Three traitors *HANGING OUT TOGETHER*

When Larry saw the pictures of his former colleagues, swinging at the end of a rope. It almost blew his mind. But then he thought to himself. They don't know what I look like. It's still best to just play it cool, then they will never know. He decided that, he was safe in Midville.

Next the media, had gotten hold of the names of all the sailors that were lost, on all the 16 ships. A few of them were from Midville, and a few more from around the area. This really incensed the people but three of the traitors were already hung by the neck. The town was really rattled up, after finding out that some of the people from their town were amongst the victims.

Larry was pretty well shaken up by the list of names, it was not because of his conscience, because he didn't have one. He was just afraid of being found out, and paying the penalty. But he was starting to get nervous enough to plan a getaway, if it became necessary. He drew $35,000 out of four banks so he had a total of under $140,000 in the trunk of his convertible. He knew that he was just as safe here is any place. They had no name, or description of the person they were looking for.

He thought back about how smart he was, in changing his name and identification three different times. He was almost thinking of putting the money back in the banks. But he decided he would wait a little longer.

Then one day he picked up the newspaper. That he had delivered every day. On the front page was a picture of four people. One was Sergeant Johnson, two girls and himself. It wasn't too clear, because the photo was small. But on the second page was a large blowup of himself alone. It was a clearer picture and left no doubt that it was him. He very quickly got dressed. He opened the trunk and check to see if his money was still there. His mind was not thinking straight and he was not sure if he had taken the money back to the bank or not.

He had the money, so he got into the car and headed out of town. Jim Benton a Midville police officer, had read the paper this morning. He had also recognized the convertible that was heading out of town. Jim was off duty but he knew what his duty was. He went back into his house and he looked up Ben Richardson's phone number. He knew Ben would be home as it was Sunday morning. Ben had a brother who was on one of the 16 ships.

Ben called some other people that had relatives on the ships, then some that just wanted to get this bastard.

Jim Benton called some friends in the next town where Larry was heading. Six or seven guys got into their cars and pickup trucks and headed toward Midville. Halfway to Midville they blocked the road, with their cars and trucks.

By now there were five cars behind Larry. When he came up to the roadblock, he just got panicky and turned off the road into the woods.

The people familiar with the area knew he wouldn't get too far in the woods. He didn't, he got stuck in a ditch. The people chasing him knew where he would get stuck, so they didn't break their butt chasing him. Sure enough there was a convertible in a ditch with the trunk open. A few hundred feet in front of the car was Larry running and carrying a suitcase. Two of the chasers had Jeeps, and they had no problem crossing the ditch. There were three or four in each Jeep.

They followed him at a leisurely pace, and just kept him running, gradually he was slowing down and then he finally fell down. They picked him up and tied his hands together, and threw the rope over a tree branch . Then pulled it up tight.

Ben Richardson said, "I had a brother on one of those ships and the bastards killed him. Thanks to you and your friends."

"I had nothing to do, with anybody getting killed. Those other guys, the Admiral the General and the Colonel, did all of that. I just gave them the time, destinations and route. Tim O'Brien told them the value and what the cargo was and how many in the crew."

"Who put the hijackers into the crew?"

"That was Colonel Maxwell and Adm. Gordon. They made the big money. O' Brian and me were small potatoes. They said they were officers and deserve more. They made millions. Me and O' Brian we only got a few hundred thousand.

Bill Grant walked up to him, and said, "My favorite cousin was on one of those ships." And he punched him in the face and kicked him in the nuts.

Bill Olson walked up to him, slacked off the ropes and said, "I didn't know anybody on those ships. But if I did. This is what I would do." Now Bill was a big guy, and anything he would do would hurt. "He said I'm not going to punch you in the face, or kick you in the nuts, or punch you in the gut. I'M not going to punch you at all. This is what I'm going to do." He took the palms of his great big hands, and with both hands and a big swing from each side of Larry's head. He hit with both hands at the same time. It seemed like he crushed Larry' head. It must've felt like it. Then he tightened up the ropes again.

Ben Richardson said, "Enough of this personal stuff." They just let Larry hang with his hands in the air.

Then Larry said, "That's enough guys let me down, my arms are hurting."

Ben said, "You have hurt and killed a lot of people, now it's your turn to hurt."

Ben went to his truck and came back with a roll of 3/8 inch rope, a coat hanger, pliers, and some handcuffs.

Some of the others asked Ben what he was doing. He said, "Getting even with this rotten bastard. Go to my truck and bring my spade, a couple of stakes and the horseshoes in a wooden box."

Jim got the shovel and the stakes, and Bob Olson carried a whole box of horseshoes.

And then he said, "I got no idea what you plan on doing with these horseshoes, but knowing you, it must be something devious enough for our good buddy that we got hanging around. So I brought the whole box."

Ben took the shovel and dug down right next to a tree, a 20" x 20" hole 16 to 18 inches deep.

Two strong guys untied Larry who was hanging from the limb.

He stretched his arms and said, "Thanks guys I thought you're going to leave me there."

Bob Olson said, "No Larry old buddy we were not going to leave you there. We're going to leave you over there he pointed to the tree with a hole dug right next to it."

"You're not going to bury me there are you?"

"No Larry we are not going to bury you there. Ben plans to bury your nuts only."

And they laid him on the ground and Ben took a coat hanger and bent it almost tight around his balls, actually around the scrotum and then bent the wire down for about 5 inches and made a loop on the end. Then they put the cuffs on him behind his back. Next they tied him to the tree with the hole. His legs were spread, and his feet planted on the edge of the hole. Then they put the cuffs on his ankles and they staked him to the ground. "Like you said Larry the bastard should be hung, by his balls. So were going to almost, follow your advice, but we will hang your balls."

When Ben attached a wire to his testicles, he didn't bother to drop his pants. He just took a big old Bowie knife and cut out the crotch of his pants and shorts. Next Ben took a short length of 3/8 line and run it through the loop in the wire five or 6 inches below that he made a big loop with a bowline knot. Now the loop was hanging down about six inches above the hole.

Larry was screaming, saying how much it hurt. Ben said, "Not to worry Larry we will call the FBI to come and cut you down. You better hope that they get here pretty soon before we hang all the horse shoes."

"What horse shoes?"

Ben showed them to Larry, a whole Dozen in a wooden box. Ben hung one on the loop. They were Clydesdale shoes (big and Heavy). Larry screamed like hell. Ben said, "Don't worry there are only 11 more horse shoes. and the hole is only 16 inches deep. You will look like shit wearing a bathing suit." Ben told the rest of the people there that if they had any inclination, to go ahead and hang a shoe.

One of the guys from Midville, just happened to be a sign painter, and he had his Van here in the woods. Ben asks Jim Ferris, "If he had poster board, and paint."

He said, "He did."

Then Ben asked him to paint a sign, which said "This is the final culprit, of the five traitors, that caused the death of 384 American sailors. Do not have any sympathy, or try to release him. Or the two gentlemen leaning against the tree opposite this one will kick the shit out of you. And they will do it because they have had relatives killed. By this prick with the long balls. Go ahead and hang a horseshoe".

The FBI will be here to pick him up in a few hours. When the FBI arrived late in the afternoon, which was five hours from the time Larry was tied to the tree. they read the sign and then noticed that the horseshoe box was empty and the horseshoes were at the bottom of the hole. There were four FBI agents, and they all agreed that he would be convicted. And hung like the other three. Except that he had a head start. He was part hung already. In a very short time he was convicted. He tried to complain to the ACLU about his extremely low hanging balls, he said that he had already been Hung Once, again would be double jeopardy. The ACLU said that they wanted nothing to do with this case.

Chapter 22

Presidential Citation.

With the criminals all taken care of, we have spent a lot of enjoyable time on Beaver Island. Every one of the crew and the martial arts people received official commendations and a medal from the President.

The President flew to Beaver Island for the official ceremony. They flew to the island in 3PBY Catalinas and landed in the harbor with 4 P51's flying cover overhead. Art threw one of the greatest fish boils, of his life. The president told him that any time he wants to come to Washington; he would appreciate a great Washington fish boil.

Adm. Leslie Ryan, a three-star admiral, Doc's good friend on the Naval staff, was part of the presidential party. Adm. Ryan congratulated Doc on a job well done and said it was great seeing Doc again. He said that the president wished to take off at three p.m. because it was a two hour flight to Midway Airport in Chicago. The presidential plane is waiting for him at Midway and he felt that he must get back to Washington.

Everybody stood on the dock, as the three Catalinas fired up their engines. Just then 4 P 51 Mustangs flew overhead in formation. Then the Catalina's made their take off run, all three of them lifted off at the same time.

Doc then said, "Party time is over I think we should get under way."

Art said, "I brought up the sea sled. You can put her aboard , you might find a use for it." Eric said, "When I need a sled, I can very easily build one."

Doc is invited the martial arts class to go with them for a short cruise to Mackinac Island and have a nice lunch at the hotel. And then a sail back to Sturgeon Bay. Art told them that a visit and a lunch at Mackinac Island is something not to be missed. And one other thing, is going under the Mackinac Bridge

One of the martial arts people, asked if the mast on the schooner will fit under the bridge. Or do they open the bridge.

Angel then said, "They will have to open the bridge, if we call ahead on the radio."

Doc said, "We can have a final dinner on board, and then hoist anchor in the morning at 8 AM."

All of Jacky's friends and Art and Linda, came aboard. Mario outdid himself with the help of Eric. Who was becoming one hell of a cook.

He said, "He enjoyed helping Mario And he learned a lot from him."

After dinner, Doc proposed a toast to Jacky and her class. Doc said, "We couldn't have succeeded without them."

Then he thanked Art and Linda, for the hospitality. Linda got up and said, "It's more like we should thank you. I now don't have to worry about Art diving in the lake anymore, looking for those logs. He has been diving for them for the last two or three years. Now that he knows where they are. He can bring in a lumber company with the right equipment to lift them out of the water and haul them away."

After that Art said, "Doc let's have one night cap. And then I'm going to take Linda home." And that's what they did. They got into their Chris-Craft and headed for their dock. As they were leaving Art said, "We will be watching you from the dock as you sail away. He said goodbye to the crew and then said, good luck to you Admiral."

Next morning after breakfast. Doc asked Angel, "If everything was shipshape and ready to get underway"

Angel said, "Everything is shipshape, and all set to go."

Then Doc said, "Angel lets show them, how a real sailing man takes his ship out of the harbor."

Angel's face shines with a great big smile on his face, And said I'll set a course of 80° to the Straits of Mackinac.

Doc issued orders for individual duties. Arch is to handle the running back stays. (All forward and aft support of the masts are stays.) When the main boom extends over the stern. The boom must clear the stays. When on port tack the starboard Main back stay must be dropped to clear the boom. At the same time the port back stay must be tightened up and locked in place. This is a lot of work so Doc had a mold maker design and build what he called lever jacks. It was a lock over Center device, that was 18 inches long but when released in the open position it gave about 36 inches of slack to the back stay. Now the opposite is done on the starboard tack

Now that you know what a running back stay is, that is Arch's job while they are tacking the ship. Plus he has to trim the sheet on the main. Eric's job is to trim the mizzen sail and the mizzen stay sail. Juan and Mario handle all the fore sails, and the anchor.

And Doc stood near Angel with a megaphone. Doc called to raise all sails. With all sails up but not sheeted in they just fluttered like a weathervane.

Art tells Linda, "Doc is Capt. But he relies on Angel as an expert helmsman. If Doc gave orders to Angel, and then to the crew, time is wasted for Angel to react. The way Doc works it. Angel gives maneuvering orders to Doc, and Doc relays that order to the crew. Meanwhile Angel has already got his rudder where he wants it.

Now he tells Linda as he sees the blue smoke come out of the diesel exhaust, "Notice the exhaust smoke. Doc always starts his diesel strictly in the case of emergency. But he won't go out of the harbor under power."

Now he tells Linda to watch and you will see some real sailing. Angel said, "Up anchor." Doc repeats this in his powered megaphone. As the ship moves forward over the anchor, Angel said, " Back the fore sail." Mario pushes the fore sail boom to the port side and into the wind. The bow starts turning to the starboard.

The harbor was rectangular. The mouth was on the east end. The depth of the harbor, was about one and a half miles to the west. The width of the harbor was a little over a half a mile. The wind was to the north east, at 15 to 20 knots. Now Angels intention, was to sail up to the north side of the harbor under full sail, come about at the West end on the starboard tack on a broad reach, **s**ail right by Arts dock with a good heel and all sails full.

After Mario backed the Foresail the ship swung to starboard, he eased out the sails for them to go on a beam reach toward the West end of the harbor (beam reach is where the wind is on the beam). When they got to the West end, Angel said, "Ready about." And he swung the ship to port. Arch unlatches his port back stay. Then quickly locks the starboard stay. Coming about worked fast and smoothly. They lost very little headway in the maneuver, and one quarter of a mile ahead on the south bank of the harbor was Arts dock. Everyone was trimming sails to get up the best speed, as they passed Arts dock. When they passed the dock, they were only 20 feet away, at full sail, and making 10 to 12 knots, with an eighty nine foot sailing ship.

Everybody waved but Admiral Hunter, General Hobson, General Turner and Sergeant Jacky Sax saluted. Then they sailed right on out of the harbor.

Art said to Linda, "That's one hell of a job of seamanship, after reversing direction in a tight harbor under full sail, then passing by our dock with his hull only 15 to 20 feet away, heeled over with all sails pulling. Linda, that is what I call great seamanship and that's why Doc has complete faith in Angel. He really feels that he is "an Angel on the helm."

Then Linda said, "She had been talking to Jacky, and Jacky said that they have a messenger from "God" aboard."

Art said "I believe it."

And they are now underway on a course of 80,° and heading for the Straits of Mackinac. Angel is in his glory, he loves being at the helm of a big beautiful Schooner like this one. He said. "She may be a big ship, but she handles like a 20 foot day sailer."

Doc told Angel, "That he did a fantastic job, of exiting the harbor. And he asked Angel if he wanted to be relieved at the helm?"

He said, "No I'm relaxed here. Arch said he would relieve me for a piss call."

Just then the five guys from Jacky's group came back to the helm. Bob the one that had asked Angel about going under the bridge, asked if he had radioed ahead about opening the bridge. Angel said, "They were about 3 1/2 hours from the bridge. When we get it in sight we will give them a call."

A little more than three hours later they saw the bridge. It was about 2 miles away. Jacky and her group were back by Angel now, so was Arch And Eric. They waited a little while, and now they were within a mile. "Bob asked Angel if they had radioed, the bridge tender yet."

Doc walked up to the group, and said, "He had just talked to the bridge tender. He said that he would open when we got there. Doc then said everyone stay back here by the helm and you will get a better view of the bridge. They were now 100 yards from the bridge, With all sails pulling like hell. Bob said, "It's not open yet."

Angel said, "Don't worry they always cut it close."

Now within 100 feet, and Bob said, "It's not open. We're going to hit the bridge."

Angel said, "Oh Shit! Hit the deck! Part of the masts are coming down, everybody hit the deck and cover Your heads and stay there, until I tell you to come up."

They came out on the other side of the bridge, Angel and Doc just stood there with a big smile on their faces. Then Doc said looking up from the stern of the vessel. "It seems like she would not fit, Cora Lee's main is 108 feet above the water and the bridge is 180 feet.

Doc said, "You were not the first ones to get sucked in on that one. Welcome to the Mackinac Bridge." They all laughed, and one of them said, "What's next?"

Doc said, "I'm getting hungry and I think we should have some lunch."

Eric said "Mario claims that he is taking the day off from the galley. Mario said he ain't Cooking and that means we had better find another lunch wagon or starve. Also Mario said for everybody to stay out of his galley."

Doc Said, "I guess we starve, unless Angel knows the way to grand Hotel."

Angel laughed and said, "Sure do Admiral." Angel always called Doc Admiral when he was happy about one of Docs orders. Angel said, "We will be anchored off Mackinac Island within the hour."

Doc said, "Okay Angel then we can do lunch at the grand Hotel. There will also be a couple of surprise friends waiting to greet Arch."

They dropped anchor on the south end of the island. They had 18 people to go ashore in the 19 foot launch, so Juan made two trips. They got together on the long pier, Juan and Angel tied up the launch. They walked up to the grand Hotel and up on the large front porch. Doc walked up first.

There were five people sitting at a large table sipping drinks. Doc headed over towards the table, one person got up and walked toward Doc. They shook hands and then Doc started to introduce everyone. When he got to Arch, Ken said, "We all know this guy. It just seems that things happen when this guy is around."

Then he introduced Ed and Linda Foley. Ed said, "You look great, Arch!" Then Linda said "You're the best thing that ever happened to us." And then Dave's uncle coming to Fayetteville. But we can let Dave tell you about that later. Then Dave Steele shook Archie's hand and said, "It is great to see you again, and Eric. I will probably see you in Chicago in another week or so."

Arch said, "By the way how in the hell, did you know that we would be here?"

Believe it or not Arch, "You and Adm. Hunter's crew are not the hardest people in the world to find. It's not too often that the president flies 600 miles to pin medals and citations on 18 people. By the way the sailors and marines involved also got citations, but not personally by the president.

Bill came over and said, "Hi Dave, how's it going?"

Fine Bill and I hear "You had your share of excitement."

"Right Dave enough to last for a while."

When Bill walked away Dave said, "Did you know Bill was a Maj. Gen. in the RAF. I found that out a short time ago, and Doc still is a three-star admiral".

Ken Jamieson said, "Okay all you people let's go inside and have a first-class lunch courtesy of the management of the grand Hotel." They went inside and were escorted into the main dining room. They were seated in a VIP area. The manager picked up a microphone and asked for everybody's attention. He said folks I just wanted you to know that this afternoon you'll have the privilege to be lunching with 18 of the people who were instrumental in the capture of the American traitors who were hanged recently.

The FBI had been looking for those traitors for three or four years. And these people made it happen. Okay people let's give them a big hand ,and then get back to lunch which they did.

After lunch Jacky's class, got together and took buggy rides around the island.

Then Doc and Bill had been talking to Jacky out on the veranda. Eric and Arch were talking to Ed Foley and Linda. Dave Steele walked up and said, "I have not been able to spend a nickel, since I've been on this island. It's time for me to buy a round of drinks at the bar. They all sat at a large table, and everyone ordered. After all eight of them ordered. Angel and Juan and Mario walked in. Dave said to include those three guys also." Dave handed the waiter his American Express card.

The head bartender walked over, took the card away from the waiter, and handed it back to Dave. The bartender said, "Sorry, we can't take your money". Arch and Ed Foley both stood up at the same time. Both thinking discrimination, because Dave was black, then Ed Foley said, "And why not?" The bartender got the idea of what they were thinking and said, "I have my orders from the management, to discriminate. Actually to discriminate against all of you people. Your money is no good here. You are guests of the management."

"We are not even allowed to accept tips. The management said they will reimburse all waiters and waitresses for tips, that they probably would have received. So enjoy yourself, it's all on the house."

Jacky's class told everybody, that they had a very interesting tour of the Island.

Bob was the first to talk, he said, "Back in the 1600s the Island was an Indian burial ground, its name was Michilimacinac. He wrote it down so he could remember."

Then Tim Christopher said, "The building which is open and now a museum, was old Fort Mackinac and later the Astor House, the headquarters for John Jacob Astor's trading company back in 1783. The building that we are in, which is The Grand Hotel, was built in 1887 and is still going strong."

Doc Stood up and said, "This was the fourth time that he had been to this island. I learned more about it in the last 15 minutes, then in all the other times that I've been here. I think that we would all like to thank our gracious hosts. The management and employees for their hospitality. I have informed the management that we intend to hoist anchor at about 6:30 this evening. For two reasons first we have a nice 15 knot wind coming out in the Northeast, which will make beautiful sailing to Sturgeon Bay, next it will be perfect timing to see a beautiful sunset under the Mackinac Bridge.

The management said, they would have a nice early dinner ready for us at 4 PM. Doc said at this time I would like to invite our friends, who came all the way up here to greet us, to a nice leisurely sail, to Chicago. This would be Ed Foley, Linda Foley, Dave Steele, Willy Baker , Ken Jamieson, Peter Chen and Jacky Sax.

They had a great dinner, in the main dining room. After they were through and had some after dinner drinks. The manager came into the room and greeted everyone. He then told of the exploits of the crew of the Cora Lee. And a martial arts class. He said all these people performed a great service to their country.

Jacky Sax then got up and spoke. "What you have said I know is appreciated ,by all. But there are two people who are not here, but back on Beaver Island. That is my former boss and friend, Brigadier General Art Hobson of the British commandos and his wife Linda, who now reside on

Beaver Island." After a final toasting cheers by the other diners, they all headed for the pier.

Juan already had the engine started on the launch. They now had 23 people to go out to the Schooner. He made two trips with no problem. They had a lot of extra help to hoist the sails. Now before they raised the anchor, Bill showed all the non- sailors to safe areas where they would not get hit by swinging booms or tangled in lines on the deck. With Everybody in place, Mario hoisted the anchor. When the anchor was off the bottom, Juan backed the fore sail. The bow swung with the wind. Sail trimmers took up on the sheets and all sails filled. The ship heeled over in Cora Lee came alive.

There was a nice 10/12 knot breeze, it was perfect sailing. On the starboard tack with the wind off the starboard quarter. Unless the wind changes, they wouldn't have to change tack all the way to Washington Island. The island is at the tip of door County peninsula. And then we change to a port tack, and go right down into Green Bay. Once into Green Bay they would head south to Sturgeon Bay. Green bay is formed by the East shore of Wisconsin. The bay itself is by the north pointing peninsula of Door County. They were on a long starboard tack. Probably 11 or 12 hours to reach Washington Island. While most of the Martial Arts class were down below playing cards, and some catching sack time.

Bill and Doc were in Docs Cabin working out next week's plans. Angel and Juan were spelling each other on the wheel. Arch and Eric were in the cockpit talking with Jacky and having a nice relaxing cocktail. It was a beautiful summer evening. They just sat and talked about what they were going to do when they get to Chicago. Jacky wanted to go to the Art Institute, and the aquarium and the Field Museum. She said that going to the Art Institute by herself is what she had planned. To the Field Museum and the Aquarium ,she would like some company. When I'm looking at artwork I may spend a lot of time looking at one picture and anyone else would become bored. So I go alone.

She turned to Eric and said you and Arch were going to visit your father were you not. I telephoned him from Mackinac and told them that we would only stay a couple days and then go back to the Cora Lee. Peter Chen, Willie Baker and Dave Steele came on deck and sat down at the cockpit table. They said they had been down below scarfing up Mario's appetizers.

They started to get up and go for appetizers, when Dave said you can sit back down because Mario is bringing some up to the cockpit. Mario stepped up to the table and set the tray down. "He looked at Jacky and said I'm only bringing these appetizers up here, because I can't resist beautiful redheads."

Angel who was now sitting at the table said "You can't resist any female."

"Does that make me stupid Angel?"

"No but you got to learn to share."

"Don't worry Angel, Mario doesn't have a share of this redhead."

"You mean I got a chance?"

"A damn slim one Angel, I don't go out with sailors."

Eric popped up with, "That's because sailors probably just can't follow Jacky's rules."

Arch said, "And that's not the least bit safe."

"You guys make me sound like an ogre."

"Well Jacky you're best looking ogre I've ever seen", was Eric's comment.

Just then and Foley and Linda came into the cockpit followed by Ken Jamieson. Ken looked at the group and said "Looks like the gang's all here. He looked again and corrected himself except Bill and Doc."

Foley asked how he knew Doc? He told Foley that Doc had a high class restaurant in New York. And as you know. I have been in the restaurant consulting business for a long time. Doc had been a Captain in the Navy before the restaurant. He resigned from the Navy and bought a restaurant. As a consultant I worked with Doc and he wound up with one of the hottest restaurants in New York.

"When the war started, they called him back as an Admiral. He sold the restaurant to two of his best employees for $400,000. They could only raise $12,000 he took their promissory note for $388,000. And went off to war. That's how I met Doc."

Foley said, "I had never met up Doc before Mackinac Island. It seems that he has had an interesting life. Come to think of it most of the people on this ship have had interesting lives."

"Actually the first time I met Arch and Dave, I got the shit kicked out of me. And damn near poisoned, all inside of half an hour."

"Then Linda spoke up and looked at Arch and Dave. Best thing that ever happened to him."

"You're right Linda. It's hard to admit that getting the shit kicked out of you, was a good thing. But it really was."

Then Ken said, "That day was the start, of your road to success."

"Then that day changed me and our lives. When Arch and Dave first walked in and I refused to serve Dave because he was black. That was the way of my life back then. Now we welcome everybody and more than half of my customers are black and most of my employees are black, we now own three great restaurants and the managers of two of them are black."

"We have a sign at the entrance of each restaurant. In large letters that said. If you are inclined to be a bigot. Check your mouth at the front door, or you will be removed. In each of the restaurants , I hire two waiters with muscles. I pay them extra to pull double duty, they are waiters first and bouncers second. If anyone uses foul language loudly or insults a waitress, black or white and professes his bigotry.

He is asked once to be quiet, and if he refuses, a waitress packs up the remainder of his dinner as a carryout. And two bouncers pick him up and carry him out the door. A waitress hands him the carryout, and said never come back again.

When the two bouncers and the waitresses come back in, they usually get a big hand from the customers. Now that is a far cry from the restaurant I used to run before Arch and Dave. I wouldn't advise everybody to go out and get the shit kicked out of themselves. But it worked for me."

"Ken then said strange things seem to follow Arch. First Foley's Restaurant. Then a rainstorm led him to Bens Bar, and he came out of that one as a messenger from God. And it doesn't stop there. Jacky tell them what happened in Hannibal.

"Basically my partner and I were trying to raise money to buy a motorcycle shop. We needed $15,000 final payment within two days. Then along came Arch. He didn't just come along he just flipped onto the scene. Arch decided to lay down in a ditch, and have his pocket picked. I just came along, and very gently apprehended the culprit and I got Arch's wallet back. The culprits in jail and some appreciative people sent me $18,000. Just in time to make a $15,000 final payment for the cycle shop. My partner and I both agreed. That Arch showing up at that time was no accident. One day later, someone else would have owned that shop. Then from Ben's Bar in Hoggsville, they said it was a "Messenger from God" Jimbo and I decided Ben was right."

Arch spoke up then. He said, "Jacky you know that's bull shit."

"If its bull Arch how come you always show up, when there's a problem. What about you and Eric in Lemont Illinois where you two guys rescued the girls. And took care of the perverts I liked the way you took care of them. And carved up their Chests with what they were. Arch said that's right ,you gave me the idea to carve up the creeps, that raped the girls."

They finally came up on Washington Island and changed to a port tack. It was about 50 miles down to Sturgeon Bay. Green Bay was a nice quiet sail on a port tack. They pulled in to Sturgeon Bay Harbor and dropped anchor. Once the boat was secured they headed in to Sturgeon Bay. They headed to Jim Shaw's Sturgeon Bay seafood house. Ken said it was the greatest seafood house in Wisconsin.

They walked into the restaurant, and were greeted like heroes. Jacky's crew of martial arts people were special heroes, because they were from Sturgeon Bay. They were home town heroes. The owner said he was proud to have the crew of Cora Lee, in his restaurant. And that it was amazing what they had done. He said anything they want is on the house.

Jacky said, "If this feeding us keeps up. I'm going to go on a diet."

Doc said, "Jacky wait till we get to the Chicago Yacht Club. They know we are coming and they intend to outdo anyone else." The Mayor of Sturgeon Bay made a speech about how honored they were for this famous group having dinner in this restaurant in Sturgeon Bay. This was during the appetizer. Mario said the appetizers are good but the chef blew the Calamari. Hey Mario it's a freebie so quit bitching whispered Angel. I ain't Bitchin, I just made a comment. Okay so shut up.

This soup which was shrimp and abalone. Everybody that had the soup said it was fantastic. Those that had the salad said the Roquefort and a crab dressing was to die for. Also Frank Sinatra, the singer did a few songs which were great. Then this three-piece group played ,Sweet Caroline and Sinatra Drew Jacky, up and danced the whole song with her. It had turned out that Jacky was a real Sinatra fan. After his gig was over he came back and asked Jacky to have a drink with him and some of his friends. He introduced her to some other people in his touring group.

Jacky was flying high for the next few days, especially after he invited her to be his guest at a local club, where he was doing a show. Doc said that they would wait to set sail till Jacky had a chance to go to the Sinatra show which wasn't for two days. Even though they planned on leaving the next day. Everyone agreed that they could find plenty to do around Sturgeon Bay.

Jacky did go to see Frankie at the club. It did take a few days for her to come down out of the clouds. They had hoisted anchor, fired up the diesels and motored through the Sturgeon Bay channel and out onto Lake Michigan. The weather was beautiful and Chicago was 230 miles to the south. They were running before the wind on a port tack on a course of 170°.Doc talked with Angel and they decided to run up the Queen fisherman.

It was smaller than the King fisherman and not quite is hard to handle with a steady breeze of 15 knots. After they got the fisherman up and set. It was a pretty sight and they were making about 13 knots. It must've been a beautiful sight, because as we passed three different sailboats they had cameras out taking pictures. It was about 2 PM when they left the channel and had hoisted sail. Angel figured that we would arrive in Grant Park Harbor at about 10 AM on a Saturday morning.

Eric Arch and Peter and Jacky, got together with Bill Turner on the Fore deck. They wanted to discuss what was going to happen, when they got to Chicago. "Bill said I know what is going to happen when we first get to Chicago. But after that I'm not exactly sure. Doc isn't sure either. But he said he will know, by the end of next week. He is waiting for answers from Washington. and commando headquarters, in England.

Until then Doc said have fun. He said you four are on salary from the government. We don't know yet ,who you are working for. Or what your monthly salary shall be, but each of you have an account, to draw from in the first national Bank of New Jersey. I will get your account numbers in a few days."

"Each of you presently have $30,000 in an account. So don't spend it too fast because as of now I don't know what your salary shall be. Each person in the martial arts class ,that assisted on beaver Island. Will receive $5000 for assistance in an unspecified government project. Art will receive some very profitable orders from Washington for his fishing business. So all people that have been involved are covered. We will be in Chicago tomorrow morning. So enjoy a nice relaxing sail. Mario is preparing his famous end of voyage dinner, so don't snack too much and ruin your appetite."

Mario out did himself. Now after Martial Artist class was gone, there were only 12 people on board. He had two large turkeys that he had thawing out in the refrigerator for the last six days.

He served his calamari appetizers. Angel told Mario, "That he was right, Mario's calamari was much better than at Jim Shaw's restaurant."

Mario shook hands with Angel ,and said, "All is forgiven."

He then had side dishes like artichokes, green beans, candied sweet potatoes and mashed potatoes and gravy. On the meat side first he served medallions of pork tenderloin and beef tenderloin.

Then came the pan fried turkey. Mario disassembled the turkey while raw. Took the breasts and wrapped them tightly with Saran. Did the same with some of the thigh meat. Then he put the breast and thighs in the freezer for an hour. When he took them out they were semi-frozen. Now they were stiff enough to cut them all into three-quarter inch steaks. He dry marinated them in garlic powder and Italian seasoning. Then with a light dusting of flour he dropped them into a couple of hot pans with olive oil till nice and brown on the surface and not overdone. Mario did not tell anyone what the steaks were. They all agreed that it was some of the tastiest pork they had ever eaten.

Next Mario brought out the other turkey, it was a 26 pound turkey. Which Mario said was cooked in the microwave oven.

Eric said, "No way Mario, hell that won't fit into the microwave oven."

With that Mario picked up the turkey on a platter and said, "Eric come with me." He showed him that it just barely fit Eric came back and said it fit.

And Foley asked Mario, where he got the microwave oven. "I never heard of any company making microwave ovens, for the consumer market."

Mario said, "He had a friend in the Army, who works on radar installations. He cobbled up this one just for me, and it works good." Mario set their turkey down on the table. Doc picked up a big carving knife, and said, "I'll carve the Bird." " No you won't Doc." Mario told Doc, that he didn't know how to carve a turkey.

"It wouldn't be the first turkey, I have carved."

"But Doc have you ever learned how to carve a turkey properly? You hired me as your Chef and said that I was a good one. So now pay attention and I will show you how to carve a turkey." Mario then took a big, 10 inch fillet knife. And carved off both breasts with just a few strokes. Then he took a Chef knife and cut 3/8 inch thick slices cross wise of the breast. They all said that was the most tender, and juicy turkey they have ever had.

After dinner Doc said, "Mario, you really outdid yourself. You really deserve a big raise in pay, But you're not getting get one."

Then Doc said, "I've got to admit one thing Mario. You do know how to carve a turkey."

They all went out to the cockpit and had a nightcap and one by one drifted off to get some sack time, as it was now about 11 PM.

It was a beautiful starry night. Lake Michigan was being a perfectly docile lady. Tonight it was smooth sailing, at other times Lake Michigan can be a real bitch. Juan was on the wheel. Angel was in the cockpit having a cup of coffee and waiting for his trick at the helm. Angel will take the helm at midnight. They were now on a port tack and at midnight, they will be 50 miles directly east of Milwaukee and 90 miles from Chicago. At midnight Angel will take the wheel and change course from 170° to 200°.

When Angel took the helm and changed course, the wind was now directly off their stern and they were running free.

Angel called Juan back to the helm they discussed the wind for a short time. Angel said, "Juan let's go wing and wing . I'll get her sailing straight up. You ease the main boom out on the starboard side. And then ease the mizzen boom out on the port side. The wind was down to 12 knots but they were still making 11 knots. With the wind off their stern, the main off the starboard and the Mizzen on the port. They were now sailing like a Square Rigged Ship, doing a pretty good job of it, sailing Wing and Wing."

They had approximately 40 miles to go to Chicago, at about 8 AM. The wind held at 12 knots, until they were about 15 miles from Chicago. It was still a steady wind but it was down to 8 kn. Sails were full. It started to get a slight fog with about 1 mile visibility. Doc had radioed ahead to the harbor master. To make sure that no one was on the Cora Lees can (mooring buoy). The harbor master radioed back and said it was clear. When the harbor master knows that a boat will be gone for a while he may give permission for a transient boat to use it.

They were about one and a half miles east of the mouth of Grant Park Harbor, when Angel got the sail handling crew to look alive. Angel turned to port just long enough to bring the main boom amidships. Angel turned starboard and let the boom out on the port side now they were on a starboard tack and heading straight for the mouth of the harbor at 240°. At this time the big speakers up in the rigging started playing music very loudly it could be heard for at least a couple of miles.

It sounded beautiful. It was "Amazing Grace" and it even looked more beautiful, as the big white schooner was coming home, in out of the fog. It was flying all sails including the Queen fisherman above the masts. It was a beautiful sight. People all around the harbor watched in awe as Angel maneuvered his ship around behind his mooring buoy. He did not drop the big old fisherman until he was ready to come up wind, to the Can. Juan picked up the pennant and pulled out the mooring line. Angel calculated it perfect as the big ship's bow stopped right at the Can.

Angel said, "A good sailor, never starts an engine to bring his ship home to its mooring." When the Cora Lee was dead stopped at its mooring, many people in the harbor knew of the crew on board the Cora Lee, so they sounded their horns saying "Welcome Home."

It was a great feeling for Doc, to be back on his mooring in his home port . By the time everybody got *Cora Lee*, all shipshape with all sail covers on, it was noon. Then by the time everybody was all cleaned up and changed into their going ashore clothes, it was 1 PM.

Doc said, "Let's go to lunch."

Eric asked, "Where?"

"We have been invited, to the Chicago Yacht Club."

Juan asked, "Should I lower the launch."

Doc said no Juan. "Call the service boat, then we don't have to leave our launch tied up at the clubs pier."

Juan blasted a signal on the horn for the service boat. The service boat picked them up, and brought them to the Chicago Yacht Club. The Columbia Yacht Club, offered VIP treatment for Cora Lees crew. Doc told them that he appreciated it but he was a member of the Chicago Yacht club.

As they walked in the door, they were greeted by cheers from the members. The crew was getting a little tired of all this hero worship, but they had to go along with it. They sat down and the waitresses just materialized and took their drink orders.

The Commodore of the Yacht Club stepped up and made a few comments on how pleased they were, to have this famous crew dining in their club.

Then he said that they had a guest speaker who was the clerk of Cook County. And the man who would probably be the new mayor of Chicago, Richard J. Daley.

After a few words of greeting. He said, "I may not be the mayor of Chicago yet, but I can offer you a key to Cook County, in which Chicago is located. It is my privilege to address you this afternoon. I ain't no great speaker, and you are probably tired of speeches by now anyway, so I say let's do something besides talk. From what I see and hear, there are seven of you here that served our country on Beaver Island and served it well. There are also two of your leaders who we will take care of later. Right now what we will do, is in the wish book of the enlisted personnel."

Chapter 23

Jacky Captures Rapists.

"While you are here in Chicago, what would you like to do?"

Juan and Angel, both said, "They would like to go to New York, and see the play South Pacific."

Daley replied that, "New York ain't in Chicago. But Midway Airport is, so you two are off to New York."

Mario stood up and said, "As long as they are going to New York I'd like to go with, and try some of their famous restaurants."

Daley said, "You're Mario The Chef, are you not? And a pretty good one I hear. Would you like to see South Pacific also?"

"Sounds good to me."

"And your two buddies, probably would like some good food too. Yes sir I train them on how to eat good food."

"We got that settled," said Daley. "Except this is the way we will do it. I will arrange for five of the best restaurants in New York to send you their menus, and their choice of their best dishes and then their way of preparation. Now you as a chef, will decide which restaurant you will go to. Then when you get back to Chicago, we will do the same thing here. Five more restaurants. After your Chicago dinner, then it is up to you as a chef, to decide which city has the best restaurants."

Daley said, "Who else has a wish?"

Peter Chen said, "I have a wish. I lived and worked on a farm in China. We did not have farm equipment like you have in America. I read about John Deere and International Harvester, so I would like to go to Moline, Illinois and I think Davenport, Iowa. I would like to visit these companies to see this machinery."

Daley said, "Nice wish, but it seems like everybody wants to just get out of Chicago."

Jacky got up and said, "I want to see many things in Chicago."

"Now there is a smart girl, and a beautiful one, I might add."

Jacky blushed and said, "There are so many interesting things in Chicago, the Art Institute, the Aquarium, your Planetarium and there are great museums.

"I see that your name is Jacky. So Jacky you shall see Chicago. Unless you have an objection, I will assign to you a personal tour guide and a limousine so you can see Chicago in the best way, also taste our good food."

Daley pointed to Arch and said, "Your name is Arch, right?"

"That's right, I'm Arch."

My question is this Arch, "Do you have a wish?"

"I have a wish, but I don't think you can solve it."

"Try me Arch, then we will decide.

Okay Mr. Daley, "But I don't think you can do anything."

"I can't until you tell me what it is."

"Well it's like this. It's about my cousin Danny. Danny Sutton is 22 years old. When he was 18, he and three other guys got drunk. They Stole a car and went joy riding in a Rolls-Royce, drank more and got drunker. Then they crashed the car through the front door of a large department store. Luckily it was 2 AM, so nobody was hurt. They drove their car down a main stairway to the lower floor. This was where jewelry and watch showcases were. They smashed many cases in trying to turn around to drive back up the staircase. When they got to the top the police were there and that was the end of that joyride."

"Well at least, they went first class in a Rolls-Royce."

"The store owner pressed charges and the Rolls owner also pressed charges. The three guys involved had long rap sheets. Danny had never even been arrested for so much as a parking ticket, but they all got the same sentence, 15 years, because of their rap sheets and Danny had none."

Daley said, "Where is he?"

"Joliet Penitentiary."

"Arch get me the name of his lawyer and any information on the case. Come to my office tomorrow, we will talk about it.

One of the club members stood up and said, "I am Justice Stanley M. Hitzman of the Court of Appeals of Cook County. I am familiar with this case and the judge that presided in the case. He is a good judge, and justice has been served, so you should not interfere with his ruling."

"Judge Stanley M. Hitzman! I have a few things to say to you. First, never tell me what I can or can't do. You may be a Cook County Judge. But I'm the Clerk of Cook County, I don't take any crap from a judge. I am also a lawyer and a good one, so stay out of my way. Just so you remember the name. It is Richard J. Daley. If you put it in your notes, make sure that you spell it right."

"Okay so much for that. Arch can you make it to my office at 2 PM? If the presiding judge is still on the bench, I don't think he should be. The second thing is this, it is a fair request from one of our true heroes who has left a trail of good deeds. He has been called a Messenger from God, so I don't think that any elected judge would want to be known as the one who denied a request from God's Messenger. Where do you stand now Judge Stanley M. Hitzman?"

The judge said, "No comment."

"Okay Arch see you at 2 PM."

"Well now that is taken care of, there is one more person on this wish list. That is Eric. Do you have a wish for Chicago, to grant to you?"

"Yes, I do, Mr. Daley, or can I call you Mayor Daley?"

"It's a little premature, but for you it is okay."

"Well, Your Honor."

"I think you're sucking up to me, but that's okay. Now tell me your wish."

"It is like this sir, I would like to see the same things that Jacky wants to see. I would like to accompany her, on her tour of the museums. I know Jacky wants to spend time in the Art Institute by herself, because she is an artist."

Daley said, "Jacky would you like Eric to accompany you after, the Art Institute?"

She said, "I would love his company."

"Okay Eric go visit your dad for a couple of days. Then come back and see Chicago with this beautiful redhead. I will have one of Cook County's Deputy sheriffs to act as a tour guide. When you return from your dad's place, where ever you decide to eat lunch or dinner, just call my office and one of my girls will take care of the reservations and the charges."

Next day, Tom Atkins picked up Jacky, in a city furnished limo. He took her to the Art Institute. She had her sketchpad and charcoal pencils with her.

She said, "Tom, why don't you go and have a beer or something. I'll meet you out in front on the steps in about three hours, which would be about 1 PM. If you hang around with me in an art gallery, you'll be bored silly. People can't understand how I can look at one picture for half an hour. See you at one and then we can go to lunch."

When Eric got home, his dad was really glad to see him. He said, "Son I'm really glad to see you, and I would like to spend more time with you, but I thought you were going to England. I've got a flight out of Midway at noon tomorrow. I hadn't got around to telling you, I've got a new girlfriend and we are going to Antigua for a week."

Eric said, "I got a limo coming to pick me up, tomorrow at noon, so I have to go anyway."

"Well we have this evening anyway, you can tell me more about Beaver Island. It seems that trouble finds you guys were ever you go."

"Yeah but Dad, it always seem to work out that way."

Meanwhile back in the city, Jacky met Tom on the steps of the Institute. He then took her to Bergdorf's for lunch. They both agreed that they ate too much, but would feel better if they walked it off. Jacky said, "Why don't you do that Tom. I want to go back to the Institute, for the rest of the afternoon."

This time when Tom picked her up on the steps it was 6:30 PM, Jacky said, "I am still not hungry, but I could go for a cup of coffee and a doughnut".

Tom said, "Okay, I know a good place for that."

Jacky said, "Cops always know where the coffee and donuts are."

"You're right Jacky, it's part of our training."

They went south on Michigan Avenue to Roosevelt Road, a right turn and there it was. A coffee and hamburger joint, called Bill's Burgers. They went in and sat in a booth and ordered coffee, both ordered cheeseburgers and fries.

"I thought we were going on a diet, after Bergdorf's."

Maybe tomorrow, but not today. They noticed three drunken muscle bound characters that came in, the one of them with a crew cut, looked long and hard at Jacky. He rolled his tongue around his lips and then he grabbed his crotch. Tom was facing the other way so he didn't see any of this. But Jacky did, she ignored them.

They sat down in a booth next to Tom and Jacky's. They weren't paying any attention to the drunks, but the drunks were listening to everything Tom and Jacky were saying.

Jacky said that she wanted to sketch the Chicago skyline, as the sun was setting.

Tom said, "He knew the perfect place for that. On the north side of the Planetarium. It would be quiet there and a good view of the downtown skyline. We could park on Solidarity drive. It's a short walk to where you want to sketch."

"Sounds great let's go."

Rick, who seemed like the leader of the three drunks, the one with the crew cut who made the obscene gestures to Jacky, said to the other two, "Come on you guys let's go and get us a red head."

"Okay" Johnny said, "I get first crack at her this time."

Rick said, "Okay, but we got to get the big guy out of the way first. Everybody got their handcuffs?"

"Yeah" Fred said, "And I got the duct tape."

"Good let's go take a ride to Solidarity drive. Nice of them to tell us, where they were going."

Tom and Jacky drove over to Solidarity drive, parked and walked over to the north side of the Planetarium. They found a good spot for Jacky to sit down on her folding chair and start sketching. Tom was sitting on the grass about 10 feet behind her. It was quiet and not quite dark, the only sounds were from traffic, some from the power boats.

The three would-be rapists pulled nylon stockings over their heads to hide their faces. They snuck up behind Tom, two guys grabbed him, as the third put duct tape over his mouth and around his head. The three of them picked Tom up and carried him to a small tree. With hand cuffs, they shackled his hands behind him and around the tree.

Rick went about 10 feet to the left of her, and Fred went 10 feet to the right. Johnny came straight at her. Jacky turned around.

Rick said, "Just make sure you don't run away, until after we have our little party."

Jacky said, "Don't worry boys, I'm not going to run away."

Tom is shackled to a tree, and he is thinking. "I was supposed to protect her. She's going to get raped by the bracelet rapists. They are serial rapists that the police have been trying to find for two years. And he thought again, that it was his job to protect her. I'm going to watch her get raped, and I can't do a thing. Then he is thinking Jacky run or dive into the lake and swim for it."

But Jacky just stands there and said, "Come on boys, I'm not running."

Johnny said, "I think she likes it." He opens his fly and said, "Come on, Baby, I got something for you that you will like." He hauls out his large, hard pecker.

"You think I'd like that little thing? Bring it over here, because I can make it go limp."

"Okay let's see you wear it out."

And she said, "That's easy," and she gives him a vicious kick in his nuts. He folds up and lays on the ground groaning.

Fred comes over to Jacky now. He's calling her a bitch, and saying, "He would kill her for what she did to his brother Johnny."

She said, "You should have taught him better manners."

"You fucking lousy Bitch, I'm going to kick the shit out of you, then fuck the hell out of you and throw your ass in the lake." He came at her with a switch blade, which she took away and pocketed.

"Hey Shit head you got a nasty mind and you talk too damn much, I'm going to fix that. I'm going to dislocate your jaw and then kick you in the nuts." She did exactly that. Now she had two guys laying on the ground, Johnny moaning saying he was going to kill her and Fred moaning, not able to talk.

Rick was taking all this in, he wasn't about to take a chance with this bitch. He pulled out a switchblade, and went at her.

Jacky looked at him, and said, "So you want to play too."

"You lousy bitch I'm going to carve you up so much your mother won't recognize you."

"You got a big mouth you creepy bastard, I think maybe I should fix you like good old Freddy over there."

That pissed him off and he lunged at Jacky with the knife. She got his wrist and with a quick twist, she now had the knife in her hand. She retracted the blade and put the knife in her jeans pocket. "I don't need a knife to handle a shit head like you." Now she looked at him again and he pulled the second switchblade out of another pocket. She said, " Ricky you just don't seem to want to learn."

Rick was more careful this time. He wasn't going to let her grab his wrist. "I'm going to get you this time, you lousy redheaded bitch."

"You're not good enough for that Ricky. Why don't you just go over and lay down by your buddies."

He kept jabbing at her with the knife. She said, "Ricky you are really pissing me off with that knife. Why don't you just give it to me or I'll take it away from you."

"Like hell, I'm going to cut you up and screw the hell out of you." Then he lunged .

She kicked his wrist. Her heavy motorcycle boot broke his wrist and the knife went flying. She caught it, retracted the blade and put it in her other pocket.

"You broke my wrist you Bitch."

"You're still talking too much and too dirty." She hit him on the side of the face and dislocated his jaw. He went down on the ground and laid there moaning. She pointed to Tom, and said, "Who has the keys for the cuffs?"

She was standing near Johnny. "Now I'll ask again, who has a key for those cuffs."

She got ready to kick Johnny in the nuts again. "He said Rick's got the key."

"Okay Rick, put the key on the ground and back away."

"I can't it's in the pocket on the side where you broke my wrist. You will have to reach in and get it yourself."

"I ain't that stupid, Ricky Boy. Johnny get over here and get the key out of his pocket."

Johnny crawled over reached into his pocket and came up empty. He said, "It's not in this pocket." She was poised to kick Johnny again.

"Are you sure? Reach in the other pocket."

"He did and came up with the key."

She said, "Rick you tried to suck me in and I don't like someone lying to me." Then she kicked him so hard in the nuts, that his ass came off the ground.

"Okay, you three, I know none of you are in shape for running right now, so don't even try, it while I go to release my partner." They agreed, but they could do no more than limp away anyway. She went over and released Tom and ripped off the duct tape.

First thing he said was "Holy Shit, and I was supposed to protect you."

"Tom we have three sets of cuffs, you have one set and they have two more." She said, "Johnny, your cuffs and keys down on the ground."

Then she asked Fred, he balked until Jacky got ready to kick him in the nuts again.

Tom said, "Jacky what are we going to do with three sets of cuffs?"

She said, "The three of you stand normally. I would put one on everybody's right wrist, but shit head here went and got his wrist broke. Okay, stick out your left wrist." and they did.

Tom said, "Jacky you really got them trained."

"Okay now, sit on the ground, everybody's left wrist to your buddies right ankle. Now snap them closed Tom. Tom how about you going to your car and calling some of your Sheriff buddies. I'll herd this fine group over to the car."

"Do you think you can handle them by yourself? Sorry Jacky that was a stupid question." Tom got back to his car and called his headquarters. He told Sergeant what happened and the sergeant laughed like hell.

Then he said, "That Jacky you're talking about must be Jacky Sax." He said he had a buddy who is on the Hannibal Police Department who said that Jacky Sax, could take on half a dozen of the big bully boys without breaking a sweat.

Next day the Tribune, Daily News and the Times all had the same headline. "Bracelet rapists captured." "Three rapists captured by their intended victim, whose name is being withheld, by her request? All three are being held in the Cook County Jail infirmary. All have received multiple injuries, two of them with dislocated jaws, one with a broken nose, one with a broken wrist and all three with serious groin injuries. The intended victim had no injuries. The rapists probably thought that things would be easy for them. Their combined total weight was 640 pounds. The intended victim was only 120 pounds. Two of the rapists were weightlifters."

"The police officer that was assigned to protect her was handcuffed to a tree and gagged and could do nothing to help her. He said, "It was the MO of the bracelet rapists." "He thought he would have to watch the three of them gang rape her. It was hard to believe what he was seeing. They threatened to rape her, one at a time, taking turns. She invited them to come to her. They thought it was going to be fun. She kicked the shit out of the first one and he lay on the ground groaning."

"Number two was mad, because number one was his brother, so he came at her with a knife. She took the knife away from him closed it and put in her pocket, saying , I don't need this to handle Shitheads like you. That made him mad as hell. Because he called her Lousy

Bitch, she said, he had a big dirty mouth, and she was going to shut him up. That's when she dislocated his jaw, then kicked him in the nuts like his brother."

"Number three came at her with a knife. She grabbed his wrist and took it away from him. Now number three pulled another knife out of his back pocket, he came at her, waving a big switchblade knife, saying you ain't going to grab this knife, you bitch. That's when she kicked him and broke his wrist. She caught the flying knife and put it in her pocket. He still tried to grab her with his unbroken hand, she warded off his hand and quick as a flash she kicked him in the nuts, and said now stay on the ground."

"She got the key and released my hands. I took the duct tape off my mouth. Then I told her that she put on one hell of a show."

She said, "It was fun. I hate rapists, that would attack a poor defenseless woman like me."

She had a special way to shackle these guys together, left hand to the other guys right ankle. They made a three-man circle. Then she made them duck walk, back to the car, to the waiting police. There were five squad cars and ten police, to take three serial rapists in. They laughed like hell when they saw these three big bruisers, limping in a monkey walk. They were all beat to hell, by one little 120 pound redhead, she didn't have a hair out of place. The police decided they had too much help, it was not needed.

Tom thought, "These guys are going to prison for a long time. They would have nightmares about the little redhead. And none of the prisoners would let them live that down. All three of them lay in the infirmary, with ice bags on their crotch."

Eric contacted Jacky and asked her, "If she was through cleaning up on Chicago rapists."

"Don't rub it in smart ass. From what I hear you and Arch did much the same thing in Lemont, Illinois, even more so. You and Arch are the kind of people that we will need for our mission. Now are you ready to go and see some of Chicago's museums? If you are, I'll pick you up at noon in a Caddy limo."

"I'll be ready, but how did you know about Lemont, it wasn't publicized."

"Doc is privy to a lot of information. That's how he decided on drafting you guys for this mission, see you at noon."

Jacky's limo picked up Eric and they went to the Museum of science and Industry, otherwise known as the Rosenwald Museum. The first thing they went to see was the coal mine. A very realistic model of a mine. First you climbed a steel stairway that was part of the mine hoisting apparatus. Next you entered a steel cage like elevator. With all the rumbling shaking and sounds effects, it seemed like you went down 2000 feet, you probably went down no more than 100 feet.

Chapter 24

Daley cuts Red Tape. Start of Musical Cruise

It was a dark mine shaft, which led to a set of narrow tracks. A small five car train rolled to a stop. Eric, Jacky and eight other passengers climbed aboard. It wound its way down through the mine tunnels. They saw all kinds of coal mining machinery, loading machinery, drilling machines and other kinds of unmanned machines. And last of all men working in the mine. It made people stop and think that this would not be the kind of place they really wanted to spend their life working. After the mine, they went through an area where there were all industrial machines. This interested Eric but not Jacky.

They were walking along in one of the rooms on the lower floor. They turned a corner, and all of a sudden they went from 1951 to 1900. It was a complete street scene. You could walk in and out of grocery stores, drugstores, clothing stores and every kind of store, that would be on a 1900 street. Jacky said, "We had better head out if we want to go to the Field Museum. It's 2:30 now and they close at 5 PM. After that, we had better head for the Cora Lee. Doc wants to see the four of us on the ship this evening. Probably to plan training in England".

They left the Rosenwald Museum. The limo was waiting for them and it took them to the Field Museum, which was only 15 minutes away. As they were riding to the Field Museum. Eric asked Jacky, "Had she had noticed this sign near the exit door? He said it was announcing, that they were bringing a captured German submarine to the Museum of Science and Industry. It was captured off the coast of Africa in 1944, then towed to Bermuda where it stayed during the war and will be in Chicago, on permanent display at the museum."

Jacky said, "Did you plan to hang around and wait for it to get here. It's only 2 1/2 years. I think we had better get back to the ship, after we leave the Field Museum".

You could easily spend a whole day at the museum and not see half of what is displayed. They only spent two hours there and were really impressed, but they knew it was time to leave and that they would have to come back again and spend a lot more time there.

Eric had been there once when was a kid, he remembered the two giant stuffed elephants. Jacky had never been there and she must have spent 10 minutes just walking around looking at the two elephants. Then there were the assembled skeletons of prehistoric animals. Also a skeleton of a large whale that was hanging from the ceiling. Jacky was so fascinated by these displays, that it was more than an hour before they got off the main floor. By the time they made a quick walk through the Egyptian room, the American Indian displays and the animal display, it was time to go.

Eric saw it first and decided that he would try to pull something on Jacky. He got her attention and was facing her, got her walking backwards until she bumped into a rail. When she turned around she was facing something very hairy. As Jacky looked up, right in front of her was a 10 foot Kodiak bear. It was looking down at her with his claw filled paws stretched out.

Jacky jumped back, and let out a scream. Eric laughed and said, "I thought that nothing scared you."

"Not much does, but that sure as hell scared the shit out of me. Eric do me a favor."

"What's that?"

"Remind me to get even with you. Now let's get the hell out of here."

The limo driver drove them back to the Chicago Yacht Club. They went inside and asked the host if he could order up the service boat, to bring them back to the Cora Lee. He said, "The service boat just left the dock to head out to the Cora Lee, it had two other people on board for another boat, so they won't be back for at least 20 minutes."

They sat down at the bar and ordered Beefeater martinis. The bartender served them. Eric put a $20 up on the bar and Lou the bartender, said, "Put your money away. You can't spend it in here, those are my orders."

"By whose orders?" asked Eric.

Lou looked at Eric and Jacky, and said with great sincerity, "By the orders of the next Mayor of the city of Chicago, I'm proud to say, Richard J. Daley. Miss Sax, the mayor, I mean Mr. Daley asked me to give you this envelope." And he handed it to her. Jacky looked at the envelope it had a return address of Clerk of Cook County, Richard J. Daley. She opened it, it was one hand written page.

It read, "Dear Ms. Sax, I have had a conversation with Admiral Hunter. He expressed concern about your safety and the secrecy of your mission. He requested there be no publicity or pictures of his people while in Chicago. I and my people will honor that and will have the media do the same. Other than that, I would personally like to congratulate you on the unbelievable job you did on capturing the Bracelet Rapists. The Chicago Police and the Cook County Police have had a detail of 15 to 20 men on this case for three years and you captured all three of them in a few hours. When you are finished with your mission for Admiral Hunter, I would like to offer you a position in the Chicago or Cook County Police Department. A position of training police officers at what you do so well. Sincerely Richard J. Daley, Clerk of Cook County. May God go with you on your mission. From what I understand one of God's Messengers is going with you. Good Luck."

Jacky read it, she handed it to Eric. He read it, then said "I'm glad we are on the same side"

They heard the blast of the horn and Lou said, "That's your ride. Come back any time, it was a pleasure to serve you."

Eric and Jacky said, "Thanks Lou." They went out and boarded the service boat. It was a short trip through the harbor and they were back on board the Cora Lee. Mario welcomed them on board and handed them a rum punch.

Then Doc and Bill came up from below. Doc said, "Good to see you guys again. Peter Chin came on board, this morning. We had a call from the County Clerk's office. Arch will be delivered sometime around noon, by a police boat. Daley said he has a few loose ends to tie up, then he will deliver Arch to the Cora Lee."

Jacky asked Doc, "What was the important thing that you wanted to talk about?"

"I have a few people that I want you to meet. First is Kelly. A beautiful blonde walked over to Jacky and said hello. Next is Sandra, another beautiful Gal, she was a platinum blonde. Finally there is Marilyn. Now Marilyn is the hairdresser who turned these gals into blondes."

"You are right, they are beautiful. But what has that got to do with me?"

"The question is this Jacky. Which one would you like to be?"

"I don't understand. I like my hair the way it is, it makes me stand out."

"And that's the problem Jacky, you've had a little too much publicity as a beautiful redhead. So now we want to make you a beautiful blonde. Your choice, blonde or platinum blonde."

"Well I always did like going first class, so I'll take platinum blonde." "Good choice." said Marilyn. "You'll light of up every room you walk into."

Doc then turned to Eric and Peter and said, "For you two guys and Arch, we have Mike the barber. He can change your hairstyle and the color of your hair. But not changing the color for Peter. I don't think that a blonde or red headed Korean would go over too well."

Then Peter piped up, and said, "How about just plain gray Doc."

"Never thought of that, but it sounds good. When they get through with you people, nobody will recognize you."

Just then a 36 foot police boat pulled up alongside the gang way. Arch came aboard, also Richard J. Daley. After all the greetings, Doc asked Arch how it went with his cousin?

"Well it was the most unbelievable day that I ever have spent. Mayor Daley, I mean Mr. Daley, but it won't be too long before he is Mayor Daley, sure does know how to deal with people in high places. You know when you want to get something done, you start at the bottom and work your way to the top. Not Mr. Daley. The first person he called yesterday morning was the President. He called the White House, told them it was Richard J. Daley and they put him right through to the President. They jawed for about half an hour, when he got off the line, he said no problem."

Then we went to court of appeals. "They told him it would take months, to get it on the docket."

"No it won't," he said, "I have all the transcripts of the trial, right here. There is not too much reading, because it was a short trial where this kid was railroaded into jail! The presiding judge in the case, as we found out, had an early golf date, so he very quickly sentenced all four to15 years in prison. Then left the court early to go play golf. As you can see the kid never had a rap sheet, not so much as a parking ticket. He got 15 years for joyriding with three other guys who had long rap sheets. The owner of the store they damaged and the owner of the Rolls-Royce pressed charges and wanted to see them hang. The three other guys with long rap sheets deserved 3 to 5 years, but the kid should have gotten a suspended sentence. Now, we need to see justice in this court today. I really don't want to create too much of a problem for any judge in the Circuit Court of Cook County. You know that I can and I will, so let's be fair. My client will not sue the county and all you have to do is sign a release order for tomorrow by noon. Also, I do not want to bring the President into this. I spoke to him this morning."

Then Daley pointed to Arch and said, "This is the gentleman that is pleading for the release of his cousin, who was wrongfully sentenced to 15 years in prison. This man has received a presidential citation just a couple of weeks ago. He and his friends captured the traitors that were hung last week, so I don't think the President will look too kindly on a wrong decision." They signed a release order for the following day at noon.

As they left the court, Arch thanked Daley and said that he was amazed at how he could cut through the red tape and get things done very quickly. Daley said, "Just doing my job. Everything works smoothly and quickly, when you start by letting them know who they are dealing with."

After telling that story Doc said, " Mayor Daley, you sure got my vote."

Mario then came up took drink orders. Juan and Mario delivered the drinks. Doc asked Daley to stay for dinner.

He said, "I may push a lot of politicians around, but on this I got to check with the wife."

Doc told Juan to show Mr. Daley to the radio room. "We have a radio phone, and you can call your wife from here."

He did that and came back smiling." She having the girls come over for a bridge party. I don't want to be around for that, so dinner sounds good and I hear you have a great chef."

"He is the greatest, I'll call him up here, he can tell us what he's got planned."

When Mario came up to the cockpit. Doc asked him and he said, "He had two big roasts, a 9 pound boneless pork roast and a 10 pound beef chuck roast. If you like tender and tasty meat you are in for a treat. The pork has been dry marinated a week with my own seasoning, wrapped in aluminum foil, in a refrigerator for three or four days and then into the oven at 150° for four hours and then back into the fridge for a day or so, still foil wrapped. Then it goes into the oven at 325° for about three hours until the internal temperature is 155° then off comes the foil, a quick browning under the broiler and now you have the most tender, juiciest and tastiest pork on the planet. Now the beef is the same way except 10° cooler. So dinner will be served about 4:30 or 5 PM it all depends on the two roasts."

Bill said, "He and Doc had been discussing what happens next on this mission. We decided that you three guys need to grow beards, before you get off this boat. It will take a minimum of two weeks to grow a half way decent beard, so we are going to take a short cruise up to Montréal. You can then get a flight from there to Heathrow in London.

Daley said, "Doc has confided in me that the four of you are going to England for training in a commando unit. He said the training is preparation for a mission. From what I have heard about Jacky, she doesn't need much more training."

"That's true enough Mr. Daley" said Bill. "Jacky will go through the same training, but she will mostly act as an instructor. You see Jacky is a commando."

Doc then said, "We have a surprise for you. Kelly and Sandra are good friends of Bill, they are both singers from a country rock group. Bill has asked them to entertain us, before dinner. They are down below right now, changing into costume."

Mario and Juan, brought another round of drinks. Then Sandra and Kelly came up in their Western costumes and guitars. They started out singing the country classics, then requests. They were really good.

Doc said, "I wish you gals could stay around for a while. You are really good entertainers."

Sandra said, "We have five days, before our next show."

Good said Doc, "How about a sail to Mackinac Island?"

Kelly said, "Great, but how do we catch a train back to Chicago, from an island?"

"No problem", said Doc, "Figured that nobody can refuse a cruise to an island, so I rechecked with Charlie the Pilot. He said that he would fly you right to the Chicago yacht club, Marilyn and Michael you're invited too."

They all agreed, then Mario came up and said dinner is served in the main salon. They all went down to the dining salon. Mario had tables set for a state dinner.

Daley took one look, and said to Doc "You really go first class."

"Why not I'm on a government payroll."

Daley's comment was, "I think I've got the wrong job."

Jacky turned to Sandra and said, "This will be great, because everybody really enjoyed your singing."

Then Kelly said, "We enjoy singing country, but really like folk singing, however, country sells."

Juan and Angel took the orders for appetizers, and came back and served them. Next came the side dishes, the potatoes, sweet potatoes and green beans, finally Mario came up with the roast pork. Juan served the roast beef. Both were on platters with clear covers to keep them warm. Mario had sliced the pork roast, it went around the table. Then the beef roast. There was a total of 13 people. The pork roast just disappeared off the platter, the beef roast almost did the same.

Everybody raved about Mario's pork and beef roasts. Daley said, "If you could teach my wife to cook like that and she is a good cook, I would never eat in a restaurant again. That was the most succulent meat I have ever eaten."

Doc said, "Mario, this is the first time, I have ever seen you run out of the main course."

"Have no fear. I looked over this group and decided that they were the bunch of hungry suckers." Mario whistles down to the Galley and Juan comes up, carrying another pork roast. "If that doesn't fill you up, I have another beef roast down in the Galley, or we can save that for sandwiches tomorrow. " They elected to save the beef roast, but they devoured the pork roast.

Everybody agreed that they were never had better roasts.

Mario said, "You two gals are really great and even if you sing for your supper, I ain't going to make these roasts every night."

Daley said, "After tasting Mario's cooking, I don't think anybody on your trip to Mackinac Island is going to want for great food. Then he said that he had better head for home. He asked Doc, if he could call for service boat."

Juan said, "No problem Mr. Daley. I'll run you in on the ship's launch." Which is what he did, after Mr. Daley said goodbye to everybody.

He wished the three guys and Jacky, good luck on their mission, whatever it is. Juan and Richard J. Daley, the next mayor of Chicago, boarded the launch and headed for the Chicago yacht club.

After finishing up that final pork roast. Six people volunteered to go down to the galley and clean up the dishes and pots and pans. Jacky made Mario a Beef Eater Martini and told him to sit on his ass and watch the galley get cleaned up.

When they finished the galley, they all refreshed their drinks, went up to the bow and sat down. Sandra and Kelly went up to the bow and sat on high stools with their guitars. They started singing some beautiful folk music and some country. Angel went over to the fore mast and opened an electrical box and switched on the fore deck light, which shined right down onto the gals. It was a floating stage.

The harbor was dead still and the sound carried throughout. The sounds of Sandra and Kelly singing and playing carried over water. Many people that were on their boats got in their dinghies and rowed over to the Cora Lee.

They tied off on Cora Lee's buoy and to each other. There got to be about 10 dingys tied off. Then Doc invited them to come aboard and join the party. They did and pretty soon there was about 50 people up on the bow enjoying the music. Doc had Juan and Mario bring up cases of beer and wine.

The party was on, some people went back to their boat and got guitars, fiddles, accordions , a saxophone and a trumpet. The party lasted till 6 AM Sunday morning. Sandra and Kelly sang folk songs and country songs. A lot of sea shanty's were sung by a popular recording star, he was good, but I forgot his name. A local nightclub comedian acted as emcee. He told a lot of dirty jokes. His name was Bobby Howard and his theme song was the Tennessee waltz. Whenever it got quiet, he's sang, "I lost my little darling" then everyone sounded off with "To The Tennessee waltz". They were loud enough for the whole harbor to hear. Then Sandra or Kelly would sing a song. Until sunrise, then the people started rowing their dinghies back to their boats. By 6 AM everybody was gone.

Mario made a big pot of coffee for a nightcap. Then they all hit the sack, there was no movement on the boat until about noon. Angel was the first one walking the deck. Mario was in the galley mixing pancake batter and Juan was frying up a whole bunch of bacon. Bill Jacky and Marilyn were sitting on the benches up in the bow, drinking the morning coffee and listening to Kelly and Sandra singing gospel music. It included a beautiful version of Amazing Grace.

When Doc heard them singing amazing Grace, he came forward to the bow. "He told the girls, that he had never heard a more beautiful version of that song. Doc told them that he played a bagpipe version, when ever leaving or returning to home port. I would love to record your voices and blend them with my bagpipe version."

They said, "Great can we do it now, it's quiet in the harbor?"

Doc got set up his equipment, they sang as he recorded. Doc picked up his equipment and went below to his workshop, he blended his recording with the new recording and it sounded great. He told Bill that he could hardly wait to play it when they sailed tomorrow morning. Come on let's go up on deck and see who else is moving about. They went up and walked back to the after cockpit.

Arch Eric and Peter were sitting at the table. Between them was a great big iced pitcher of bloody Maria's (with tequila) Bill asked how everybody was moving this morning?

Eric said that he was having some bloodys, to work up enough ambition to go diving this morning.

Doc asked, "Why?"

"Remember Sam? The guy with the trumpet. As he was leaving he set his trumpet on the rail, he bumped it and over it went. The sax player was below, standing in the dinghy. He reached to catch the trumpet, lost his balance. He missed the trumpet, while doing that, he lost the sax. Now both are on the bottom. I told them not to worry, I'll find both of them in the morning. After they dropped the instruments, Angel checked position with the Peloris, so that we didn't have to check the whole bottom of the harbor."

Arch then said, "What's this we stuff, it seems to me that you very graciously volunteered your services. Once Angel shows us the location we can all cheer you on."

Just then Jacky stepped into the cockpit wearing a sexy looking bikini.

"Sandra", Arch said, "As much as my eyes are blurry this morning, you looked great last night, but even better this morning."

"Arch your eyes must be blurry, because you are talking to Jacky not Sandra" said Bill.

Next words out of Arch's mouth were "Wow you sure do clean up nice. You sure are one sexy lady."

"Back off hotshot, or I'll have to make an example out of you."

"I know you could, but you wouldn't, would you Jacky?"

"No just fooling with you Arch."

Kelly and Sandra walked aft from the bow. They stepped in the cockpit and they stopped. Kelly said, "Holy shit, another Sandra."

Jacky looked at Sandra and said, "I think I look too much like Sandra. Being a platinum blond, I'll just have to punch out too many guys."

"Jacky from what I heard you already did that in Chicago when you were a redhead. Then, I also heard you put three of them in a hospital. Keep the platinum, then we will be a pair."

Jacky said, "Okay Sandra, I think I will."

Angel came into the cockpit, with a giant cup of coffee. He said, "I came to tell you guys that Doc said, we will be underway at 10 AM tomorrow."

Eric asked Angel, "If he intended to leave the harbor, under sail?"

"Yes we will sail out of the harbor."

"But the wind has been blowing straight in, through the mouth of the harbor. I have not seen one boat sail out, since the wind was in that direction."

Don't worry Eric, "As long as everybody is sober, handling sheets, and sails, it will be a piece of cake. Then Angel said, "Just to make you feel better, when we have to tack in a congested harbor like this, I start both the diesels and keep them running in case of an emergency. You never know what some idiot may do. Somebody may pull right out in front of you and those diesels can save your ass"

"Sounds good to me," said Eric.

Then Eric said one other thing. "Angel, you said that you plotted where the two horns were dropped. Can you point out where that is, because I don't want to swim around in half the harbor."

"I'll do better than point, Eric. Go and put on your swim suit and mask. It is only 20 or 25 feet deep, so you won't need a tank. We will take the launch, and I'll put you right over the spot." They went out a ways and stopped the launch.

Eric said, "It didn't seem like we were out this far."

Angel said, "Dive right here, and if you have your eyes open, you will find two shiny brass horns." Eric went over the side and was back up in less than two minutes with two brass horns.

Angel and Eric went back to the Cora Lee, they lifted the launch back up on the davits, then set the horns down on the cockpit table and grabbed a nice cold beer.

Doc walked over and picked up the sax and asked us if these horns were the ones that went over the side last night or actually this morning. "Who got them off the bottom?"

Eric said, "He did."

"Very good thing you did. These are not cheap ones, they are expensive professional horns. Have you got their names?"

"No, but I have the name of their boat. "*The Dancer*" I was going to take them over after a while.

Doc said, "I have to go in, and see the harbor master. I can take them with me and drop them off." Doc lowered the launch, got himself and the two horns aboard, then fired up the engine and headed for the harbor master's office. Doc was going to see the harbor master to let him know his can would be empty for 3 to 4 weeks."

The can may be used during this time. But they would be responsible for the pickup line, and a stainless steel mooring cable attached to the mooring buoy. This would be for transient vessels, that the harbor master (Herb Eldeen), deemed responsible types.

Now with that out of the way he asked him where The Dancer was located in the harbor. "The Dancer," he said, "Is Bud Sachs' 55 foot sloop." He showed Doc on the harbor chart. Doc thanked him, and headed for The Dancer. He found her, a sleek red and white sloop.

There were two guys in the cockpit drinking coffee. They invited Doc aboard for a cup of coffee. They introduced themselves as Richie and Lester. They said they were just boat sitting for the owner, Bud Sachs, who is out of town for three weeks. They had been working for Bud for last six months, in a nightclub he owns on Rush Street. A new group has been signed, so we have to find a new gig. Ritchie said that he plays the sax, accordion and Banjo and Lester plays the trumpet, guitar, violin and trombone.

"I heard you guys play last night, and this morning, you are pretty good. You just had the Sax which was great and so was the Trumpet. You both play these other instruments too?"

"Yeah we do"

"As good as the sax and Trumpet"?

" No much better."

Doc said, "I've got a great idea. How would you like to go for a nice musical cruise to Montréal and back. That's if you don't have any existing problems with Canadian customs."

They said, "Yes to the first, and no to the second question."

Doc said, "What we have here, is five or six weeks of beautiful weather. A great boat, musicians, great singers and enough time. We have a piano on board. Which we move up to the bow now and then. Juan plays a mean jazz piano. He also plays classical piano. Mario plays classical violin and guitar."

Lester said, "It seems like every one of your crew does something. What does Angel do?"

"The most important thing of all. He runs the ship and does that very well. Angel is a sailing master, a damn good one. He is the only one on this ship, that I will take any orders from."

"All this music can be picked up by four different microphones up on the bow and then up to the big speakers up near the top of the main mast. I had the speaker's custom-made, they will carry for miles."

"Sandra and Kelly planned on getting off on Mackinac Island, but if I can talk them into hanging in for a round trip from Chicago to Montréal and back, we can light up the Great Lakes and part of the St. Lawrence."

"From what I gather, they are not too happy with the people they are working for now. I have many connections in Chicago and New York . With their talent, I can get them into some of the top clubs in New York, or Chicago. Probably at twice what they're making now, with no agent to pay."

Doc put it to the two gals and they both agreed. Doc also told them that they are aboard a nationally famous ship. Now with this musical cruise, the publicity won't hurt a bit.

Chapter 25

Jacky Saves Commandos

Doc got everyone together, for a little cocktail party before dinner. He told them about the plans for a musical cruise. He told him that Ritchie and Lester will join them, Juan will go and pick them up, so they can join us for dinner.

Bill said you know Doc, "Jacky is not a bad singer. She can really belt out a song if she wants to, and she has a beautiful voice."

"I forget exactly where but it was somewhere in France, near the coast. My Spitfire was hit by flak in 1942 June or July. I went down near where 12 commandos had just completed a mission. They got me out of my plane, before the Krauts got to me. We were surrounded by at least 100 Krauts. They were looking for me, but they didn't know the 12 commandos were there. The Krauts used flashlights, to find me. Soon as a Kraut turned on his flash he was very quietly made dead. After a while they got wise and did not use the lights anymore. They got into a line and beat the bushes. If they kept that up they would find us, because we had two wounded men that could not walk. They had to be carried. Jacky was not one to give up. She told us not to move and she took two of her best men."

"We waited in a ditch, then we heard some beautiful singing. We didn't know where it came from. Until Gary one of the wounded said. "Believe it or not boys. That's Sergeant Sax. Then we heard the silenced Sten gun. And sometimes no shot just a scream. Then we heard the same singing voice, from a different location. Then the shots and the screams.

Or no shots just screams. Then another location and more screams. After a couple more times she must have gotten their leader. Because now we could hear them shuffling through the weeds toward the road. Then truck engines started and away they went."

"I can't imagine what they said in their report. But I know they were short about 20 people. We all made it back to the pickup point. We made it back across the channel. Jacky was our leader, when asked what happened, she said I just felt like singing. That was the last time I heard her sing, she was the Loralai of their Unit."

Chapter 26

Bob& Jim Attack Jacky& Eric.

Jacky said, "Bill you are making a big deal out of a minor incident."

"It wasn't so minor, for those who got out alive. Including Art Hobson who was being carried out, or for the people that awarded you the DSC."

Doc then said, "That's enough haggling about heroes. Jacky I would like to ask you if you would join our group of musically talented people and singing the Great Lakes alive."

Sandra said, "Jacky you're platinum now."

"Well if you put it that way, I guess I got to sing for my supper."

Kelly said "Now we got a real group."

Doc said, "Juan, how about you and Mario bring up the piano and get it mounted on the deck. Bill you're the electronics guy, how about rigging up the microphones. We want to be all set when we sail out of the harbor in the morning. That's all I've got to say." Then Doc said, " Now let's have a toast to some great music"

Then Bill said, "I'll drink to that." They all spent the afternoon getting everything ship shape and ready to get underway in the morning.

Mario addressed the crew and guests. He said, "For the last night in Chicago I'll give everybody a democratic choice, for dinner tonight." He passed out slips of paper and said write down your choice and hand them back to me. They filled them out and gave the slips back to Mario. He opened them up looked at them, they read Prime rib, roast pork, chicken pot pie, roast beef, porterhouse steak, liver and onions, fried shrimp and a few others.

Mario then said, "As long as this is a democratic vote it wouldn't be right for me to read them off. So Doc would you do the honors and read off the choice of our fellow travelers."

Mario walked over to Doc with the slips in his hand as he walked behind Arch. He put the slips in his left shirt pocket and took a new set of slips out of his right shirt pocket and he handed out to those slips to Doc.

Doc read them off, "Angel hair pasta with Mario's excellent pasta sauce. Angel hair' with Mario's great Italian pasta sauce. Mario's special Italian dinner the last one was Mario's choice. Doc finally quit reading and said Mario have you ever thought of going into politics."

"No Doc, bad enough being a chef. Okay dinner will be served in one hour. Best damn pasta sauce you ever tasted".

Mario was right it was the best damn pasta sauce they ever ate. They all decided that a legitimate vote ain't always the best. They had their dinner drinks, some went to their cabins, some walked the deck and some went to the aft cockpit to drink and talk.

Mario, Kelly, Sandra, and Jacky went up forward to the cushioned benches in the bow. They talked about the trip they were about to take. Kelly and Sandra said that they are glad that Jacky decided to sing with them.

Mario said "I'm also very glad that you are going to sing. You have not only a beautiful voice, but a very powerful voice. I know this because I heard you sing on Beaver Island. You were walking on the shoreline and you started to sing. I just happen to be close by picking blueberries for the next day's breakfast. I heard this beautiful voice singing. I came closer and then I saw it was you sitting on a rock and singing. I did not want to invade your privacy. So I've never said anything and I know not saying something now, would not be right."

Jacky said, "No problem Mario. I just made a stupid vow years ago. I was studying opera and I had a personal trainer that I fell in love with. We were supposed to get married when he dumped me for another girl, he married her. He wanted to keep training me. I told him to go to hell, and vowed never sing again. Then I joined the Army and then the commandos. I never had any urge to sing again until Sandra talked me into being a platinum blonde . I think I will enjoy being in this plan, of music across the lakes."

Kelly said, "Jacky, Mario has come up with another plan. He said he has heard you sing, and he knows that you can do it, to sing Amazing Grace."

Mario said, "Doc always plays Amazing Grace when leaving or returning to the home port, which is Chicago. He plays a recording, the sound is from a loudspeaker up on the main mast. The recording is with bagpipes. Then after a couple of minutes, the volume of the bag pipes are lowered. You three girls come in for a short period and then, Jacky you go solo. I know you can do it I've heard you sing. I think they will be able to hear you all the way to Milwaukee. I've written it up the way you will play it. We can't practice it because we want to surprise Doc."

It was Sunday morning the last week of July at 5 AM. Mario said, "It was a serve yourself breakfast buffet." Mario had a lot to do before they set sail at 9 AM. He had to let Bill in on the plan. Bill and Mario rigged the microphones in the bow. Mario had told Doc that he would take care of setting up the recording of Amazing Grace. It was getting close to 9 AM, the three blondes came up on deck, wearing shimmering gold evening gowns. All three of them walked toward the bow.

Doc saw them and said, "Those gals have really dressed for the occasion. Then he said Bill, "I think we have the most beautiful crew in the harbor."

"You're right Doc.

Angel asked if all positions were manned. He said, "Then let's get underway." Mario dropped the pennant and the mooring line. Cora Lee was now free. Juan pushed the jib boom to the starboard and the ship swung to the port, they were now on a starboard tack. All of a sudden the bagpipes started playing amazing Grace. Angel sailed the big ship expertly through the harbor, through a maze of boats and then they were heading right for the Chicago yacht club. The volume is lowered on the bagpipe recording . The three girls were singing amazing Grace as they passed the club. There were hundreds of people on the docks and the public walks above the club. All the people standing ashore and in boats were waving.

It was an impressive sight, to see Angel maneuver the big schooner between the moored boats , then with a hard right rudder, Angel came about and put her on a port tack. Just at that time Jacky started singing solo, her strong and beautiful voice carried through the harbor. By now Cora Lee was under full sail, toward the mouth of the harbor. Angel was smiling, as he was having the time of his life.

Doc came back to the helm, and told Angel that what he did, could only be done by a master sailor. Angel said, "It was fun Doc."

Then Doc said, "Those girls were also fantastic. I've got to go and congratulate them."

Just then Juan came over to Doc and said, there was a call on the radio. Doc went down below. He talked on the radio for a few minutes, then he came back up and went forward to find the three girls. They were sitting on the bow talking with Mario.

"Doc said that what he heard this morning, was absolutely fantastic, it was more than beautiful. Remember what I said about you girls when you first agreed to go on this musical cruise. I said that a little publicity couldn't hurt. Well that radio message I just got was from a guest at the Chicago yacht club. He is from Sun Records and he would like to see you when you get back. He also said, it was the most beautiful thing he has ever heard."

Then Doc said, "Look at the recognition that you got and we were not even out of the harbor. Can you imagine how much publicity you will get after sailing 2400 miles."

They were sailing up the west side of the lake, on the Wisconsin side. The wind was coming from the North West and they sailed as close to the wind as Angel felt his ship could sail efficiently.

The Cora Lee was making about 9 knots and was about 85 miles out of Chicago at about 7 PM. They were overtaking what looks like a 50 foot sloop. As they got closer both Lester and Richie said, "That's The Dancer." Just then they heard The Dancer's PA system playing The Tennessee waltz. Doc played back The Tennessee waltz in answer. All of a sudden the dancer fired off a whole series of flares . These flares were to be used only in an emergency. Doc said, "Angel cut back and stay with them in case they do have an emergency. If they didn't have an emergency, they do have one now because here comes the Coast Guard helicopter."

Doc then said, "It's Illegal to fire off emergency flares for the hell of it. The Coast Guard won't take it lightly."

The helicopter was one with floats and could set down on the water. They used their hailer to ask what the emergency was?

Bud Sachs got on his hailer and said in a drunken, sarcastic voice, "I said we ain't got no problem what's your problem."

Doc said, "Wrong answer."

Lester said. "Sounds just like Bud."

Doc then said, "They have trouble now."

The Coast Guard then ordered them to drop their sails and prepare to be boarded.

The people on the dancer, ignored the order. Instead they went on a port tack and headed east. Somehow they had this stupid idea, that the helicopter couldn't touch them.

Bill said, "Doc, are you keeping score. On how many stupid mistakes these ass holes have made?"

"No but I see a big fine. Time in jail and the impound of one nice sloop."

Dancer was on a reach heading east. The pilot of the helicopter decided that he had enough of this ass hole on the sailboat. He came within a few hundred feet over the boat, then dropped fast. When he judged that he was close enough, he hit the throttle full power and then full pitch. It didn't take much of that Whirlybirds wind, to tear up dancers Main and then the fore sails .

Then they started the engine, turned around and headed for Milwaukee. That didn't work either, because just about 2 miles off, was the Coast Guard 83 footer, out of Milwaukee coming at flank speed. The people on Dancer saw that and just shut down and waited. The last they saw the dancer was it being towed to the Port of Milwaukee.

Doc said, "It doesn't pay to be a stupid wise ass."

Angel had the crew, trim the sheets and they were on their way again. It was early evening and a full moon was coming up. Mario cooked a fine dinner. He made 6 good sized meat loafs, with mashed potatoes and gravy and green beans.

A few of the people went forward, most of them to the cockpit and some stayed below. The three girls, Richie the Sax man, and Lester with his Trumpet went forward. The Sax man and the trumpet man started playing. They played for a little bit and then the gals started singing.

Doc was sitting with Eric, Arch, Juan and Bill in the after cockpit. They said, "You know, we've got the nicest music on Lake Michigan."

Doc said, "So let's share it." They were about three quarters of a mile off of Kewaunee. He said, "Juan turn on the speakers and turn them up high, we will let them know we are here." Right after Juan turned on the speakers. Lights came on around Kewaunee. A few bottle rockets, then a couple skyrockets.

Bill said, "At least those rockets were not shot from an emergency very pistol."

Doc said, "At least they know we are here. You know Bill our musical crew, sure does sound beautiful."

"And Doc you know something else 3/5 of them look beautiful."

"Bill I agree with you but I didn't think you would notice that."

"Doc when I get too old to notice a beautiful woman I ought to be dead."

"Well, all five of them work good together. You had a good idea when you invited Richie and Lester."

Then Doc said, "The most surprising thing was, you telling us Jacky could sing, she is great. Let's go up to the bow, so we can get better seats for the show."

Bill and Doc got up to the bow. It was kind of dark up there until your eyes got adjusted. Marylyn grabbed their hands and led them to their reserve seats. Everyone knew that they would be coming up to the bow. They did a great show and Mario had set up a bar. He also had some after dinner snacks. The three gals sang and the guys played. Richie and Lester also did some singing. The guys sang On Top of old Smokey and Mule Train. Kelly and Sandra sang Mockingbird Hill and Goodnight Irene. Then Jacky sang Come On A My House and Music, Music, Music. Then the three of them sang the Tennessee Waltz as a finale.

It was a great show and it lasted two hours. Doc told everybody, "What a great job they were doing. He said that Cora Lee is the "Original Lake Michigan Showboat" and that tomorrow they should spend a day at Beaver Island, they would be treated to their greatest fish boil on the Great Lakes.

He said that he hoped they wouldn't mind doing a show like this for the local residents. Then he asked Juan if he had his piano ready to play some jazz?

Juan said, "Not yet but I'll be ready in the morning."

Angel said that we would drop anchor in Beaver Island Harbor at about 8 AM. It was about 11 PM when everyone decided to hit the sack. Except Bill and Doc who went back to the after cockpit. They no sooner sat down when Mario showed up with a tray. On that tray was three very large Beefeater martinis and a plate of boiled Shrimp in some of Mario's own cocktail sauce. Mario sat down with Bill and Doc.

Doc, said " Mario, You must really be psychic, you always show up with food or drink at just the right time."

"It's my job boss. To tell you the truth, I was going to drink the 3 martinis myself and eat all the shrimp, but my conscience wouldn't let me do it. So have a martini Boss and you too Bill." They worked on the martinis, and talked about the St. Lawrence seaway.

Doc said, "He had made the trip to Québec, once before. When he was an ensign. At that time on a 165 foot minesweeper. He said some of the areas past Cornwall are very tough on props, if you are not careful."

Bill said, "Sounds like an interesting trip."

"You like fishing Bill?"

"I love it, but never seem to have enough time."

"You will have time, if you want to fish. Ever fish for Muskie? Or would you rather fish for bass?"

"I would like to try to fish for Muskie."

"We can stop in Clayton, New York, I know some people there. I can arrange for licenses, boats and any other gear that we would need. We have a lot of tackle on board but anything else we need we can get in Clayton."

"Mario is a diehard Muskie fisherman, he has caught some big ones. He has become quite antsy, since he heard that we were going to thousand islands, which is where Clayton, New York is. Record Muskie's have been caught there. It is also great for small mouthed Bass, that's what I like to fish for."

"Bill why don't you get names and information for license's for anyone who wants to fish and Bill don't forget Mario, or you will starve for the rest of the trip. If Mario can't fish, you won't eat. When Mario fishes for Muskie he catches Muskie. He is he is not like most fishermen, who catch a record breaking fish and then have it mounted. Mario smokes them, best smoked fish you were ever tasted."

"Most smoked fish are oily, and some of them taste oily. A Muskie is a wet fish and most wet fish do not smoke well. But there is not too much that Mario can't do."

Bill said, "My glass is empty, so I think it's time to hit the sack." They said goodnight, and the three of them went down below to hit the sack.

They woke up the next morning, at 5 AM to Juan playing some real great jazz. He played jazz for about 15 minutes, then some blues for a while and back to jazz. It was now almost 6 AM and they were just coming up on Whiskey Island. This is about 8 miles northwest of Beaver Island. At this point they headed east southeast on a port tack, which would bring them to the mouth of the harbor in about one hour . Then Angel would make one more maneuver , to come about, go in on a starboard tack and sail right into the harbor and drop anchor.

By the time they were ready to go on a starboard tack, the three girls were up on the bow, looking fresh, beautiful and singing the Tennessee waltz. Now Ritchie was playing his Sax and Lester his Trombone. They were in the harbor, almost to Arts dock. Then Angel came up into the wind, they had enough headway that it carried them about 200 yards, at that time Mario dropped and set the anchor.

While the other guys dropped sail and put on the sail stops. Mario started playing his violin. It was something that was of the classics and was perfect for the end of a trip.

Art and Linda, got into the Chris-Craft runabout and headed out to the Cora Lee. When they got out to the Schooner, Juan lowered the stairway and welcomed them aboard.

Mario has now quit playing and the three girls were singing. Ritchie was playing the Sax. Bill and Doc came aft and sat down at the cockpit table. Mario served them all coffee and Drambuie as an eye-opener. After some small talk Mario said he had to go forward for a bit. Doc said, "Art we have a hell of a surprise for you."

What kind of surprise Doc?

Then they heard Mario playing the violin and the girls started singing with the one powerful voice, of the lead singer. Mario and the singers started walking to the stern of the ship as they were singing. It was hauntings the sound carried over the harbor. They finished their first song, Be My Love. Mario played the violin and Jacky sang Mona Lisa, there wasn't a dry eye in the group. When she was through with this song everyone applauded.

And then Jacky walked over to Doc. Art said, "Doc where are your manners, how about you introducing me to this beautiful blonde."

Just then Linda said "Hi Jacky. These men are blind, they wouldn't recognize their own mother, if she wore her new hat."

Art said, "Holy Shit is it really you Jacky? Is there anything you haven't done?"

"Well I haven't caught a Muskie, but Mario said he is going to change that."

"Not here." said Art.

"No, at Thousand Islands."

Then Art said, "That's the place for Muskie and small mouth Bass. Knowing you Jacky, you may be the first person to catch a Muskie, with your bare hands."

"I don't think I'll try it, Art. I hear they have big sharp teeth."

Well Doc, "What brings you back here."

"Art it's like this, we are on our way to Montréal. Before we left Chicago, I told everybody about your great fish boils. Now they have refused to eat Mario's cooking, until they get some of your famous fish. Look at them Art they are just wasting away."

"Yeah and it looks like you and Bill, have been doing all the eating."

"That's just leftovers Art."

"Okay Doc, "We will have a fish boil, this afternoon. But now it's time for one of Mario's good breakfasts.

"You got a deal Art let's go talk to Mario. Mario agreed to swap breakfast for fish boil."

Eric asked Art, "If he still had the sea sled, and if they could use it to show Jacky how good it works."

"Of course you can. You can use it all you want."

"Okay Jacky how about after breakfast? With Aqua Lung or without said Eric?"

"Without, Eric."

After breakfast Eric and Jacky went to the work shed to get the sea sled . After they went into the shed, Eric looked around and found the sled.

Jacky took one look at the sled and said, "You claimed it was simple, but I never thought anything this simple would work. If you say it does, I guess I got to believe it." They went back to the dock with the sled.

Art came out of fish shack and said, "Where are you going to dive with the sled.

Eric said, "Jacky wants to see where we found the logs and the plane."

Art then said, "I've got two Aqua Lung's in the fish shack and three full tanks. Take the Canadian freighter. The logging company is supposed to start raising the logs next week."

"Have they made a deal with you, for the logs?"

"They gave me an offer, but I told them to wait until they raise some of them."

"They insisted, that they wanted to make a deal first." Art said, "I told them to forget it. I finally got another company to raise the logs. I know the owner of this company, I told him what the offer was. He said that it was much too low, even for third-grade logs. I have been told that someone has been diving to look at the logs. I think it was somebody from the company that made the offer."

Jacky and Eric loaded up the sled and Aqua Lungs in the Canadian freighter. Art got a chart of Beaver Island and surrounding area. He marked the area where the marker buoy should be. They headed out to the area and found no buoy.

They hooked up the sea sled and Eric said, "You want to try this sled, or do you want me to go first?"

She said, "You have me so intrigued by your sled, that I've got to try it."

"Okay Jacky get your tank on and get into the water. She put on her tank, then rolled into the water and got on the sled."

"Jacky, I know we have explained this sled, but you have never physically tried it, so it's best to practice some maneuvers first before you go deep."

Jacky did the up-and-down, the right and left, the inverted cruise, then she came up to the surface. She gave Eric the okay signal, then down to the bottom signal. Eric ran parallel courses for about 20 minutes. When a marker buoy popped up, so did Jacky.

She said she found the buoy anchor and some logs. Eric said, "Let's get the sled out of the water and go down to check it out. I don't think the buoy would break loose by itself. It was either run over by a boat or cut on purpose."

And Jacky climbed aboard and had a cup of hot coffee out of a thermos."

Jacky said, "I think the anchor line was purposely cut, I think I know why". Then she asked Eric if he had a knife with him.

"He said yeah I've got my hunting knife."

Jacky said good "Let's go down and check something out." They had the boat anchored by now. They went down and found the logs There were some big pine or spruce logs, then there were a bunch of smaller logs about 12 inches in diameter. Some were 20 to 30 feet long. The small logs were on the bottom. Jacky went to the small logs and hacked at one of them. She got a small chip and put it in the pocket of her wetsuit.

As they were coming up they noticed another boat alongside of their boat. Someone was hanging over the bow and then their anchor line was dropped into the water. Jacky pointed to their boat, Eric got the idea and swam to the stern of the freighter. Jacky swam under the intruder boat. It was about 16 foot, Jacky saw that it was a laminated Hull and that it was double planked. When double planked on a small boat, the planks cross diagonally, but are very thin. Jacky pried out a few inches of the outer planks, amid ship. Then she poked her knife through in two places and ripped out a hole about 3 inches, the width of the plank.

They had fired up their out board engine just at the time Jacky ripped a hole in their boat. She went down to make sure she cleared the prop. When they saw Eric get in the boat, they turned their boat around to attack Eric. Then they saw Jacky climb aboard and they changed their mind because it was even odds. They changed their mind again when they saw Jacky's female profile in her wetsuit jacket, besides their boat was sinking.

One guy had a knife, the other had a hatchet. The Guy with the knife decided he would go after the gal first because she would be easy (Mistake) he went down fast. She had his knife and he was face down in the bottom of the boat. The second guy saw his brother lying face down and he went after Jacky with his hatchet. (Mistake number two)

Eric said "Jacky I guess you don't need my help."

"Yeah I do Eric." and she handed the confiscated knife to Eric. She said cut their anchor line and tie it to the freighters line, which is what Eric did. Then Jacky found some more rope lying in the bow of the Canadian Freighter and she tied them face-to-face. She had them so tight with a rope around their necks that they were almost kissing each other, they didn't like it. One guy really smelled of garlic, the other almost begged to get his face away from his.

Jacky said, "Suffer you bastard you didn't mind killing us." She took her foot and pushed them off the seat and were now laying down in the wet bilge

Eric then said, "Jacky you really know how to treat the bad asses."

"Eric I have met enough of them, it seems that I attract them. After I while you get to dislike them very much. They have the idea that since I'm a gal whatever they want to do will be easy. They never learn."

"Well look at that Jacky, their boat is going under. Looks like poor maintenance."

Jacky said, "Looks like we will have to give them a lift back to Arts dock, then call the sheriff".

"Jacky what did you find down there on the logs?"

"Eric those small logs came from South America. Have you ever heard of Lignum Vitae? It is a very dense close grained wood. It is very wear resistant and does not absorb water. It is more than twice the weight of Mahogany and much more expensive."

"Eric when I was down under on the sled, what I saw were not logs that were dumped by one errant log boom. These logs were dumped purposely. They have not been there for 60 or 70 years. These Lignum Vitae logs were dumped at the north end of Beaver Island during the war. Care to ask why? She said the reason is, this is a very expensive wood, there was a lot of duty to be paid on it. It came from South America, so there would be duty to be paid to the Canadian government. Then as it entered America, there would duty to be paid to US customs."

"They loaded up somewhere in the Gulf of St. Lawrence below Québec. With Lignum Vitae, and a pile of pulp logs on top. The lumber carriers, which are very common on the St. Lawrence, are called Guallettes. They are shallow draft and flat bottom. The bottoms of the boats are made of 12 by 12's, so they can run up on shore at low tide to be loaded or unloaded, in an out of the way place, away from prying eyes of the Canadian Customs."

"The shallow draft boats are capable of navigating the Ottawa River. All the way to North Bay, and then to Georgian Bay, which is on the northern side of Lake Huron. Finally through the Straits of Mackinac to Beaver Island, the dumping ground. The South American country where the wood came from, also knew of its value. They put a fantastically heavy Duty on every log taken out of their country, so it was smuggled out of Brazil, smuggled into Canada and then smuggled into the US. After the war the need was not so great. The guy that set this up is dead. Only a few people know about it."

Eric said, "Jacky I don't doubt anything you said, but how did you know about all of this."

"I knew about it back in Chicago. You were talking about the sunken logs, that went down in a storm 70 years ago. I didn't buy it. I knew about Lignum Vitae and its weight. Remember when we went to the museum, you were playing with some machines. I was checking out Lignum Vitae, its specs and where it came from."

"During the war many ships were built and Lignum Vitae was used as a prop shaft bearing. It was used as a water cooled outer strut bearing, was wear resistant and did not absorb water. It was as good, if not better, than Bronze, which was in short supply during the war. Jacky said that she had talked with Doc about it. He checked on who used it during the war and who is using it now. The who is using it now, may lead us to who hired these hatchet men."

"Let's get these guys back to Arts and get hold of the sheriff."

"Jacky, it would be good if we got these guys to talk before the sheriff gets there. Once the sheriff has them, they will have a lawyer to protect them. You think Art will let us use the famous fish gut trick?"

Jacky said, "I think that will work pretty good. It will just piss Art off, knowing that these two creeps tried to kill us.

"You know what their big mistake was?" asked Eric.

"What was that?"

"They attacked you first."

"Well Eric, I never told you this before. I'm going to be your trainer when we get to the Achnacarry Castle, which is the commando training area. I am going to teach you and Arch to be hand to hand warriors. You will be so damn tough you will scare yourself."

"Now let's get these two creeps back to the fish shack." They got back to the harbor and saw Art's Chris-Craft tied to the Cora Lee. Eric pulled alongside of the boarding ladder and secured the freighter. Jacky went aboard and found Mario and Angel in the after cockpit sucking on a beer.

She asked Mario to roust up Doc and Art. Art, Bill and Doc came bounding up the stairwell and into the cockpit. She said, "We were right Doc, this is a shit load of Lignum Vitae on the bottom. Art, we have two guys in the bilge of your boat, who didn't want us to tell you about what was down there."

"The two gentlemen I am referring to, using the term loosely, Eric and I have decided to request the use of your fish guts interrogation system."

Doc said, "Jacky it sounds like you have everything under control".

"I think so, Eric is in the freighter keeping our guests quiet."

Art then said, "I think that Bill, Arch, Peter and I might want to help with the interrogation."

Doc said, "Than maybe Art should get a hold of the sheriff."

Jacky then said, "Tell him not to hurry. I like to know who was trying to kill me and why."

"It's just noon right now," said Art, " I'll tell him to come by for a fish boil at 5 PM. I think that a couple hours in the fish guts, they will tell you anything you want to know."

Jacky said, "Okay Art, we will head to your dock." Jacky got into the freighter and pointed to the dock. "Okay you to bilge rats, as soon as we get to the dock you can get up off your face. When we get to the dock we just want you to climb up and just stand there for a few minutes."

Eric said, "Up on the dock and stay there." The big guy started to run, Eric stopped him. Their hands were just tied in front of them, so they were not too incapacitated and they knew it.

Jacky said, "We just want to talk to you two guys. First-your names." The bigger of the two said, "Fuck you bitch." And he took a side swing with his hands tied together. As he swung to the left she avoided his fist, but pushed around to make a 180° turn, then she kicked him in the back of both knees, he folded up. She kicked him in the butt and he went down on his face.

He got up and said, "If my hands were not tied, I'd kick the shit out of you bitch."

"Didn't I tell you that I don't like to be called that, you piss ant." she said, "Hold your Hands out." she untied his hands.

He backed away real quick, reached in his hip pocket and came up with a switchblade, moving it from side to side. She reached into her pocket and came up with another switchblade. "I took this blade off a rapist in Chicago, then kicked the shit out of him. I like your knife better."

She threw her knife in the water. He figured that this was his chance and lunged at her. It was so quick that Eric didn't see what happened next, neither did the guy with the knife. He was down on his face, she had a new knife. She cut off the corners of his ear lobes, off both ears"

She said, "Now get up, I'm through playing games with you."

Eric said, "Let's bring them in the back, where they clean the fish." They made a rope harness for each guy, just like they did for the General and the Admiral. When they got them harnessed up, they lifted them so they were standing on their tiptoes, then tied them face to face.

Eric asked, "Why face-to-face?"

"You didn't see what happened to the Admiral and the General." She said, "Fish guts really get bad, especially if you're in it. One of them is bound to heave his guts out, right in the other guys face, then a chain reaction. We may not even go that far before they start talking. The shoe trick worked pretty good with the Admiral." She explained it to Eric.

Just then Doc, Art And Bill came in as Jacky was saying, "We got to take their shoes off or Art will be pissed off."

Art caught what she was saying. He said, "Damn right I'll be pissed. If you get those big clod hoppers in my brand-new blades, take off their shoes." Eric and Jacky did that.

Jacky said, "First off, let's get some names." The big guy said, "Go screw yourself." The other guys said, "What's this about taking our shoes off."

"Art doesn't want his cutter blades ruined if we lower you too far into those fish guts."

"My name is Jim Wagner and he's Bob Wagner. What else do you want to know, I ain't going in no fish guts."

Bob then said "Shut up you ass hole they can't do this, it's illegal."

"So is trying to kill us you bastard "

Jim said, "What do you want to know? I ain't going into no fish guts."

"Shut up Jim, they ain't going to do it."

Art pressed the up button on the pendant and lifted them 4 feet above the floor. Art said "Check their pockets for anything metal." They patted them down and said, "Okay." Art pressed the lift button and Jim started to scream.

Bob said, "They are bluffing."

They were now swung over the tank and Art lowered them. When their feet hit the fish guts, Bob said, "I'll talk." Bob was singing like a canary and Jim was crying his eyes out.

Just then Linda came into the fish shack, and she said, "Art, When are you going to start setting up for the fish Boil." Then she walked further back toward the fish cleaning area. she saw two guys hanging over the fish gut tank.

Art what's going on? Art started to explain, when Linda burst out with, "Bob and Jim what in the hell are you doing? Are you going swimming in the fish guts?"

Bob said "I hope not Linda."

She said, "Set them down on the floor. Hose them off and untie them, they are my cousins."

Jacky said, "You sure got some weird cousins ."

"I know that, Jacky but they are harmless."

"They tried to kill me, and Eric."

"But you are both alive. See what I mean, harmless." Linda asked them what they were doing out on the lake where the logs were.

They said, "Their dad, Linda's uncle Lou, told them about some valuable logs that were dumped in the mid-and late 40s. Lou said that before he broke his legs in a truck accident, he used to work as a deck hand on a riverboat. He worked for the Le Blanc River Transport. He said maybe once a month they would take a load of logs from Rimouski, then Pulp wood would be piled on top. Paul LeBlanc knew someone at Algona Mills in North Channel. He would load the pulpwood at Algoma Mills."

"Then he would go through the Straits of Mackinac and head for beaver Island. He would then dump half his load of Lignum Vitae at the north end of Beaver Island. Paul LeBlanc then delivered the rest to some company in Green Bay and collected cash, half to be paid to his contact in Canada. LeBlanc screwed his Canadian partner. LeBlanc told Lou he would wait two years, then they could go back, raise the logs and make a lot of money."

"Lou never did believe LeBlanc. LeBlanc was killed in a Quebec Saloon. He told his sons Jim and Bob that someday he would go looking for the Lignum Vitae. He knew it was north of Beaver Island, Garden Island, Whiskey Island or Hog Island. One day Jim and Bob spotted a marker buoy. They got some SCUBA gear and went back and dove on this site. They found the logs, marked the site on a chart and cut the buoy free. Bob and Jim had figured that these logs were their inheritance. Lou would be surprised when they brought some of these is logs home. When they found Eric and Jacky's boat at the site Jim and Bob thought they were being robbed of their rightful inheritance."

Linda then said, "What gives you the right to attack somebody, because you think some logs are yours."

Bob said, "Those logs were my Dad's because he and LeBlanc dumped them there.

Doc said, "If what you two guys say is true. Then doesn't that make your daddy a smuggler. They smuggled it into two countries. That would make him wanted by Canada and the United States."

Art said, "Linda didn't you say that your uncle lived on Hog Island? Jim does your dad have a boat? He did, but now it's sunk by the logs."

Doc said, "Linda why don't you let Juan take you to Hog Island and bring your uncle here for the fish boil. Then maybe we can get this log thing all straightened out."

Art said, "It's only seven or 8 miles to Hog Island so you can be there and back in 30 minutes." Linda and Juan took off in the launch, Linda directed him to the dock. There was a giant of a man about 6'6" standing on the dock. He looked to be a friendly sort.

He seemed agile enough, but he was balancing on a crutch. He said,, "How are you Linda? You sure are looking good."

"I'm fine Lou how are you?"

"Can't complain, but Art said those two of the boys of mine got themselves in some kind of trouble."

"Yeah they did Lou, but I think maybe you and I can iron it out and everybody will come out the better for it. I really don't think it's any big problem, other than them trying to kill a couple of our friends."

"Well it sounds like they didn't succeed, did they have a good reason?"

"Well both Bob and Jim thought there was a good reason. That's for you to help iron out, but right now let's get to the fish boil." Lou got into the launch. Juan tried to help but he waved him off with his crutch. "Six months ago, I would have said give me a hand, but the more I do things the easier it gets."

"Linda asked Lou how he screwed up his legs."

He said, "It was on a construction site. I was directing a truck that was backing up to get loaded. It was muddy clay, I slipped and both legs went under the rear wheels, I was lucky he wasn't loaded."

Juan was running flat out and the big old Chrysler engine was really purring. They were back at Arts dock in a very short time. Linda got out of the launch and tied the bow line, Lou was up on the dock using his crutch like he was a pole-vaulter.

Linda said, "You do that pretty good Lou."

"I am getting used to this damn crutch. When the doctor says that I don't need any more, I may just tell him to go to hell."

"Well I guess I had better go and find them and find out what kind of trouble they gotten themselves into." Lou walked over behind the fish shack . Art was setting up for the fish boil. "He said hi Art, how are they hanging?"

"Pretty good Lou. How's it going with you?"

"Also pretty good, but I don't know about Jim and Bob."

"Nothing too serious Lou. At least they didn't kill anyone."

"Yeah but I heard, they tried to kill two people."

Art said, "Come on let's go listen to their side." Art, Linda and Lou walked over to where Doc and Bill were talking to Eric and Jacky.

Linda asked, "Where's Jim and Bob?" And she introduced Lou.

Jacky said, "She would get Jim and Bob." She went to a storage shed, opened the door and said, "Come on you guys time to see your father." She heard them say, "Aw Shit ." "Get out of There or I'll come in and get you."

"Okay were coming." And they walked over to the group and said, "Hi dad, how's it going."

"Don't try to sweet talk me. I hear you got yourselves into a lot of trouble."

"Well not really."

"What do you mean not really? Didn't you try to kill a couple of people, who were they?" "This guy here named Eric, and a gal named Jacky."

"Jim you must be shitting me. You tried to kill this beautiful lady."

"Well she kicked the shit, out of me and Bob."

"Was that before or after you tried to kill them?"

Then Bob said meekly. "It was after . She's a one-woman fighting force."

"You mean that pretty little gal, kicked the hell out of both the you big strong boys.

"What about Eric what did he do?"

"He watched."

"That's hard to believe."

"Eric said believe it or not Lou, she could kick the hell out of a half a dozen guys like Jim and Bob. I've seen her in action before."

Linda explained how they thought, that Eric and Jacky were claim jumpers, trying to steal your logs, that you and LeBlanc had dumped there years before.

Doc said, "Whoever raises these logs will have to pay the duty owed. That would be both to the Canadian and the US government, plus I think there would be a large fine to be paid by Lou."

Lou said, "That it sounds like the logs would hardly be worth raising."

Doc said, "I've got a lot of clout in Washington and some in Canada, I think I can get them both to forget the fines and duty. That is if we can get Art and Lou to work together on this project."

Art came over and said, "I think I heard my name is called. So, what's up?"

They explained what they had been talking about and Art and Lou agreed to a partnership, then Art said let's eat."

Lou said, "That sounds good but something's got to be done first. Both of you boys have to apologize to Eric and Jacky in front of all of these people, by the way where is my boat?"

"On the bottom."

"What do you mean on the bottom?"

"It's sunk, but we know where it is and we can get it up."

"Okay, so now go and apologize. Where is Jacky?"

Doc said, "Here she comes with Sandra and Kelly."

Three beautiful gals, were walking down from Art and Linda's house. They were dressed in sexy evening gowns. Doc got up in front of all the people and called their attention. " Folks this is going to be a great night. Art and his crew are in the process of doing a great fish boil, but before that, we have three beautiful gals who are going to entertain you with some great singing."

Sandra, Kelly, and Jacky sang a few songs, then Ritchie soloed on his Sax. By now everybody felt that they were in Orchestra Hall. The sun had gone down and the moon was starting to show itself. The weather was perfect at about 80°, the fish were ready to eat. Almost everybody who lives on the island always came to Arts Fish boils. Art didn't have to call anyone. He had an 80 foot tall flagpole on the corner of his dock. All he did was raise the fish boil flag and very quickly word would get around. The women brought pies cakes and other desserts. The men brought beer and booze.

Art cooked the fish, small onions, small potatoes and little Brussels sprouts. Linda went into the fish shack and melted the butter to dip the fish and to put on the veggies. Everyone knew when Arts flag goes up, it's feast time.

It was a great meal and now it was desert time. After dinner drinks, Mario played some enchanting music on his violin. After Mario came the three gals again to sing a few songs, then asked if there was any requests. They did quite a few requests and finally Sandra addressed the people and said, " By special request of Kelly and myself, Jacky has agreed to sing a song that you all will love."

All the lights were turned down except two of them, which were kerosene lanterns. They were set on each side of her and slightly behind, it had a beautiful effect. There was dead silence, Jacky sang the most beautiful rendition of Ava Maria. When she finished you could hear a pin drop, then a fantastic applause.

Lou turned to his two sons and said. "And you two idiots tried to kill that Angel."

"But Dad we didn't know, we thought they were claim jumping, trying to steal your logs."

"They never were my logs, but thanks to Doc we may wind up with part of them."

"Now you and your brother get up there and apologize to Jacky and Eric, make it nice and loud, so everybody can hear it."

Jim and Bob got up on the platform where the three girls were standing. Kelly looked at the two guys and said, "It looks like we got two more singers here. "

Bob said, "No ma'am, we just have something to say to Jacky and Eric."

Jacky said, "Okay boys what have you got to say?" She knew what they were up there for, she was going to drag it out and make the guys suffer a little more than they planned on.

Bob started to say that he was sorry about, then he quit and said, "You tell her Jim."

Jim said, "Why don't you Bob?"

"I can't I got something in my throat."

"That's a lot of bull Bob."

"Well Jacky, Bob and I just want to apologize to you and Eric."

"Step up closer to the microphone, so ever everybody can hear you."

He got closer to the microphone. He talked into the mike, and said it again. "We want to say that, we are sorry for what we did.

"Do what, Jim?"

"You know what we did."

"I know what you did, but nobody else does."

"Come over by the mike Bob, you tell everybody what you did loud enough so they can all hear. Bob said, "We're sorry that Jim and I, almost killed you and Eric."

"That's much better. I think that we both can accept your apology." Jim and Bob then started to walk off the platform.

When Jacky said wait a minute boys. "You're not through yet. You ain't getting off that easy. While it seems that you boys are afraid of the mike, bashful I would say. So before you get off this platform , you're going to sing a couple songs for all these nice people."

Jim said, "We can't do that, we ain't never ever sang in front of a bunch of people."

"You're going to learn real fast, because Mario has got some sheet music for you."

Mario stepped up with some sheet music and said, "Take your pick boys. Richie and Lester will accompany you." He walked away. They looked at the music, then said, "Mule Train." Richie and Lester nodded their heads and started to play. Jim and Bob started to sing, very low at first, then louder and better. They started to get the feel of the music and pretty soon they were singing real good. It sounded like Frankie Lane. When they finished Mule Train, they said That Lucky Old Sun. After doing a great job on that, they were really getting into it and sang On Top Of Old Smokey.

Then Jacky said, "Okay boys that's enough punishment, I think you're enjoying this too much. By the way I think you boys are pretty damn good. Just then a stranger walked up to the platform and introduced himself as Roger Witco . He said that he was the one that called from Chicago yacht club. He was from Sun records and what he heard tonight, is exactly what his company is looking for new, great voices.

Jacky said, "For the girls you will have to wait, till we get back to Chicago. These two are through with their punishment tour, so ask them."

The boy's agreed to meet Witco at Sun records new office in Nashville. He gave them 10 $100 bill's. He said, "This is for airfare and new clothes which you will need. One thing you want to do, even before you audition for the big boss is to make a good visual impression. But if you sing like you did tonight, you will be cutting records in a short time."

The boys then thanked Jacky. And apologized again then stepped down off the platform. They walked over to where Lou was standing and apologized to him as well.

Lou just smiled and said, "As always boys, all is well that ends well."

"I just hope you guys still remember me, after you get rich and famous."

"Don't worry you will always be number one, Dad."

Bill and Jacky came over, and Bill commented to Jim and Bob. "You are the luckiest bastards alive. You guys are not the first ones that have tried to do in this beautiful gal here. I wish you luck in Nashville." Jacky said that she holds no grudge against you."

Jacky grabs Bob by both ears, looks him straight in the eyes and held them there for a few minutes. This scared the hell out of him. Then she said, "Both of you get your butts on that plane tomorrow, when you get to Nashville, do your old man proud, or maybe I'll have to kick your ass again." She smiled and let Bob go. Then both Bill and Jacky laughed and wished the guys the best of luck."

"Jim looked at Jacky and told her, that she had to be one of the nicest people he had ever met. After what we tried to do, you should really hate us."

"Maybe I should but I don't. I had a talk with your cousin Linda, she said that you are really nice guys, who were trying to protect what they thought was their dad's property. When their dad had broken both of his legs, they picked up the slack. They refused any charity, or family help. They hired a private nurse to take care of Lou, then they worked for anyone that would hire them. So I got to say Linda was right. From what I heard tonight you guys will be big in Nashville."

It was now about 10:30 at night, Doc and Art came over and talked to Bill and Jacky. They were both bombed out of their minds. They finished a bottle of Arts Drambuie, after a few shots of scotch. Doc sent Juan back to the Schooner, for a bottle of Docs Green Chartreuse. Juan saw what shape Doc was in, so he tried to talk him out of getting the hundred and ten proof, Green Chartreuse. But Doc was the boss, so he got into the launch and headed for the Cora Lee .

When Juan got to the schooner, and climbed up on deck. He saw Mario in the cockpit drinking coffee. Juan explained his problem.

"Doc is the boss, but he is blasted out of his gourd. This hundred and ten proof booze . Will put him right over the edge."

Mario said, "Okay Juan, let's change the booze. Mario got a bottle of Green Chartreuse, and an empty Chartreuse bottle. Using a funnel, he poured more than half of it, into the empty bottle, and put that bottle on the table. Then he told Juan to bring the bottles. And come to his laboratory."

They went down into Mario's galley. "Mario said to pour some more chartreuse into the second bottle." Number one bottle was one third full. The second bottle was two thirds full. And then Mario added a cup of clear Karo syrup, to each bottle. Then he added some mint sauce and some peppermint. They tasted the mixture and they liked it. So they added it to number one bottle. Number one bottle was about 2 cups short of being full. So Mario added more karo syrup it tasted pretty good but it needed a little bite. Mario added some more karo and some clear hot spiced sauce, again he added a quarter of a cup of a mixture of water vanilla and almond extract. Green food coloring, mint sauce and some peppermint. The bottle was now full, but only 30 proof. They tasted it and pronounced it not too bad.

Juan took the bottle, he got into the launch and headed for the dock. When he pulled up to the dock. He could see Art and Doc were sitting at a table with empty glasses. Juan brought the bottle over. He Poured some in each class. Doc said, "Prosit." and they both picked up their glasses.

They were both smacking their lips, as if they were trying to make up their mind. Art reached out and grabbed the bottle and poured two more glasses. "You know that's not half bad," Doc agreed, "but it does have a pretty good bite."

"Well Doc you sure know how to pick a good liquor". Juan just stood there smiling.

The party ended and Art staggered home, everyone else headed out to the ship. Mario brewed gallons of coffee and most everyone was in the after cockpit, sucking it up like there was no tomorrow. Bill and Jacky grabbed some coffee and walked up to the bow. They sat down on the bench seats and looked out over the harbor. It was a beautiful moonlit night and it was a wonderful view. "Jacky remember what you did, after you saved your çommandos and myself in France?"

"After we got back to England I tried everything to find you. But you just seem to have disappeared. Nobody could or would tell me how to find you."

Chapter 27

Bill pops the Question. Kelly's Reuben.

"After a war I was discharged from the RAF. I looked all over for you, I finally found that you were discharged and left the country. They thought you went to the USA I had no idea where you would go in the US." Before I left England. I went to see Art Hobson, who was a general in the commandos. He said that he would contact me as soon as he heard of your whereabouts."

"Art contacted me and told me of Admiral Hunter's plan to pick you up in Sturgeon Bay. As soon as I heard this I got ahold of Doc and signed on. Doc agreed for me to come aboard, but made me promise not to do anything that may affect the mission."

"I heard through the grapevine, that you had been looking for me. Doc just casually mentioned, that you would be aboard. When Doc said that he was sending a plane to pick us up in Sturgeon Bay, I was excited and anxious to see you."

"When we got to Beaver Island. and we met for the first time in almost 5 years, you just didn't seem too enthusiastic. So I decided that what I heard through the grapevine, was just a rumor."

"It was no rumor. I had been looking for you. I was just honoring that agreement that I made with Doc. Maybe I just went a little too far, but I'd like to change that if you will let me. I knew that you were going to commando training school in Scotland and I know you are to train, Eric and Arch and Peter. After you get through with that mission, I will be back in Chicago. I have a motorcycle shop in Chicago. I just found out the other day while talking to Arch that you are in the motorcycle business in Hannibal Missouri."

"I have a partner in that shop in Missouri. I talked to him on the phone while we we're in Chicago. I called Hannibal today, before we set sail out of Chicago. Word had already gotten out about the bracelet rapists, also the people in Hannibal had already heard about the traitors that were hung. With all these people knowing that I was Jimbo's partner, it did not hurt business at all. He said he had to hire another mechanic because he couldn't keep up with all the work. I told them that I was considering not going back to Hannibal, then asked him if he would consider buying me out."

"He said that he would rather that I come back to Hannibal, but if I wanted out, it would be not a problem. He said my share has tripled in value."

"I told him that I just wanted what I originally put in the shop, because I had been away ever since we first opened the shop. The increase in value has happened while Jimbo was running it by himself."

"Jacky you have always been well known, around Hannibal. Your Buddy Rich on the Hannibal PD, has a friend on the Chicago PD. That's how the people here found out about the Bracelet rapists. There are pictures of Jacky Sax all over town and in Jacky and Jimbo's bike shop. People come to hang around and want to know what bike that you rode. When I told them that you rode a Vincent Black lightning everybody seemed to want one. I've sold four Vincents in the last three weeks and four more on order, all "Black Lightnings."

Jimbo then said, "Your bike was sitting out in the shop, and people just had to sit on the seat, that Jacky sat on. So I moved it up into the front office. Actually in the front window. People would come in and ask if that was Jacky's bike. I spent so much time explaining about your bike, that I finally decided to put up a sign next to your bike."

"Everybody knows they can buy a new Black Lightning for about $16,000, but I've had offers of up to $26,000 for your lightning. So when you say that you only want what you put in the shop, you are actually adding value, just by using your famous name. Thanks to you Jacky, business is great and your share has at least tripled."

"Okay Jimbo good talking to you and I'm glad you are doing good. I'll call you when I get back to Chicago. That will probably be in the spring."

"Bill I just wouldn't feel right, about taking more than I put in the shop."

"I understand how you feel, since you left shortly after you and Jimbo started the shop. Then again I can see Jimbo's side. Your name has it made it grow."

"Jacky I think I have the solution, to your dilemma. You tell Jimbo that you will only accept the amount of your original investment. He pays you that amount, then you are no longer a part owner of a Hannibal motorcycle shop. Then you can become half owner of a Chicago bike shop, namely Bill's bikes. What I'm asking you Jacky, is to marry me and Bill's Bikes. You get half a bike shop, and me thrown in as an extra bonus."

"You know that was the worst is marriage Proposal, I have ever heard of. I should have recorded it so we could play it back for our kids someday. I guess my answer is just as weird as your proposal. The answer is yes, I would love to become Mrs. Turner."

"Back during the war there was a field in France, where a beautiful girl, singing so very beautifully, saved the lives of 12 people. I said right there, that someday I'm going to marry that gal."

"I have one obligation to complete first, then after that you can set the date."

"That's one of the things that I've loved about you Jacky. No matter what you want to do, you will always complete your obligations first." He then took her and held her close and kissed her very deeply, Jacky responded, as she realized that she was truly in love.

"Bill I would really like to tell Doc, about our decision to get married."

"I was thinking the same thing, but we may have to wait till morning. Art and Doc have drinking enough Drambue and Green Chartreuse to paralyze a whole platoon of commandos, but let's go see if we can find him."

And they did find Doc sitting at the table in the after cockpit he was just saying goodnight to three other people, as they staggered off to hit the sack. He was now sitting alone nursing a drink. "Hi ! Where have you two been, we thought we had left you on the beach. Juan was just about to take a run in to see if you were still on the dock."

"Doc Jacky and I have something important to tell you. We just wanted to make sure you were sober enough to hear what we have to say."

"Bill when the captain of a ship drinks so much that he doesn't know what the hell going on around him on his ship, then he shouldn't be captain. I believe right now that I am speaking, to the future Mr. and Mrs. Bill Turner." Jacky just leaned over and kissed Doc on the cheek.

Doc Then poured three shot glasses of Mario's mixture and said, "This deserves a toast." After they did the toast, Bill said, "Doc this is pretty good stuff, where have you been hiding it."

"I thought it was green chartreuse but it's not. I don't know what it is, but it is good, we will have to ask Juan in the morning . Meanwhile congratulations are in order for you two. We can let everyone else know at breakfast and have a party tomorrow night. On second thought we had better wait till noon to make the announcement. Probably only half the people, will make it for breakfast, including me."

"Bill I know that you have been looking for Jacky, for a long time. I couldn't believe, how long it was taking you to pop the question."

"Doc I was just trying to honor, the agreement that we made when you told me that Jacky was coming aboard."

"Bill I only meant for you not to talk her out of the mission, that she agreed to do."

"Doc I agree to do the mission, then back to Chicago to make sure that Bill doesn't change his mind."

"Jacky that will never happen, besides I'm going with you as far as Achnacarry Castle. The powers that be won't let me go any further on this mission, because I'm still in the RAF reserved."

"But I will be waiting for you, when you get back. I'll be at Achnacarry, ready to take you back to Chicago."

"Once we get back we can have a quiet wedding and get on with living our lives, like ordinary people."

"Jacky," Doc said, "With you I don't think it will ever happen. Nobody will ever forget what you have done for your country. So now let's go hit the sack, see you in the morning."

"Bill I really don't want to say goodnight, and head to my own cabin. But I think we have to stay respectable, for a while anyway. Goodnight Bill." Bill grabbed her, and kissed her hard and fierce.

"Goodnight Jacky, I'll be dreaming about you."

Next morning Jacky and Bill were up at 6 AM, the only other person was Mario. He brewed coffee and baked rolls for breakfast. Mario, Jacky and Bill sat down at the cockpit table having coffee and rolls. It was a perfect morning, the three of them were just sitting back looking at the mouth of the harbor.

Bill said, "In the British Isles, there is no large freshwater lakes such as the American Great Lakes. It is really fascinating to sail, swim and be able to drink the water of the Great Lakes."

"Mario looked at Bill with a curious look on his face. "Bill where you come from, is an island, with hundreds of Inlets and Coves, nothing but water all around it."

"You're right Mario. But it's all salt water. You can't drink it. This water you can drink."

"If you guys are through talking about water."

"I have something much more important to say."

"What's more important to a sailor than water?"

"What is more important, is that I am going to change my name."

"What's wrong with Jacky and why change it?"

"I am not going to change Jacky."

"I'm going to change my last name."

"Mario said why change Sax? It's a neat name. Mario was becoming exasperated. You don't like it anymore? So what the hell are you going to change it to?"

"Mario you and Doc are first ones to know, I'm changing it to Turner."

"Now what makes you think that Turner sounds better than Sax? Oh wait a minute you mean Mrs. Turner, Mrs. Bill Turner.

"You got it DUMBO."

"Mario it sure took you a long time to figure it out."

Mario said, "Bill, it takes Jacky a roundabout way, of telling something."

"When I asked her to marry me, it took me a little while to decide, whether she said yes, or get lost. I finally figured out what she said, was yes."

"Well Bill, your asking wasn't the simplest thing, to figure out either."

"Mario then said that the question and answer period, worked out on the plus side. Congratulations to both you, I can hardly wait to tell everybody. It's the best news heard in a long time."

"Mario you have to keep it quiet, Doc and Jacky have decided to announce it at dinner tonight"

"Bill most everyone was hung over this morning, and didn't show up for breakfast. They will be hungry as hell by noon. They will be surprised, because I'll only be serving a light chicken broth and some small finger sandwiches. They will think of it as appetizers, but that's all they get. They will be smelling roast and all kinds of good things cooking, also a couple of banana cream cakes with fresh raspberries on top. This will be for your engagement party dinner. It will be a beautiful dinner for a most beautiful couple. Doc will make the announcement at a great dinner. I will send Juan ashore to invite Art and Linda to a celebration dinner. They will never forgive Doc, if they are not invited."

Precisely at noon. Doc picked up the microphone. "Now hear this, now hear this. This is your captain speaking, get your butt close to a speaker, because I'm only going to explain this once. I have heard rumors that Mario is trying to starve you, while you smell wonderful aromas coming from his galley. He has locked everyone except Juan and Angel, out of the galley. Mario has a method to his madness. He wants to starve you to the point of being hungry as hell. As Mario said, "I want everybody to be hungry as hell, for tonight's extra special feast."

Later Mario and his crew, were bringing the food into the main dining salon. He said, "It will be ready for all of you to go down into the salon in about five minutes."

Juan had taken the launch ashore to Art and Linda's house about three hours before the feast, early enough to make sure that they hadn't eaten yet. Juan told them that it was for a special occasion, a great feast. Juan told them that he honestly didn't know any more than that."

Linda had just gotten out of the shower when Juan arrived. Linda said, "Art get your butt into the shower, Juan looks like he is anxious to get back."

"Yes, I have to get back to help Mario in the galley."

Art then said, "Take off Juan, we can take the Chris-Craft out to the schooner."

"Okay thanks Art, I better get going."

Art and Linda arrived 20 minutes later.

Mario came up from the galley, dressed in his immaculate whites and his tall chef's hat. He said, "I will seat everyone at the large dining table." Which he did. Doc and Art at one end with Linda around the corner from Art. Then he seated everyone down each side of the table. The two Blondes at opposite ends from Doc and Art, but on each side across from each other, the obvious seats still empty. The two at the end of the table. The lights went almost completely out when the door opened to the galley. Bill and Jacky came in and sat down.

Almost completely unnoticed. Then Mario came in carrying a candelabra and set it down in front of Bill and Jacky.

The lights came back on and Doc stood up. "Mario you did two great things today. First you did a great thing in organizing and cooking this great feast, second great thing you did, that I didn't think you could, you kept this whole thing a secret, from last night till now. Since you have done so good in keeping quiet I'm going to give you the privilege of making the announcement."

Mario stood up and said, "Thank you, Boss, it is a privilege to make this announcement. Folks, I am a man of few words so I would like to introduce to you the future Mr. and Mrs. Bill Turner." Everyone stood up and cheered.

Jacky with tears in her eyes, stood up and said, "Thanks Mario", kissed him on the cheek, then sat down and kissed Bill.

Doc stood up and said, "This is an engagement party so let's celebrate, but let's eat first." Everybody cheered again and they did eat, it was a real feast. Everybody started filling their plates with roast beef, pork, turkey and fried chicken. Then came the potatoes gravy and a variety of vegetables. Mario outdid himself.

Before they started eating Kelly and Sandra got up, went to Jacky and Bill, congratulated them, kissed them both. Everybody got up and formed a line to congratulate the couple.

It finally got to Doc, he said, "He couldn't be more pleased , if it had been his own family."

"Jacky and Bill both spoke at the same time, saying, "We are family doc." Then he hugged them both and kissed Jacky.

Then Linda and Art wished them the best and kissed them both. Art said "Jacky when did you first decide that you and Bill would be married?"

"When I pulled him out of his bloody spitfire."

Bill turned to Jacky and said, "This is a fine time to let me know. If you told me back then, it would have saved a lot of looking for you.

"Well Bill if I knew you were interested, I wouldn't have gotten myself lost."

"Well I found you now and I'm not going to lose you again."

"I promise not to get lost again, now let's party." Everyone did party, it lasted till 3 AM. Everyone finally hit the sack and nobody got up till 9 AM, not even Mario. The galley was dead quiet, with only a night light on, an empty 12 cup coffee pot, a canister of ground coffee and a note saying, " Make your own, I ain't getting up till noon." signed Mario.

Actually Mario was up at 9 AM with a slight hangover. But once he got back to doing his thing which was cooking, his headache disappeared. To Mario cooking was a sedative more so than aspirin. He was making biscuits and gravy which everyone loved.

Although Bill asked Mario about a month ago, if he had ever made potato pancakes? Mario never gave Bill a definite answer. So Mario decided that this was the day to do it.

Jacky had also mentioned, "That before she was killed in an air raid, one of her mother's big treats after church on a Sunday morning was potato pancakes, with applesauce or apricot preserves on top."

Mario then said to himself, nobody makes better potato pancakes than, Chef Mario Fiorentino. He decided he would make his own special compote, instead of applesauce to put on top.

Mario got busy making his biscuit dough, and then he made the so-called gravy. When made in many restaurants it was biscuits and gravy. Gravy which could be poured. Mario's gravy was very heavy meat sauce with Italian sausage, pork sausage, onions, celery, and mushrooms. It was considered the best biscuits and gravy on the planet.

One by one the people started to arrive on deck. Once it was spread around that Mario was making biscuits and gravy. Everyone became immediately alive, ready to eat.

Bill was up earlier than most people. Mario told him about the potato pancake, Bill then went to Jacky's cabin and told her about the potato pancakes. She was up, showered and dressed inside of 10 minutes.

She met Bill up on deck and asked him when Mario was serving the pancakes?

"Right now Jacky," and they headed toward the dining cabin.

Most everyone was taking a couple of biscuits and covering them with Mario's meaty gravy. With that in one hand and a cup of coffee in the other, they headed up on deck to eat. Some of the people got their biscuits and gravy and parked their butts at the dining table.

Bill and Jacky sat at the end of the table and Mario served them potato pancakes, with his tasty compote of apricot , raspberry, lemon and orange wedges.

"Jacky said that her mother was a great cook. But she had never tasted potato pancakes and sauce as good as this." Bill agreed, they kept eating and Mario kept Cooking. Finally they were full and told Mario it was fantastic, but they could eat no more.

Mario said, "It was about time you quit. There is just enough left for me. I love potato pancakes and I am now getting hungry." Mario went into the galley and came back with a big serving plate full of pancakes. He sat down and polished them all off.

Everyone was so stuffed that they could hardly move. But a bunch of people got together and told Mario what a great job he did. They rigged up a hammock in the bow, from the foremast to the fore stay. They told Mario to go and take a nice leisurely nap, they would clean up his galley. He protested until they told him that Juan would be there to supervise. He agreed and climbed in the hammock and was sound asleep in less than a minute. Everybody worked in the galley and made it spotlessly clean. Juan said, "Mario will approve of the galley."

Then Kelly said, "Has anybody noticed how hard Mario works to feed us all some fantastic meals?"

Sandra spoke up, saying, "I would love to cook something for Mario, but he is such a professional that I couldn't cook anything that he would feel was made properly. I wouldn't think that Mario would complain, but I would feel bad if it didn't make him something real good"

Angel was standing there, and he asked Juan, "What does Mario like best."

One of Mario's favorites, "Is a Reuben sandwich."

Kelly smiled and said, "My last name ain't Bergman, for nothing. My folks owned a Jewish delicatessen and I've made more Reubens, than I care to count. When I make a Reuben, its known as unforgettable. It's too big to have a second one and you don't want the first one to end."

Juan said, "Mario has some corned beef in the freezer, that he was saving for corned beef hash."

Kelly asked Juan "If there was sauerkraut, and provolone or Swiss cheese. What about good rye bread."

He said, "There was about a dozen loaves of Rosen's rye, in the freezer."

"Let's get everything together and I'll get the meat thawed and sliced. And then we just wait for Mario to wake up. He has been sleeping for four hours. When he wakes up just keep him topside for 15 minutes and I'll deliver him the best Reuben he ever tasted."

Sandra walked over to Kelly and said, "You never told me that you were Jewish."

"You never asked."

"But you are a natural blonde."

"Is there any law against that? My mother is a Swede."

Mario woke up at 3:30 and Kelly went down to make his Reuben. When it was finished she put it on a large plate cut it in half and put a large slice of dill pickle on each side it was a thing of beauty, it weighed at least one and a half pounds. She found a candelabra and lit the candles.

They talked Mario into going to the rear cockpit, sitting at the table and having a beer. Sandra carried out the candelabra and set it down in front of Mario. He was totally confused until Kelly set the Reuben down in front of him. His eyes lit up and he flashed a great big smile.

He studied it for a short time said, "It's beautiful.", picked up half and took a big bite. He put the sandwich down and Mario sat back, fully chewed and savored the taste.

Mario then said, "I have always told everyone that there was only one place to get a Reuben that tasted this good and that is in Chicago."

Then Kelly piped up and said, "At Bergman's delicatessen on West Ontario." Both at the same time, said in unison. "Now I remember".

Mario said, "About three years ago, you were the blonde behind the counter who made my Reuben while I watched. I spent more than an hour eating that sandwich, it was wonderful."

Then Kelly said, "You came back to the counter and thanked me for a great Reuben, you Tipped me with a $20 bill. At that time I said I would never forget the customer that tipped me with a $20 bill. It wasn't till today, at this very moment, that I realized you were that customer."

"Don't feel bad Kelly, it didn't dawn on me either, until I tasted your fantastic Reuben. Whatever you do makes a difference, between good and fantastic."

"Mario, you get the goods, and I'll teach the world's best chef, how to make a great Reuben."

Mario said okay, "I'll call ahead for whatever you need and we will pick it up in Detroit, at the fire dock. After Detroit we will have a great Reuben Holiday. Mario finished his sandwich and said, "I can hardly wait till we get to Detroit." Then he got up and said, "I better go and come up with something for dinner."

Relax Mario and this is your day off. Juan and Angel are going to rustle up some cold cuts, for sandwiches and everybody can make their own.

It was a lazy sunny afternoon, everyone was just taking advantage of a sunny summer day. They were all just laying around doing nothing, because tomorrow we hoist sail.

Bill, Doc, Jacky and Angel were walking around the deck, just taking a leisurely stroll and looking things over. They were talking about Bill and Jacky's future as marriage partners and partners in the motorcycle business. They both agreed that it would be very interesting, a big challenge and a great experience.

Doc said , "Somehow word got back to Chicago, that you were going to get married. When you return to Chicago, The Clerk of Cook County, Richard J. Daley, insists on throwing you the biggest wedding, seen in Chicago for a long time."

Bill and Jacky agreed and said. "Okay if it makes him happy."

Doc said, "Angel let's move on out of here tomorrow."

"What time boss?"

"Not too early, about 8 AM after breakfast. So Angel talk to Juan and they spread the word about the departure time."

Next morning Mario had breakfast ready at 6 AM corned beef hash and scrambled eggs. After that everyone was up on deck and ready to move out. All sail stops were off and the booms were free. All that was needed was to raise the sails and then hoist the Anchor. They raised the sails, Then Mario went forward and turned on the anchor winch. About 30 feet of chain came in and then it stopped. Mario went aft and talked to Angel They decided to kick in the diesels and move ahead across the anchor and try to raise it from another direction. They did the same thing, in two more different directions.

Nothing worked. Eric and Arch said they would go down and check it to find the problem, they got their gear and went over the side. Eric found it first and then pointed it out to Arch. It was about a 60 foot steel boat, the anchor was snagged in the open engine hatch. They swam around it and found it had Coast Guard marking on it. It was a buoy tender.

Art and Linda, had come out to the schooner early that morning, to say goodbye to their friends. "Art said that he thought that the boat on the bottom was the Shaw, a Coast Guard buoy tender."

Arch said, "It looked like that was the name on the stern."

Art said, "The Shaw was on a South course, She passed between Hog Island and Garden Island which are north of Beaver Island. She was going to pass on the east side of Beaver Island on a course to Petosky, which was straight east.

It was two years ago in late fall. A stormy night with high winds and rain. Shaw just passed Hog Island, which was probably why she didn't show up on radar. Most ships at this time had radar, as did the Des Plaines a 290 foot freighter, out of Escanaba on the East Coast of Wisconsin. She was on an eastward course passing just north of Beaver Island, when she struck the Shaw about midship.

It sprung the hull plates, and blew the engine hatch cover over the side. It looked like she was going to go down fast. The three-man crew decided that they had better launch a lifeboat in a big hurry. The petty officer at the helm, decided to lock the wheel in place and keep the engines running and the screws turning. This was to keep this Shaw stable while launching the lifeboat. The Shaw's crew spent the next two hours in the lifeboat, when finally the Des Plaines found them and picked them up.

The next day the storm died out, and it was a sunny day. And the Shaw was not to be found. The Coast Guard and the Navy had about five ships searching for two days with electronics equipment for searching underwater. They had thought it would be easy to find. She was supposedly sinking fast, direction of the wind was Northeast, she should have been somewhere east of Hog Island. Instead she wound up in the opposite direction and into Beaver Island Harbor."

"So what must have happened, is that the engines kept running, she stayed up long enough to get to this spot and then sink. Art then said. "I will report it to the Coast Guard. I think you had better get your anchor and head out of here before you find any more sunken treasure."

"I think you are right Art. From what Eric said only one fluke of the anchor is in the engine compartment." Doc said, "Ease out another 50 foot of scope on our anchor chain. Angel, fire up the diesels and over run our own anchor until it stops. Mario let go of the anchor number two and let it out till it hits bottom, now take the 30feet log chain, which had been lowered on a half inch rope and wrap one end of it around the protruding anchor fluke. Then pull it tight and take the log chains grab hook and attach it to the number two anchor chain. Now hoist number two anchor, which should pull the fluke out of the engine compartment, next lower the anchor back to the bottom and remove the log chain. Now both anchors are free. The half-inch rope is still tied to the log chain and it is hauled aboard. Number one anchor is hauled up."

Then Art said, "See you in Chicago for Jacky and Bill's wedding as he and Linda headed for the dock."

They got all the sails up and everyone at their station, Angel at the helm. Mario hoists anchor number one. Juan backs the jib and the ship slowly turns toward the mouth of the harbor. She picks up speed and is making about 12 knots, on the run to the Straits of Mackinac, almost straight east, with the King fisherman flying for about 140 miles, then south on a beam reach to Port Huron, to Lake St. Clair and to Detroit.

Mario went aft to the helm to talk to Angel.

He asked "How far to Detroit?" "

"Angel said about 375 miles give or take a few, 75 of that is up a river into Lake St. Clair and then the Detroit River. We will tie up at the fire boat dock. It will take 42 and 44 hours. And this being 11 AM Sunday I would say that we will be docked in Detroit at about 7 AM to 9 AM Tuesday."

"I've got to order some supplies and have them delivered to the firehouse in Detroit. Doc told me we were going to tie up at the fire boat."

"I thought that he just wanted to say hello to his friend Chief Bishop."

"But you probably have something else planned, haven't you Mario?"

"Just great Reubens, Angel. Doc has invited the whole fire crew for lunch."

They were now on a run towards the Straits. It was just a little short of 40 miles to the bridge. It started out as a beautiful sunny day. When they were about 10 miles from the Mackinac Bridge, fog started to close in, it kept getting Thicker.

Most of the fog on the lakes was a sea fog, or a ground fog. This was caused by warm air passing over relatively cool water. Since this fog was generated at water level, the top of the fog would not necessarily be too high. The fact that Doc had been a sub commander, he did what any clever submariner would do and being that he was an admiral in the U.S. Navy, he could get favors done by Navy technicians. This of course was all done for experimental purposes.

At the top of the main mast they had mounted a new design of an electronic periscope. The optics had a wide angle lens. The image seen by the optics was transferred down to a receiver that was in a metal box. This was mounted on a pedestal next to the compass. The box had a key lock cover. When opened there was a viewing screen about 8 inches square, with a switch to open the cover over the optics on top of the mast, 108 feet above the water line.

On the key locked bronze cover, engraved in large clear characters, it said, 'Property of U S Navy, Authorized personnel only.'

Angel opened the cover and looked into the box and said, "Looks like a sea fog. I can see over the top of it." Just then off in the distance, there was a sound of a foghorn. Angel reached behind the wheel, flipped open a small door on the side of the wheel pedestal. Inside was a lever, which he turned to activate the automatic foghorn located on the fore mast of Cora Lee. The ship made timed blasts of her horn and so did Cora Lee.

The fog was very dense by now and Angel sent Juan and Eric up forward as Bow watch. By holding his last course toward the bridge and keeping track with his newfangled periscope box, Angel felt confident and secure in his placing the Cora Lee on a safe course. At this time very few private yachts had radar.

Angel then said, "I have her in sight." What he saw was the masts and funnel of a large freighter. When they passed alongside of the freighter, she let go with a blast on her foghorn. It was so loud and piercing that is scared as hell out of everyone on the schooners deck.

Arch was standing next to Angel. He asked, "How did you know that it was a freighter before anyone else could see?" Angel explained the periscope rig and then showed him. Off in the distance, the outline of the bridge started to show.

Then they heard another foghorn. Not as loud and piercing as the freighters horn, probably a yacht of some kind. As they got closer to the bridge there was music being carried by the fog. It was the Tennessee waltz. Without any hesitation the three gals went to the bow and answered with their rendition of the Tennessee waltz. That sound carries for miles in the fog. The schooner and a 60 foot yawl passed, as if it was choreographed to perfectly meet under the bridge.

As they were going under the bridge, with people on both boats singing the Tennessee waltz, at least 20 shutters on cameras snapped. The singing could be heard very clearly up on the bridge and the traffic was stopped . From up on the bridge looking down, both sailing ships could be seen very clearly. A sight and sound that people won't forget for a long time. Luckily it was vacation time and many people had their cameras with them.

After they cleared the bridge, Angel set a course of 110°. They would stay on that course for about 100 miles. With a 13Knot breeze and with the fisherman flying they were making 12 kn. They were now in lake Huron, whoever was in charge of Huron weather decided that they should have sunshine, which is what they got.

It was about 11:30 PM when they reached a point about 100 miles east of Mackinac. At this point they dropped the King fisherman. They made a course change to 170° and headed for Port Huron. They were now on a beam reach and it was 175 miles. It was 1:30 AM when they reached Port Huron .

The crew lowered and furled all sails, they would be under diesel power all the way to Lake Erie, which was approximately 80 miles. With both diesels chugging along at under half power, they were making about 5 knots Cora Lee entered the river with Port Huron on the starboard side and Sarnia (Canada) on the port side. On the Sarnia side there were refineries, quite a few of them, or one great big one. It looked like Saudi Arabia with all the tall stacks, belching gas and flame. It was a beautiful sight on a very dark night. On the starboard side was Port Huron where you would see the typical shore lights, nothing spectacular. What is more interesting is a large ship heading toward you in a narrow river at night, even more interesting was a ship coming up on your stern.

Chapter 28

Stupid Fisherman on Lake St. Clair.

She was coming up on the Cora Lee pretty fast. Angel was running at 5 to 6 knots, he kicked it up to 8 knots, the ship was still moving closer. They made a turn in the channel, at that time they had a quick side view of the ship. With the lights from the refineries, they could make out that she was black, she had large white letters on the side, there were two or three words. The last word was Dixie. Angel and Doc talked it over and came up with the conclusion that she was the Ben Dixie, a 200 foot cement boat out of Chicago. The Dixie was a bulk carrier, that delivered bulk cement all over the Great Lakes.

A few years earlier.Doc got into a hassle with the captain of the Ben Dixie in Manistee, Michigan. They were just starting to tie up the Cora Lee to a wharf. At that time the Ben Dixie was empty, she came barreling through a no wake area at about 12 kn. It's wake caused some damage to Cora Lee, but a lot of damage to the 50 foot yacht tied in front of the Cora Lee. It was dark and the ship was black.

She went by so fast that nobody saw the name of the ship.

Juan and Mario got into the launch, and caught up with her and the big white letters on the side said Ben Dixie. Doc contacted the owner of the yacht, and together they reported it to the Coast Guard. Ben Dixie owners paid for damage to the yacht. The captain and the pilot received a reprimand.

The pilot on the Dixie actually spotted Cora Lee in Lake Huron before they entered the river. The Captain of the B'en Dixie remembered the Cora Lee and his reprimand. He felt that now was his chance to get even. He decided that he would scare the hell out of them, by almost ramming them and then drop back like nothing happened.

Angel now had Cora Lee running at 9 to 10 knots. and Ben Dixie was still gaining. Juan flashed a bright light at them, it made no difference. When Doc found that it was the Ben Dixie behind them, he figured that the pilot was looking for revenge.

Doc radioed the Coast Guard. There just happened to be a 43 footer, that had entered the river at Port Huron. They went flank speed, till they were alongside of the Ben Dixie's pilothouse. With two spotlights shining at the pilothouse, they announced, this is the Coast Guard on their amplified megaphone. They told him to slow down to 5 kn. and to tie up at a commercial wharf in Marine city 10 miles ahead.

Angel asked Doc "Where the Coast Guard came from?"

Doc told him , "I called the Coast Guard."

Mario then said, "The Captain will probably lose his license."

Probably not, "If I don't agree to witness against him, but I doubt if he will be pulling any more of his tricks. He may not be charged, but the report will still go on his record. Let's forget about it. Angel go get some sleep, I will take a trick on the wheel."

"Okay Doc." Angel went below. Most everyone on board had been sleeping. The sounds of the increase revolution of the engine and the sound of the rushing water on the side of the hall got some people awake. But the sound of the Coast Guard's loud hailer brought everybody up on deck.

The Dixie slowed down and dropped back, Angel cut his speed to 6 or 7 kn. Then the Coast Guard boat pulled alongside. An officer came out on the foredeck with a megaphone and said, "Not to worry folks all is well. Be on your way and thanks for calling, we are here to help."

All the guys were up on deck and waving to the Coast Guard crew. But Coast Guard crew were not paying much attention to the guys. They were waving at three sexy looking blonds in shorty night gowns. They were arm in arm underneath the spreader lights doing the shimmy. The Coast Guard helmsman stayed right alongside, until the girls were through with their dance, then they pulled away, with the Coast Guard crew cheering and clapping. After that the girls put on their robes that they wore, when they came up from their cabins.

The three of them walked to the after cockpit. All the guys were sitting around the table drinking coffee. Bill was now at the helm. As the girls approached the cockpit the guys all cheered and clapped.

Doc looked up from his coffee mug and said, "We definitely do not need to bring in any outside entertainment. We have it all right here."

It was now almost 3 AM and Mario suggested they hit the sack because he would be serving breakfast at 8 AM. Everybody went below except Jacky, she went to the helm and was going to stand watch with Bill. Bill said that he enjoyed her company, but felt that she should hit the sack.

He said, "That he had Juan on bow watch and Angel will be back at the helm at 6 AM." Jacky decided to stay and talk to Bill for half an hour and then hit the sack, but as she was leaving, Bill told her that you three did a great job of entertaining that Coast Guard crew. "That's part of our job Old Boy. Cheerio and good night."

Angel was at the helm at 6 AM and they just entered Lake St. Clair, which was about 25 miles wide and about the same length. It was a shallow lake and a channel was dredged the full length of it to the Detroit River. It was well marked with buoys which were right at the edge of the channel. You definitely did not want to go outside of the channel. Lake St. Clair was only 8 to 9 feet deep in some places and the Cora Lee drew 11 ½ feet.

It was a nice sunny morning, there were a lot of fishermen out on the lake. Many of the fishermen like to fish the edge of the channel. They would line up a couple of buoys and drop their anchor, back away from the channel, then drop a second anchor off their stern. Now they could cast into the channel. If they were lucky they would catch some nice walleyes right at the edge of the channel, but then there was one fishermen that was not too bright.

He went past the buoys and went quite a ways out into the channel. He dropped his anchor and backed up to the edge of the channel. With him that close to the channel and his anchor line going down at an angle, he was in a dangerous position. Any boat or ship going by, near the edge of the channel with a fairly deep keel, could drag him under unless he was quick enough to cut his anchor line. His anchor was in a bad place, but if he let out more line and backed his boat away from the channel he would probably be safe.

"Juan spotted the fishermen and went aft to tell Angel and to suggest moving to mid channel, to miss the guys anchor rode."

"Sounds like a good idea Juan, but I think we will have a problem with this freighter coming at us from downstream. It looks like he has already decided to take his share of the channel, out of the middle. He is much bigger than us, so we will have to take the starboard side of the channel. If that fishermen stays where he is, his anchor line will drag on our Keel. Where we will pass his line is probably no more than seven or 8 feet down and we draw 11 ½ feet. We may just slide over or we may drag the line and drag his boat under."

"Juan take a couple guys up forward and try to get him to move back. Take the handheld signal horn to get his attention."

Juan, Bill, Peter and Arch went forward. Juan signaled and they all waved to get him to move back. He heard the signal and then returned his own signal. His answer was a single middle finger. It looked like the freighter and Cora Lee would be passing at the fishermen's location at the same time. Cora Lee could not slow down and lose headway or the freighter's wake would wash them out of the channel and run them around. So Angel told him to try and wave him back again. They got the finger.

Just as Cora Lee's bow passed the smart assed fishermen, he laughed and gave his finger signal again. At about midship of the Schooner, his anchor line was struck by the keel. As the line dragged to the deepest part of the keel, his boat was dragged under. The forward part of his boat was decked over which kept the boat from going to the bottom.

The boat and the wise assed ,wet as hell, fishermen popped to the surface, just as Angel passed him. He was no more than 15 feet from Angel and he had a scared astonished look on his face. Most of the crew were now in the cockpit. When he popped up six people gave him the finger.

Two other fishing boats pulled up their anchors. One boat picked up some of the gear that floated away, then one went over to assist the guy in the half sunken boat, maybe tow him to shore. The second boat went after Cora Lee. Everybody figured that he wanted to get a name to claim damage, but this was not the case.

He pulled up alongside the cockpit and said, "That was beautiful. He was a friend of ours, but we had been warning him for a long time not to anchor in the channel. He wasn't hurt but I'll bet he never anchors like that again."

Doc said, "Good, he wasn't hurt, thanks for telling us."

Then Doc said, "Angel we had better kick it up a bit, Mario's anxious to get to the fireboat. Mario had radioed to his supplier in Chicago, who in turn contacted a first-class restaurant supplier in Detroit. They said they would deliver 200 pounds of prime corned beef, sauerkraut, 40 loaves of Rosen's Rye and 50 pounds of Swiss cheese."

It was a nice quiet morning as they motored through southwestern portion of Lake St. Clair. Everyone was enjoying the weather and the scenery. As they entered the Detroit River, they came upon Belle Island. Detroit on the starboard side and Windsor, Canada on the port side.

Chapter 29

Detroit Fireboat, Salt Mine, Niagara Falls

Shortly after Belle Isle they saw the fireboat moored at its station. Angel had been here before and he knew just where to tie up. The fireboat was moored on the west bank facing south. It was right next to the fire station. Their living quarters were on shore. Their crew were both firemen and seamen, they could be underway at a moment's notice. An engineer was aboard at all times with the engines running. Their normal duty was with 24 hours on 48 hours off. They were on call for any fire or disaster along the shoreline or any ship disaster. Angel laid the Schooner alongside a long wharf and behind the fireboat.

The fireboat was impressive, she was 108 feet in length and her name was the Robert Kendrick. She was built to fight fires and do rescue work. With two powerful snorkel cannons mounted up near the bow, her pumps could move 16 to 20,000 gallons per minute. She also had two smaller snorkels on platforms that were mounted midship. This was a ship that could handle most any fire on a ship or on shore.

As soon as they were tied up, Capt. Jim Bishop came aboard and greeted Doc who he had known for a few years. Bishop was captain of the fireboat and was in charge of all ship handling. The fire marshal, Bob Richards, handled the firefighting crew. Doc introduced everybody aboard the Cora Lee to Bishop. Then they all went into the fire station. The fire station was where the fire crew and the ship's crew lived, ate and slept.

There was a minimal amount of crew living space aboard the fireboat. She was a workboat, meant to put out fires.

Jacky asked Bishop, "What does the fire crew and the ship's crew do all day, when not fighting fires."

He told her, "That the crews do not lay around watching soap operas on TV. There is a lot of equipment to be maintained, also continual training exercises.

We will be going out tomorrow morning for our monthly test of the fire pumps."

"You are welcome to come along. It will only be a 20 minute run down the river and we anchor in a wide area west of fighting island. There is a small park where hundreds of kids show up for a water bath. We put a notice in the local paper and on radio news programs. The kids have a ball and so do our fire crews. We aim the monitor pipes in the air so as not to hurt the kids, so you can come with us tomorrow and watch the fun."

"What might be interesting is to go with Bob Richards tomorrow afternoon . Bob is going to take a group down into the diamond salt mine. Have any of you ever been in a salt mine?"

Everybody said no except Peter. "Who said that he had been sentenced to work in one for two years in China. The last place in the world that I want to visit is another salt mine."

"Kelly also the declined saying that she has heard enough about mines from her parents who were under the thumb of the Nazi's."

"Bill, Jacky, Sandra, Arch and Eric said they would like to go. Bishop said that there was room for two more in Bob Richards car."

When they said they were going to purchase a brand-new fire marshal's car from Buick, he told them to save their money, that he would purchase a used car and send them the bill. Which he did, he bought a two year old Cadillac limo from a livery company going out of business. He then had it painted bright red, put lights and sirens and added the Detroit fire marshal painted on both front doors. It was a first-class piece of equipment like no other fire marshal had.

That night and they had a lasagna dinner courtesy of the fire departments number one Chef. It was excellent. Tomorrow afternoon everyone will get to try Kelly and Mario's Reubens.

After dinner they all sat around and told stories. The Cora Lee's crew told about their adventures in sailing, but not about their Beaver Island adventures. The firemen had great fire stories, the best happened right here at the firehouse. Two of the stories probably been told many times.

"There is a large cruise ship the White Lady, she makes a round trip from Cleveland, Ohio to Muskegon, Michigan once a week. Downriver going south is no problem because she is going with the flow, but going north against the flow is a problem as she is large and moving fast. The whole river seems to move in front of her."

"As you may have noticed, there is a small bay along the north end of the fire station. The mail boat that delivers mail to the ships out on the river is tied up on the north side and a public launching ramp is on the south side. This ship caused the water level to raise and lower three times, by the time the ship goes by. First it raises the water about 2 feet above the mean level. Then it Goes back down to one and half feet below the mean level. She does this in three separate waves, the ship comes through at pretty close to noon. This is also a time when many people are launching their boats. The local people know about this ship and what it does to the water level in the launching ramp."

"The firemen know what can happen so if they see someone backing down the ramp and it is close to noon, they take a quick vote to see if they like the guy or not. If they decide he is a good guy they warn him and he waits for the ship to go by. If he gets a no vote, he backs his boat into the water when it's at the lowest point. By the time he wakes up he is sitting in his car with water up to his neck, then the firemen become good Samaritans and tell him not to try to start his car they will tow him out.

Dave, the number one engineer said, "What about Linda and Louise and their trip across the river?" When Dave said that, the firemen bust out laughing.

Bishop then said, "You know, that episode was a real classic. The Keystone cops couldn't have done it any better. Most of the guys just saw the last part of the fat ladies ride. But Dave saw it from the start to the finish. He can tell it best, if he would quit laughing."

Dave started with, "Well the story goes like this. It was a beautiful summer day, about 2 PM on a Sunday. I was just walking back from helping the guy on the mail boat tie up, after making his run out to a passing ship. As I was crossing the public ramp, a big black Cadillac with a 17 foot boat in tow pulled up. The two rear doors opened up, and two big ladies stepped out. When they got out the Caddy Rose about 2 inches. They were each about 300 pounds. The driver got out and he looked to be about 350. He surveyed the ramp, got back in the car and backed it up toward the ramp. Backing a boat trailer down the ramp was not one of his greatest skills. After about four tries I walked over to him and I told him that I would help."

"He started to get out of the car, to let me back it down and I said no you do it. I'll help you. You just watch me, with hands on the wheel at three and nine o'clock I will simulate with my hands the same position. I told him to back slowly, watch my hands and do the same motions as I did. It went smooth as silk and the boat was in the water. He got the boat off the trailer and tied it to the dock. Next he pulled the car and trailer out of the ramp, but before he pulled out of the ramp he unloaded two big coolers out of his trunk. When he came back he carried the cooler down to the dock and put them in the boat. The boat had four seats number one seat being in the bow."

"After talking to him for a bit, he thanked me for helping them. He offered me a beer, which I declined saying I was on duty. I introduced myself, he said his name was Sam and the two gals were sisters Linda and Louise. He said that he had just bought the boat and trailer that morning. They showed him how to start the outboard, which was a brand-new 35horse power Evenrude, but nobody showed him how to back a trailer."

"He lowered the beer cooler aft of number three seat. Then he loaded the food cooler forward of number two seat. Next he got the gals in the boat Linda looking forward on numbers three and Louise looking aft on number two seat. Surprisingly the boat did not settle down too much with all that weight. Sam would add another 350 pounds. Luckily Sam had delt with someone who knew boats and sold him a 17 foot Lyman with a lapstrake hull. A good strong sea boat, one that would carry a lot of weight."

"Now Sam got into the boat, after untying it from the dock. He was standing up to start the engine. He pulled out the choke and squeezed the bulb on the gasoline line from the auxiliary tank. Sam kept pulling, getting no fire from the engine. Dave told him that he had flooded the engine. Now close the choke and hold the throttle wide open to clear the flooding, then when it fires, shut it down to an idle. Sam had it wide open and in gear. It started with a roar and being in gear, the boat took off like a banshee. Sam did a Brodie over the transom and landed in the water. "

"The boat made a straight shot out of the ramp area, out into the river. The river was very wide in that location and two screaming women went flying across the river. Sam climbed out of the water, up on the dock. There was nothing they could do but watch."

"By now about 10 other firemen were watching. There were two ships coming, one southbound and one northbound. One of the ships was giving a series of quick blasts, indicating a danger signal. The Lyman as if on autopilot passed close in front of the northbound ship and close behind the southbound ship."

"The Lyman then ran up on the beach, under a giant willow tree. Because of the northbound ship being in the way, the Lyman had run aground before the northbound ship had passed. After the ships had cleared, they could see no boat on the other side of the river. Sam and Dave figured the worst had happened."

Dave asked, "If they had life jackets on?"

Sam said, "No but there were plenty of flotation cushions, and they were both good swimmers."

"Dave and Sam headed for the fire department launch, Sam and Dave jumped in and Dave started the engine, two more firemen got into a launch. Dave opened the throttle full bore. They were almost across the river when they started looking for swimmers or wreckage."

"Dave was thinking that they could have gotten tangled up with a screw on the southbound ship. Then everyone noticed the transom of a boat with an Evinrude outboard on it."

"Dave brought the launch up to the beach next to the big willow tree. Everyone jumped out and ran under the willow tree. They found two women eating chicken and drinking beer."

Louise said, "Sam that was one hell of a ride, but why didn't you tell us you didn't want to go with."

Linda looked at Sam and said, "Now Sam how did you get so wet." And everyone laughed.

Then Louise said, "Sam let's get this boat out from under this tree and go boating."

Dave said, "Sam we took the launch out to possibly rescue someone. What do we put on the report?"

Sam said, "Malfunction."

They all thought that both of these stories were pretty interesting and Doc asked, "If they had ever seen Sam again?"

Bishop said that, "Sam is a regular here now. He has a bigger boat now with an inboard engine. He does not want to go over the stern again." Linda and Louise always come with Sam.

"Sam owns five pizza places in the Detroit. And Linda and Louise own a big bakery in Detroit."

"This is one fire department, that has plenty of good pizza and first-class bakery goods. If they stop by tonight we will introduce you to some nice people and two funny gals."

Mario then said, "We can also invite them to have some of the best Reuben's this side of Chicago."

Bishop said, "After talking to Sam and the gals. Good Reuben's will entice them to come." They did come the next day, enticed by the thought of Kelly's Reuben's. Kelly told them where to go when in Chicago to get the same Reuben's. Sam said that they go to Chicago 3 to 4 times a year, and now they would have reason to go more often.

The party finally wound down, but nobody really wanted it to end, because Linda and Louise never seemed to run out of jokes and funny stories. It was 2 AM when Linda finally said, "They had better get shuffling off, because they had to be at the bakery at 5 AM."

Sam laughed and said, "He had to be at his pizza place at five also, 5 PM and laughed again."

Cora Lee's crew also decided that they had better hit the sack. It was two thirty and they had to be up at six. At least one thing on the plus side about having a fire house party, alcohol was not allowed, so no hangovers. They were all up at 6 AM. It was a fantastic sunny morning. The guys all wore shorts and T-shirts. The three gals came up to have morning coffee in the after cockpit. They walked down the steps into the cockpit, side-by-side, it looked like a scene out of the Ziegfield Follies.

All three blondes dressed alike, in light summer sun dresses. They were beautiful and could have passed for triplets. If they intended to impress the fire crew, they were sure going about it in the right way.

Doc asked, "How they got all the same identical dresses."

Sandra said, "While in Chicago Kelly and her went shopping and found a store that had closeouts. There were 10 identical dresses on one rack, all the same size, our size."

Mario said, "I see three visions of beauty, I think I should write a song about it."

After a great breakfast, they all went ashore to meet with the fire crew and the boat crew. When they went aboard the fire boat, the boat crew and the fire crew all crowded around three sexy looking gals. It seems that all the guys figured that the only ones that would be interested in the functions of a fire boat would be the three gals. They just wandered around for a while until Jim Bishop and Bob Richard walked over to them.

Bob Richardson said, "Well it looks like our horny crews don't think you guys look sexy enough for fire training. Jim and I have decided to show you guys around so that your education about fire boat is not completely ignored. You guys really just don't look nearly as good as those three girls, but somebody has got to do it."

"First let's go to the after engine room, which is our main propulsion. They went down below and Bishop pointed out two large V/ 12 diesel engines. He told them that these engines could be completely controlled from the engine room or from the wheelhouse."

Bishop said "Now follow Marshall Richards and he will explain the real guts of a fire boat." They went forward into the next compartment and they saw that there was another V/ 12 diesel but one and a half times the size of the propulsion engines.

"This engine drives a 5000 gallon per minute pump. These first three engines can be started from top side. So what say we wind them up." Jim picked up a microphone and said, "Wheel house, this is Capt. Bishop. Fire up number one and two engines. Then wind up number two pump." All of a sudden it seemed that all hell broke loose when the three engines started.

Richards said, "Think this is noisy, wait till hear the big one start. The big one pumps 15,000 gallons per minute. It has to be started from the engine room . It does not have an electric starter like the other three. It has a separate pony or starting engine. It is a small engine that is started first. Then through gearing and a clutch, it engages the large engine to start it. It can't be started from the bridge, but it can be throttled or shut down from there."

They move forward to the next compartment, which was directly below the bridge. This engine was a V/16 that was at least twice the size of the number two pump engine. Marshall Richards walked over to the bulkhead and pressed a button and a small engine started. He then went to the big engine and pushed the lever which engaged the small engine to the large engine. The big one slowly started cranking over.

When it fired up it made so much noise, That Sandra let out a scream. Arch said, "At least now we know where the girls are." They were coming down the stairwell to the engine compartment that the guys were in. The gals walked over to the big diesel.

Kelly took a real hard look walked around the engine with a real serious look on her face, she backed away a little, as they were all watching her. "Pretty sure that that is bigger than the one in my Ford."

Bishop then the said, "On that note I think we should adjourn top side."

Kelly said, "Come on you guys ain't you seen enough engines for today. Let's get this show on the road. We need to go and spray some kids with water."

While the guys were down below Bishop called Dave, the first engineer, to drop the lines and move the boat out.

The three gals turned around and went back up the companionway. They turned around and faced the guys that were coming up the stairs. The gals hassled Bishop and Richards, "Jacky asked them if it always took them this long to get under way to get to a fire."

Bishop answered saying, "It's never taken this long before, but with three beautiful gals like you three, it always will."

"You gals are a sunrise vision not to forget."

Then all three realized that they were at the top of the stairs looking down and the guys were looking up, the gals had their light summer dresses on and their backs to the sun.

Sandra asked, "Are all firemen as horny as this crew?"

Then Bishop said, "I'll have to look into that."

Richards turned to Bishop and said, "Bob let's get this bucket moving a little faster and go and cool off some kids."

Jim stuck his head in the wheelhouse and said, "A few more rpm Dave, let's make 12 knots." They went downriver for about 45 minutes, pulled into a small cove, turned the boat 180° and dropped an anchor from the bow. Then let her drift back with the current. When she was back far enough they dropped an anchor off the stern and then took up on the bow anchor, now they wouldn't drift sideways when they were pushing 15 or 20,000 gallons per minute out of their water cannons. It was now 8:30 AM., the paper said 9 AM for the water show. Now that the fire boat was in place they came.

Small kids, big kids, white kids, black kids, girls boys and some adults. Most of the kids wore swimming suits and some of the adults did. Some of the adults just wore street clothes.

The strangest thing was the three stretch limousines. We all figured that they came to watch. The doors opened and six people got out of each limo, three guys and three gals, in tuxedoes and evening gowns. Eighteen of them headed right for the middle of the field, formed a conga line and started dancing. Other people got into the mood and joined the conga line.

This went on for ten minutes when another limo pulled up. This time the bride and groom got out and went over and joined the party.

By this time the crew got the 5000 gallon per minute pump going. They started to shoot water out of the two smaller cannons. Everyone on the field was getting wet as if they had been in a big downpour.

It was bright and sunny, about 95, it felt hot as hell on deck. Eric said, "Why are we roasting here on deck, they are all cool down there."

Bishop said, "If you people want to go and cool off, one of my guys will run you in shore on the launch."

Arch Eric And Bill said, "Let's go."

Bishop said, "Ladies are invited too."

The three gals looked at each other and said, "Why not." and they got into the launch.

When they got to the shore they headed for the center of the field where the wedding party was . Kelly walked over and talked to a very wet and laughing bride. Kelly asked why they were here? She said, "That it was almost impossible to get reservations for a hall unless you paid a lot of money under the table. So we had a 2 AM wedding and a 3 AM reception. People came to reception but when the air conditioner quit everyone went home except the wedding party. Somebody remembered about the shindig here and we are getting cooled off"

Just then the big cannons let loose, when the big guns let loose, you knew that you were going to get more than just a little wet. The crew aimed the streams up in the air and swung them around. A direct blast would knock somebody off their feet. The fire crews have both pumps and four water cannons going full blast. The kids and the adults were having a lot of fun running between the light showers of the small cannons, and a deluge of the big cannons.

Everyone was having a ball, including the wedding party. Also the guys and gals from the fire boat. The girls of the wedding party got together and had a confab. Next thing they did was all nine gals, plus the bride walked over to a large trash can. They pulled off their bras, and threw them in the can, then they went back to the heavy downpour.

The three blondes saw what the bridal party did. Then Kelly said, "You think we ought to chuck our Bras?"

Sandra said and Jacky agreed," That if they got back to the boat all wet and braless, it would be a problem. Jacky said that horny crew wouldn't be able to find their way back to the fire station and we will get blamed."

So at about 10:30 the fire crews shut down the pumps and the bridal party got back in their limos wet and happy. The kids headed for home, along with some happy wet adults.

The three gals and the guys climbed aboard the fire boat. There were some whistles from the fire crew, but as good looking as these gals were, they were used to it. Dave the engineer said, "We will be underway in about 10 minutes. When we get moving stand up in the bow, you will be dry in a short time." Which they did and they were all dried out, by the time they get halfway back to the fire boat dock.

It was 11 AM when they tied up at the firehouse. Before they went aboard the Cora Lee, Bob Richards said, "There were five of your people that wanted to see what a salt mine looks like. I'll be leaving at 1 PM, and we should be back no later than three. We will meet in the firehouse game room."

Sandra said, "She didn't want to go." She decided to stay and help Mario, and Kelly make the Reubens. "I figured that I can help and I would really like to learn how to make the Reubens. This is the best chance I'll ever get." She went down to the galley and talked to Mario."

"He said that he and Kelly would appreciate the help. There was a lot of work to do in preparing about 50 Reubens."

Mario said, "Kelly told him that 50 Reubens would be simple. She felt that they should cover their butt and make 70 of them. If there were any left they could be re-heated in the oven for breakfast. We could make the last 20 sandwiches minus the sauerkraut and the sauce, just put the kraut and sauce on it as needed." Mario and the two gals got busy making 70 Reubens .

It was getting close to 1 PM. After a light lunch Bill, Jacky, Eric and Arch met Bob Richards in the game room. He asked, "Is everybody ready to go to the salt mines. He said the mines are interesting place to go if you have never been there before. They have two tours on the weekends, but it's just a ride through a tunnel. That's why I wear my official uniform and cap and with my fire marshals limo I can go any place and see anything." Eric then said, "Not too much that can burn in the salt mine is there?" "No but a lot of safety concerns"

"Most people have never been in a salt mine, I'm usually the one elected to take people on the tour. "

Jacky then asked, "If there is anything interesting in the mine, or is it just a big pile of salt."

"Well if you have never seen it before, it could be interesting for a short time. It has 60 miles of tunnels and if they didn't have signs you would never find your way out. With this limo and the separate drivers compartment, you people can refresh yourselves with beer, wine or little gin for a martini."

They arrived at the diamond salt company. It had a cyclone fence around the property. We stopped at a guard shack, the sign said no admittance. Employees and mine personnel only. Richards pulled up and the guard waved him through.

After about half a mile, they came to the mine entrance. The sign said, "Mine entrance lights on. Down graded to 1000 foot depth. Use second-gear, maximum speed 20 mph, for the next 3 1/2 miles." They did the switchbacks until they reached 1000 feet in depth . Now they were in the mine and they came all the way down the wide two-lane switchback Road .

They were in an amazing snow white cavern, except it was all salt. It was bright as day, the roadways wide as a highway, with traffic signs, traffic lights and trucks were coming and going. There was all kinds of heavy equipment, boring machines, undercutting machine and front end loaders.

Jacky said, "If she knew it was this much work to get salt, she would probably feel self-conscious about picking up a salt shaker."

Richards said, "Very little of this salt goes for table use. It is mostly used commercially. Over in Windsor is another mine, there they get more table grade salt. One day they figure that these two mines will run into each other. That will make one great big mine."

Bill who hadn't said much for the first hour, came up with a suggestion, "Before those Windsor people punch through and we wind up in Canada why don't we head back to the exit and go to the Cora Lee's after cockpit. I think I could use a martini."

Everybody agreed that it was a good idea. Bob Richards said, "It sounded good to him because he will be off duty in one hour."

Eric then said, "When he got back he would go and see if the two girls and Mario needed a hand, that is after he had a couple martinis." Now that they were all thirsty for a drink, they could hardly wait to get back.

Richards took his Official hat and jacket off, and said, "Now I am a thirsty civilian." He climbed back out of the mine at 30 mph. Making the switchback turns a little hairy.

Jacky flew across the seat on one turn and said, "Bob you sure are one thirsty fire Marshal."

"No, Jacky, just a practicing a high-speed run, to get to a fire." They were out of the salt mine, heading to the firehouse. Bob had his lights flashing and running at about 50 miles an hour in a 30 mph zone. A police car came up behind him with lights flashing, they pulled alongside. The police officer on the passenger side asked, "Is this an emergency sir."

Bob now had his white marshals hat back on, "It's not a fire emergency, it's an assimilated operation, to take place in 10minutes on the Schooner Cora Lee, which is tied up behind the fire boat"

"Follow us sir, we'll have you there in 10 minutes." They did, with lights flashing and sirens wailing from both vehicles. They made it in eight minutes.

Bob got out of his car, put his Marshals jacket back on and walked to the police car and said, "Thanks guys, you sure as hell did great, anytime you happen to have a fire, give us a call."

Bob said, "I don't do that too often, but sometimes it comes in handy. Now let's see if we can find our way to the Cora Lee's after deck." They all sat at the after cockpit table.

Then Bill got up and said, "I guess I'll do the honors and make the drinks."

"No Bill you keep Jacky entertained, I'll do the drinks." said Arch."

Eric said, "While you're doing that I'll check with Mario and the girls and see how much help they need."

Arch came up carrying a tray, and a towel over his arm like a waiter. He had four double Beefeater dry martinis and one wine glass with a carafe of red wine. Bob tested his Martini and looked at Arch, licked his lips, and said, "Great martini Arch. You are to be condemned."

Jacky said, "You mean commended."

"No I mean condemned, because if I have two more of these. I won't know my own name, but damn they are good." They sat around and bullshitted for a while, had a couple more drinks. Eric then went to help out in the galley. After his third drink Bob still knew his name, but decided that he had enough double martinis. They all decided that Bob was right. Bob headed to the firehouse and everybody else headed to their cabin for an after booze nap.

They all got up at 4:30 at the sound of the Klaxon. Everybody showered, shaved, did whatever they had to do, then dressed for a party on the Cora

Lee. There was four big coolers on deck. Two with beer Marked Off Duty. And two coolers with soft drinks Marked ON DUTY. Nobody ever thought of breaking the rules.

A big black Cadillac pulled up at the firehouse, Sam got out then Linda and Louise and they were all dressed for a party. Sam whistled up a couple firemen and ask for a little help carrying something. Sam said "I got 10 of my best Pizza's for your freezer."

"Linda and Louis, have got a bunch of cakes and pies from their bakery, these are dessert for the party." The guys rousted up three more firemen and carried pizza to the firehouse freezer. The bakery goods went to Mario's galley.

Sam, Louise and Linda were led aboard the Cora Lee by Arch and Bill. They explained that she was a two masted staysail schooner with a length of 89 feet 6 inches.

Louise said, "If I knew we were going to party on a pirate ship, I would have worn my pirate costume."

Linda said, "I've never been on a sailing ship before have you Sam?"

"No and it sure looks like it would be pretty complicated to sail a ship like this."

Just then Angel walked by with a beer in his hand. Bill called Angel over and he explained that Angel was the sailing master aboard this ship. He introduced Angel to Sam and Louise and Linda.

Then said he knew that Angel would be glad to explain, anything about a sailing ship. Angel said, "He would be glad to do it." He said, "Follow me and I will show you what makes a sailing ship work."

Meanwhile Arch had gone over to a beer cooler and brought some back for Linda, Louise and Sam which they gratefully accepted. Bill pointed out where the beer cooler was, just reach in when you run out.

Then Angel took them all over the ship. They were fascinated as Angel explained the points of sailing and how they tacked into the wind. Louise said, "She thought that a sailboat could only go the way the wind blew. It sure does ease my mind, I always thought that when the wind was blowing to the west all sailboats went west and they didn't come back till the wind changed to the east. That's why I always thought that sailboats were stupid, but I guess I was stupid. Did you know anything about that Sam?"

"Louise, I never even thought about the way a sailboat works. I have enough problem with my own boat and I just have to turn the key to start it."

Then Angel took the three of them down into Mario's galley. They greeted Mario, Sandra and Kelly. Linda said, "This is my kind of place. It sure is a beautiful galley."

Sam said, "Something really smells great, I hear you are making Rubens, one of my favorites."

"Sam", Linda said, "All food is your favorite."

"But Linda these are supposed to be the best."

Mario then said, "These Rubens are being made under Kelly's supervision, she is the Reuben expert."

Sam asked Kelly, "Do you mind if we hang around to watch?" "That is if Mario doesn't mind."

Mario said, "No problem ."

"You see I own this Italian restaurant, not a full Italian menu and I'm not Italian, but we have the best pizza in Detroit. We've got spaghetti and lasagna with the best pasta sauce in town. We also have great quesadillas and chimichangas and enchiladas and I ain't Mexican either. I am a fat Greek, but we don't serve Greek food. I learned how to make really good mat'zoh ball soup. A lot of people come in just for the soup. They keep telling me to serve Reubens with the soup."

Kelly said, "Okay, Sam, since you are a nice guy, you can watch us assemble Rubens. The corned beef has already been roasted, then steamed and that's most important. I'll tell you about that later."

"Maybe we can trade off ideas that your folks place might want to use. Linda and Louise have a bakery shop that does specialty baking. I know that most places that make Rubens use Rosen's rye which sure as hell is good, but the L and L bakery makes a seeded rye that is even better, perfect for Rubens. They brought a big box of Rye bread and the Rye rolls that you can try out on some of your Rubens today."

Doc, Bill and Jacky were sitting at the after cockpit table, just having a beer and talking. Doc asked, "What they were going to do after Jacky gets back to Chicago besides get married?"

"We will both be back in the motorcycle business again."

"Jacky is selling out her share of her Hannibal, Missouri motorcycle shop. Then we will run the Chicago shop together."

"Sounds like a good idea, who is running your shops now?"

Jacky said, "She had a partner and he is doing good."

Bill said, "His old RAF friend is running his shop and he's doing good. So it looks like we will be back to doing what we like to do."

Jacky asked a question of Doc, realizing that he probably won't or can't answer. She asked him, "If he had any idea what the mission is about."

He said, "There are two reasons that he can't tell her right now. The first reason is that it is very top-secret. And the second is that I don't know anything about the mission . Other than, they want you to carry it out and they would not explain why. They did say it was important and your recent actions, have confirmed their thinking."

"I've been following orders before and I'm still in the reserves, so I guess they will tell me when the time is right. Right now I guess it is time for Reubens and beer."

Jacky and Bill got up and told Doc that they were going up to the bow and watch the ships going by, have a Reuben,and maybe some of Sam's great matzoth ball soup."

Eric brought a table up to the bow. It was a three by six folding table on the port side next to the cabin. The legs dropped into sockets on the deck so that would not move. The top of the table was compartmentalized for 24- 8 inch plates. Eric and Sandra brought up enough plates of Rubens to fill the table. They were all gone in 10 minutes. They filled the table again this time it didn't go as fast. They brought up another 3 x 4 table and set it alongside in the first table this table held 30 soup mugs and a big pot right in the middle of the table. It had a big ladle and was full of Sam's matzoth ball soup.

The Reubens were moving fast, but very few people could handle a second one. Eric came up from the galley with a knife and cut some of them in half. Some people came back for half of a Reuben. The Matzoth ball soup went slow at first, until word got around about how good it was. Sam knew that would happen, so he already had a second pot almost done. That pot was finished in a short time and by 8 pm everyone was stuffed with food and beer. The duty section were also stuffed but just with food. It was a great party.

The firemen went back to the firehouse at 9:30 pm. Some of Cora Lee's crew were sacked out by 10 pm and some stayed up drinking and talking till about 1:30 am. The next morning no one got up until 10 am, even Mario did not shake loose until 10:30 am and got in a 20 minute cold shower.

Mario went to the galley, when he got there he found one of the firemen, Bill Fries, who was on the duty roster yesterday and he did not drink. so he was bright eyed and bushy tailed this morning. He complimented Mario on the Reubens and said that he had 1½ sandwiches.

He told Mario that he heard that he loved fish and loved to cook fish. Bill asked if he liked Walleye and Mario said, "Not much of a challenge to catch, but they are great to eat."

"Fries told Mario and that he knew that they were headed to the Welland Canal and with a slight detour to an island just north of and between Port Clinton and Sandusky, there was some great Walleye fishing."

"Sounds great to me. I'll check it out with the Captain. I decide how to cook the fish but not where to catch them. I'll check it out today."

Mario checked it out with Doc. "Doc told him that it is starting to get a little late in the season to make too many side trips. He said that we would have to head straight for Welland and we will leave no later than noon today."

"But, Mario, we do have to stop at Clayton, New York, as I have an important meeting there . While we are there you and some of the rest of the crew can go fishing for Muskie or Small Mouth Bass and you know Thousand Islands is the Muskie capital of the world, that's were Clayton is. We have a lot of fishing gear aboard ship. If any more gear is needed it can be purchased in Clayton and charged to the company."

"Sounds great Doc and you know what, Muskie is a real tasty fish when smoked. You've got to know how to do it because a Muskellunge is what is called a wet fish, usually oily fish are used for smoking. Even if you don't get to eat a Muskie, it is a very challenging game fish."

At about 11 am, Angel went down in the engine room and checked the old engines visually to see if there was any leaks or anything out of the ordinary. Then he checked the fuel and water filters. Next he started them up and ran them up to 1500 RPMs. Satisfied with them he shut them down. Up on deck, Juan pulled all the covers off the sails and stowed them in the sail locker. Then he came back up and checked the sheets and halyards. He was getting everything ready to hoist the sails tomorrow when they reached lake Erie.

At 12 noon, everyone said their goodbyes. Sam, Louise and Linda had come back again earlier that morning and the two women brought pies and cake and some of their excellent rye bread, which Mario agreed was better than what he had been using. Sam brought a case of frozen pizzas. They thanked Mario and Kelly for their work in the galley and then thanked Doc and the crew for inviting them to join in the festivities last night. Before the ship moved out everybody sat down and ate pies and cakes and drank coffee, no beer today.

Angel restarted the diesels again and backed down away from the fire boat, he put it in gear and headed down river toward Lake Erie. They were all up on deck and glad to be moving again. At 6 knots plus the current they were making about 8 knots over the bottom. In 2 ½ hours they were at the mouth of the Detroit River, setting sails to cross Lake Erie. Once they had the Main and Mizzen sails up, Angel shut down the diesels.

It was quiet and beautiful, just gliding across the lake. It was approximately 250 miles to Welland. The wind was a perfect wind for the King Fisherman. It was coming out of the west at a steady 13 knots. The guys were now very adept at handling the sails, the big fisherman came out of the sail bag and was up and pulling in about five minutes.

The three girls went up to the bow where Juan had just finished putting down a custom padded 7' x 10' blanket. Doc had it made for people to sun themselves on the deck. It had grommets in six points. There were recessed rings in the deck that were used to tie this pad down so it didn't blow in the wind. Angel said that they would be tied up in Port Colborne anywhere from 10 am to Noon depending on the wind. If the wind holds we will be there by 10 am in the morning. It was a sunny day and it was relaxing to just soak up the sun. Sandra all of the sudden sat up and looked at Jacky and Kelly and said, " I were wondering, were you really a full-fledged commando?"

"Yeah, I was and still am in the reserves."

"We know what you did in Chicago, but then there was Hannibal, Beaver Island and France. You sure as hell are one tough lady. Even Bill said that he wouldn't want you to get pissed off at him!"

Jacky laughed. " It was in during the war when my fiancé dumped me shortly before our wedding. I felt I had to do something, so I joined the Army and then applied for commando training. They hesitated because they figured me for a desk job, but finally gave the okay. In order to be in the group, you have it take a certain amount of training. When I beat their big tough guys they sent me for advanced training. After advanced training, they made me a sergeant and then a combat group leader. We were sent on many missions inside occupied countries and that's where I first met Bill. After the war I came to the U.S, but they seemed to have found me again."

"I heard that somebody wants you to go on a mission," said Sandra.

"What it is, I can't say because I don't know what it is yet. The Admiral doesn't even know. All I do know is that I have about 10 days to train Arch, Eric and Peter and that's not much time for training."

Kelly said, "Being you are so good at what you do, Sandra and I were wondering if you could train us enough to protect ourselves from an attacker?"

Jacky looked at the two blondes and made this comment, "You gals are too damn sexy looking to walk around untrained. You probably attract creeps like flies to dog shit!"

"That sure as hell is true! Would you give us some training?"

"I will but have to follow the rules, if you do it by the time we get to Montréal you won't be a commando, but you won't have to worry about the run-of-the-mill creeps."

Sandra said, "When can we start?"

"How about right now, as soon as I get my training book. I'll be right back." Jacky took off and was back in a few minutes. She had a paperback novel and a deck chair. She said, "This is my training equipment. I used it to piss off my trainees. I would be reading and drinking an ice cold beer, with another beer next to me on ice. I did this while they trained for a couple hours in the hot sun."

"Okay with you two sexy blondes, if we are going to make you safe from the assholes of the world in the short time that we have, I think I can teach you how to kick butt."

"First off, we have to harden up some of your flabby muscles. We will start off with 10 push-ups." Which they did.

Jacky said, "I think you guys are in a little better shape than I thought you were. Now 25 squat jumps. She showed them how and then they did the 25. Now I would like you gals to run around the deck from bow to stern and back, do 10 laps at 20 seconds a lap. That's about an 11 minute mile."

Kelly said, "Is all this necessary?"

"Kelly, girls as good looking as you and Sandra need all the self-protection you can get. By the time we get to Montréal, you should be able to handle at least one attacker and if there are two attackers you put the first one on the ground and hurting. The second one will think twice about hanging around. Does that answer your question?"

"I think so. So let's get moving okay? We run."

After they ran about six laps, Doc came forward and walked up to Jacky and said, "What's with the running, Jacky?"

"Well, Kelly and Sandra asked me to help them with their self-protection program. Can you imagine gals as good-looking as those two not being able to protect themselves from some sexual predator? They both said that it was never safe for them to walk to their own car by themselves at night and sometimes it's not even safe in daytime. If I had a couple of months with them they would be safe

anywhere, but I only have the time from here to Montréal. By then I should be able to teach them enough to handle any single attacker."

"Sounds like a good idea, Jacky. You sure proved yourself in Chicago," then Doc said, "The last I heard was that those three guys will spend the next 60 years in prison with no chance of parole. By the time they get out, they ain't going to have any interest in sex anymore." Then Doc said that he heard that one of them has already lost interest. He's still in the hospital they had to remove both of his testicles.

Jacky said, "That must've been Rick he got kicked the hardest. He was the leader and a real lousy bastard. So all's well that ends well."

The gals did their 10 laps and said that it wasn't too bad. Sandra said, "I could do that every day."

"You do and you will pretty soon be known as the toughest blondes in town."

"Not really, there is a commando here," said Kelly.

Then Jacky said, "She is really a redhead."

Kelly told Jacky, "She was not sure that she could really kick some guy in the nuts."

"All you have to do is stop and think of what this creep wants to do to you and it should make you mad enough not to hesitate. Mad enough to put him temporarily or permanently out of commission. You have to think that it was his decision to attack you and if there is more than one guy, your attack should be quick, permanent and painful. The first one has to go down quick and not get up or you will be the next to go down. Now come on, you two trainees, let's go and have a beer."

They went back to the after cockpit table. It was close to dinnertime and Mario said he had enough left for one round of Reubens, so they drank some beer and ate their Reuben sandwiches. After that, Kelly and Sandra decided that they would go and take a shower and hit the sack early because they were up late last night. Jacky knew that they were just tired because they were not used to exercising. Jacky said to herself, "We will change that."

Jacky went back to the helm where Bill was pulling a two hour trick on the wheel. She gave him a kiss and said, "I'll be glad when are back in Chicago."

Bill said, "You know, it's really hard to believe that we will be married in the Holy Name Cathedral in Chicago." He asked if she had ever seen the Cathedral.

"No, I never have."

"It's at about 600 N. State Street, it is very huge and also very old. It was built back in the 1800s. Also the only people who get married or buried there are rich and famous."

"Bill, are you telling me that we are not famous enough to get married in a cathedral?"

"No, I'm not saying that. I'm saying that once the famous Jacky Sax gets married there it will become more famous than ever. The clerk of Cook County, Richard J. Daley, said that he would take care of the guest list. He hasn't said where the reception will be yet. He said he will take care of that, so why worry."

"I wish I knew what this mission was about and why they specified me to carry it out. Doc said he doesn't know at this time, but he will let me know as soon as he finds out."

Angel, Juan and Mario sat down at the table with a beer in hand. They asked Angel when he thought they would get to Port Colborne, which is where the first lock was located. Doc came over and sat down at the table, he was carrying a drink in each hand. Mario asked if he had become a two handed drinker.

"No, one is for Bill, who was about finishing his trick at the wheel."

Juan got up and took the wheel from Bill and Bill took the drink from Doc. He turned to Mario and said, "This is your green chartreuse recipe that you dreamed up on Beaver Island. It's pretty good."

"Doc asked Angel what time he thought they would be in Port Colborne."

"We have been making good headway, Doc, we should tie up at the first lock at about 10 am. By now Eric, Peter and Arch had joined the group.

Peter asked a question directed to no one in particular. "I have never seen a lock and never had a reason to ask about them. Right now I understand that we are headed for some locks. Is this a good thing or a bad thing, I have no idea."

No one said anything for a minute or so. Then Doc opened up with, "Peter it's a damn good thing. The purpose of a lock is to raise or lower a ship to another level of water. In my time I have been through many locks. I never pay too much attention to the specification of each different lock but luckily for you, I just happen to find a book at the fire station about the Welland Canal, so I should be able to answer your questions. First off we are now sailing on Lake Erie and we wish to sail on Lake Ontario. The problem is Ontario is 326 feet lower than Lake Erie so in order to get this ship down to the level of Ontario we have to go through the locks in the Welland Canal.

By the time we reach Ontario, we will go through eight locks, and 27 miles. Each lock drops the ship approximately 41 feet. The first lock is on the Erie side at Port Colborne. The last lock on the Ontario side is Port Weller. The locks themselves are 80 feet wide and 766 feet long. One or more vessels may go into a lock at the same time, depending on their size. After you go through the first lock it takes about seven hours to go all the way through to the end. The canal was started in 1913 and completed in 1932. Now you know everything about the canal that came out of a book. Tomorrow you will see the real thing."

Then Doc said that we will probably tie up opposite of St. Catherine's. "We will only be about 10 miles from Niagara Falls, if we go by without stopping and the gals found out how close we were to Niagara Falls and did not stop, I think they would be really pissed off. So we will stop."

Arch decided that he would have one more beer and then hit the sack and Eric agreed. Doc said, "Bill I think we deserve another nightcap."

Mario then got up and said, "I'm just the guy to make them and I'll have one too."

After about 15 minutes, Mario showed up with a tray with three large drinks and a and a bowl of boiled shrimp, a saltshaker and some cocktail sauce. Doc said, "Good man, Mario, you deserve a raise but you probably won't get one."

Then Mario said, "I really don't need one. I am what you call satisfied, but someday I would like to open up my own restaurant." A different kind of restaurant, almost as if you were inviting someone to your home, strictly reservations and no menus. People would call to make a reservation and they would ask, "What's for dinner?" they would be told, then they would have to decide whether or not to come that night, everyone in the restaurant would eat the same meal. The only variations would be choice of side dishes and dessert. Everybody pays the same even if some people asked for second helpings. It would be much simpler to order food and much less waste."

"I got this idea from listening to a radio talk show. It was about this 75 year old colored woman who owned and ran Ruby's restaurant in

Kansas City, Missouri. That was just the way she ran her restaurant. Many people called a radio show and they all said how great Ruby's was. A lot of people called and said that many times they would make a reservation and not even bother to ask, "What's for dinner?" Sometimes it's nice to be surprised and they knew that whatever it was, it was always good. Boss, I would love to have that kind of reputation."

Doc said, "Mario, you already have that reputation. All you need now is your own restaurant and as I said before, when we haul *Cora Lee* out of the water for renovation and repair, I'll help you financially to get started, providing you start it in Chicago. I like to have a good restaurant to go to, I also think Ruby's idea would be great. Now let's hit the sack."

The next morning Mario got up at 5 am, thinking of his planned restaurant. Mario decided that he had better get some of his recipes on paper. He had never used a written recipe. They were all in his head, so he decided that he would start writing down recipes as he cooked. This morning he would make his one-of- a-kind great frittatas. He would write everything down as he cooked, it would be the start of his recipe file.

He made three 18 inch frittatas. By 7 am, everybody made it into the main dining area, they all agreed that Mario made the greatest frittatas in the world. Mario decided that frittatas would be on his menu. It was about 8 am when people went up on deck. Bill had spelled Angel at the wheel while Angel sat down at the cockpit table to eat his breakfast.

It was another sunny morning with a slight haze over water. Angel was now back at the helm again. He pointed and said, "About six or 8 miles off the port bow is the entrance to the Welland Canal. It looks like a Navy ship is going to beat us to the entrance. It looks like it is a Destroyer Escort or D.E. We will be following the destroyer into the first lock, if there is nobody ahead of them. It could take hours to go through the first lock. After the first lock it will be quick."

When Cora Lee was a half- mile from the entrance to the Welland Canal, Angel fired up the diesels. The crew dropped and bagged the Fisherman sail, and then dropped and furled all the other sails.

Now they were under diesel power, which they would use for the next 27 miles. The D.E. entered the canal first and Angel followed her to Port Colborne and the first lock. When they got there they found that you did not lay up to shore. When you got to the locks you tie up and waited till the southbound ships cleared the lock.

The waiting ships tied to large posts that were lined up like a fence. These posts were two feet in diameter, and stuck out of the water about 12 feet. On each side of the canal, were concrete blocks, that sloped down and went about 20 feet below the surface. With a ship tied up to these posts it was about 25 feet to dry land.

Each ship or boat had to put some people ashore to handle mooring lines going through the locks. The D.E. ahead of them was in the process of putting a man ashore. They had a man in a bosun's chair, which was a board seat with a sling of rope underneath it. It was attached to a long boom that reached over the water to dry land. The jury rig boom collapsed and down he went. He should have swam to shore but he didn't. He stayed in the chair and they hoisted him back up.

It was a summer cruise for reservists and nobody seemed to know what they were doing. They had more than twice the normal compliment of crew on the ship. When you have too many people everything goes wrong. They tried to get him back in the bosun's chair, but he would have no part of it.

The people on the *Cora Lee* were up on the bow watching this and jawing with some of the Navy crew who were on the after deck of the D.E. After seeing this, Angel said, "Put your guys on the schooner and we will put them ashore."

Angel went aft and started the diesels. He told Juan and Mario to ease off the lines. Then he brought the bow sprit right up to the stern of the D.E. and four sailors from the D.E. came aboard by bowsprit. Angel told Eric and Peter to handle the lines for the schooner. Eric asked Angel how he was going to get six guys to shore. Angel said, "Just watch and you will learn."

Angel then asked Mario to get six pairs of canvas gloves from the paint locker. Mario got the gloves and Angel told him to give each of the line handlers a pair. Mario did and Angel said, "Stick them in your back pocket and leave them there until I tell you to take them out."

Angel told Juan and Mario to release the mooring lines. He backed out and then swung the schooner to Port 90° to the shoreline. Now he had the bow pointed to the shore. He moved the ship forward until the bowsprit was over dry land and said, "See, no problemo."

One of the sailors said, "How do we get back on?"

Angel just said, "Keep the gloves in your back pocket."

Now the line handlers were on top of the locks, they still had to wait for the lock to open. Just then a loudspeaker sounded and announced that it would be another 45 minute wait. The guys on the stern told the *Cora Lee* people on the bow that the D.E. had run aground last night and they think they tore up the starboard screw. The captain wants the engineer to take a look at it.

Next they dragged out a portable compressor, and a couple of hundred feet of hose. When Arch saw the pile of stuff on the after deck, he said sarcastically, "Are you sure that you have enough equipment to go down 5 feet? Because that is about how deep your screws are."

One of the sailors said, "Chief said that we've got to do it by the book."

Arch said, "Forget the book we have snorkels masks you can borrow."

And then the Chief showed up. He had enough hash marks on his arm to say that he had been in the Navy for at least 25 years. They put a ladder over the side and someone started up the compressor. Then the engineer put on his face mask with the air hose attached, went over the side and down the ladder. No problems so far. He was just under the surface when the Chief came over raising hell. He said, "Are you guys try to drown him? Give him some air!" And he threw a pile of hose over the side. It landed right on top of the engineer and he was all wrapped up in hose and had lost his mask and his grip on the transom. He went down with the weight of the hose. The Chief then said, "You guys are trying to drown him." And he disappeared. Arch saw the problem, dove in and went down to the bottom. He untangled the engineer and brought him up to the surface. The guys on deck pulled him up.

Arch went back down to check the screws. He was back up in a little over a minute. He told the guys on the D.E. "He Starboard screw is wiped out to the hub and the Port screw is banged up but salvageable." Then Arch got back on the Cora Lee and he said, "I need a beer, on second thought, I need a martini." Which he got and enjoyed it. Then Arch turned to Doc and said, "Peter asked you what the locks were, but you never told him about this. But at least the martini is good."

Doc pointed out that he may be right about the martini. "What do you think, Bill?"

"Well, it's worth testing."

They both got their martinis and sat down and took a sip. "He is right, Bill, the martinis are good."

Just then the horn on the locks sounded and the gates opened. Two ships came out, a small tanker and a freighter. The D.E. started up and moved in slowly. They only had one screw so they did not have too much control. The D.E. tied up portside to, so did Cora Lee. The gate behind them closed and water started going down. When they reached the bottom and the gates started to open, the sailors asked how they were going to get down. Eric said that Angel told them that this is the time to take the gloves out of your pocket. Eric said, "Put on your gloves and follow me." He took off running, leaped off the edge, flew about 12 feet, grabbed the main center shroud, swung around and slid down 41 feet to the deck.

As soon as he hit the deck he looked up. He saw Peter flying off the lock. Eric hollered as loud as he could, "Keep your legs together."

Peter heard him just in time. Arch looked up and saw the four sailors looking down. Arch said, "Piece of cake, but keep your legs together."

One of the sailors, Jerry said, "When I saw you leap off the lock, it scared me shitless. But after two more guys, it was my turn, I found that it was great flying through the air and heading for that shroud. I would even like to do that again sometime."

"Don't worry, Jerry, you will have the privilege seven more times. There are eight locks in the Welland. We can tell your people that we don't want to pick you off the stern of the D.E. for each lock, so you should stay aboard until we get through the canal," said Arch.

Then Eric said, "We have beer, good food and three beautiful girls aboard. Would you rather go back to your D.E.?"

"Hell no!"

"Our Captain has decided that we are going to stop and tie up for a short time near Sorrel or St. Catherine. He said that the women will never forgive him if we passed within 8 miles of Niagara Falls and they didn't get to see it."

The D.E. and the schooner went through four more locks, going through the same procedure as the first one. They found a place to tie it up at Highway 406 that goes through St. Catherine's. Most of the people aboard had no idea why they were stopping at this spot. Doc had talked to the Captain of the D.E. and they both agreed to stop at this point, so that the D.E. could retrieve their four line handlers. It was a public, temporary, overnight docking area which had slips for 10 boats. They also had a dock that ran parallel to the canal, to tie up ships the size of the D.E. The four sailors were getting ready to go back to their ship, when Mario came up from the galley with a large tray. On the tray were four big steak sandwiches and four bottles of beer. He said, "Just so you guys remember the *Cora Lee*."

The sailor Dave, said, "They would never forget and took their steak sandwiches and headed for their ship."

Doc asked, "If anyone knew where they were at."

Arch said that he saw a sign right before they pulled into the slip that said "St. Catherine's, 3 miles", but what is in the opposite direction of St. Catherine's? It seemed that no one knew.

Doc told them, "Eight miles that way is Niagara Falls."

"You're kidding," said Eric, "Niagara Falls is in New York."

"You're right and eight miles that way is Niagara Falls."

"Doc, if what you say is true, are we going to visit the falls?" asked Sandra.

Doc said, "Sandra, if we passed this close and we didn't stop or even tell you about the falls, what would you gals have said when you found out about it?"

"I don't think you would really want to hear that, Doc."

"That's what I thought. Transportation to the falls will arrive at 1 pm. It's Noon now, so everybody go to your cabins and get ready quickly and get back up on deck. Mario has some real good rib eye steaks that are almost ready. Mario and Angel are staying with the ship. They have both been to the falls before."

Everybody was back up on deck in record time. They wanted to get their steak sandwiches while they were hot. Doc was right those sandwiches were really good.

The transport showed up early at 12:45 pm and everyone was ready to go, so they got in the van and headed to the falls. Kelly asked the driver if this was his regular run of Niagara Falls. "I must see Niagara Falls four or five times every day. I pick up people in St. Catherine's some of the time, but mostly at the Niagara Falls airport."

"Then you must know a lot about the falls."

"When it comes to the falls, I'm a walking encyclopedia."

"If that's the case I think we probably have a lot of questions, if you don't mind."

"My name is Tim, ask away."

Doc said, "Tim is not only our driver, but he is also our tour guide. He will be with us all day and into the evening or until we are ready to go back to the ship."

Tim then started making like a tour guide. "First I would like to thank you for coming, mainly because I make my living here by showing you some fantastic natural wonders. There are two Niagara Falls. There is Horseshoe Falls which is on the Canadian side and then the American Falls which is naturally on the American side.

There are also two cities of Niagara Falls. One on the Canadian side and one on the American side. Like I said before this is a very popular attraction. Which makes me happy and keeps me working. We have about 4 million visitors annually. As long as I've worked here, I have never seen anyone go away disappointed."

Tim pulled into a parking lot. "We will get out and walk over to the viewing area and what we will see is Horseshoe Falls. It is very large and very noisy. It is 162 feet high. The curving crest gives it the name "Horseshoe", at the crest is 2600 feet wide. The American falls, which we will see later over on the east bank, are 1000 feet wide and 167 feet high."

Bill asked, "What would be the chance of survival for someone going over to falls? And if you were going over, which falls would you choose?"

"Neither. Your chance on either one would be close to nothing. If you didn't drown immediately or the fall didn't kill you, the suction at the bottom would keep you tumbling underwater until the falls decided to spit you out, all beat up and drowned. People have gone over and survived but most don't. The ones that have survived, do it in heavy wooden and cushioned barrels, some were steel barrels that were completely cushioned on the inside. The non-survivors just tumbled at the base of the falls till they were finally spit out but no one was alive. Then there was that tightrope walker Charles Blondin, who walked across 160 feet above the falls. Then he did it again the following year with his agent on his back. There were a lot of people who did weird things to attract attention. If there are no more questions about Horseshoe Falls, then let's go to the Maid of the Mist."

"Hey, Tim, where is that boat going down there?" asked Arch.

"Into the mists."

Then Eric and Peter piped up, "You mean into the falls?"

"No, the boat is only going into the mist and the people will get rained on."

Sandra said, "I hope they come back out again."

The Maid of the Mist went into the mist on the Canadian side, heading toward the American side, so they were waiting for the Maid to come out on the eastern side of the falls. It did not. But it finally came out at the same place it went in.

Jacky said, "It looks interesting. Are we going to go down there?"

"We will be on that boat within the next 15 minutes. We have reservations."

Bill turned to Doc and said, "How would you like to take the *Cora Lee* through that rainstorm?"

"Only with Angel at the helm."

On that note Doc said, "Let's get back in the van. Time to get the show on the road."

They went down some curvy road and came out at a small parking lot. They parked, got out of the van and followed Tim to a house that was right next to a lake.

There are was a long dock and the boat was tied up to the dock. On his transom it said "Maid of the Mist Number Two." They looked into the haze and saw the Maid of the Mist number one coming toward them out of the haze, they noticed it was coming from Horseshoe Falls. The Maid of the Mist number one turned until her stern was pointed toward the shore and she backed down and made a perfect landing at the dock right across from Maid number two.

The people coming off the boat were all laughing and singing they were also wearing raincoats and fishermen Sou'Wester hats. There wasn't anyone that was not totally drenched. They were coming off and the crew was going aboard. A few of them stopped to talk to them, they said it was interesting and fun. But be sure to wear your rain gear which they will give you before you leave the dock. It looked like about a 40 foot twin screw diesel powered boat. It had a large cabin about amidships. There was a bench seat in the cabin to accommodate about 50 people, a raised wheel house forward of the main cabin and had windows all around.

The wheelhouse had about an 18 inch long hood extending over to the windshield and a big windshield wiper, it looks like they planned on a rainstorm. They went aboard and the mate told them to go into the midship cabin. There were lockers all around the walls he told them to pick a locker and put in your coats and hats and anything that you do not want to get wet. He said to put your things in, lock it and take the key. If you're wearing a coat, put it in a locker because you will be wearing a slicker and you will sweat like a pig if you wear your jacket. Someone said, "Pigs don't sweat." The mate then said, "Neither will you if you do what I say."

Bill said, "All accounted for Captain."

The Captain said, "Okay we will get underway then." There was a total of 29 people aboard. "We have three rules. No climbing on the cabin top to take pictures. No running on deck and no diving over the side to go swimming. Let's go out on deck and up to the bow. To non-sailors, the bow is the front and the stern is the back of the boat. We are now in the Maid of the Mist pool. It is deep here so there is not a lot of current. That is, not for about 2 1/2 miles downriver, then it gets stronger and stronger and if you would be in it 7 miles downriver, that would be a real wild ride. Just to make sure that it doesn't happen we have two engines. If one fails the other one will get us back to the dock. We are going down stream right now but only for about 1 1/2 Miles, then we will turn back toward the falls."

The Mate said to Sandra, "No Ma'am, we are not going under the falls we are just going into the mist. Trust me, the Captain has made this trip a few thousand times and he knows what he is doing. He's not going to get too close to the falls. He values his hide too much for that."

They headed toward Horseshoe Falls. The closer they got, the louder the roar. Everybody was standing on the bow of the boat and the roar is louder now. The mist is very heavy, and everyone looks like they have been in a rainstorm. They keep heading towards the roaring sound. The water is becoming more turbulent and one very nervous lady asked the Mate how the Captain can tell how close he is to the falls.

"He can tell by the sound."

She said, "It sounds to me like we're already there."

He said, "Ma'am, we are just in the mist right now. If we were in the actual downpour of the falls, you would know it. It would scare the hell out of you. I've been there once and I don't want to do it again. The mist was getting heavier the roar louder. Then it got a little quieter, finally there was sunshine and everyone cheered. The boat headed away from the falls out into the bright sunshine. The Captain turned the boat 180° so they were facing the falls. The Mate said that they were now in the center of the horseshoe. He told them to look up and they could see the whole crest of Horseshoe Falls. It was a beautiful view, better than you can see from up on top. It looked immense and powerful. Only an idiot would go over that in a barrel.

The Captain turned the boat around and headed to the dock. When they got there, Tim was waiting. He asked how the trip was, some said it was beautiful and others said it was scary. Sandra asked him how many times he had gone into the mist.

He said, "Never. It's too scary for me."

The Mate said, "Don't let him pull your leg he has more time in the mist than anyone I know of! Tim used to be a Captain on one of the original Maid of the Mist boats."

Tim said, "Back when I was young and stupid. Some tourists that had their own boats, thought it would be interesting to take their own boats into the mist, they said they would pay me $100 to guide him. I told him it was stupid and dangerous not knowing anything about the falls. Then they offered me $200 and I said no, they said they would go without me, so I said okay. There were two17 foot boats with 40 HP Mercury outboards. One had a driver and three passengers and one with a driver and two passengers. I went with the two passengers. I said that I would guide them, so I told the second boat to follow me. We went into the mist, going along all right, until the guy in the second boat decided to scare his passengers by getting closer to the falls. He got too close, where the water was so turned up that his props were not taking a bite and they were getting slowly sucked in. I told the driver in my boat to get his anchor and a long line, to get in the rear seat and secure the anchor line to the cleat, get ready to throw the anchor to the other boat and hope to hell they will have enough sense to secure it, as we cross their stern and immediately turn away from the falls."

"We crossed and threw the anchor. The anchor just dropped in over his transom and hooked and we damned near pulled her transom off but we got him out of there."

We got back to the dock and they just couldn't stop thanking me. "I told him that I should not have taken them there." He said, "They would have gone without me, if they did that, some of them would not have made it back." He said, "He would send me a check for $1000."

I said, "Don't bother, I'll tear it up." A couple of weeks later I received an envelope that was certified mail. There was a short note that said, "You can't tear this up. If you throw it away, only the restaurant will benefit."

It was a $3000 gift certificate for one of the best restaurants in Niagara Falls. There was a Post-it note attached to the gift certificate that said, "Spend it. It's already paid for and thanks for saving our stupid asses. Signed, Larry Masters." Well, thanks to Larry Masters, I have been eating pretty good. But now a days I stay out of the mist."

"So now we go to the American falls."

"We don't take another boat in the mist again do we?" asked Sandra.

"No, we walk, but first we ride in the van to the American side. We will cross over on the toll bridge, then go to the overlook," said Tim, "Do you see that little island down there? That is Goat Island. We are now at Prospect Point which has some good views of the falls. There are a series of coin-operated binoculars which cover the falls and down river."

After leaving Prospect point they drove down to Rainbow Bridge. They spent some time looking at the lower part of the falls and down river. They came off of Rainbow Bridge and went over to the footbridge and then headed down to Goat Island. From Goat Island they took an elevator to the foot of the falls. Then they headed to the Cave of the Winds. The Cave of the Winds was behind the curtain of falling water. After spending a short time there, everybody agreed to head back to the ship.

While driving back, Tim said, "As much as the falls are for recreation and sightseeing, the falls also serve a very useful purpose. The power plants that are down river from the falls are fed by four large turbine tunnels and produce 4,000,000 KW of electricity. This is shared by the U.S. and Canada. Now that you know all about Niagara Falls, you are back at your ship. She sure is one beautiful ship. May I come aboard to see what a real ship looks like?"

Doc said, "Tim, you are welcome to come aboard and you may stay for dinner if you would like. We have one of the greatest chefs afloat. I talked to him on the phone and dinner will be ready in half an hour. Tonight he is making the world's greatest lasagna."

They all went aboard, including Tim. Doc showed him around the ship, they had a good dinner and sat around having a few drinks. Doc told them that their next stop would be Clayton, New York.

Tim asked Doc if he was interested in antique boats? Doc said he was. Tim told Doc, "There is an antique boat Museum in Clayton."

"That is one place I will visit in Clayton, I'm glad you told me about it."

Tim said that it was time for him to go. He thanked Doc for the tour of the ship and the dinner. Doc had already paid him for his service as a tour guide and thanked him for a good job. On his way to his cabin he thought about what Tim had said about the antique boat Museum in Clayton.

Doc used to own a big old Hacker Craft. He had a 1937 Chris-Craft speedboat and he decided that he had to see this museum. Both Angel and Mario were also interested in old boats. In fact Mario has a 1939 Chris-Craft in perfect condition. They would jump at the chance to see some of these old boats. He would tell them in the morning. Right now, Doc headed for the sack.

The next morning after breakfast, Angel fired up the diesels and headed downriver toward the last two locks. They went through the locks, then downriver to the mouth and out into Lake Ontario. Now they were only 150 miles from the St. Lawrence Seaway. It was 2 pm and by the time they reached Lake Ontario it would be another 15 hours to the head of the seaway. This would put them at about 5 am when they made it to the St. Lawrence. It was about 20 miles to Clayton, New York and the Thousand Islands. They didn't know if there were actually 1000 islands, but there were a lot of them.

Chapter 30

Jacky, Arch and Bill Capture IRA Guys

Doc asked Angel and Mario if they were interested in going to an antique boat Museum in Clayton. They both said yes they would . It was about 6 am when they reached Clayton. Angel brought the ship into a small harbor and Mario dropped the anchor. Everybody except Juan got off the ship. Doc took them to the boat and bait shop. It was a place where you could rent boats and fishing gear. They sold bait and were very knowledgeable about where to fish for Muskies. There were also some good places to fish for Small Mouth Bass. Mario picked out a nice Muskie rod and some surface lures, then he saw some deep diving gear, which he bought. Doc told Jim, the owner, to put everything on one bill including the boat rentals. That would be three boats and outboards.

Doc asked about the museum. Jim said, "It's a great museum and has some beautiful boats in it, but today is Monday and it's closed on Monday. It's open tomorrow though, 10 am to 5 pm. When you go out on the water to go fishing, take a look at the tour boats out there. There are a lot of them. Most of them belong in the museum. They are all in fine shape and well taken care of, the big old Garwoods, Hacker Crafts, Century's and Chris-Crafts."

Doc and Angel decided to go back to the boat today, they would fish tomorrow. Angel said that he liked to eat fish, not catch them.

Mario said, "We will catch some Muskie today and I'll smoke them tomorrow."

Jim said, "You're going to smoke a Muskie? You can't smoke a Muskie. It's not a smoking fish."

Mario looked at him and asked him if he had ever smoked any fish.

"Sure, lots of times."

"What kind did you smoke?" Jim named off a lot of different fish.

Mario said, "Those are all oily fish, some even saltwater fish."

Jim said, "The Muskie is a very wet fish which does not lend to smoking."

Then Mario said to himself, "I don't think that the Muskie knows that and I'm not going to tell him."

Mario then said, "Jim, if you don't think a Muskie can be smoked, then come out to the ship tomorrow night. I'll send a message as to what time."

Jim said, "Okay, I'll be there."

They rented two 18 foot boats with 25 HP Evinrude outboards and they got all the fishing gear they needed to catch the Muskie. Jim gave them a couple of maps for the area and marked off some good spots to catch Muskies. Eric, Peter and Mario took the first boat.

Mario was anxious to start casting for Muskies, so they headed straight north to an area pointed out by Jim. Peter was in the bow. Eric handled the outboard, he shut down the engine and Peter casted toward the shore. Eric also casted toward the shore of Wellesley Island. Mario was sitting between them, casting toward mid-channel with a diving Pike Minnow lure. He no more then started his retrieve on his first cast when he had a strike.

Mario had fished for Muskie many times before and he knows that with a Muskie you have to set the hooks quick and hard. Muskies have a very tough mouth and if you don't set quick and hard, the Muskie will clamp down on the lure and just play with you until she decides to spit it out. Many people fished for years without catching a legal Muskie. The minimum legal size is 30 inches. Most people catch the smaller ones, which are thrown back. The bigger Muskies get bigger because they learn how to outwit the fisherman and usually the biggest Muskies are female.

On his first cast Mario had hooked into something that seemed to be good size. Mario played with the fish for about 30 minutes . By now Mario knew he was well hooked and getting tired so he started bringing the fish closer to the boat. Then it dawned on Eric that he still had the outboard in the water. If the fish gets the line wrapped around the lower end of the outboard, it's goodbye fish. Eric lifted it out of the water. Just then the fish flashed by alongside of the boat, then it dove down. But the fish was tiring and Mario reigned it in. He told Eric to get the net ready, which Eric did. The fish came up to the boat, Eric got the fish in the net and they got the fish in the boat. The Lure was snagged in the net so Mario just cut the line.

Mario said, "This is a big one! At least 42 inches and about 16 to 18 pounds. It's not a good idea to keep fishing with that big sucker in the bottom of the boat. Let's keep the fish in the net, and go back to the ship. I'll take it to the galley, clean it and put it in the cooler."

They got to the *Cora Lee*, and Mario carried the fish up the ladder. Doc was standing there and said, "Nice! Who caught i?" "I did, first cast, now I'm going to get it ready to put it in a cooler for tomorrow," said Mario.

Doc said, "Let's measure and weigh it first." They took it down in the galley, measured and weighed it. It was 45 inches long and weighed 19 pounds.

Mario cleaned it and put it in the cooler. "Now I got to get back to fishing. I have had only one cast so far."

They headed back to fish again and Eric was heading for the same spot that Mario caught his fish. Mario said, "No, where there was one large Muskie, you won't find another. They are a solitary and territorial type of fish. Other fish, even other Muskies stay away. They have a vicious set of teeth. The Muskie is considered a freshwater Barracuda."

They fished for three hours without a strike, they were about ready to pack it in when Peter got a hit. He set the hook hard four or five times as Mario had shown him. Peter played with the fish for about 45 minutes, finally got it to the boat and Mario netted it. It was a good-sized fish but not as big as Mario's. It looked to be about 36 inches long and probably weighed 10 to 12 pounds.

The three of them took a quick vote and decided that they would head to the Cora Lee. Mario said, "Tomorrow we are going to have some delicious smoked Muskie."

"Mario, I have a question to ask you about smoked Muskie. My dad smoked cold water Carp and there are a lot of people that won't eat Carp, but when he smokes it, that Carp is great!" said Eric.

"Eric, do you know why his Carp is great?"

"Why?"

"Because he knows what he's doing, same as with the Muskie. You will see tomorrow. Muskie is a great tasting fish. Most people that eat Muskie bake it. That's not bad, but not as good as smoked Muskie."

Right after breakfast, Mario took a boat to one of the Forested Islands, when he got back to the schooner, he had all the greenwood that he needed to smoke the Muskies. While sitting at the after cockpit table drinking coffee before breakfast, Eric asked Arch how he did fishing yesterday. "Bill caught one that was 33 inches and 8 pounds. Jacky and I each caught one under the 30 inch minimum. Bill gave his fish to Mario to smoke. Jacky, Bill and I are going to try our luck again this afternoon, after we go to the boat museum."

Eric said, "I am going to take Sandra and Kelly out to fish for small mouth bass. After seeing Mario's big fish they decided against fishing for Muskie."

At 10 am, they all headed over to the museum. It was not a fancy building, though it looked to be very well constructed. The closer you got, the better it looked. As they were standing outside admiring the workmanship on the doors, the curator of the museum came out. He walked over to the group and said, "I can tell when someone appreciates quality work. This building was financed by a rich publisher back in the mid 1930's. He hired a ship's carpenter to build it, as you can see, if you put this building in the water it would probably float."

He introduced himself as James Hamilton. "I do this part-time. I'm really in the hardware business. I do this all year long with three other local people. We are all volunteers, we like boats, particularly old boats. We only have one paid employee and that is Peter Gustafson. He is a ship's carpenter. He puts some of these old boats back together. He is very interesting to talk to, he is very knowledgeable about ships and boats. I will introduce him to you, but once you start talking about anything that floats, you will have a difficult time getting away."

Hamilton brought them into what looked like a large warehouse. The first thing that caught Doc's eye was a 28' Garwood. It had a front cockpit for the driver and a couple of passengers. There were three sets of seats, two sets behind the driver's cockpit. A big engine compartment and another seat in the stern. Basically this boat had four cockpits plus an engine compartment.

Hamilton showed Doc another boat and asked if he had ever seen a boat like this Hacker Craft.

"Yes, I have I owned one for a few years. A great boat for its time."

They walked around a bit until Mario spotted the old Chris-Craft like the one in his garage. Kelly came over to where Mario was standing and asked him if she heard him right, that he had a Chris-Craft just like this one?

He said his was like new. Inside and out had been refinished and the engine was in perfect shape, a six-cylinder Gray Marine engine.

"Aren't all boat engines painted gray?"

"No. Chris-Craft painted them blue."

"But you just said it was painted gray."

"No, I said it was a Gray Marine engine. Gray is the name of the company that makes the engine."

"Now I know," said Kelly.

"Now that you know, would you like to take a ride in a beautifully restored Chris-Craft?"

"I would love to."

"That sounds good, after the boat ride, I would like to take you to a great restaurant that is owned by a friend of mine. He has decided to retire and wants to sell it to me."

"That sounds great. When are you going to do it?"

"After we get the Cora Lee back to Chicago. Doc has at least a year's work in Washington. Angel, Juan and three other guys are taking it south. They will take a charter group to the Mediterranean. I will get off in Chicago and start my restaurant." said Mario.

"I was talking to Doc and he told me about your plans for a reservations only restaurant and you deciding what the menu is for anyone who gets a reservation. I really think it is great. Want a partner?"

"I thought you would never ask. I never considered a partner before, but that was before I met you. Yes, of course, you would be perfect partner. After we go through the rest of the museum I have to get back to the ship and check my fish that are smoking. I put them in at six o'clock this morning. They should be ready for dinner tonight at six."

"I'll go back with you, but first I have to stop at the store and get some toilet articles."

"Okay, I have to go and see Jim at the bait shop to invite him to dinner. I will meet you at the dock in about 30 minutes."

Kelly turns to Mario and said, "Okay, Partner."

Mario said, "It's got a good ring to it hasn't it?"

"I believe it does."

Kelly and Mario made a quick walk through the rest of the museum and then headed to the schooner. Kelly was thinking that Mario and her may become more than just partners in business. That was a good thought.

The rest of the crew checked out the old Chris-Crafts, there were three of them. There were a couple of Hacker Crafts and another bigger Garwood and an old Hinkley Cruiser. There were all different kinds of canoes, including the Canadian freighter.

Then Hamilton took them into the back, which was the workshop of the museum. There were about five different types of boats being worked on. One that looked almost completed, was a 36 foot Matthews single screw cruiser. Next to the Matthews was a real first class antique, she looked to be about 45 feet. An AC&F (American Car and Foundry), with a 420 HP Liberty engine. It was a double cabin with nice workmanship, but the cabin design looked like something that should stay on dry land. It was 45 feet long and only 7 feet beam (width).

They were all looking at the AC&F when Peter Gustafson came out of the cabin. He climbed down the ladder and walked over to Doc. "I am Peter Gustafson and you must be Admiral Bob Hunter."

Doc agreed and introduced the rest of his crew. Gustafson said, "That's a right smart Staysail schooner you've got anchored out in the harbor. Looks like she was designed by Cox and Stevens back in the late 20s and built by Wilcox Crittenden."

"Right on all counts. How come you know so much about my boat?"

"I used to work for Wilcox Crittenden. The original name of your boat was Jezebel."

"Right again. My wife didn't like the name, so I named it after her."

Eric told Gustafson, "This is a neat museum, but Peter and I have to go. We are going back to the boat to pick up Sandra. She wants to go fishing for Small-Mouthed Bass."

"You want Bass, just go right out behind the museum and you will get all you want. Bring a few big net bags. If you put them on a stringer, the Muskie will get them. I've got three big nets bags that I used to lend to my relatives. Just put them by the front door of the museum when you get through with them. The channel to the museum starts just north of the bait shop."

So Peter and Eric headed out to the schooner to pick up Sandra then headed to the channel. Gustafson was right. All three of them were catching Bass as fast as they got their lure back in the water. Sandra started wondering who was going to clean all the fish. Then she wondered out loud. Eric said, "I am and I'm going to teach you how to clean fish too."

"Sounds good to me. I think that we have about 30 pounds of fish now, maybe 10 more pounds would make a good fish fry."

They went back to the ship and brought their catch aboard. As they came up the boarding ladder, Doc greeted them, as they carried three nets full of fish aboard. He said that it was a very good thing that everybody liked fish. They brought the fish down to the galley and Mario asked what was in the nets.

"All Small-Mouthed Bass, about 3/4 to 1 pound each," said Eric.

"Nice fish! That is a lot of good eating," said Mario.

Eric said, "How about Sandra and I fillet them and put them in the freezer?"

"Good we can have a fish fry a few days from now."

"I have about 28 pounds of Muskie smoking now. It will be ready at about 6 pm. Jim from the bait shop is coming out to try the Muskie that he said can't be smoked. Also, Doc invited Gustafson. He agreed with Jim that Muskie don't smoke too good. Maybe we will have smoked fish tomorrow again, if Bill, Jacky and Arch do any good. The three of them went out to the area were Jacky lost a big Muskie. If you miss a Muskie and go back to the same area, you might get that same Muskie. Like I said before Muskies are territorial and keep going back to the same area."

Bill, Jacky and Arch were back casting for that big Muskie. Bill was in the middle, Jacky in the bow and Arch in the stern at the outboard. Bill was casting towards the shore, Jacky and Arch were casting deep out in the channel. They were anchored off of Northern Island. There was another boat in the channel, which was half a mile wide. The other boat was a float boat. It was anchored off the island on the south side of the channel. There were two people on the float boat, but only one person was fishing. The one fishing looked like a girl. Behind the float boat was a 19 foot Chris-Craft with two guys in it. It looked like they were casually fishing; not working at it.

All of a sudden Jacky got a strike. She set the hooks at least four or five times. She said that she was not going to lose this one. Jacky played with it for about 30 minutes, got it up to the boat, Bill netted it and got the fish into the boat. She didn't lose it this time. End of story, almost that is.

There had been a third boat. Not a fishing boat, it was a fast speed boat. It had two guys in it who were doing much the same kind of fishing as the guys in the second boat. The third boat drifted close to the second boat and all of a sudden there was a sound that Bill and Jacky recognized immediately. A silenced high powered pistol. Two pistols - three shots.

The two guys in the second boat had been shot. Boat number three raced over to the float boat. One of the bad asses jumped out of the speed boat and onto the float boat.

As soon as they heard the shots, Bill hollered to Arch. Arch headed to the pontoon boat full bore. They were now close enough to see that one guy was struggling with what looked like a 16-year-old girl. He was just about to shoot the older woman that was on the float boat. The girl kneed him right in the in the place that hurts the most. He fell backwards into the speed boat, but he had the girl by the wrist and she landed in the speed boat too. The driver pushed the throttle forward and the speed boat took off.

Jacky said, "From what I saw, I think she hurt the bastard pretty good. This boat isn't fast enough to catch them. We don't have a chance to catch the bastards at all. They pulled up to the float boat, Bill and Jacky jumped off. There was an Irish woman on board and she was pissed off. "Lousy IRA bastards, they kidnapped the daughter of the American Ambassador to Ireland. That little girl just saved my life. He was about to shoot me. He knew that I recognized them and now they will threaten to kill her if I inform on them. Also the Ambassador is negotiating with England."

Bill said, "We will get them."

Arch said, "How?"

"With that helicopter over there."

"Who does it belong to?"

"To the Ambassador," the Irish woman said. She said that she would call the Ambassador on her radio.

"Forget asking. You call and get some help for the two guys in the boat. Are they Secret Service?"

"No private security firm."

"Tell the Ambassador to hire better security. Where is your rope locker?"

She showed him and it looked like there was about 100 feet of five eighths inch line. Bill said, "Take it and let's go."

Jacky said, "To rappel," and she noticed a wool sweater. "Can I borrow this?" She pulled her big knife out of the sheath and cut both arms off the sweater. She said, "Sorry," and threw one of the sleeves to Arch. "Now hang onto this. Let's go, Arch. Fire up the outboard."

Bill said, "Put her up on the beach next to the helicopter." Arch did exactly that.

The three of them ran over to the helicopter. Bill got into the pilot's seat, turned on the ignition and started spooling her up. The pilot ran over and asked Bill what he was doing?

Jacky said, "Emergency! We need to borrow your chopper!"

"Not without permission from the Ambassador."

"They have it Jack." That was when they noticed a beautiful red headed lady standing barefoot in the grass. With an Irish accent, she said, "And may God go with you."

Jacky then said, "We have God's messenger with us now."

That's when Bill lifted her off the ground and they headed after the speed boat. Jack asked the ambassador, "Who were those people?"

"Those are the people who are going to rescue Heather. Damned IRA have just kidnapped her. The reason I know is that Peggy called me from the float boat and she said not to worry, it looks like some good people are after the bad guys and I think the IRA guys bit off a little more than they can chew this time. She said Heather saved her by kneeing one of them in the gullonies and that he probably wouldn't be able to walk straight for quite a while. She asked me to radio the schooner Cora Lee that is anchored in Clayton Harbor and ask for Admiral Hunter.

I guessed that it must be Admiral Robert Hunter of the U.S. Navy. I called and talked to Bob Hunter, whom I have known for quite a few years. I told him the situation and that there were three people in a boat who were fishing when it happened. Peggy is the gal who was with Heather when it happened. She said that the three of them scared the creeps off, but they got Heather anyway. One of them must have been a pilot with an English accent, a beautiful blonde and a big muscular guy."

"Crystall, you couldn't have picked a better group to rescue your daughter. The pilot is RAF and the blonde girl is one of the toughest commandos you have ever seen and the big muscular guy is a Messenger From God, so Crystall, the only ones to worry about are those IRA guys. They will be needing medical attention."

The Ambassador told this to Jack and he felt much more relieved. "The Admiral also invited us to his schooner for smoked Muskie dinner and asked if we could take that big Muskie out of their boat that Jacky had caught and left behind because she wouldn't want to lose it since it was her first legal Muskie. I had told him there was a big fish in the boat, caught by the female aboard, on my channel."

After about 20 minutes, Bill, Jacky and Arch spotted the boat. There were two guys and a girl. Bill told them to get the rappel line secure and for both of them to go out the same door so he can keep an eye on the two of them. "We don't want them shooting at you, so I think it's best to run them out of ammo and make them real nervous."

"From what we have seen of that little girl down there, it's not going to bother her at all. I think she will enjoy it. Okay, here is what I'm going to do. I am going to buzz them real low from behind, from the front and from each side. I'll be so low that they'll feel like they are in a hurricane. They will be both afraid and pissed off at me so they should be shooting and wasting ammo, till they run out."

Arch asked Bill what he considered an important question, "What if they hit a sensitive part of the engine or control?"

"What they probably don't know is that this model of a chopper was built for police and military. Everything on this puppy is armor plated. They can't put a dent in this machine with those hand guns that they have, but they can put a dent in you rappelling down those lines, unless I run them out of ammo first."

Arch said, "Good thinking, Boss."

"That's why I'm sitting up here nice and comfortable and you're going to jump out of that door and tangle with a couple of nasty people."

"Yeah, but we get to rescue the princess."

"Make sure you do."

Jacky said, "Why don't you guys quit jabbering and let's get this show on the road."

"Right you are, Beautiful Lady," and he dove at the boat. Right before he got over the top of it, he pulled full pitch and full throttle. Both of the kidnappers were firing their automatics at the chopper as it was coming at them. Bill decided that he would hit them from the side and then from behind again. He came over the boat and did the rotor down wash trick again, then headed behind and was going to come up from the rear.

The boat was rocking violently from this side run. The guy in the back seat, supposedly guarding Heather, was now firing at the helicopter, trying to hit the pilot. There was nothing but a click and he threw the pistol over the side. Heather saw that he was reaching for something on the floor. It was a rifle he had just got his fingers through from the trigger guard, when Heather stood up and stomped on his hand as hard as she could. He screamed and held his hand. The boat lurched and he fell to the side away from Heather. The two guys in the boat were no longer thinking straight. The only one that was thinking right was Heather. The next thing she did was reach down and grab the rifle and threw it over the side. Bill had been hovering behind him for a couple of minutes. He was watching as the guy in the back threw his automatic over the side and then he saw Heather stand up and stomp on something, it was on the bad guys hand. Then she threw his rifle over the side.

Bill said, "The driver must be out of ammo as well as the guy in back. I'll just make one more run to make sure. Which he did and came over the boat from each side, it slowed them down to a crawl. Jacky unhooked one of the lines, coiled it and threw it over her shoulder. "We will need this line to tie up those creeps. We can both go down the same line."

Arch said, "We better get down there before Heather kills those guys."

Bill held the helicopter right over the boat and Jacky went out of the door followed by Arch. They landed on the boat in a matter of seconds. Jacky in the front seat and Arch in the back. The driver was fighting the steering wheel because of the helicopter's down wash, but he came up with a 9 mm automatic. He had almost pointed it at Jacky when she reached over and ripped it out of his hand. She ejected the cartridges and threw the gun on the floor. He got up out from behind the wheel and was standing there on the seat. The boat was stable now as Bill had pulled away. Jacky asked Arch how he was doing back there. He said, "No problem, Heather has already made him a cripple. How's it going upfront?"

"Going okay. I took away his shootin' iron and now he wants to play with a knife."

"Give me that knife or I'll carve IRA on your ass." He lunged at her and Jacky dodged his pass. "Well, I guess you like the idea of IRA on your ass." He lunged again and this time he caught her blouse and made a slight cut on her belly. She caught his wrist and took the knife away. With her other hand she twisted his wrist, and laid him face down on the seat.

"Arch, throw me the rope that I threw into the backseat." He did and Jacky tied the creep's hands together right after she coldcocked him with the butt of his knife. He was out like a light, with his hands tied, she brought the rope down and hogtied his ankles. Next, she unbuckled his belt and unzipped his fly, she picked him up and laid him belly down on top the front seat with his head toward the back and his feet toward the front. She pulled down his pants exposing his bare butt. She said, "Heather, do you want to do the honors and carve up this bastard's butt?"

"With pleasure!" and she climbed into the front seat. Jacky asked Arch how his buddy was in the backseat.

"He ain't doing nothing, he's all tied up."

"Hold this other guys arms and I'll hold his feet while Heather carves a reminder in his ass." Heather carved "IRA" on a his left cheek using his own knife. "I promised him "IRA," so you can carve whatever you want in his right cheek. Not too deep, maybe a quarter of an inch, but big letters." Heather laid the big knife down and reached into the pocket of her jeans and came up with a small razor sharp pocket knife. She then carved a (NO) sign over IRA and in small letters below IRA (Crystal Quinn). Then she put away her small knife and picked up the big knife.

Jacky said, "Heather haven't you carved enough?"

"I just have to carve one more thing on his left cheek. If you had seen what these bastards have done to some of my friends.:

"I have, Heather, more than you know."

So Heather carved "ASS" on his right cheek and while she was carving, he woke up screaming. "What are you doing to me?"

"Just trying to let people know what you are."

Jacky wrapped his bloody butt in a blanket and threw him in the backseat with his buddy. Arch climbed into the driver's seat. The three good guys in the front seat and the two bad asses in the back. Bill had been circling overhead to make sure all was well. The two girls and Arch waved to Bill. Then they turned the boat around and headed back toward Clayton.

Bill radioed ahead and talked to the Ambassador. He told her that all was well. Bill asked how the two security guys that got shot were? She said, "One is serious but not critical and the other is minor. They are both on their way to the hospital." Bill landed in the same spot the helicopter was in when he took off. By the time he landed, the pilot, Peggy and the Ambassador were there to greet him. He knew what they were going to ask him, so he said, "Good guys, good shape, bad guys not so good shape. They are both going to need a little medical attention. Would you notify the local police to hold these guys for the FBI and give a call to the Admiral and let him know what happened?"

About 10 minutes later the boat pulled in and tied up to the Ambassador's dock. Heather jumped out of the boat and ran over to her mother. The Ambassador was stunned when she saw the blood on her blouse and arms. She had washed it off her hands in the river. Heather looked at her mom and then grinned, "It's not my blood, Mom. It's their blood," and she pointed to the two culprits tied up in the backseat.

Arch and Bill lifted the two out of the backseat and laid them on the grass. Peggy said, "I know these two."

"You recognize them, Ambassador?"

"Yes, I do, and they have been on the wanted list for a long time. This one is Davy O'Rourke and the other one hog-tied is Timothy Fitzpatrick. The law will be loving to get their hands on these two!"

Bill asked the Ambassador if she had a camera. "Now you have asked a question that I can give you a good answer to. I am what you would call an amateur photographer." She named off a bunch of cameras.

Bill said, "The Argus C-3 and the Polaroid; have you got film for them?"

"Of course, the camera is no good without film" The Ambassador then asked Peggy to go up to the house and get the two cameras and film for each. "Top shelf in my office."

Peggy was back in a short time with the cameras. Bill turned to Heather and said, "We have the criminals and what we need is a heroine."

Jacky walked over to Heather and put her arm around her and said, "Heather here is a victim. But those two found out she don't go easy. So I think Heather should be the heroine in this production."

Okay, Heather it is," and Bill brought Heather over to stand behind the two culprits that Arch had placed on a bench. The Ambassador took a series of pictures with the Argus C-3 (35MM) and then the instant camera, the Polaroid . When the ambassador said that she had enough pictures, Jacky and Arch said that she had to take one more picture of her daughter's handiwork. She said, "Okay, what's the picture?"

Arch said, "Wait till we get our guest of honor all set up."

Jacky asked the ambassador if she had a bottle of alcohol. She said no but she has some Jack Daniels. The Ambassador asked 80 or 100 proof? "100 proof. And a small towel."

Bill and Arch picked up Timothy Fitzpatrick and laid him over a back rest of the bench. This guy was the leader of these two.

Jacky said, "He tried to shoot me and when that didn't work he tried to carve me up with a knife. I told him to give me a knife or I would carve IRA on his ass."

The Ambassador asked, "You didn't do it, did you?"

Jacky looked directly at the Ambassador and said, "No, I did not, but your daughter did."

At that moment Bill pulled down his pants it was all bloody and you couldn't read what it said until Bill took the bottle of Jack Daniels and soaked the towel with it and Bill wiped off the blood so it could be read. Timothy's butt must have burned like hell because he was screaming and saying this is cruelty and torture! The Ambassador pulled Heather to her and said, "You did this?"

"I did good?"

"I think you did a very artistic job, except for one thing - you spelled my name wrong. My name, Crystall, has two L's in it. This bastards feels he is being mistreated. He thought it was amusing when they showed the burned up bodies in the news, caused by the bombs he and his friend had set. I have no sympathy for the vermin. Peggy, would you please go up to the house and get my speed graphic camera? I want a real good shot of this."

Peggy brought the camera and a tripod down. She took a picture of his carved butt and then his face, then the two culprits together. Finally one with Heather standing over them. She also took the same pictures with the Polaroid camera. When the photography session was over, Bill and Arch sat O'Rourke on a heavy cast-iron bench.

"Tie his hands behind him and to the bench," said Bill.

Heather taped a splint to his two broken fingers. Peggy would not help. She said, "The bastard tried to kill me."

Heather said, "I broke his fingers, so I guess I ought to do it." And she did. When they sat Fitzpatrick down on the bench he howled like hell. Heather said, "Wait." And she went to the house and came back with a pillow and put it under his butt.

Arch asked why she was doing this for him. Heather looked at Arch and said, "I may be a rotten kid, but I'm not totally mean person like these two guys."

Bill and Arch got them all tied up and Bill said, "Now we wait for the police and the FBI."

Then Fitzpatrick started screaming about his rights, "What about a doctor? We are both injured."

Bill said that if he didn't shut up, Arch would give him some more medical attention on his butt, with some more Jack Daniels, that shut him up. Just then the police launch pulled in and tied to the Ambassador's dock with four FBI men and the local police from Clayton, plus one medical aide.

John Norton, the head FBI man asked for two things. First the bathroom and next the two culprits. But bathroom first. Norton came back looking refreshed. "Now let's get down to business, where are the bad guys?"

Jacky took him to the bench. He took one look and said, "Looks like you hit the jackpot, we have been looking for Fitzpatrick here for a long time. His buddy over there is also wanted, but not as much as this Fitzpatrick, but we will take them both."

They loaded the two guys into the police launch. "We will take them, get them processed and come back tomorrow to make out a report," Norton said. "Good job, we will see you tomorrow." And away they went.

Bill said, "We had better get over to the Cora Lee. Mario has probably got his Muskie smoked by now, it is getting close to 5 pm."

Jacky said, "What about my Muskie? It's not in the boat."

Peggy said that she had taken it out of the boat and put it into a cooler alongside Heather's Muskie. Peggy pointed to a big cooler that was on the dock and there were two big Muskies each over 20 pounds. Heather decided to give hers to Jacky and they could bring them out to the schooner for Mario to cook. He would be glad to cook this Muskie because it would be too late to smoke it. Bill said that he could call Doc and have him send out the launch."

"No need for that," said Jacky, "We have our boat, plus the IRA boat."

The Ambassador said, "Heather, Peggy and I should go up to the house and get cleaned up for the visit to the schooner. You people probably want to do the same and you will want to give those fish to your chef."

Bill and Arch loaded the cooler into the fishing boat. Bill looked at Arch who was getting settled down in his seat. "Let's get this puppy started. I've got a hell of a taste for martini."

Jacky said, "There are more people in his boat who could probably use a martini. In fact I think I need a double."

They arrived at the Cora Lee, the two guys carried the cooler up on the deck and then down to the galley. Mario was in the galley when they got there. Bill opened the cooler and Mario reached in and picked up one of the fish and said, "Beautiful. I heard that you guys had a busy day out there. How the hell did you find time to fish?"

Arch said, "Jacky caught one and Heather, the Ambassador's daughter caught the other one."

The Ambassador and her daughter and assistant will be here for dinner. "Did you ask them if they like smoked fish?"

"I told them that you were smoking Muskie," said Bill.

"What did they say when you said that?"

"They said you can't smoke Muskie, but I told him you could and they said they would be here."

"Well, I am going to bake these two fish. No time to do anything else. I would appreciate it if you would give me a hand to get the fish in the oven," said Mario to Arch.

"I have seen you fillet jumbo perch."

"The big Muskie are easier. I want the bones and the head to make a broth, with which to make a sauce. You get them ready for the oven. Look in the cooler. In the back corner are some herbs. Bring out what will make a cup of dill. When I get the broth ready, I will make a dill sauce. The Muskie will go into the oven for a short period, then under the broiler with lemon and butter to get them nice and brown. We will put the dill sauce on top. I can taste it already."

While Arch filleted the two 20 pound Muskies, Mario went up on the after deck, where he and Juan had rigged the two big smokers on planks that extended over the water. They made them so the smokers could be swung in board to load them or to take the smoked meats out. Mario checked the Muskies and determined that the smoking was finished and the Muskies would be delicious.

He then got Juan to round up Eric and Kelly. He wanted them to get the big platters and carry the fish to the midship dining cabin. Then he and Arch would finish the Muskies being baked and broiled. The Muskie fillets had only been in the oven for 20 minutes. Now he was going to broil the fish with lemon and butter on top. When the fish got nice and brown on top, he would take the fish out of the oven and put his fish broth flavored dill sauce over the top. He would cut the fillets into smaller pieces and add more dill sauce. Then he would bring it out and put it on a large serving table.

Mario went up on deck and located James Hamilton and Peter Gustafson, who were talking to Doc. Mario walked up to the three of them and said, "Time to show you what smoked Muskie tastes like. There is also a broiled Muskie with dill sauce. It's down in the dining cabin already."

He found Jim from the bait shop who was talking to Heather, Peggy, Jacky, and the Ambassador. Mario said Jim, "The Muskies that you said can't be smoked are on the dining table."

Jacky introduced Mario to Heather and Peggy and then she said, "I would also like to introduce you to the American Ambassador to Ireland, Her Honor Crystall Quinn."

Mario said, "I'm very glad to meet you and I am really impressed that Jacky knows people in high places."

"Hell, Mario I know a lot of people. I shook hands with the President and the soon-to-be Mayor of Chicago is my good buddy. He insists on Bill and I get married in the Holy Name Cathedral and he said that Chicago is going to spring for the reception.

The Ambassador said, "There is only one person who could and would do something like that and I've known him for years -- Richard J. Daley, am I right?"

"You sure are."

"Am I going to be invited to your wedding?"

"You sure are!"

Just then Hamilton, Gustafson and Jim came up from the dining cabin. "The smoked Muskie is great and the broiled Muskie has a flavor that I have never tasted in any other fish," said Gustafson.

Jacky asked, "Do you want to know why, these particular Muskie tasted so great?"

"Why?"

"Because they were cooked by a great chef!" They all agreed.

Gustafson asked Jacky if she thought that Mario might tell him how to smoke a Muskie. "If he would tell me, then I would spend more time fishing."

Everyone enjoyed themselves and got stuffed with Muskie. After a few hours of eating, drinking and talking, the party came to an end and the guests got in their boats and went home, after complimenting Mario.

Doc, Bill, Jacky, Mario and Kelly sat down in their favorite meeting place; the aft cockpit table. Bill looked at Doc and said, "Doc, you do throw some pretty good parties."

"You can't blame me for that, Bill, it was Mario and Kelly that put together this fine feast. It was pretty good, wasn't it? But Kelly has got to share the blame for all that wonderful food."

"I accept my share of blame and I think Mario has put down the non-smoking of Muskie myth in Clayton. I think he has made some believers. Doc said "Mario you and Kelly make one hell of a good team, of cooks."

"That's what we were thinking Doc. Remember what I was telling you about a reservations only restaurant. Well Kelly likes that idea too .She likes it enough to become my partner"

Bill says, "Business partner or full time partner"

"One thing at a time Bill, Kelly and I have talked about it, but for right now it's to get a restaurant going."

"Have you come up with a name for the restaurant yet?"

"We think we have Doc, we tossed it around for quite a while. We thought of Mario and Kelly's – Kelly and Mario's, you can't make anything out of Fiorentino and Bergman, so we decided to call it Doc's Place. No just kidding! We finally settled on something that we both like, "THE HOME PORT". xx

Doc said, "That's perfect . You are both from Chicago and that is where your restaurant will be."

Everyone agreed that it was perfect. Jacky said, "You two are perfect and if you decide to tie the knot, wait till I get back to Chicago. We can make it a double at The holy Name Cathedral and the reception, wherever Richard J. Daley decides."

Both Kelly and Mario said that it sounded great, but first things first. "Right now, let's have a toast to your new restaurant and whatever the future brings."

They made the toast just as Juan walked up and told Doc that there was a radio message for him from an Admiral in Washington. "He said that he was on the Naval staff, Admiral Leslie Ryan."

Doc said, "Sounds like we're in business. Admiral Ryan doesn't just call to chitchat."

Chapter 31

Meet with Fathers at the Yard. Into Ireland.

They all figured that it was about the mission that Jacky was to lead. As of now nobody knows what the mission is to be. They have gone to a lot of trouble to keep it quiet. Juan came back over to the table and asked Jacky to go to Doc's cabin. She went and he was sitting behind his desk with a chair set in front of it a brandy snifter in front of him, another one on the other side of the desk for his guest.

Jacky sat down and her opening words were, "Your good brandy, that means this is not a social call."

"Didn't think I could fool you, Jacky. I got a call from my friend in Washington, Admiral Leslie Ryan. He had a call from Senator Matthews who is head of the anti-terrorist committee. The Senator had gotten a call from George Talbott of Scotland Yard. The Yard has a few questions for you. They patched her through to London. They wanted to ask her some questions.

Question 1: "Do you know Brian McPhail?"
And the answer was, "Yes, but I don't know if he is still alive."

Question 2: "He is still alive in Ireland. Have you ever been a friend of his, and if you were, are you still friends?"

The answer was, "No -- No and No. He was assigned to my commando
Group. I accepted him for a few missions into Germany because he knew his way around there and he hated Germans. Actually he hated most everybody. Except young girls. He was a pedophile. I saw the way he treated young German girls in front of their parents to get information. He got information but he also got his jollies out of sexually abusing the German girls. I told myself that the next time he did, I would put a bullet through his head. But it never happened. He was never assigned to my group again."

Question 3: "Do you have any idea where he is now?"

The answer was, "Yes."

Question 4: "Do you think you would be capable of bringing him out of Ireland?"

The answer was, "Give me what I want and let me do it my way and I'll get him out. Probably not in perfect condition."

Question 5: "What will you need?"

The answer was, "I'll tell you when I get to London."

Doc said goodbye to the Admiral and signed off. "Jacky, do you really think you can find him and get him out?"

"Doc, I won't have to find him, he will find me. Doc, there is something that you have not told me."

"There is Jacky, they told me not to tell you, but he has four girls that are kidnapped. Three daughters of members of Parliament and one daughter of an industrialist, who was going to school in England. They did not tell me what his demands are or what he threatens to do to the girls."

"I know this guy and what he is capable of doing. I know that we plan on going to Montréal by water and then flying to London, but that will take too long. He planned on getting the Ambassador's daughter and being that didn't happen yet, he may be taking it out on the four gals that he already has. Doc, tell them if they want their girls back they have to play by my rules."

"First pick us up in Clayton by helicopter and bring us to Montréal International. Then, an immediate charter flight to London. Next a meeting with the Yard without delay. Tell them to get all the information on the girls including their pictures. Shut down any publicity on the capture of Fitzpatrick and O'Rourke. Now we need to get Bill, Eric, Arch and Peter up to speed on what is happening. Doc, see if you can work it out with the FBI to spread the word that the Ambassador's daughter was killed in a boat explosion, along with two unknown men who were trying to abduct her. That way McPhail will not be thinking that we are getting information out of Fitzpatrick and O'Rourke.

They called Bill, Eric, Arch and Peter to Doc's office to brief them on what he knew. He told them to be ready to get into the launch at 7:30 am tomorrow morning. "The helicopter will pick you up at 8 am. You will be on a charter flight to Heathrow at 9 am. You will be at Gatwick Airport at 6 pm our time - midnight London time. We hit the sack and meet at Scotland Yard at 9 am."

Bill asked if they had figured all this out since they talked to them an hour ago. "No, Jacky did." He said, "If you left it up to them, they would have to call a committee meeting and they would get back to you in a few days. It's best to tell them what you want and then they do it."

The four guys and Jacky said their goodbyes to everyone. Jacky told them that the mission was top secret and they could not say where they were going or what they would be doing. "When it's over, I'll call Doc and he will let you know all about it. You aboard *Cora Lee* will be the first to know."

Mario cooked a great dinner with Kelly's help, and an early breakfast. After breakfast, Jacky and the four guys got into the launch and headed to Clayton. Juan dropped them off at the dock and they had a short walk over to the park in front of the museum. It was 7:45 am and a pickup was scheduled for 8 am. There were three people standing under a big maple tree.

"When they got closer, Bill said that it was the Ambassador, Peggy and with them was a teenage boy. The boy was none other than Heather."

She said, "I'm dead you know. I got blown up in a boat explosion. Couldn't you have done me in in a nicer way? While I only have to act it, it's a lot nicer than being really dead, hurry up and get those bad guys so I can be Heather again."

The Ambassador said that Admiral Hunter called her and explained the situation and why Heather had to play dead for a while. "We will pray for the four other girls that bastard has abducted. The Admiral said he has total faith in you people succeeding in your mission."

They heard it first and then looked up and coming down for a landing in the middle of the field was a big Sikorsky H-19 helicopter with US army markings on it. After it sat down, a side door opened. A sergeant jumped out and came over to the group and introduced himself and said, "We had better get moving you have a plane to catch in Montréal. As they headed to the helicopter, the Ambassador said, "May God go with you."

Bill put his arm around Arch and said, "His Messenger is right here." And they climbed aboard.

The helicopter lifted off and headed northeast. After they were airborne Eric said that this was a great way to travel. It was about 8:45 am when they descended to the Montréal airport. The pilot landed in the commercial area next to a large hanger. The passengers got out of the helicopter and walked toward the hanger. The helicopter lifted off and headed out of the area. They looked around and the only plane on the ramp with a large four-engine Lockheed Constellation. A fuel truck was parked alongside and a fuel hose was attached under the wing.

A mechanic was on a rolling ladder platform, he had just closed one of the engine covers and was coming down the ladder. Bill and Arch walked over and asked if he knew of a charter flight that came in from London. He said that he thought that this "Connie" came from London. He pointed to an office. The crew went over into the hanger office.

All five of them went into the office and found the three crew members and two stewardesses. The captain asked if they were waiting for a charter flight to London.

The Captain said that he was told that it was an important flight. The copilot said that it must be, to send a Constellation to pick up five people. One of the stewardesses said, "At least we can give you first-class treatment."

"Looks like they are through fueling, we can board any time."

When they got up into the cabin, Eric said to Arch, "How would you like to explain this one to your class reunion. A whole Constellation for five people. One of the stewardesses asked if anybody was thirsty? Bill asked for a Beefeater martini. "Make that two," said Arch. "Three," said Eric, "all doubles." Jacky asked for wine and so did Peter. All agreed on surf and turf.

The flight attendant that took their dinner order asked if anybody minded if they fed the cockpit crew first. "They have been going since 11 pm last night."

They all agreed that the cockpit crew were the most important on this plane and to feed them first. After the first martini, they all felt a little better. Bill said that it was only about 9:30 am. "We have just had martinis and wine and have ordered a second round and we had a big breakfast three hours ago. Now we are ready to order surf and turf. Is anybody really hungry? No, I didn't think so. We have a nine hour flight ahead of us, why don't we just wait a few hours before we order a big meal."

No one could say they were very hungry so they decided to wait. Sally the stew that was serving drinks, brought their second round. Jacky told her that they had better ease off a little on the booze because they had an important meeting in the morning. They told their second stew that they would order their food in a couple more hours . It was too early for them to eat a big meal. She said to just let her know if anyone gets hungry. They sat back and nursed their drinks. Jacky reminded them of their mission to rescue the four girls, and to bring back McPhail.

Jacky asked if anyone had any second thoughts about completing this mission and if so, they could stay in London until the mission was completed. Nobody had second thoughts. Peter said, "Jacky, you trained me and I'm not about to let that training go to waste."

Jacky looked at Arch and Eric. "You two guys didn't get as much training as I wanted but we did a fair amount of training on Beaver and Mackinac Islands. We didn't have a lot of time, but luckily you guys are natural street fighters. The reason I'm saying this is that the original plan was to go to Achnacary Castle, the commando training site but after finding out that McPhail is involved and he has kidnapped four girls who are daughters of important people, we don't have time for any more training. I think you guys can handle yourselves really well already."

"What makes things much more urgent is the message from Doc. I talked to him on the phone while we were in the office in Montréal. He said he was talking to Dick Johnson, the FBI agent that came to Beaver Island and picked up those two traitors. When Johnson heard about Heather's attempted kidnapping and the people from the *Cora Lee* had captured the culprits, Johnson pulled some strings and got the Clayton police to hold the two IRA culprits and to stay quiet about their two guests. If there was any questions, they were to be called drug smugglers. When Johnson and his partner, Bob Masters, arrived in Clayton, they went directly to the office of the Chief of Police, Tom Marston. He said that he was holding the two prisoners incommunicado and as far as anyone knows, they are drug smugglers. John Morton said that you would be coming for them and not to release them to just anybody who shows an FBI badge. Then Johnson turned to the Chief, who was 6 foot five and 250 pounds, he looked him straight in his face and said, "Tom, you are one ugly bastard."

"You are right and the prisoners are yours."

"After seeing your size, I was not too sure. As far as using that as a code, it seems to be perfect. I can't see anyone walking up to you and calling you a big, ugly bastard." Then Johnson said, "You big handsome guy, can I use your phone? I have to arrange for transport of these two guys."

"Where are you taking them, Dick?"

"You would be much better off not knowing. Then you won't have to lie if anybody asks you." Johnson pulled the card out of his wallet. It said "Charlie's Air Service". He called and got Charlie on the phone. Charlie said he was taking the day off, but he agreed to fly to Clayton. Charlie asked, "Where to from there?"

Johnson said, "I'll tell you when you get here."

Then Johnson called Art Hobson on Beaver Island. He told Art what he wanted and Art said that if he had anything to do with Admiral Hunter, it must be important.

"Yeah, no problem, Dick. I won't ask you what you want to do, but I'll have everything ready."

Charlie flew to Clayton and tied his plane up to the municipal dock. Johnson came out to greet him and told him where the flight was to go. Charlie agreed. "Haven't seen Art for a while."

Johnson brought the prisoners out to the plane. They were handcuffed with shackles on their ankles. Fitzpatrick started screaming that he can't fly. Johnson asked how we got here from Ireland. "That was a big plane."

"Get in the backseat, Fitzpatrick." He started screaming again. Charlie came up behind him and wrapped duct tape around his head and covered his mouth. Charlie made a couple more turns with the tape and said, "That will shut him up."

Charlie held up the roll of duct tape and said, "Don't leave home without it."

Johnson, with Charlie's help, got the two of them into the plane, handcuffs behind their back and legs shackled. Then Charlie wove seatbelts up and through their arms and back down. "Don't want any problems in the air."

Charlie taxied out into the river and opened the throttle. After a few bumps crossing some wakes, Charlie bounced the Beaver into the air. The De Haviland Beaver had a 450 horse power engine, so she climbed out quickly. O'Rourke complained that he was uncomfortable with his hands behind his back. Charlie said, "Just lean back and enjoy the ride. We have a three hour flight."

Johnson said, "Why don't you be nice and quiet like your friend Fitzpatrick."

"But he's got duct tape over his mouth."

"If you want some, I think Charlie has some more duct tape." After that O'Rourke was quiet.

After an uneventful flight Charlie landed on Beaver Island Harbor and taxied over to the dock. Art was there waiting on the dock. Charlie shut down the engine and was drifting to the dock when he got down onto the pontoon, threw Art a line and Art pulled the plane in. Charlie went to the stern and they did the same thing. Once the plane was tied up to the dock, they got the guys out of the back seat and on to the dock. Johnson then took the duct tape off of Fitzpatrick.

He said, "This is against the Geneva Convention."

"If you keep complaining, I'll put the duct tape back on."

"Art, have you still got the tape recorder that we used when we interviewed the General and the Admiral? And do you think Linda could be a stenographer?"

The two IRA guys had no idea what they were talking about, but they would learn soon enough.

"Okay, you two guys follow Art through that door."

"Aren't you going to take the shackles off so we can walk better?"

"And run better too? I don't feel like chasing you. I'll take the shackles off when we get inside."

They walked all the way back to the fish cleaning room. They placed the two guys back-to-back and put a three-quarter inch line under their arms and around their bodies. Then Johnson took the cuffs off one wrist of O'Rourke and told him that he would cuff them in front, O'Rourke held out his hands and Johnson cuffed him. Johnson did the same with Fitzpatrick, but soon as he released one cuff, Fitzpatrick took a swing at Johnson with the loose cuff and hit Johnson across the shoulder.

Johnson said, "You will wish you hadn't done that." Johnson grabbed the loose cuff and slapped it on his other wrist. Then Art picked up a steel double ended hook that was about 8 inches long and snapped it over the cuff chain. Fitzpatrick laughed as he moved his wrists up and down. Then Art went over to the room where he stored his gill nets. He grabbed a 50 pound weight that he used to anchor his nets. He hung the 50 pound weight on the hook and said, "Now laugh."

After they were tied close back-to-back, Art took a second rope and hooked it under their arms. Johnson brought the electric hoist right directly over their heads and lowered the big hook, he took the rope that went around their chests and under their arms, brought a loop up between their backs and put the loop onto the hook. Art pressed the up button and it started to lift them off the floor. Then Art stopped lifting with their feet still on the floor, Johnson asked Art if he should take the shackles off. Art started to lift again until he got their feet about two inches off the floor and then he lowered them back down to the floor. Art said, "Dick, take off their shoes, socks and shackles." Which Johnson did, and he lifted them until their feet were dangling five feet off the floor.

O'Rourke asked why their shoes were taken off and Art told him, with a straight face, "Shoes just tear up the cutter blades at the bottom of the tank in the fish gut grinder."

They didn't know what Art was talking about until all of a sudden they were over the top of a large vat containing one hell lot of stinking fish guts.

As they got over the tank, Art started lowering them into the stinking fish guts. Art said, "Dick, the grinder ain't running. Go push the red button on the switch box on the wall."

Dick pressed the button and the fish guts start vibrating and quivering and making a lot of noise. Art said, "It's okay now, the chopper is running."

Actually, the noise and vibration was from a vibrator mounted to the side of the tank. When a truck from the fertilizer company comes to load up with fish guts, the slide is opened on the bottom and the vibrator is turned on, so everything goes down smoothly, but O'Rourke or Fitzpatrick didn't know that.

"We just want you to answer some questions, if you answer, you will survive. If you don't, won't, or can't you will be fertilizer. First off we know that you are one of Brian McPhail's top Lieutenants and we would like to know his location."

Fitzpatrick said, "Screw you."

Art lowers them until they were up to their ankles and then to their knees and then stops. "When did you last see McPhail?"

O'Rourke said, "Two weeks ago."

Fitzpatrick said, "Shut up, you idiot, they are bluffing. It's against FBI policy, it's illegal, against the Constitution and the Geneva Convention."

Just then, Art's wife Linda comes in and said, "Art, you can't do that. Pull them out."

"You're right, Linda is my wife and my lawyer."

Kilpatrick said, "See she knows the law, that she does."

Art lifts them out and puts their feet on the floor. Johnson takes the handcuffs off both of them and they shake their wrists in relief. Fitzpatrick said, "And now the ropes."

Instead, Art presses the up button. "You can't do that, your lawyer said that you can't."

"She is also my wife and she knew that handcuffs would wipe out those expensive blades."

Linda said, "Up, up and away."

Art swings them back over the vat and Johnson turned on the vibrator again. Art lowered them to their waist.

"Tim, I don't want to die," said O'Rourke.

"Shut up, you idiot, I told you, they are only bluffing," said Fitzpatrick.

Art lowered them to their chest and Johnson said, "You ain't got much more time. As far as anyone knows you are already dead, blown up in a boat explosion along with the Ambassador's daughter."

Now Fitzpatrick is thinking, but he couldn't make up his mind.

When Johnson went to the office earlier, he had called Linda and asked her to bring down her Osterizer, or some kind of a kitchen blender. She did and Johnson filled it half-full with fish guts and blended the guts. Then he poured the ugly mess into a large bowl.

Art had almost gotten Fitzpatrick to talk, but not much. Then Johnson walked over and showed them the bowl of blended fish guts. "I thought I would show you what comes out of the other side of this vat. This is what you will look like, it will be a lousy picture to send back to your family."

Just then Fitzpatrick heaved his guts out and O'Rourke was crying. Fitzpatrick said, "I'll talk." And O'Rourke said, "I'll talk too."

Art lifted them up and set them down standing on the floor. Johnson hosed them down, he said, "This is the best deal you're going to get. If you lie you will go back into the grinder."

Johnson said to them, "Actually what you guys are going to do is help us rescue the four girls your leader has kidnapped. We will either capture or kill Brian McPhail and we want to destroy his organization. You are going to help us do this."

We have some good people and you guys have met one of them. "The blonde"

"Yes, and she is good. If you help us complete the mission and they get the girls out, you guys will go free. The blonde hates McPhail so much, I don't think she will bringing him back alive. It's up to you, a failed mission and you go back in a vat to make fertilizer. You will be locked up in a very secure prison for now, as far as anyone knows, you are dead, so don't screw up. You lie and you will be fertilizer."

"Okay you guys time is of the essence. We have to work together both to save the girls and to save your lives," said Art.

Timothy asked Dick, "Would you really put us back into the vat and grind us up?"

Dick said, "Timothy, I would rather not do that. I would rather set you free. Everyone thinks you are dead, so nobody will be looking for you. It's up to you. Right now you can take a shower, put on some clean clothes and we can have some lunch. Then we can get started on your giving us the information that is going to save the girls and your lives." They had coffee and sandwiches, then Dick said, "Let's get down to business."

They were up in Art and Linda's house, sitting in the dining room at a large table. "I have decided not to handcuff you or put on shackles. It's your life that you are trying to save, plus the four girls. There is nothing to stop you from trying to get away except Art's and my nine millimeter automatics. "Linda has a 45 Colt and never misses her target. She won't kill you, she will shoot you in the back of the knees as you are running. She won't miss, so let's get down to it. First anybody want another cup of coffee?

Linda served it all around. Everyone noticed that Linda had her shoulder holster on with a big Colt 45 in it. Art said, "I might mention that Linda hunts ducks with her Colt 45, gets them right in the head while in flight. Don't tempt her. Now what we have here are some questionnaires. One copy for each of you."

Question 1: Where is McPhail's headquarters?

They both answered, "Toome, in Maguire's friendly pub which belongs to McPhail."

Question 2: Where are the girls?

Don't know. Someplace on Lake Beth."

Question 3: How many people are armed at the pub?

They both said, "All of them."

Question 4: How many people are usually there at 10 pm?

"8 to 10 people. More on football night."

Question 5: Do they check out strangers?

"Yes."

Question 6: How?

"They pat you down and question you."

Question 7: What else will they do to check you out?

"Three or four guys will go through your vehicle, inside and out."

Question 8: When is McPhail most likely to be around the pub?

"Mostly on Sunday night when him and some of his blokes get together."

Question 9: Usually how many?

Eight or Ten

Question 10: You were on the wanted list. How do you get into the country?

"By private plane, belonging to Vincent Darby imports of New York."

After the two Irishmen talked things over and agreed on all the answers, they said they would try to remember anything that might help make this mission successful.

Johnson said, "I don't think I need to remind you that you really want this mission to succeed because you will be saving your own life."

Timothy and Davy now seemed like changed people. They not only were trying to save their own lives, they wanted Jacky's crew to win. They both said that they never did like that bastard McPhail. "It was the thing to do in Belfast where they grew up - to join a group like McPhail. Once you are in you could not get out."

Davy told Johnson that there was one more thing. The entry code when you walk into the pub. "Immediately ask, "How far to Belfast?" and somebody will say 18 Kilometers. You say, "Close enough" and you are in. They change it every month. But it's okay now for two weeks".

"If we think of anything else we will let you know."

Linda was recording all this. Art will get a secure line to Admiral Leslie Ryan. The Admiral will get it to Senator Matthews and he will, in turn, get it to George Talbott, the Chief Inspector at Scotland Yard. He will get it to Jacky.

The Constellation landed at Gatwick airport and taxied over to the commercial area. A rolling staircase was wheeled over to the plane. When they got off the plane, there was a Bentley limousine waiting for them and they headed directly to Scotland Yard in London, a forty Kilometer ride. Jacky figured that Talbott should have a message for her by now. They headed north towards London through Croydon and then to the south end of London. The limo crossed the Thames on the Waterloo Bridge and made a left turn on Victoria Embankment and headed for the Scotland Yard office.

When they got there, George Talbott, the Chief Inspector was waiting outside for them. Talbott introduced himself and Jacky introduced the others. Talbott said, "I want to talk to Jacky before the Parliament members or anyone else started trying to question any of her people.

"The message I received from Senator Matthews said "Top Secret - For Your Eyes Only." Do your people know that I have this message."

"They know and I would like them to go with us to a conference room where we can all look it over and study the message. I believe it will tell us where McPhail is. We have devised an excellent way of getting information from some of the people we have captured. This is where the information you have received came from. You, myself, and my four people are the only ones who know about this message. There will probably be another message with more information."

Talbott asked how they got the information? "It's an old commando trick. You can beat it out of a person or threaten them with death. It does work, but if you get answers, you don't know if they are true. With our method, we get the truth and they are willing to help us in any way."

Talbott gave Jacky three 9 x 11 sheets. She passed them around as she read them. Bill said, "It looks as if we have enough information to get the girls out."

Jacky said, "This guy McPhail is no dummy. He may be cruel, but he is not dumb. We have to be very careful in dealing with him. When we get to Ireland I'll call back and see if there's any further information, the more information we have the better for us."

"Okay, George, let's get together with the fathers of the girls, so we can get this show on the road."

They went upstairs to another conference room. In the room were four men and four women. Jacky said, "I know who you men are, but who are these women?"

Seems like they all said in unison, "They are our stenographer's."

"They will have to leave."

"Who will keep track of the meeting?"

"No one will."

Then Talbott introduced the members of Parliament. Lord James Foxglove, Sir Robert Dean, Sir Jonathan Graves and the Industrialist, Terry Palmer of PKM Technologies. Jacky then introduced her crew. Sir Robert Dean said, "How do you plan on rescuing our daughters? They are probably in a very anti-British area."

"I don't intend to tell you anything about this operation except its outcome, and that is getting your daughters away from that bastard that has kidnapped them. Just so we start off on the right foot, the reason I'm not going to tell you anything about how and where, is because that is the way the wrong people get killed. One word to the wrong person could mean the life of your daughters and my crew. So I won't take that chance," said Jacky.

Foxglove said, "Then why are we here?"

"To give me the information I need, the equipment I need and the funds for this operation."

Fox glove said," I'll be damned if I'm going to give you anything. That is, unless you tell me what I want to know. I was a colonel in the British Army and we didn't do anything, until we had all the information on any operation."

Jacky said, "Fox glove with your attitude you might blow this whole operation and get the girls killed. By the way what was your job in the Army?

"I was the head of a finance unit."

Jacky said, "It figures."

Terry Palmer said, "Fox glove why don't you go along with the rest of us. Jacky Sax came to us to save our daughters. She comes highly recommended and has information about the kidnappers that we don't have. She also had good reasons for not divulging this information."

Sir Jonathan Graves said, "I think we should do what Jacky Sax wants, and do everything to help her get our daughters back. Sir Robert Dean and Jerry Palmer agreed.

Sir Graves asked Fox glove, "If he would agree?"

Foxglove said, "No I don't agree, and if you proceed, I will go to newspapers and let them know what you plan on doing."

Jacky asked Tallbot, "How much power do you have?"

"I can do most anything if it involves the lives of these four girls. We also have two more members of Parliament who agree with however you wish to run this mission.

Jacky said, "I cannot risk this operation , with Fox glove running loose, jeopardizing the girls and my crews lives. Talbott can you hold him incommunicado until this operation is over?"

Talbott said, "I can do that." He picked up the phone and said a few words.

Two men with side arms came in and stood at attention inside the doorway.

Fox glove said, "You can't do this."

"Yes I can" said Talbott.

"I'll sue you for everything you own."

"No you won't said Sir Robert Dean. If you even try it, you will never see the inside of Parliament again. You are a member now, only because your father was."

Tallbot said, "Take him away, down the back elevator. Make sure he is totally incommunicado until I say different."

"Shall we cuff him?"

"I don't think it's necessary."

"You can't get away with this Talbott, I'm a member of Parliament. I'll be out of here before lunchtime."

"Cuff him and take him down the freight elevator. I want him held incommunicado. Put him in solitary, he talks to absolutely no one."

Jacky said, "Now that we have that taken care of, let's get down to the business of rescuing your daughters. I think we wasted enough time with Foxglove. I think we could trust you men if I told you what we know, but it is too easy to make a slip."

They all agreed.

"Let's get down to finding what you need."

"First: A 12 person short takeoff and landing aircraft. Bill recommends a DHC3 De Haviland Otter."

They all agreed. No problem. "You can have it tomorrow morning."
"Second: A Sikorsky - H19A helicopter on standby with a 700 hp engine. This may be needed to get the IRA leader, who is the kidnapper, out of Ireland. The helicopter should have no military markings.

Third: 60,000 in British pounds and 80,000 in Irish Punt. This is to be used for bribes and equipment and will be returned if not used. We will call Scotland Yard when we need a pickup by plane or helicopter. We will need weapons delivered to Balleymena, five 9 mm automatic hand guns, five Uzi's, 1000 rounds of ammo for each weapon and six grenade launchers. This can be arranged by Talbott. Then, five combat knives (K –Bar), 16 small charges of C–4 and 16 detonators.

Fourth: Field maps covering 100 mile radius around Belfast.

Fifth: Irish made clothes and identification."

They all agreed to furnish what Jacky asked for.

"How soon do you need it?"

"Time is of the essence. I know this man who has kidnapped your daughters and you would not want any of your girls under his thumb for too long. If you can, and I know you can arrange for everything that I'm asking for, I would like to get underway at noon, the day after tomorrow."

At first they said, “We think we can do it, then they change their mind and said we will do it.”

Jacky said, “That’s good, you will be happy with the outcome. Mr. Talbott remember one thing. Keep foxglove under wraps until we get back. No communication with anyone. If he says he needs a doctor get a volunteer and keep the Doc locked up too.”

On the second day at noon, the crew had everything that was required. The Otter was on the ramp, all fueled up and loaded with gear. They had a 380 mile route to Renfrew Airport, which was outside of Glasgow. It was a two hour and 45 minute flight. After getting to Renfrew airport, they went the auto rental desk. Jacky asked him for a large Mercedes van.

The man behind the counter said they had one, “But it was reserved. Reserved For someone named Jacky.”

She said, “That’s me. It was reserved by George Talbott.”

“Right that’s it, you won’t need any identification.”

“I don’t suppose you rent motorcycles?”

“No but there is a Triumph shop in town.”

He told her where it was. “Now you call them, and tell them to get a triumph trophy all gassed up. Then call me a taxi and that Bill would settle up with the paperwork, then handed him $1000 in cash to pay the rental fees.” She said, “Load the van, but leave room in the back for a small motorcycle”.

The taxi showed up and Jacky went to town. She got to the cycle shop. Jacky told him that she wanted to buy a triumph trophy. They tried to show her a Thunderbird and some other models. “I asked to have a trophy all gassed up. Do you have it gassed it up?”

“No the fuel station is closed for dinner.”

“Drain the gas out of other bikes. I want a full tank.” She said that she wanted to take the machine she pointed out. She asked the price as is, that the trophy goes for?

“3600 pounds plus tax, which is a little over 10%, we have a plan of financing which is very reasonable.”

She handed him 4000 pounds and said, “That should cover it. Give me a receipt and hold the door open.” Jacky got on the bike, started it up, flew out the door and headed back to the airport. When she got there they loaded the bike in the back of the van. The trophy is a very light bike, which is why she wanted a trophy. With the 500 cc engine, it was still fast. A perfect bike to get it in and out of the van.

With Eric driving, they headed south to Stramraret a town, in the Bay Loch Ryan. When they arrived they went directly to the ferry dock. When they got there it was not there. A uniformed man was sitting on a crate with a small fishing pole in one hand and a large beer in the other hand.

Jacky and Arch walked up to him, after the greetings going both ways, he said that his name was Tim Macky. "Your local Irish customs agent. The ferry will be here in one hour and will depart for Larne 30 minutes later. We might just as well get all the customs over with before the ferry returns. He asked the usual questions and why visiting Ireland?

"Mostly as tourists and to visit some friends in Londonderry."

Then he asked, "Why the motorcycle in the van?"

Eric said, "His friend in Londonderry, races bikes in Ireland and I race in the states."

"He challenged me to a race in Londonderry."

"So I needed a bike."

"It looks almost new."

"It is new. I bought it a few hours ago, he showed him the receipts."

"So he said, if you are bringing it into Ireland you'll have to pay a duty." He told him the amount of duty. Eric paid him and he signed the receipt as paid. While they were waiting for the ferry, Arch and Jacky talked with Tim Mackey about Ireland . Jacky said that a friend recommended a restaurant in Balleymena.

"Gary Hooker's family restaurant, have you heard of it?"

Tim said, "I have not only heard of it, but I take my wife there, three or four times a month. I'll be taking her there again, the day after tomorrow. Hooker serves good food at fair prices."

Arch asked if it was a large place, and if there was a secure place around the back. The motorcycle dealer said not to leave the trophy showing. Someone will follow you and when they get a chance, they will break into the van and get the trophy. Arch actually wanted to find out, if there was a safe place to load the guns.

Tim said, "There was a covered loading dock."

That sounded good. The ferry came in and they loaded up. It was 5 PM and Tim said that it was the last group to Ireland today. It was a three hour trip. So they arrived in Ireland at 8 PM.

Bill is back in Renfrew Airport. He parked the De Havilland in a military area. It was arranged by George Talbott, that he would stay in the military office, and wait for a call from Jacky. While Bill was waiting, at 7 PM a Sikorsky H. 19 helicopter came in and landed on the ramp.

The pilot walked over to the office and handed Bill a logbook. They told me to tell you, not to fill out anything in a logbook. It will be taken care of after your mission, they said it was training .

"Is there anything strange about your bird, that I should know of?" Not really, she is fairly new, but there is one thing, the light on the altimeter goes out sometimes. It's okay if you are not flying at night."

"I plan on flying at night, in some strange places. Why didn't you get it fixed."

"I told the crew Chief to fix it, he said it would be down for three days. They said they needed an H. 19 at Renfrew right away, so here I am."

"Yeah with a broken bird."

"Not to worry, I stopped off at a novelty store this morning and picked up a small flashlight and some clay. It works good. Is there anything else? She's a good bird."

"Well I hope so, I've got to pick up some pretty important people."

"She will do you good."

The Mercedes rolled off the ferry and by Tim's directions they headed for Gary Hooker's family restaurant. It was only a 20 minute ride to Hookers. They pulled into the parking lot, which did not look too busy. They went into the restaurant which was also not crowded. It was only a 8:25 PM and Toome was only 10 miles away. It was decided that 9:45 PM was a good time to get to the pub.

Tim the customs man said Hookers lamb stew was the best, he said the lamb chops are a little more pricey but Irish lamb could not be beat. They ordered and then asked the waitress if Gary Hooker was around. She said no, but not to worry. I've had you pegged the moment you walked in. I used to work with Talbott and he asks a favor now and then. Gary had to go to Belfast to talk to some of our suppliers, I will get the equipment you need after you finish your dinner. By the way I am Jill, Gary's wife.

When they were ready, she told them to pull the van around the back, and into the loading dock. Which they did but with the trophy in back, it was too crowded to put the cases of C-4, detonators and a rocket grenade. Jacky said unload the bike and she will ride it to Toome. When they got to Toome, Jacky headed for the pub and found it in a wooded area on the edge of town. Jill had told Jacky that Brian McPhail drove a black and silver late-model Bentley. Jill said that she knew him because he had dinner at hookers quite often. She knew his car, because when he had a girl with him, he liked to brag about going first class. Jacky knew that that was Brian McPhail.

He probably threatened someone who he was paid to assassinate, got him to sign over to Bentley and then killed him anyway. He would do this with a smile on his face. Eric parked the van in the woods. She told them what she planned on doing. She was going to the pub by herself to tell them that she wanted to meet with McPhail the following night at the pub.

Chapter 32

Pushers and Mcphail Captured at Pub.

She went to the pub, she knew that he couldn't resist. She told them, "It was Jacky that wanted to see him."

One of the guys got off a barstool and walked over and asked what she wanted McPhail for.

She said, "I didn't come in here to be questioned. I just want to leave a message for McPhail."

Another guy came over and asked if she knew McPhail.

She said, "No more questions."

This second guy said, "I am McPhail, now what do you want to bitch."

She grabbed him with a finger hold, spun him around and said, "Don't call me bitch. Because you ain't shit, you ass hole." She planted a foot on his butt, with a swift kick he landed with his face on the foot rail. The first guy reached over to grab her arm, he landed on the foot rail looking up.

"Just tell McPhail, that Jacky will be here at 10 PM tomorrow night. Tell him to be here."

"Are you coming alone, asked the bartender?"

She answered, "I don't need any more than me."

He said "I guess not,"

Then she left. She took off to the north cranking it on pretty hard. After going down the road for a couple of miles she came back to the wooded area, where the van was. If they were listening to Jacky taking off on the trophy, they would figure that she was long gone. Instead she was right across the road in the woods. All of them made themselves semi comfortable for an hour's nap.

Then at 10:30, they took turns watching the pub . Each person sat on a log just inside of some brush, it was a good view of the parking lot. At about 11:15 the black and silver Bentley showed up. Peter went back to the van and told Jacky that Brian McPhail went into the pub by way of the side door. He was carrying a sack that didn't look too heavy. An upstairs light went on, two minutes later it went out. He must have brought something upstairs in that sack . That needs checking out.

Eric remembered that Jill said, amongst other things, he was also into drug dealing.

After McPhail came down the stairs. He went up front to the bar. He told the bartender to give him a double shot of Jack Daniels. He sat down at the bar and said, what's new for today.

Mike told him that there was a blonde looking for him. She said she would be back tomorrow at 10 PM. She was a real good-looking broad.

"That makes it all the more interesting. Did she have a name?"

"Yeah, she said to tell you that Jacky was here." He stopped to think and said to himself, no it couldn't be her, he left her for dead in France.

Then Mike said, "She kicked the shit out of Joe and Ralph." McPhail looked at Joe and Ralph, they both look pretty banged up.

McPhail looked at the two of them, and said, "Don't feel bad. If she is who I think she is, she could take care 10 guys like you, without breaking a sweat."

"Are you going to be here tomorrow night?"

"I've got to be here, because if she is looking for revenge, there ain't no hiding from her. I want all eight of you guys here tomorrow night, with pistols in your pockets."

Mike the bartender said, "She was coming alone."

"Like I said, I want all eight of you in the bar tomorrow night, with pistols in your pocket, that lady is dangerous."

Later that night at about 11: the last car had left the parking lot. Except the Bentley. And then at midnight all the lights went out. McPhail got into his Bentley and drove away. Jacky said, "It looks like we are leaving in class tonight guys."

"The Bentley?"

"Yeah the Bentley."

They waited until about 1 AM. Since had Peter worked for a locksmith in Shanghai, he opened the side door with ease, in about 50 seconds. Three of them went upstairs and Peter went into the bar. He went behind the bar and found (3) 12gauge shotguns strategically placed, under the bar. There were two double barrel shotguns and one sawed-off Winchester model 12, Pump shotgun. He looked around some more, and pulled open two drawers.

He found a 45 caliber colt in one, and a 9 mm automatic, in the other. Peter worked on a 9 mm first. He brought two pairs of pliers and with practiced dexterity he pulled the lead bullets out of the cartridge cases. Then he dumped all the powder into an ashtray, he put a small amount of powder back into the cartridge cases. Next he put all the lead slugs back into their cases, he did the same with the 45 Colts ammo. Then he put them back in the drawers, after he reloaded them. Next he emptied the shells, out of all three shotguns. Then he took his knife, opened the front end of the shells, then dumped all the pellets down the drain. He closed the front of the shells and put them back in the shot guns and put the shotguns back under the bar. He went back to where he worked on the handguns, picked up his pliers. He dumped the gun powder that was in the ash tray down the drain. Now if someone fired any of McPhail's handguns, the slug wouldn't do much more than a BB gun. The shotgun would still make plenty of noise, but they would only be firing blanks.

Peter looked all around in the bar area, and found no more guns. He then went upstairs where the others were.

Jacky said, "They had found the bag of heroin and marijuana. We will get it when we come back, and burn it in front of the bastards. Then they checked out all the windows overlooking the bar area. Peter found four more hand guns in a file cabinet, he made them as useless, as the ones behind the bar.

Seeing the layout, they knew what they were going to do. Four people went in the side door and four came out. But tonight about 9 PM only three people will go in the side door and one in the front door. When they got back to the van they knew that they had to get back into the side door by 9 PM. There would have to be a distraction so they could get in, into position , without being noticed.

Eric said, "Why don't we set a car on fire, across the empty field, on the street that is about a block down from the front door of the bar?"

Arch said, "There are no houses or cars on that street, so I guess we can put one there."

They took a ride in the town, and found a used car lot. Eric and Peter got out at the lot and found an old Land Rover. Peter opened it up and jumped the ignition, then started it. At 2 AM the streets were deserted, a perfect time to steal a car. When the car was parked on the side street, Eric attached a small piece of C-4 to a detonator and a timer. He put it in the gas tank with a string attached to it. He would use the string to pull it out and set the timer tomorrow afternoon. He had to do it in the late afternoon, because there was only six hours on the timer clock. Then Peter picked him up and they went back to the woods to wait. The plan was to wait for the explosion and the car fire, to distract everyone in the bar. They would be looking out the front door and three guys, would sneak in the side door, each one carrying an Uzi and a handgun. Eric and Peter would go upstairs and sit down on the chairs that were set by the windows with a clearer view of the bar area.

Arch would go to the back room behind the bar, there was a small storage room in the back. He would stay there just in case, somebody went to the back room. At a few minutes after nine the detonator went off, the car was ablaze. All the people in the bar came out the front door, to see what happened. Peter, Eric and Arch, went in the side door. Peter and Eric went up the stairs to watch for Jacky. Arch was looking into the bar through a hole he had carved in the wall, when they were there earlier. The guys lost interest in the car fire. The local fire brigade was putting it out. They went back into the bar and ordered a beer. Brian McPhail showed up at 9:30. He told Mike and Todd to get behind the bar and handle the shotguns that were under the bar.

Mike said, "Brian there are three shotguns under the bar."

"Good, Jim you get behind the bar, with the other two guys. Mike get the two hand guns out of the drawers behind the bar and give them to me." McPhail took them. He kept the 9 mm automatic and handed Joe the 45 Colt. Bob, Art, and Jack were still unarmed. McPhail did not want them carrying weapons around town. The local police had a habit of stopping McPhail's friends and frisking them.

McPhail said, "Bob go up in the office, check the top drawer of the green file cabinet. There are four brand-new 9 mm Beretta in the drawer with loaded clips. Bring them down." Bob brought the Beretta's down, he gave them to Brian, who gave one each, to Art, Jack, and Bob.

He put the extra one in his coat pocket. Brian said, "Who knows how many people she is bringing, even though she said that she was coming alone. Looks like we have enough firepower to handle whoever comes in that door." What they didn't know, was that they were basically unarmed.

Jacky walked in the front door of the bar. She said, "That sign outside said closed. I thought maybe that nobody was here."

"We are here Jacky, it's just that we figured this would be a closed meeting."

"Good thinking Brian, I wouldn't want to be distracted by your local customers."

"No problem. Jacky you look real good as a blonde, but I liked the red head better."

"Then why did you leave me in that swamp to die."

"I didn't want to take a chance of the two of us being dead, Jacky."

"You always were a practical thinker."

"Is that why you are here, revenge"?

"Brian if I just wanted revenge I could have killed you long ago. Just like I killed your flunkies Davey O'Brien and Timothy Kilpatrick."

"I came here to make a deal. I've got 2 million in my backpack, you get the 2 million US cash. And I get the four girls you kidnapped."

"Jacky you should know that you can't bargain with me. I already have the girls, now I have the case and I also have you. Jacky you know, "I've always wanted you and now I've got you. Drop the pack Jacky. What you think about our little deal? We've got the four girls to bargain with, we have an extra 2 million and I got my favorite redhead commando."

Jacky said, "Think again asshole, as she dropped the backpack, she pulled a 9 mm out of the side of it."

But Brian also pulled out the 9 mm he had in his pocket. "Jacky you should know I don't take chances. I've got a double layer of bulletproof vest on. If you pull the trigger it will hurt a little, but if I pulled the trigger you're dead."

Think again shit head I've got real bullets in my gun, she points the gun down and fires at his big toe.

He said you bitch and fires his 9 mm at her belly. The bullet hits her jacket and falls to floor. Then Jacky shoots and out his other big toe.

Art, Joe, Jack and Bob had their handguns out and Mike, Todd , and Jim brought up the shotguns up from under the bar. When Peter and Eric see the guns out, with just a few bursts from the Uzi's, they shred the gun hands of all of McPhail's crew. Meanwhile Arch came in, and shoved all of the guys with the bloody hands, down to the floor and up against the bar.

Arch asked Jacky, "What next."

"Go out in the back room, and see if you can find a piece of rope, to tie up our good friend here. And grab a towel so he doesn't bleed all over my new Bentley."

Brian said again, "You bitch."

Jacky turns to Brian and said, "You know I don't like being called that and you still have eight more toes."

She asked Eric to bring down the bag of dope. He did and she said, "Dump it on the floor." There was about a kilo of marijuana and about 100 nickel bags of heroin. These are the small bags, the bastards sell to school kids. I think they should try out what they sell. Arch found a bunch of towels and he threw each one a towel so they can wrap their bloody hands. Also a couple towels for the guy with the two sore toes.

Jacky said, "Before we leave, these dope peddlers need to be taught a lesson." She walked over to Mike who had a towel wrapped around his hand and sitting on the floor. She said, "You like selling dope to kids."

"It's a living."

"Arch bring over those nickel bags, and Eric a big glass of water . Okay, what's your name?" she gets no answer. She rapped him across his bloody hand.

He said "Mike."

"Okay Mike, you are going to have a little snack. Open your mouth Mike." He doesn't, she shoots the off the end of his shoe, narrowly missing his big toe. "Do you like your big toe Mike? Ask Brian how it feels."

"No, I'll open,"

She threw in a nickel bag. "Now have a drink of water to swallow it or your toe goes bye-bye. Now one more bag and you're home free."

"No I can't."

"The big toe Mike," and he opens and in goes another nickel bag, some water and he swallowed the bag. "Now that wasn't hard was it? Then she told the other guys that they had seen the routine. I'm not going to waste any time. I'm going to ask you to open your mouth if you don't, off goes the big toe. I'm not going to ask twice."

They saw that she meant what she said and it went smoothly. That is until the last guy, he was a big guy. He did not like being told what to do by a woman. He reached out and grabbed her gun arm. She lifted him off the floor, and kicked him in the nuts. He was now holding his groin, with his right hand, with a bloody left-hand on the floor. She shot off the tip of his pinky. By now Mike was having stomach problems. The big guy got three nickel bags.

Peter, Eric and Arch had them all tied up to the bar foot rail. Jacky said, "Let's get the hell out of here." She dumped out the rest of the heroin on the floor, and the marijuana. Then she called police and told them that a half a dozen drug dealers needed to be picked up.

"It looks like they will need to have their stomachs pumped. It seems that they have been swallowing their own heroin." There is no rush, in another five or 10 minutes they will be in too much pain to walk. These people whom you should not be in too much of a rush to pick up, should suffer for a while. Their vehicles are not in running condition, so they are not going anyplace.

"These people are at Mcguires Friendly Pub. , Their boss will not be available now or ever. After three days, call George Talbott at Scotland Yard. He will fill you in, goodbye for now. (a friend.)" Then she ripped the phone lines off the wall.

"Okay guys let's go, times a wasting. Brian give me the keys to the Bentley."

"You can't take my Bentley."

"We are taking you too Brian."

"I ain't going to give you the keys."

"Have you counted your toes lately." He handed her the keys. "Peter tie his hands behind him, I don't need any problems in the car." They went outside and Jacky told McPhail to get in the back. Eric had gone to the woods to get the van. He pulled the van next to the Bentley. "Arch you drive the Bentley. Peter go with Eric and tell him to follow us. There is a hardware store, on the right side stop there first."

They stopped, Jacky got out, and went inside. She was back, inside of 10 minutes with a block and tackle, and 200 feet of five eighths line. She threw it in the van and got back in the Bentley.

The man in the store said, "It's on this street, up two blocks. Charles MacLean Realty. Talbott knows MacLean, and he said this warehouse, is what we need." Arch stopped in front of the real estate office and Jacky went in. She and the agent came out. Jacky got in the Bentley, the agent got in his car. Arch followed for about half a mile. He pulled up to a building, that had a large garage door in front. Jacky went inside with the agent and came back out through the large door. She waved goodbye to the agent and told Arch to pull in. She told Peter to go inside with Arch and guard their guest .

She went back inside and said, "Arch and Peter, watch McPhail, don't listen to him, he's a con artist, and he will try to talk you into anything.

Trust me stay away from him. I have one more small errand, I will probably be back in 15 minutes."

Jacky and Eric took the van, and drove to an area about 10 blocks away. This is where the real estate agents said there was a pet shop with exotic animals. He found the address in the phone book. Eric pulled up in front of the designated address. A sign in the window said, "Beth Murphy exotic pets." The whole area looked like any big cities depressed area, drunks laying in the doorstep and teenage gangs just standing around doing nothing. Soon as he parked the van and got out, he walked around and stood by Jacky.

Then about eight guys ranging from 16 to 20 circled around Jacky and Eric . The oldest looking guy, walked right up to Jacky had said, "What have you got in that purse lady."

"She said about $60,000 Shit head."

"Don't give me no shit bitch."

Quicker than the blink of an eye, she pulled a 9 mm out of her purse, and rapped the barrel across his teeth. She broke the front ones out. He brought up his right hand to grab the pistol, she got a hold of his hand and bent it backwards until he was down on his knees.

"She said while you're down there, you had better pray, because I'm either going to blow your brains out or your balls off. Your choice which one?"

He said, "Balls."

"No I don't think you got brains or balls" as she put the gun away. He got up and tried to grab her. She hit him on side of the head with her fist, so hard that he went down on the ground and stayed there.

While all this going on, one of the other guys had a revolver stuck in Eric' s ribs. About the time Jacky smashed the guys teeth, Eric made a quick turn, grabbed the gun and twisted it till it broke the finger that was in the trigger guard. Eric then removed the cylinder from the gun, threw the frame into the sewer. Then he handed the cylinder back to the guy he took it from. He said, "Now go and try to shoot someone with this."

Jacky turned to the group, and said, "Pick up your buddy and carry him home. By the way tell him to get his front teeth fixed, he looks like shit."

Eric looked at the guy holding his right hand and said, "Never stick a gun in a guy's ribs, its irritating and you better fix your Finger. When that guy on the ground wakes, tell him to never ask a blonde what's in her purse. We will only be in the store for a few minutes. Stay away from the van." They all moved off leaving their good Buddy, lying on the sidewalk.

Eric and Jacky went into the store. The lady came up to them and said, I'm Beth and are you the lady that called about the rats and snakes?

"I am the one that called. We also need about a 50 gallon aquarium."

"We got that, we have a 50 gallon octagonal. It was brought back because of a small crack near the bottom, which I will fix if you can wait a few hours."

"We can't wait, and we only need this for a few hours. It's just for a demonstration."

"I don't rent animals or equipment."

"We will buy your animals and your aquarium, but after a couple hours we have no more need for any of this. You can have them back."

"I don't buy anything back."

"I didn't say buy. You can have them back. Wait at least three hours and go see your local real estate man Charles MacLean and he will take it to where the aquarium is."

They settled on a price for 20 wild rats, which Beth sold for snake food. There was six King snakes. They carried out the aquarium put it in the van from the side door, then they carried out two ventilated cartons with rats and snakes. They went back to the warehouse and pulled inside.

Peter had climbed up, rigged the block, on an overhead beam and run the 5/8 line through it, secured one end to a post and the other to a concrete block. Arch and Peter had found a four-wheel flat material handling cart. They put McPhail on it. Then they wheeled him over next to the wall. He could see everything that was going on. Now there was a rope suspended over the aquarium.

Jacky came over to Brian McPhail. She said, "One last chance, where are the four girls?

"I'll never tell you Jacky. Even if you kicked the shit out of me and I talk, you will probably kill me anyway, so why should I tell you."

"Okay, Brian, you want to go the hard way. Peter you are the one good with rope. Secure his legs to the rope. Then Brian saw 50 gallon aquarium, so it looks like you are going to drown me. If you do that, you will never find the girls."

"No Brian, a lot of people would like to kill you, but not me . Hoist him up guys."

They did, and he was hanging over the aquarium.

He looked down and said, "There is no water in there. "

"No there isn't Brian. But look what we've got for you," and she dumped 20 rats in the aquarium.

"You can't do this Jacky it's cruel and inhumane. It's against the Geneva Convention."

"Don't be so squeamish Brian. Those rats won't last forever. Arch lowered his head to one foot the above the top of the aquarium.

Then Jacky dumped in Six King snakes. "Look Brian the snakes are going to eat up all the rats. It will take them three weeks to do it. Meanwhile the rats will do anything to get away from the snakes. The rats can't climb the glass but as we lower you they will jump up and grab your hair or, oh, that's right you are bald. They will dig their claws into your scalp and bite you as they climb, these rats are hungry, so are the snakes."

"By the time they have eaten half your face off, you will be glad to talk. I have heard they favor testicles. This may be cruel, but I can't think of a nicer person to do it to."

Arch, "Lower him another 6 inches."

Arch lowered him and now the rats were jumping up and were getting about 3 inches from the top of his head, they just let him hang there for a while to see how he liked it. He didn't

Arch asked Jacky, "If he should lower him anymore."

Jacky said, "I don't think so Arch he seems to like it where he is. Okay, Arch, maybe one more inch." Now the rats were getting closer.

Finally Brian said "Anything you want. Get me out of here and get me to a doctor my toes are killing me."

"Eric here is a pad of paper and a pen to write all this down. Arch raise him up which he did."

Jacky said, "Answer the questions, or you go all the way down and those rats will make you talk."

"First -- the location where the girls are."

"They are in Ballyroma, about 20 km from here on the west side of the lake."

"Second -- what kind of house?"

" It was a large mansion once owned by, and still called The McGinty House."

"Third – I've known for a long time that you had been kidnapping girls all over British Isles and selling them into Asian prostitution houses. Some really choice ones to Middle Eastern harems. Besides the four girls that we have come for, how many more for prostitution."

"Usually 25 to 30 sometimes more."

"Fourth -- how many people are guarding the girls?"

"I ain't going to tell you no more."

"Lower him into the snakes Arch."

"Okay, okay it's 12 to 15 guys and sometimes some from the Asian houses."

"Fifth -- are they armed?"

"Yes."

"With what?"

"Mac tens and UZI,s"

"Sixth -- Brian I've already got your butt, do you really give a damn about those other 12 and 15 guys? Because if we don't get those girls I am not going to take you back to England and you won't be in a comfortable cell. You will be living with snakes and rats."

"All right there are cameras on the driveway and they can be switched off by a switch behind the no trespassing sign."

"Seventh -- Brian you are going with us"

"I am?"

"That's right, is the lane mined?"

"Yes but in my Bentley there is a sensor, that deactivates the mines.

"There must be a switch, where is it?"

"In the glove compartment."

"Eighth -- is there anything else we should know?"

"No."

"Ninth -- is there enough space, to land a large helicopter?"

"Yes"

Jacky said, "Okay guys, looks like change of plan. We are going by Bentley and we will leave by helicopter. Let's take some of the things out of the van that we might need and put them in the Bentley. We might need the C-4 and detonators, the grenade launchers, the four UZI's and hand guns. Jacky said there are two pair of handcuffs in the glove box, get them. Let's go back to the real estate office."

Arch and Peter got in the back seat with Mc Phail. Eric drove and Jacky was in the passenger seat.

Jacky said to McPhail, "We will get you to a doctor as soon as possible. Here are some aspirins and she handed him a bottle of soda to wash them down."

"Sorry I shot you in the foot, but you shot me first."

"But I shot you with blanks."

"You didn't know that when you shot me."

"Well, I guess I deserved to lose a couple of toes."

They went back to the real estate office. Jacky got out and told everyone that she would be right back. She went inside and talked to Charles and asked to use the phone to call Scotland Yard. She asked if he had Talbotts number. He said he did and that he would get him on the line for her. He got Talbott and handed the phone to Jacky. She explained what had gone on. He told her that the Irish Police had gotten the message that she had left in the bar. All of the guys that were tied to the bar rail made the police laugh.

"None of the guys tied up were laughing, they were sick as hell from eating heroin. I can't imagine who made them eat it. One guy said she made them eat it or lose a toe. Another guy was missing his big toe and another with the tip of his pinkie gone."

Jacky said, "It served them right. Their boss is missing two big toes."

"McPhail?"

"Yeah, McPhail, I'm bringing him back, but right now we have to get the girls." Jacky asked how long it would take to assemble a group of about fifty first class Irish Police. She explained that this was a bigger organization than we thought. They have about thirty girls that they have kidnapped all over the British Isles, then they sell them into Asian Prostitution or Middle East Harems. It is in an old mansion in Ballyroma. The mansion is called the McGinty house. Let the police know not to drive up the lane, it's mined. Tell the police to be well armed. I will meet the police at McGuires Pub in Toomes in one hour.

Chapter 33

Rescue 4 Girls and 45 More.

Jacky said, "We have an hour to wait, let's get something to eat."

McPhail, now sounding friendly or defeated said, "There is a good place to eat a couple of blocks over, Jimmies Bar and Grill." Eric headed the way McPhail said, they saw Jimmies Bar and Grill.

Jacky said, "Pass it up. One of those guys just going in was at McGuires Pub when I first went there. We will find another place." They found another place, Dog and Suds.

After they finished eating, they went to McGuries. Arch and Jacky went inside where there were about forty police officers. They were all well armed, all with hand guns, some with shot guns, some with rifles and some had Kalisnikovs and UZIs.

Jacky told them about the lane being mined, and the 15 armed people inside. "We will go in first since we have a vehicle, that they recognize. We will disable their vehicles and we will try to separate them from the girls. You guys with the rifles, can you hit what you aim at? If you are good, you should stay back as snipers in case they hold some hostages. Don't come in till you hear some explosions, then come in full force."

"Sergeant Murdock said that all his men are in uniform and they won't shoot each other. We will all have on bullet proof vests. We have ten extra vests, so put the vest on and when shooting starts, take off your jackets to show your vests."

Sounds good said Jacky, "We had better get moving."

They all put the vests on with their jackets over them, got into their vehicles and headed for the mansion.

The Bentley turned up the lane, and stopped "McPhail said, in the glove box, move the switch to the left and you are home free." Jacky moved the switch and they went up the lane with no mishap.

They got to the rear parking lot. There were about 14 cars in the lot, all very high priced cars. A little bit of C-4 will make a mess out of them. Jacky and Arch went over to the big box truck and opened the rear doors, the walls were about three inches thick and insulated. The floor and walls were padded. This is how they transported the girls. It was sound proofed, so the girls could scream and not be heard. Arch got McPhail out of the car, took him over to a small patch of trees and sat him on the ground leaning against a small tree. He handcuffed him with his hands behind the small tree. Then he put some duct tape over his mouth, just a precaution in case you want to call one of your buddies for help.

With the C-4 right under the differential or the engine, whichever was easier to get at on all fourteen cars, the detonators were radio activated. Once initiated, they would go off one after the other. Now they had to get inside.

They went in through a main door. Once in, Jacky and Eric went down one hallway and Arch and Peter went down another. They wore fairly large coats with the UZI's in an inside pocket. The four of them met where the halls intersected. There was a lighted room on the right. It was a kitchen and somebody was looking at something in a pot.

Arch snuck up behind him and hit him over the head with a Sap, laid him on the floor, put his arms behind him and around a leg of the stove. He pulled a couple of wire ties out of his pocket and put them around his wrists like handcuffs. All four of them carried wire ties just for this purpose. Then he put duct tape over his mouth.

In the next room was a stroke of luck, there were twelve of them having dinner. They were all comfortably sitting at one large table. First Jacky and Arch, then Eric and Peter rushed into the dining room with their UZI's up and pointed at the dinner crowd. Jacky said, "Sorry folks to break up your nice dinner, but we came here to release some girls that you people have detained."

"What we don't need is you people interfering with our mission, so we are going to ask you to go to sleep for about an hour . Jacky took some very large pills out of her pocket. I have here some very powerful sleeping pills, they will put you to sleep in about three minutes."

"You can't make us take those pills."

"No, I can't, but I can give you a choice, one of these pills or a lead pill out of this UZI. The choice is sleep for an hour or sleep forever, your choice."

"One guy said, you cannot tell me what to do, I will take no pill."

"Quick as hell, Jacky reached over on the table and grabbed a loaf of bread, stuck the barrel of the UZI in it (said I don't like noise), pointed it at his head and pulled the trigger."

"After that, she passed out the pills one at a time. She said, now no cheating, if you don't swallow the pill, then you won't be asleep in three minutes and then I will have to give you one of these lead pills."

After she said that, one guy said, "I think I dropped mine, would you give me another one?"

"I think you are bullshitting me, you spit it out but I'll give you another chance, here is another pill." He put it in his mouth, took a drink of water and swallowed it. In a few minutes they were all sound asleep.

"That's thirteen of them, can't be too many more." They went down the hall a little further, and came to a room with computers, and three people looking at them. Jacky explained the pill routine to them and the alternative.

The Caucasian guy said," I'll take the pill."

She gave him the pill and a can of pop. He swallowed the pill and sat down in his chair.

The Chinese guy and the Chinese woman were yacking away in Chinese and she was telling the guy to act like he didn't understand English, then Peter started talking Chinese to them and they said they would take the pill. They did and now there were sound asleep. Jacky then said, set off the C-4. Eric punched the radio transmitter and 14 cars were put out of commission. Arch said, I heard and outboard start.

Arch went out and checked. There was a boat pulling away from the dock with two people in it. Arch went to the Bentley, reached in on the drivers' side and punched the button to open the trunk. He pulled out one of the grenade launchers, went out on the dock, lined up on the boat and fired. It landed right behind the boat and blew off the transom of the boat. They swam ashore and Arch was waiting with his UZI.

Now the Police arrived, put cuffs on these two wet people and put them in one of their vehicles.

Arch went back in and saw Jacky talking to one of the top police officials and Peter was explaining what was on the computer in Chinese.

He said, "It was negotiating the sale of these girls to some Asian dealer in flesh." He said, "These two Chinese won't be deported, they will go to trial and prison here. They will probably get life for kidnapping".

The Police got into the barracks where the girls were kept imprisoned. There were actually forty-five girls. Plus the four that Jacky and her crew came for.

After a couple of hours, the military came in and cleared the mines out of the lane. Then they brought in prison vehicles, to haul the prisoners away. They brought in plush motor coaches to take the forty-five girls to a fine hotel to stay until they went home.

After all that, Bill landed the H-19 helicopter in the yard behind the mansion. They loaded McPhail aboard. Jacky got into the copilots seat. The four girls, Eric, Arch and Peter got in the back.

When they landed at the airport Bill said, "He made a swap. Instead of the ride back to London in the Otter, he conned someone out of a nice corporate DC3." It was much more comfortable, and had a stewardess aboard. She served soft drinks and alcoholic drinks, also food. It was a nice flight."

When they got back to London, they went directly to Scotland Yard. George Talbott greeted them. "You people did a wonderful job, much more than was expected. If it wasn't for you and your crew going to rescue the four girls, we would never have known about this despicable, ring of criminals."

"The Irish Police have been thankful, and helpful in working with us. All of the men picked up in McGuires Pub are in custody and are being charged with a variety of things. Their charges range from dope dealing, dope smuggling, kidnapping, murder and a few other things. Strange thing though, they all had shot up right hands and one had his big toe shot off, another a pinky finger. With all this shooting, how come none of you or your people got hit?"

"She said, we are just better shots, no, to tell the truth, it was and unfair fight. It was fixed. We made an adjustment to all of their ammo. That way all we had to do was incapacitate them, because they were shooting blanks and didn't know it."

"They are all in the prison infirmary now, but there is one person that is in the prison infirmary in London. He is the one you brought back, McPhail is the name. He is the leader of the McGuire's Pub kidnappers, also part of the girls for sale group that were captured at the mansion."

"He is guilty of a lot of things, he even tried to kill me. He shot me in the stomach with a nine mm Beretta from a distance of one foot, point blank at one foot distance. That was his problem, he pointed a gun with blanks at me. The slugs hit my jacket and fell to the floor, then, he lost his two toes. It just made me mad that he would shoot me in the belly like that."

"The forty five girls that had been imprisoned at the mansion have been staying in a first class hotel in Belfast and now all but eight of them have gone home."

"The seventeen people that were captured at the mansion are being sent to England for trial. You had originally captured sixteen, the police found the seventeenth one upstairs in an office hiding in a closet. It was a beautiful Chinese woman. The girls said that she and one other guy were the ones in charge. She made the deals for the girls and ordered the kidnappings. She will get life in prison with no chance of parole."

Talbott said, "You and your crew did one hell of a job. The strange thing is, there was only one person killed in this whole operation. The one killed, you shot through the head."

"We had no choice, our job was to free the girls."

"The problem was, this one you killed was a mid-eastern Sheik. His government complained, but our people told them to go to hell. The government office told them that they would charge their government with complicity in kidnapping. They shut up and went away."

"The Sheik was just window shopping for his harem. He got what he deserved and it made an example for the other bastards. They followed the rules after that little episode."

"Now, there are some people that wish to meet you and your crew." Jacky, Bill, Eric, Arch and Peter walked through a door into a large room. They could hardly believe their eyes. In that room was Princess Elisabeth II, the Prime Minister the four rescued girls and their fathers, who were members of Parliament.

The American Ambassador to Ireland came with a very popular Chicagoan, Richard J. Daley.

They all congratulated the rescue crew and the fathers and mothers thanked them profusely.

Then Jacky said, "I have $65,000.00 left that I did not spend, it belongs to the fathers of the girls." The fathers all said to share that between you and your crew.

Lord Foxglove came up to Jacky and apologized for what he said was his stupid actions. "I just did not believe that you few people, could do what you did. I will now belatedly contribute my share, which I now feel is not enough for what you have done. I wish to donate another $50,000.00."

The other three fathers said, "Good show Foxglove, we feel we should do the same."

Then Foxglove said, "For what you people have done, this is the least we can do."

The Ambassador to Ireland said, "It was just a short time ago in the Thousand Islands, New York, that I was thanking you for saving my daughter. Now I am thanking you for saving four more daughters, plus you also rescued 45 more girls who were someone else's daughters. On top of that, you put a dope ring and prostitution ring out of business."

Richard J. Daley then steps up, and said that he is proud to be here. And hands Jacky a fresh copy of the Chicago Tribune. Then he said, "Chicago is also proud of you and your crew." The headlines, which were printed in green said, "Jacky and crew do it again in Ireland." Then there is the story of what happened. We are all proud of you people.

Then Princess Elisabeth came over and said, "It is my understanding that you had done a great service for England as a commando." You have done it in the colonies as well (the USA) and now you have done it again over here. It's amazing what you people have done."

"As a well-known person has said, "Never have so few, done so much for so many." The Princess said, "I hear that you are getting married when you get back to Chicago. I also hear that he was one of our fine RAF pilots."

Jacky said, " He flew us on this mission, and she introduced Bill to the Princess." She didn't bat an eye when she said, "Going to marry Rex Harrison?"

Bill said "I'm really Bill Turner."

"That's great, but are you going to quit the movies?"

"No Ma'am, I was never in the movies."

The Prime Minister thanked them and wished them well. He said, "Anytime I can do something for any of you, just give me a ring." He handed them each a business card. "This is my private direct number, but please don't give this number to anyone else. You are all amazing people and we are much better off after what you have done. Thank you all."

They talked with George Talbott for a while after the dignitaries had left. Bill said, "I think we should go back to the hotel, we're going to have to arrange for a flight to Chicago."

Talbott said, "Don't worry about it, I'm arranging for the flight for the Irish Ambassador and Mr. Daley and I was told to arrange for your flights, also to cover your hotel bill. Your flight is at 1:00 P.M. London time."

"Princess Elisabeth said that she would like to see you off, but she has her royal duties to attend to in the morning. She will send her royal limousine to pick up you and your party, also the Irish Ambassador and Mr. Daley. You are all on the same flight. You are also booked into the First Class Section as VIP. The limo will pick you up at 11:00 A.M. and the royal limo will go right to the plane. I have already informed the Ambassador of the limo and the flight."

"The Ambassador and Mr. Daley would like to meet us in your hotel bar and have a bon voyage drink. We should meet them in 30 minutes."

The stretch limo picked them up to take them to the hotel. The concierge met them at the door and took them to a dining room instead of the bar. Arch said that they had just eaten and that they wanted to go to the bar. "Sir, the word had gotten out that you people were coming here, so now there is no room in the bar."

The Ambassador and her friend are seated in the dining room and are waiting for you. As they approached, the Ambassador and Daley started to get up. Bill said, "Sit down please and relax, you are probably as tired as we are and thirsty too. It seems like when you are around Royalty, everyone drinks wine."

Talbott then said "Goes with the territory. I used to drink beer and gin. Beefeater Martinis, that was my favorite." The waitress came by and asked for their order.

Bill said, "He would have a dry Beefeater Martini on the rocks with 4 olives, a double. Arch said the same, Eric the same Peter said I'll have the same."

"Talbott said make that five.

When she got to Jacky, she said, "I think I need something different, I'll have a half pint of Guinness and a double shot of Chevez Royal Salute.

Eric asked her, "If she knew how the Chicago Cubs were doing."

She said, "The only thing I know is that they just swept the Yankees in a four game series, and before that they swept the Phillies."

"That sounds good, looks like they may win the Series."

Their drinks arrived and Jacky and Daley were talking about how things were going in Chicago.

Daley said, "He had only been gone for four days, but he will be glad when they set down at Midway Airport."

Talbott then said, "He had been informed that $300,000.00, has been transferred to a bank in Chicago. In the names of Jacky, Arch, Peter and Eric, to be divided evenly."

Everybody was so tired that after the second drink, they decided to call it a night. The next morning, everybody was up bright eyed and bushy tailed. The Ambassador and Daley joined the crew at a large table.

Eric asked Jacky, "How is the beef in London."

She said, "The beef was never that great in England but this is considered a high class restaurant and they might get imported beef, you can ask the waitress. If you happen to like lamb chops, they more than likely get their lamb from Ireland and it's the best."

They asked the waitress, and she said, "The beef comes from the Chicago Stockyards, and the lamb from Ireland."

Bill ordered a porterhouse steak and so did Daley. Jacky and Crystall, as she asked to be called, ordered a rack of lamb. Everybody else had the house special, lamb chops and fried eggs. They all said it was one hell of a breakfast and the tab was picked up by someone else, which meant the price was right. They finished their coffee and English scones . No sooner than they relaxed and somebody said, "Your limo is here."

Chapter 34

On the Constellation with Tony, Patti

Everybody loaded up in the stretch limousine and they headed off to the airport. When they got to the airport, the Royal Limousine was waived right through the main gate. The driver headed right down the ramp and parked within thirty feet of a four engine Lockheed Constellation. All seven of them climbed the rollaway stairs and headed directly to their seats. All seven of them were seated in the First Class Section.

There were only ten seats in First Class and their group used up seven seats. Finally, two other people came into the cabin and sat down in First Class. The head stewardess came into First Class, and welcomed everybody aboard. Then she asked if anybody had flown on a Constellation before, everybody said that they had. She then asked if they had flown First Class on a Connie? Peter said, "The last flight we had on a Constellation, five of us were the only passengers on the plane, boy, did we get good service from the stewardess's."

"Well you will get good service on this flight."

Peter said, "He was sorry, he did not mean that they would not get good service."

"Many famous people fly on the Constellations, such as the famous Mr. Tony Bennett and I almost missed, the famous Patti Page."

Then Patti Page said, "Not near as famous as your other guests in First Class."

Tony said, "You are right Patti, we're just singers, but you people are the real heroes. He asked the stewardess if she read any papers or watched the news in London. Well these are the people that rescued forty nine girls in Ireland that had been kidnapped by a prostitution ring. These few people did what the police could not do."

Jacky then said, "We had an advantage, I knew who we were looking for and where he was."

Then Tony said, "If I remember right, you are Jacky Sax. I was at the Chicago Yacht Club, we all watched as you stood on the bow of a large schooner, as it sailed out of the harbor, you were singing "Amazing Grace." It was beautiful to see and to hear. Jacky, you are an extraordinarily talented person, have you ever thought of going into show business?"

"No and I don't intend to go into show business. Bill and I are in the motorcycle business and we are are getting married when we get back to Chicago."

Daley said, "Once Bill and Jacky make up their mind when, I have a lot of people organizing the wedding and the reception. The wedding will be at the Holy Name Cathedral in Chicago. We have not decided where the reception will be. We will make suggestions and Bill and Jacky will decide. The City of Chicago will foot the bill for the reception. Once word had gotten out about this wedding, everybody wants to donate something. Eight different Bridal Salons want Jacky to wear one of their gowns, even tuxedos for Bill and anyone in the wedding party. The Bridal Salons will also custom make gowns for Jacky's bridesmaids."

"You would never believe how many caterers wish to donate their food, Mexican food, German, Chinese, French and Italian. We will have enough food to feed and army.

"I had been talking to the people at the Merchandise Mart about renting their large show auditorium. They said we couldn't rent it, but they would donate it for the reception. Nobody wants money."

There have been a half dozen top bands that wish to donate their services, also some of the top singers, Nat King Cole, Frankie Lane, The Andrew Sisters, Theresa Brewer and Pat Boone.

Tony Bennett said to Patti, "Don't you feel left out?"

Patti asked Jacky, "Is there was any room for two old troopers willing to sing for their supper?"

"Only if you sing the Tennessee Waltz, with two of my friends Sandra and Kelly."

"I heard they were really good, they were a trio, not a duet and you were the third." Patti said, " If the four of us sang, we would be a blonde quartet."

Tony said, "I still feel left out."

Patti said, "Tony you are a better solo."

Tony agreed and said, "I guess nobody wants to sing with me."

Jacky said, "I'll sing with you."

Tony said "How about Amazing Grace."

"Sounds good to me."

The stewardess said, "It is now 6:00 P.M. in Chicago and we will be landing there in ten minutes at Midway Airport." It felt good to be back in Chicago and Eric could hardly wait to set foot on solid ground.

After they landed, Daley asked everyone where they were going after they left the airport. Tony and Patti hadn't made up their mind as to where.

"Can you suggest a good hotel?"

"None better than the Drake, that's where we are going. There should be a stretch limo waiting for us on the ramp. You are welcome to join us, the limo has room for 10 and we are only 9."

"We could pick up a hitch-hiker."

"We would have to get our luggage."

Daley said, "No problem, I had no idea how much luggage we would have, s I had one of my people bring a station wagon. It's nice to be the boss. Give the driver the description of your luggage, he will pick it up along with ours and bring it right to the Drake."

Tony said to Dick, "It seems like you make everything work easy."

"That's what I do for a living, I make everything work easy." They got to the Drake. Everyone got separate rooms except Eric and Arch. Peter said he wanted his own room.

Crystall said, "Jacky, why don't we bunk together, I get lonely in hotel rooms."

"I agree, I'd rather have somebody to talk to. I guess we had better shower and get ready for dinner, remember we agreed to meet in the lobby in one hour."

"Jacky why don't you shower first, I want to make a call to Heather."

Jacky showered, got dressed in a casual but sexy skirt and blouse. She laid down on the bed, then she heard someone singing an Irish Folk tune. It was a nice song and she was wondering who the singer was. She looked around and finally spotted the radio. She went over to turn up the volume, but the radio was off. It was coming from the bathroom and she didn't notice a radio in there when she took a shower. It dawned on her then. It was the Ambassador. She was one hell of a singer. From the sound of it, she thought she probably could really belt it out.

Crystall came out of the shower. Jacky said, "Crystall, you sure do have a great voice."

"I like to sing in the shower, I used to sing with a group in Belfast and all around Northern Ireland."

"My husband was a Lieutenant in the police department in Belfast. He was killed in a skirmish with the IRA. Heather was five years old at the time. Things were getting bad in Belfast, so Heather and I came to the USA, joined some Irish groups in the states, got into politics and I was finally appointed the US Ambassador to Ireland. Now I don't sing anymore, I just talk to people."

"So, let's go and eat, I'm starving and tired of hearing your life story."

"I'll say no more." They headed down to the lobby. The whole crew was in the lobby, all showered and with fresh clothes.

The hotel manager recognized Richard J. Daley as soon as he walked into the room. He came over and asked if he could be of any help. Daley told him they needed a table to seat nine and would like it to be with a good view of the stage and we would like dinner and cocktails before the show starts. "Would you mind having a cocktail in the bar on the house while our people rearrange some tables so you will have a good view of the stage? We have to treat VIPs as a VIP should be treated. I have noticed Tony Bennett and Patti Page are in your group. We are very honored to have you here."

Daley said, "Then you should be as much honored by my six other guests. First, the American Ambassador to Ireland then if you had read the newspapers, you would recognize these other five people."

"Oh yes, I recognize them now, the newspapers never show good pictures. All I can say is I'm sorry I did not recognize you, but I'm very proud to have met you. You shall have the best seats and the best food that the Drake can serve."

Arch said, "I've been here once before, I can vouch for the Drake's food."

"I do remember you, a couple of months ago we were told in advance of your pending arrival. Everyone was on pins and needles waiting for you. We were told "A Messenger From God" was coming and when you arrived on a golden motorcycle, everyone knew who you were. As far as I know, you received the best treatment from all of our staff."

"That I did." said Arch."

"If I remember right, you had a first class suite, dinner and breakfasts all prepaid for two days. You gave all this away to a honeymoon couple that you had never seen before. That's why as they saw you ride away on your golden motorcycle, they knew they had met the "Messenger from God", we are honored to have you back."

After they had a cocktail, the headwaiter came into the bar and asked if they wished to be seated in the dining room? The table amazed them, it was a large curved table with everyone seated on the same side facing the stage. They were all seated on the convex side so they could see each other and the stage too. "We only have two of these tables, they are our VIP tables."

They had an excellent meal and were having an after dinner drink when they noticed that the dining room was full, not an empty seat. The waiters were trying to squeeze in some small tables for late comers, then they closed the lobby doors and the lights went down. In the shadows someone was coming forward from the back of the darkened stage and the sound of the beautiful stains of Mona Lisa. A voice over a speaker said the incomparable Nat "King" Cole and he did his most beautiful version of Mona Lisa.

After a few more songs, he said, "Folks, I have been told that we have a lot of singing talent in the audience. To start with, Tony Bennett is here." Tony stands up and gets a lot of applause.

"Then there is the American Ambassador to Ireland and it was just found out tonight, that she is a singing Ambassador, Crystall Quinn." Crystall stands up and gets a polite applause.

"And last but not least is the Singing Commando. A very successful one I might add. Those German troops just could not pull the trigger when they saw this beautiful blonde. She sings as well as she shoots."

"Now that you are all tired of listening to me sing, I'll take a rest and let Tony Bennett entertain you." He promised that he would sing only one song, but Tony liked to sing and the crowd wanted more so after three songs he said "I gotta go now."

Then Nat said "Now one of my favorite singers, singing a song that she made a hit record of, but she said that she doesn't want to sing it by herself, so it will be Patti and Jacky singing the "Tennessee Waltz". Mind you folks, these two gals have never sung together at any time or place. The girls say that if you people will listen they will try singing." They sang the "Tennessee Waltz" and the crowd gave them a standing ovation.

Nat then said "Next we have something that you have never heard before, a singing Ambassador, but she said that she also wants to sing with Jacky." They sang "Amazing Grace" it was another hit, a standing ovation. They kept clapping and asking for an encore. She said "Nat, one more song, one of Patti's songs "Mocking Bird Hill" with Patti as a duet." They did it to another standing ovation. Then Jacky grabbed the mike and said, "Now I want to do something that I came here for and that is to listen to the Master, Nat "King" Cole." There was a thunderous applause and Nat said, "I never enjoyed a show so much, but now I better get back to what they are paying me for." After that everybody enjoyed a fantastic show by Nat "King" Cole.

After the show Nat came over and sat with them. He said, "I just want to let you know that tonight was fun. After doing so many of these shows it gets to be work. I enjoy it, but it's work. Tonight you people made it fun." The manager who was now sitting with them said, "The audience enjoyed it too." Nat said, "Good thing this is my last night here otherwise a lot of people out there would be expecting the same show tomorrow." The manager then said that their tab in the dining room will be taken care of by the house.

Daley told the manager, that he had one little problem and that is arranging for a nice place to show some bridal gowns. When the word got out that Jacky was getting married, especially when they found out that the ceremony would be at Holy Name Cathedral, all the high class bridal salons wanted to get in on the action for the publicity. Eight of them donated their expensive gowns providing their names were mentioned. Two of them are from Paris.

Daley said "I know you have a room where you do fashion shows. Would you have an opening for that room to show these bridal gowns? That way Jacky can decide which one she would wear."

"Yes, we can do that at no charge, but you must allow the media to be at this event or I will be on the carpet in front of the directors of the hotel."

"That sounds agreeable, when would you have an opening?"

"Four days from now, then not another opening for three weeks."

Daley said, "Tentatively, four days from now, but I'll check with Jacky." Jacky agreed to the four days, but only if they were all there on the same day and that they had the prices on all of them. They had to be complete with nothing to be added later. Daley told Jacky that he would get them in line.

"Well Mr. Daley, if anybody can get them in line, it would be you." The next day Dick Daley made his calls and they all agreed to Friday afternoon.

Everybody went home. Arch to Minneapolis, Eric to his dads place in Chicago, Peter to Kansas City, Mo., Jacky and Bill to Bill's Bikes in Chicago, Crystall went to Thousand Islands, N.Y. and Tony and Patti to California.

Eric had called his dad at the machine shop and told him that he was back in Chicago. He said that he would be home that afternoon. "Okay, Eric, I've got to get off the phone a customer just came in, we will see you when you get here."

Eric thought, "Who's we?"

Daley arranged for a limo to take Eric home. The limo pulled up in the driveway, Eric got out. The limo left and he walked to the backyard. Art was there stoking up the charcoal in the Webber Grill. Art said, "Where you been? I'm ready to put the steaks on. Oh, by the way, meet your new mother, Kathy. We got married down in the Caribbean while you were out gallivanting on that big schooner. You and your friends sure did make a name for your selves, seems that every time you called you were just going off on another adventure. We figured no sense in waiting for you to get back home, so we just got married."

"Are you going to hang around for a while or are you off on a new adventure?"

"Arch and I are going to take a little bike ride.

"Where to?"

"Down to Phoenix."

"Going to raise a little hell?"

"We plan on doing that."

"By the way, don't plan on calling your girlfriends, Janice and Wendy, they both got married while you guys were gone. They married twins, had a double wedding. Kathy and I went to the wedding."

"Speaking of weddings, you will be invited to one at the Holy Name Cathedral."

"Boy, that's high class, who is getting married?"

"It's Jacky Sax and Bill Turner."

"Jacky Sax! Is she the Ex commando that they say is tough as hell. She can take on a half dozen bully boys at once and lay them all out. She must be all muscle, built like a bull."

"No Dad, she is a 120 pound doll. A beautiful doll at that, she is marrying Bill Turner, an ex RAF pilot, the guy I bought my bike from."

"Sounds great, when is it going to be?"

"Pretty soon, but I don't know exactly when. The reception will be at the Merchandise Mart."

"Sounds pretty classy, but who is paying for all this?"

"All donated because of what Jacky and us have done."

"Yeah, I guess you have been pretty busy lately."

"How are you going to pay for your little ride down to Phoenix? If I remember right, you were pretty broke before your boat ride."

"Not to worry, dad, I've got $75,000.00 in a Chicago bank and so has Arch. We would take $5,000.00 in travelers checks and when that's gone, come home."

"Where did you get all that money from?"

"From the fathers of the girls we rescued in Ireland, so dad, we are going to party for a while."

Then there is Peter, he went home to Kansas City, Mo. to see his parents. His parents own a Chinese restaurant. They were not doing too bad in the restaurant business, but it was still tough paying for his sisters college tuition. They paid for Peter's tuition and now it was his turn. He gave his mother a check for $25,000.00.

She said, "Where did you get all this money? This is enough to cover the last three years of Lu Ann's tuition and have $10,000.00 left."

"Then go and buy yourself a new car."

"But we don't want to take all your money."

"Don't worry, mom, I've got more than enough left over, in fact I'm going out today to buy a new Ford Convertible."

She said "From what I hear, I think you earned it."

Then there was Arch. He could hardly wait to get on his big old Indian and head South to Phoenix, but first he had to make a call to New York before he left the Drake.

He called the number that Jenny had given him. The receptionist answered with one word, "Cindy's, then asked how may I help you."

He asked for Jenny and she said, "Oh Mrs. Marshal" and connected him. "Mrs. Marshal was what he heard next."

He said, "Jenny?"

She said, "Yes, this is Jenny Marshal."

He said, "This is Arch Mueller, you told me to give you a call if I got to New York or Phoenix. Well, I am going to be heading for Phoenix in a couple of weeks."

"Well Arch, I'm Mrs. Jenny Marshal now and I don't go to the ranch, with the girls anymore, I go on cruises with my husband. Although we still own the ranch and we have six girls, all unmarried models, if you are going down to Phoenix, I will have them leave the welcome mat out for you and your friend."

Then Arch was saying to himself, "Well old boy, can't do much better than that."

Then Jenny asked Arch, "If it was true that he and two other guys, were with Jacky Sax in Ireland?"

"He told her that it was, and the guy going with him to Phoenix, was one of the other two guys."

"Is he as good looking as you?"

"Much better looking."

"I had better not let the other girls know, or they will all want to go. Nobody will be here to work, because all these gals love heroes. I'll let the six girls know who you are and that you will see them in Phoenix. Have fun Arch."

"I have one thing to say Jenny, your husband is a lucky man. Goodbye and have fun on your cruise."

Then Arch went over to Bill's Bikes and picked up his golden Indian Chief. Bill and Jacky were not there at the time so he just left a message. "See you at the Wedding." He headed up to Minneapolis to see his parents. They were very glad to see him. They were happy when he told them that they were invited to the wedding of the year in Chicago. The wedding of Jacky Sax and Bill Turner. When he told them that he was taking a ride to Phoenix with Eric after the wedding, his mother tried to talk him out of it.

His dad said, "You only live once, have at it."

Jacky and Bill headed right to Bill's Bikes. Bill said, "You haven't seen where I make my living. I have an apartment above the shop, where I'm living now. It's not fancy, but it's comfortable. I'm having a nice tri level house built in River Grove. We can move there when it's finished, in a couple more months. Jacky, I think we are going to have to decide on a date for our marriage, how about tomorrow and a justice of the peace."

"I Think that would create a riot, how about two weeks from today?" said Jacky.

"You have about three more days before you have to decide on a wedding gown."

"I've already decided, Bill."

"I just have to make a call." She called Hannibal, Missouri and connected with Paula Jensen. "Paula, this is Jacky and I have a couple of questions for you. Remember when you used to make me some dresses? Do you still have that dress form with my size?"

"Jacky, I could make any dress you would want, even without the form."

"What kind of dress?"

"A gown, a wedding gown."

"A wedding gown, are you getting married?"

"Why else would I want a wedding gown?

Next question is, can you do it in twelve days?"

"That's tight, but I could do it."

Then Jacky explains that the wedding would be at the Holy Name Cathedral in Chicago, a lot of important people will be there, including yourself and your husband. "Your favorite singer will be there, Tony Bennett. I know he will sing a song for you."

"Jacky, with all those people there, it's really got to be a first class dress."

"You will see your dress in every newspaper and in the newsreels." You will be famous, Paula."

"Then I can't do it in twelve days, it will take eighteen to twenty days."

"Okay Paula, max, twenty days."

"You're on."

"Paula, one more thing, cost is no problem, make it your best."

"For you, Jacky, it will be."

"Paula, I just want to let you know that I'm going to have the pleasure of turning down some of the fanciest, most expensive bridal salons in the country and Paris. They want me to wear their gowns so they can get the publicity."

"Bill, can we change the wedding to three weeks from Saturday and I better call Paula to tell her 21 days is okay."

Bill said that day would be good for him.

"Now I better call Daley and tell him of the date and find out about the gowns at the Drake." She got his office and his secretary said that he was not in, but should be back shortly. She asked who was calling? When Jacky told her, she said to hang on, I'll find him and she did. Daley came on the line. Jacky said, "Three weeks from Saturday, okay?"

"It Sounds good to me, now I've got to get everything rolling."

Jacky asked Daley how he was going to get all these different things organized in such a short time. He said, "No problem, Jacky, I've got some pretty good secretaries. They look over all the things to be done and then each takes a share. I trust them implicitly. They can and will do a good job."

"Jacky, now about the wedding gown, do you really want to go to the Drake and choose one of these over-priced and probably ridiculously designed wedding gowns? It seems that they only want to compete, with the rich person's idea of a Paris Designer. And they want the publicity they will gain, by getting you to wear one of their gowns."

"Remember the one thing that I said. The gowns are to be on mannequins, I won't try them on. There are many wedding gown salons that are fair and reputable and many others who con these girls who are very easy to manipulate when they are about to get married. They sell them highly over-priced gowns that they or their parents go in hock for. If they don't get them too bad on the initial cost, they hit them up hard on the alterations. It's a money making racket and I don't want to be part of it. What I'm saying here is not true of all Bridal Salons, there are some that are very fair."

Daley said, "Jacky, I agree with you, so I would like to be there Friday when you look over these gowns."

"I would like to see you there, you and the media."

"Jacky, the media will definitely be there. If you want to be able to keep some of them out, be there Friday at noon."

"Bill, you want to go with Friday to the Drake to look over those gowns?"

"Jacky, this is your thing, I'm not into wedding gowns and I don't want to cramp your style by being there." So, Friday noon, Jacky took Bill's Lincoln Continental and drove to the Drake.

She was met by the manager who brought her to the showroom. He said, "All the gowns were on mannequins, some of them look pretty wild. Especially the ones from Paris and New York. Another thing that is wild, are the prices. The French did not want to post their prices. They wanted to announce the price as you looked them over. I told them to go by the set rules or pack up the dresses and take them back to Paris. They posted the price. It would cover France's national debt."

Jacky, Daley and the manager went out to the fashion showroom. There were nine mannequins. Jacky, Daley and Dan, the manager walked back and forth in front of the display of gowns. Jacky already knew what she was going to do. She already had said that she wanted no representatives, from the Bridal Salons in the room. She asked Dan if the mannequins could be moved to form a semi-circle with the front facing her. Now it was possible to look at more than one gown at a time.

Next she asked Dan if he could spare about eight girls from their duties, a mixture of office girls, maids and one supervisor. Dan said he could do that. Now we need eight clipboards for the girls. Can we get someone to list all nine of the Salons. Then a column to number, from one to nine, the best and the least quality of workmanship. Then a column from, one to nine, for the most attractive design. A column for high and low prices and one to put in your own estimated price. Also, one question, "Which one would you choose to wear, if you could afford to pay the Salons price?"

"Considering these three factors; quality of workmanship, the most beautiful design and the factor of cost using their own judged cost, which gown is the best value?"

One of the office girls brought out the clipboards, with the listings of the Bridal Salons. Jacky noticed how well dressed, and neat this girl was, she asked Dan if this girl could be one of the judges.

Dan said, "No problem, we have one secretary and one supervisor. We need seven more girls. The girls name was Julie. She said she could help by picking out the other seven girls.

She said, "I know the maids and the office girls."

Dan said "I'm sure we can trust Julie's judgment, with your approval Jacky."

"I don't think you need my approval. It seems that Julie knows these girls and she knows what we are trying to do." Julie selected seven more girls. Now, before the girls came into the showroom, they invited the media to come in to take their pictures, of Jacky and the wedding gowns. While they took their pictures, the prices were still on the gowns.

Then Jacky, Daley and Dan removed all the prices from the gowns and Dan explained to the media what was going on. Dan told them that these gowns were going to be judged by girls, that could be the possible buyers of wedding gowns. It would be fair judging. They told the media they could discuss anything with the girls, after the judging. But not to speak to any of them while they are in the process of judging. Jacky then told the media that the agreement was that after this shindig was over, whichever ones that were not chosen, would be auctioned off with the proceeds going to a charity.

All the girls came into the room. Jacky told them to look at the gowns, to look at them very closely and that they would be judging them. The eight girls walked around the mannequins, Dan gave them the clipboards and explained what they should do.

The girls started listing what they thought was the best looking design. Most of them said that the best was easy, second and third was not too hard, the least attractive was easy and the next least attractive was also easy. Now they had four left, the choices varied quite a bit, but everything was to be averaged out.

Next came the judging of the quality of workmanship. Again the first, second and third were easy and even the fourth. The bottom two were also easy, but the three in the middle varied quite a bit and again it was averaged out.

Then the girls were supposed to estimate the prices for each of the gowns. They were given the salon's top price of $12,600.00 and the bottom price $3,200.00. The girls top price was less than half of the salon's price and was not awarded to the salon's top price holder.

The clipboards were given to Dan who brought them into the accountant's office. He averaged everything out, and gave the sheets back to Dan. He gave the new sheets that had a column of the bridal shops, a column of best workmanship, a column of most attractive gowns. Then a column of the averaged out prices the girls came up with. The last column was empty and the girls were to compare the workmanship, the attractiveness of design and then the averaged prices that were judged by the girls. Then, putting all three considerations together, they would each decide which was the best buy. Dan brought these final sheets to the Accountant. He made a final sheet.

This final sheet included the salons' name, the Salons' prices, the quality of workmanship graded for each salon, quality of design for each salon and the girls estimated prices of each salon. Finally, the best buy, the 2nd and 3rd .

Dan took these finals into the office and made Xerox copies after the best buys were averaged out. Jacky gave the media people copies of the results and told them it was okay to question the girls who judged the gowns. Along with the media people, came the owners or the representatives of the salons. The media people were amazed at the prices and the ratings in quality of workmanship and the quality of design.

The French salon owners would not talk to the media other than to say they were insulted. Both of the French salons were rated at or near the bottom in the judging. Both George's Girrard and Pierre of Paris, said they would pack up their gowns and go home. Dan told them to go but their gowns stay to be auctioned off for charity as agreed on from the beginning. The French went home. Kenneth of Chicago, who was awarded the best, was happy with the publicity, so was Yolanda Judd of Chicago, who was second, as was 3rd place Golden Glow of New York.

The media people asked Jacky, if she had made up her mind yet. She said that she had, "They would see her gown on the day of the wedding. She then told the media that the reason, that she did what she did had a purpose. Too many young brides or her parents, have been ripped off by a slick sales person in a bridal salon. They would convince this gullible bride, that for this important occasion, the bride deserves the very best. So the bride or the parents go in hock, sometimes deeply, for a gown that is very much over-priced."

"As you can see, with these eight unbiased girls doing the judging. The highest salon priced gowns, were not necessarily the best quality, in either design or workmanship. I believe that most wedding gowns should be priced in the hundreds of dollars and not in the thousands. That's my opinion, it's up to you people to do whatever you want with it. Now I'm going home."

She pulled up in front of the bike shop, and noticed that something was missing. It was the big neon sign "Bill's Bikes." It was gone, but the crane was lifting a new sign. It had a protective covering on it so she could not see what the sign said. She went inside, Bill was talking to Benny, his shop foreman. He was also one of the best English bike mechanics in the city. It seemed that they both agreed on something. Benny walked back into the repair shop.

Bill said, "How did it go at the Drake, Jacky?"

"We wound up with some unhappy salon owners and some very happy ones."

"Well, who's did you pick out of the happy ones?"

"None of them, Bill, I've already got Paula Jensen, in Hannibal, Missouri making my gown. I think you will like it."

"How do you know I will like it, you haven't been to Hannibal for months."

"I trust Paula Jensen, she is a skilled seamstress and a very talented designer, so whatever she makes will be better than anything that I've seen at the Drake."

"Bill, what are they doing to your sign out front?"

"They are making a change, Jacky, something I should have done a long time ago."

The foreman from the sign company came into the shop and said, "Bill, your sign is up and it looks great, come out and take a look."

"Come on Jacky, let's go and have a look." They went out the front door and looked up, the sign said "Bill and Jacky's Bikes".

"It's beautiful, Bill, but I don't want to be just a partner on paper."

"Got that all figured out, Jacky, remember that I told you I owned the whole building. I had intended to rent out the end section, to get some better cash flow. I talked to my banker and told him I might want to expand. He said that he would consider it. Remember you said that you would like to get a franchise for some English bikes? I told the banker that it would be run by my future wife. He said that he would have to discuss this loan with the directors of the bank. Then asked me to fill out a form that he said was required when a loan was to be reviewed by the directors of the bank. He picked up the form and saw the name Jacky Sax. "This is not the same Jacky Sax who is about to be married in the Holy Name Cathedral?"

"There is only one Jacky Sax." The banker then took the form that Bill just filled out and tore it up and threw it in the waste basket. He said, "No need for this, Bill, the loan is approved with the amount still open."

Then Bill contacted some British motorcycle companies. The first company he talked to was Vincent, they told him that they would send him an application form to fill out. He remembered the banker's reaction and mentioned Jacky Sax and they forgot the application. They just asked how soon and how many. He decided that he had better talk things over with Jacky before he talked to any more motorcycle companies. The first thing Jacky said was, "Forget the loan, Bill, we don't need it."

"We will when they start shipping the bikes in."

"We are partners, Bill and will be in more ways than one. I've got $75,000.00 in a Chicago bank and a check from Jimbo for my share of the Hannibal shop. A total of $115,000.00 and, as you said, we are equal partners so I will put in $100,000.00 and keep $15,000.00 for pocket money."

Bill said, "Okay, Partner, I think we have everything settled, now let's go out for dinner."

"Where would you like to go, Bill?"

"Jacky, remember that Mario and Kelly were going to start a restaurant? Well, they did and it seems that they are doing quite well. The reservations only and the no choice menu seems to be working out pretty good. The name of the restaurant is "Home Port."

Jacky said, "Bill, you know the rules, you're going to have to call for a reservation."

Bill called and Mario answered. Bill said, "Hi, Mario, this is Bill Turner, Jacky and I would like to come for dinner, what's on the menu?"

"Well, Bill, what would you like?"

"Bill, we haven't started cooking yet, so what would you and Jacky like?"

"Well, Mario, Jacky said that she has a hell of a taste for Kelly's Rueben sandwiches."

Chapter 36

Visit Cathedral and Daley's Office

"Hey Mario, you have me confused. I understood that you and Kelly decided on the menu, and the customer just got whatever you cooked."

"That's true, Bill, and tonight they are getting Kelly's Reubens and matzoth ball soup."

"Mario, I also understood that some of the people that called in asked what the menu was. What was the menu?"

"It was Yankee pot roast, cornbread and Mario's New England clam chowder."

"What happens when a customer shows up and the menu is different?"

"It's happened a few times before. When people call to make a reservation, I ask them to leave their phone number in case there happens to be a change. I call and tell them. If they get huffy, I recommend another restaurant. I tell them that we have plenty of agreeable customers and we don't need any hard asses. This same guy called back half an hour later and apologized profusely, then he and his wife came to dinner. As a matter of fact, he will be here tonight. His name is William Lublin. Mr. Lublin is a Judge in the Cook County Appellate Court and as it turns out, he is a pretty nice guy. I will have to give him a call along with some other people."

"You really don't have to do this, Mario."

"Kelly would kick my ass if I didn't. See you tonight at 7:00 pm, Bill, I've got to get busy."

Mario told Kelly that Bill called and that Jacky had a taste for Kelly's Reubens and Matzo ball soup. "You're right, Mario, I would have kicked your ass, but with a pair of fluffy slippers on. Thanks Mario, for your consideration. But now, Mario, you're going to have to explain to the customers of the change in the menu."

"Of the 22 reservations, only nine asked what the menu was, but I know how to make them all happy."

"How are you going to do that?"

"I'll just mention who had a hell of a taste for a Reuben and that I would introduce them to Jacky.

All the customers agreed to the change in the menu. Mario had asked Bill if Jacky would object. Jacky just said, "Anything for a Reuben."

When Bill and Jacky got to the restaurant at 7:00 pm, most of the tables were occupied. After they sat down and cocktails were served, Mario brought some of the guests over to Bill and Jacky's table and introduced them. Mario then brought a couple over with the man pushing a wheelchair. In the wheelchair was a teen-aged girl. Her folks said that she was a high school senior and that she was in an auto accident. Her right leg was in a cast and her left leg and right arm were bandaged. The mother said that since the accident she refuses to be seen out of the house. She even refuses to go to school and we home tutor her, but when she heard that Jacky Sax was going to be at the restaurant, we couldn't hold her back. She loves to sing and has done so in school shows, but she hasn't sung a note since the accident.

Jacky asked the girl her name. She said, "Patti."

Jacky said, "I'll just bet God sent you here tonight to sing. Just last week I sang with Patti Page at the Drake Hotel. Patti told me that I would probably do this again. I think tonight's the night. How would you like to sing with me?"

"Sounds great."

Then Jacky said, "I think we could make it a trio." Jacky called Mario over and she asked him something.

Mario then addressed the customers. He said, "Are you folks so hungry that you would rather have food right now or listen to some good singing by Jacky, Patti and my head cook, Kelly."

They all cheered and said, "Singing, the food can wait."

Kelly came out of the kitchen, took off her apron, walked over to Bill, gave him a kiss and a big hug for Jacky. She said, "Okay, Jacky, what do we sing?"

"Well, we have Patti here, so why not start with *Tennessee Waltz*." Patti started to say something when Kelly said, "We will start and when you get ready, just start in singing." It worked out great, Patti was pretty good and was having a ball. The customers loved it and kept asking for one more song, which they did.

Mario finally said "Singing's over and soups on. All this singing has got the kitchen in a little stall, so it will take a short time to get things going again."

Just then three women got up and said, "Mario, help has arrived, you have three new waitresses here."

"Great, let's get the food out." The three women started serving the Matzo ball soup. Then they went back in the kitchen and helped Kelly assemble the Reubens and served them. Everyone sat down and ate.

After everyone ate, people wandered over to Bill and Jacky's table and told them how much they enjoyed the singing and some asked for autographs. Then Patti's mother came over and said that Patti has now decided to go to school. She can't wait to tell her friends about singing with Jacky and Kelly. She wants to show them the Polaroid pictures that Mario took of the trio.

Their dinner of Matzo ball soup and Reuben sandwiches were great. All the customers raved about Kelly's Reubens. After dinner, Bill and Jacky sat down with Mario and Kelly. Mario found some nice scotch for himself and Bill and an after dinner drinks for Jacky and Kelly. Kelly asked Jacky when the wedding was. Kelly had already sent a message about not doing a double wedding. She said that she and Mario are planning to get married, but not at this time.

Mario then said that they were spending too much time in the restaurant. Kelly said that they considered hiring enough help so they can take the time for a nice honeymoon. Mario said that it would take time to train someone reliable enough to leave for a week or two.

Jacky said, "That could take a long time."

Kelly said, "We have come up with a solution. We have talked with some of our good customers and they agree that we should just close down for a couple of weeks."

"That's what we will do, but we will definitely be at your wedding. As soon as you let us know when, we will put up a sign. "Closed for Bill and Jacky's Wedding."

After a couple more drinks, Bill and Jacky went home. They stayed in Bill's small but comfortable apartment. Jacky asked Bill if he would mind them sleeping in separate beds until after the wedding. Bill said, "If that's what you want, but I'll be damned horny by the time of the wedding."

"I will be horny too, but it was my mother's wish. We lived in London at the start of the war. There were a lot of soldiers and sailors roaming London looking for girls on the loose. She made me promise that I would wait till I got married. I'm probably the oldest 26 year old virgin you have ever met."

"Jacky, you are perfect in every way and I'm sure your mother was right. You said your mother died in a bombing raid? I would think that she died happy knowing her daughter followed her wishes. It will be worth the wait, Jacky." They kissed and said that they loved each other, went to bed with a smile on their faces.

Next morning, they got up and ate a good breakfast. Jacky made grits, eggs and pork sausage. After breakfast Bill said, "I contacted Doc, or Admiral Robert Hunter, in Washington and asked him if he could break loose from his job in Washington for a few days to be my best man at the wedding."

Doc said, "I would be more than honored to be in the wedding at that capacity, although I think Jacky knows who the best man is. He said to let him know the date and he would be there with bells on."

Bill had talked to Jimbo Scott many times since Jacky decided to sell out to Jimbo. He asked Jimbo if he would be a groomsman. "I would be honored, Bill." Then there would also be Mario, Eric, Arch and Peter.

Bill asked Jacky if she had organized her bridal party. "Well, I have talked to Art Hobson and he has agreed to give the bride away and his wife, Linda, would like to be a bridesmaid. Sandra, who is making records in Nashville, will come in to be a bridesmaid and Kelly will be maid of honor. The final two bridesmaids will be Crystall Quinn and her daughter, Heather."

"Then there is Charlie, the pilot, and his wife. He will pick up Crystall and Heather in Thousand Islands and fly to Beaver Island, pick up Art and Linda and fly to Chicago anchor the plane right off the Chicago Yacht Club, then head to reserved rooms at the Palmer House. There will be many Chicago dignitaries, such as the Police Commissioner, the Fire Commissioner, the Chief of Police, the Mayor and many others. The Holy Name Cathedral seats two thousand."

"Jacky, how are we going to organize all these celebrities, bands and caterers for the reception?"

"Not to worry, Bill, Richard J. has his people handling everything."

"What about your gown?"

"Paula said that she will be here with the gown on the 13th at Midway airport."

"Tell her to call when she is finished or knows exactly when she will finish. I will rent a plane at Midway. I have a friend who has a flying service. He has some nice surplus military planes on hand. They cruise at over two fifty, so I could make a round trip in about four hours."

Jacky said, "Okay, I will tell her that she is to be piloted by an RAF Reserve General, just to make sure that she knows you are a qualified pilot."

"Thanks, old buddy."

"By the way, Bill, have you looked into getting a tuxedo?"

"No" Bill said.

"It's only about ten days to the fifteenth and I am told that you are an important part of this wedding."

"Well, Jacky, I have talked to Doc and he is a three star Admiral on active duty, Art is a Brigadier General in the British Commandos. They both said that they were going to wear their first class dress uniforms and they told me that since I'm a Reserve General in the RAF, I should wear my dress uniform."

"Good thing that I was only a Sergeant or I'd be wearing a uniform too."

"Never in a million years, Jacky, you are going to look beautiful in your wedding gown."

"One thing for sure, it's going to be one hell of a brass wedding. You and Art are Generals, Doc's an Admiral, about four officers from the Chicago Police and two officers from the Fire Department. Daley just informed me that representatives for the Army, Navy, Marines and the Coast Guard wish to attend. They are all Admirals or Generals. Daley told them Okay. Like I told you, Bill, one big brass wedding. You look pretty sharp in your uniform."

Jacky called Hannibal and talked to Jimbo. She told him that the wedding would be on the 15th of November at 1:00 pm. Jimbo said, "Jacky, unless it's snowing, I'll ride your Vincent Black Lightning up to Chicago for you."

"Sounds good to me, send your tux by UPS and I'll have it all pressed and ready for you."

"I'll have your Lightning all tuned up for you, see you on the 15th."

Richard J. called and talked to Bill. Daley told Bill that everything is on schedule, even the weather man is agreeable. He said it will be a sunny day and warm for November.

Daley said, "Even with a seating capacity of two thousand the church will be full. It seems that everyone thinks they are important enough to qualify for a seat in the church. I have had to tell some self-important people that they didn't qualify. I can honestly say that I almost had fun doing it. The best part was telling them that there was seating for two thousand people and yet, they didn't qualify. The reception should be able to handle about three thousand."

Bill said, "I would hate to have to pay for this wedding."

Daley said, "Not to feel bad about someone else paying for this wedding, with all the things that you, Jacky and your other people have done. They know that they owe it to you."

"We have six days before the wedding, the days seem to be going pretty slow. Let's go downstairs to the shop and see what's happening." They got down to the shop and Benny came over to them and said, "Boss, there are six crates out on the loading dock."

"Benny, I ain't the boss anymore, Jacky here is the new boss."

"Nah, you're kidding ain't you, Bill?"

"Yeah, I am, but Jacky and I are partners. Jacky is going to run the foreign bike side of this business."

They went back to the inside loading dock. One of Benny's helpers had opened up three of the six crates. There was a Vincent Black Shadow, a 1000cc 140 mph bike. Next came another Vincent, a 500cc single cylinder. Then there were two Triumphs, a 655cc Thunderbird and a 500cc Triumph Trophy. There was one case from Norton. When they opened it up, they saw it was the 850cc Commando. Bill said that it looks like they couldn't think of a name, so they named it after you. They finally got to the sixth case. It looked like it came from Italy. Bill said, "He did not remember talking to anybody from Italy."

Jacky said, "She hadn't either." When it was opened, they found that it contained a bright red single cylinder motorcycle. The unusual thing about it was that the single cylinder laid down horizontally, but even stranger yet was the outside flywheel. The fly wheel was polished and plated so that it did not snag on pants or shoes. It was a Moto Guzzi. Jacky asked, "Why the outside flywheel?"

"The reason," Benny said, "Is that this machine is built for road racing. A 500cc machine that does in excess of 120 mph. With the outside flywheel, the cases can be made smaller and stronger, strong enough to withstand a fourteen to one compression ratio and still hold together."

Bill said, "Well, that's enough talk about engines, you understand engines, but most people don't. Let's just park all these bikes on your side and forget about them for a while."

"Well, Bill, we have the whole afternoon left so what should we do?"

"Well, one thing we should do is go to the church and talk to the priest that is going to marry us. It's a good thing we are both Catholic, it will make the priest happy and save one of us a lot of studying."

After arriving at the church, they were directed to the priest's office and introduced to Father O'Malley. He greeted them warmly and said something unexpected. He said, "Miss Sax, may I have your autograph?" He handed her two nine by twelve pictures of herself that were taken in Ireland after the release of the girls. He said, "It was a request of his twin nieces who are great fans of hers and want to be like her.

Dick Daley came to see me and he said that he is organizing this wedding. May I say that you couldn't have a better organizer.

He said, "You will sing *Ave Maria* after the ceremony and then *Amazing Grace* with your two friends."

Jacky said, "Father, I would prefer to sing *Ave Maria* before the ceremony and *Amazing Grace* at the reception."

"I agree with you, Miss Sax, besides it's your wedding, we will do it your way."

Then Father O'Malley said, "Now let me show you this lovely church. I'll give you the twenty five cent tour." The three of them walked out of his office and into the church itself. It was huge. It seemed that the rows of pews were unending. When O'Malley saw that they were counting the benches or pews.

He said, "She seats a little over two thousand people. It's a big church, but from what I hear, it will be standing room only. The Fire Commissioner will be a guest, so it will be up to him when people should stop coming in. I never have officiated at a wedding this size and this popular. Some shindig!"

O'Malley said, "Look up and you will see a ceiling that is one hundred and fifty feet high."

Bill said, "I would never volunteer to paint it."

"Well, it hasn't been painted in a long time, are you sure about not volunteering?"

"I'm sure."

"We have two organs in the church. The large one has seventy one stops, whatever that means, I'm not sure the salesman who sold it knows."

Jacky said, "I could tell you what it means, but then you wouldn't be able to use that line anymore."

Bill asks, "Do you really know?"

"No, but that's my line."

"The second organ has nineteen stops and I won't say any more about organs other than the big one was made in the Netherlands and the small one in Canada. Now let's go outside, that is, if Bill will help me open these big bronze doors. They weigh twelve hundred pounds each." Bill and O'Malley pushed on the doors, they moved fairly easy.

On the outside, the church looked like a Cathedral. Bill and Jacky were looking at the front and the sides, O'Malley said, "Two hundred and thirty three feet long and one hundred and twenty six feet wide." Next they looked up and he said, "That spire is two hundred and ten feet high. "The original church was smaller, it was destroyed by fire in 1871. A new church, this one, was built and dedicated in 1875. This is a Catholic Church. It's at 735 N. State St. and there is a bullet hole in the corner stone, put there in 1926 when Capone's men killed Hymie Wiess. That's the twenty five cent tour. Thank you for your kind attention. You know, I'm getting pretty good at this. I'm going to start collecting the twenty five cents."

"Bill said, I guess we will be seeing you on the fifteenth."

"No Bill we will see each other before that. There will be a rehearsal a few days before the wedding."

"It's more complicated than I thought."

Jacky and Bill both thanked Father O'Malley and then said, "I guess we had better check with Richard J. Daley. He seems to know what's happening and we should just follow his schedule."

"Well Jacky, let's go over to Daley's office, he said that he would be in all afternoon." When Jacky and Bill walked into Daley's outer office, the secretary, Ellen, immediately recognized both of them.

She said, "We have been waiting for you, all the office staff have been dying to meet the two of you. Mr. Daley has had us busy organizing your fantastic wedding. It's amazing how many famous people have already been invited, so far there are fifteen hundred. There is room for five hundred more and about one thousand more have asked."

"If someone asks personally and is a nice person, push him through. If the request is made by his secretary, forget him. Are you three girls going? It's going to be a hell of a shindig."

"I don't think we could."

"Why not?"

"We couldn't ask Mr. Daley if we could go."

"Well, I'll ask him." Jacky opens the door to his office and said, "Dick, could you come out here for a few minutes?"

"Okay, Jacky, be right there." When he came out, she pointed to the lists of names and different kinds of people that were on the girl's desks. She said, "Dick, that's a lot of work they have been doing to organize this little party. After all their hard work, I think they should be invited."

"Jacky, do you really think I would forget my hard working staff? If you gals would look back into your lists, at about thirteen hundred, you will find your names plus your husbands."

"Jacky then said, "I think maybe I misjudged the Clerk of Cook County. So, in appreciation of all the hard work, you girls are doing, I'm going to kick in five hundred dollars for each of you to buy a gown to wear at this party."

"No need to do that Jacky."

"Why not?"

"Because I have, the County that is, has already appropriated a six hundred dollar bonus for each of them. I just figured that I couldn't have my secretaries going in rags. One of you girls write out an expense chit for the rental of tuxedos for your husbands. I'll sign it. Jacky, do you think we have that settled?"

"Looks like it is."

"Come on Bill and Jacky, let's go into my office before these three gals convince you that they need a raise in pay. It seems that everyone that you and your people have helped want to be at your wedding. There are even two Germans who were in the German Army. One was Lieutenant Joseph Richter and his friend Sergeant Hans Retzer."

They said to me, "We were in a platoon of German soldiers ordered to find the pilot of a crashed spitfire. It was a wooded area, we had troops spread out sweeping the woods. We heard a beautiful song ringing through the woods. Eight of us headed to where we thought it was, in a shallow ravine. All of the sudden there were eight of us on the ground. There were only two of us alive. Hans and I were hit and bleeding quite a bit. We knew that we could not survive unless the bleeding was stopped and we had fairly quick treatment. Then there was that beautiful singing voice now speaking to us in German."

"She told us to be quiet, I thought she would cut our throats, instead she took her first aid kit and patched me up as good as she could. Then she got another kit from one of her soldiers and fixed up Hans. Then she said, "We would be all right if we got aid soon enough. We thought that she was an angel, she sang like one. Next, she did something totally unbelievable. She gave me one of her emergency flares."

"This is so your people can find you before you bleed to death. I could have killed you, but I didn't, so now I expect you to honor my wish and not fire that flare for fifteen minutes, which is enough time for me to get my troops to the pickup point."

"She asked if I had a watch, I said no it was smashed by a bullet." She gave me her watch and said, "Remember, fifteen minutes."

"I told her I would abide by her wishes, but I did not wait the fifteen minutes. Hans and I both agreed that the fifteen minutes might not be enough for them to get to the channel, we waited 30 minutes. We found out later that this angel had made it. I know this because the watch that she had given me had an inscription of the back that said To Jacky from (?), a name I could not make out but Jacky was clear. Now I would like to return her watch."

Jacky said, "I'd really love to get that watch back. It has sentimental value, also I would like to say hello to my former enemy."

"There are many more that I would like to see. The reasons can be explained later at the reception. There is Ed Foley and his wife, Linda, Ken Jamieson and Dave Steel. Dave Steele's uncle, Robert Johnson. These people have done good in many ways."

"There are probably many celebrities and dignitaries that you know about, so just use your own judgment . Meanwhile I think we should go back home and get ready for this wedding. Bill, what do you think?'

"I think you are the most amazing woman I've ever met . I take that back, the most amazing person I've ever met. You are beautiful, smart, the most capable and on top of that, sexy as hell and in three days you will be my wife. Let's go home, Jacky."

When they got back to the bike shop, the UPS truck was there. The driver handed Jacky a box. The shipping ticket said that it was from Hannibal. It was Jimbo's tuxedo. She said, "I will drop it off at the cleaners to have it pressed. Bill, are going to fly down to Hannibal to get Paula and my wedding gown tomorrow morning?"

"Jacky, I talked to Jimbo yesterday and wanted to pick him up too." He said that he was just getting ready to leave on your Black Lightning.

"When are you going to leave for Hannibal?"

Bill said, "I talked to Paula this morning and she said that she could be at the airport at 1:30 p.m." Bill told Jacky, "He would be at the field at 1:45, pick up Paula and be back in the air, on the way to Midway by 2:00 pm., land at Midway at 3:45 pm, check the plane in and be back to the bike shop by 4:30 pm."

"There is a rehearsal tomorrow night at 7:00 pm, so it looks like you will have plenty of time." Bill got up at 8:00 am. He and Jacky had a leisurely breakfast, then went down to the bike shop and talked to Benny.

He told them that two more bikes came in from England they were Indian Warriors, something he had never seen before. They went over to the new shop to take a look. There were eight brand new bikes on the floor.

Bill said that it was a good thing that the windows were painted over, otherwise we would have to spend all our time explaining these new bikes."

Benny stuck his head in the door and said, "You've got a phone call, Jacky." Jacky went over to the wall phone, picked it up and said, "Hi."

"Hi, Jacky, it's Sandy and I'm at Mario and Kelly's. Kelly said that we should get together tonight at their restaurant."

"What time?"

"Eight pm at the Homeport."

"Okay, Sandy, as far as I know we will be there, if not, I'll call." Jacky told Bill and he agreed.

When they arrived at the Homeport, they found a sign on the door. It said, "Closed For Business This Week Only Thursday through Sunday".

Bill rang the bell. Kelly opened the door and said, "Hi, guys. The gang's all here."

After walking into the dining room, it was not hard to see what she meant. Art, Linda, Charlie, Beverly, Crystall, Heather, Sandra and Doc, even Dick Daley land his wife. Daley said, "That he had told his wife so much about Mario's cooking that he knew this would be a real treat for her." They all decided that this would be a rehearsal dinner.

After one of Mario's great dinners and some desert, they just sat back and talked. Art said that they brought a barge with a crane on it to Beaver Island. The Lignumvitae Logs are being picked up and sent to a processor.

Linda and her uncle each get ten percent of the sale. We won't get rich, but it sure helps the budget.

Bill asked Doc what the Cora Lee was doing right now. Doc said that right now he is not sure, Angel hired on three of his friends and they are on a charter to the Mediterranean. Right now they are probably in the Mid-Atlantic and will spend all winter cruising the Med.

Daley said, "Jacky, you went through a bunch of bridal gowns and turned them all down. The Parisians went back to France mad as hell. They insisted on taking their gowns back home with them. Dan, the manager at the Drake, told them no, that all gowns stay at the Drake to be auctioned off for charity. Dan said that it didn't make much difference, the French gowns went pretty cheap."

Daley then asked Jacky how her Hannibal made gown came out. "Don't know yet, Dick. Bill is flying to Hannibal tomorrow to pick it up."

"That will only give you one day for fitting and alterations."

"Won't need any, Dick. Paula is good."

Mrs. Daley said, "I've been to a lot of weddings and I've never heard of a bride having her gown delivered the day before the wedding and not having any alterations."

Jacky said, "Mrs. Daley, tell your friends to have their gowns made by an artist like Paula and they won't have a problem."

Kelly said, "Jacky, I have been to a lot of my friend's weddings and I have never seen anyone as calm as you are two days before."

"Kelly, tomorrow we have a rehearsal, nobody is getting dressed for a wedding. I don't know why we need to rehearse. I think once is enough. So why even do it?"

Bill said that he thinks it is just to satisfy the priest."

Jacky said, "Bill, I guess we are going to do it anyway."

Doc asked Bill where they were going on their honeymoon. Bill said, "Doc you wouldn't believe how many places we have been offered, gratis, plus transportation, yachts, planes and motor homes. So, Doc, we have no idea where we are going. We may just get on a couple of motorcycles and take off a long ride. I could do without the rehearsal and Jacky feels the same way, but it's expected and we only have to do it once.

The one on Saturday, "Now that's for real. Jacky is looking forward to that." "All women do, Bill, also you had better not be late with her wedding gown." "No problem, Doc, I'll make it back with time to spare."

Sandra said, "All the bridesmaids are here. She counted them off, Crystall, Heather, Linda, Kelly and me. Now for the groomsmen we have Arch, Eric and Mario. Peter called and said he would be here in the morning. Everyone should be at the church by 5:00 pm for a 7:00 pm rehearsal." Kelly told Sandra that she had missed one groomsman.

Sandra, "Then asked Jacky if she had heard from Jimbo."

Jacky said, "That she hadn't heard from him but his tux is here at the cleaners getting pressed."

Mario said, "Okay all you people let's go home. Tomorrow is another day. I've got to clean up this mess that you people have made."

Eric said, "Mario, set your ass down. Everybody pitch will in and we will have everything cleaned up in no time." They did and then went home.

Next morning after a leisurely breakfast, Bill headed for Midway Airport. He stopped at the cleaners and picked up Jimbo's tux, so that he didn't forget it on the way back home. He got to Midway at about eleven thirty. His buddy, Lou, had the B-26 all gassed up and ready to go. Bill had made a deal with Lou to use it for this flight. He had already filed a flight plan and was ready to go. He made his preflight checks and asked and received clearance from the tower to taxi.

The airfield was not busy and this time, so he taxied to a takeoff position. He got clearance to take off and was on his way to Hannibal. At about 1:40, Bill landed at Quincy Airport which was about fifteen miles from Paula's house. Paula was waiting in the office of the private section of the airport. Bill taxied to the ramp up next to the office. He shut the engines down and locked the parking break. He got out of the plane and went into the office. Bill knew Paula immediately from Jacky's description. Five feet one inch and silver blue hair and she had a big cardboard box in front of her which must have been the gown.

Bill said, "Hi, Paula. Is that the gown?"

"Sure is and be careful with it."

"Okay let's get this show on the road."

She said, "You know my name, but I don't know yours."

"I'm Bill and Jacky is my bride to be."

"Oh, great, Jacky didn't tell me that you were coming. I just thought that she was sending a charter pilot."

"Well, Paula, I guess I will just have to tell you, I'm not a charter pilot."

"Well, Bill, let's get moving. Jacky's waiting for her gown."

"Okay, Paula, I'll carry your box and let's get on the plane."

"What kind of plane did bring, Bill?"

"A twin engine Douglas B-26."

"Nice plane, Bill."

"Have you ever flown, Paula?"

"Used to, but not since my husband died. He was a charter pilot."

Bill put the box in the storage compartment and they climbed aboard. He fired her up and they were on their way to Chicago. While they were cruising along, Bill asked Paula if she thought the gown would fit Jacky.

She said, "Not a problem, Bill, I've made dresses and gowns for Jacky before and she told me she hadn't gained or lost a pound. I make them to fit the first time. Most Bridal Salons make them with alterations in mind. There is lot of money in the rework and some salons make these brides pay up front for what they claim are most probable alterations."

"Jacky has a lot of confidence in you, she thinks that you are the best."

She said, "She has enough faith in your designs and workmanship that she just told you to do your thing."

Paula then said, "I think that Jacky's judgment is pretty good, but I can't understand why anyone would take what looks like a fully armed Bomber to come and pick up a wedding gown."

"Well, we also had to pick up an important dress designer named, Paula, so this ship is fully armed in case of bridal gown pirates. Actually, my buddy, Lou, who owns this machine, asked me to fly it up from Texas. He intends to preserve it just as it was set for battle. He has some friends that are starting a war museum in Ohio. I went down to Texas while Jacky was at the Drake. I told Lou that I would do it if I could use it for one short trip. This little war buggy can handle two tons of bombs and has a total of ten fifty caliber machine guns and they happen to be fully loaded. I would fire one of them to show you, but the slug may drop on someone's head."

Paula said, "I'll take your word for it." They landed at Midway and taxied up to Lou's office.

"You know something, Paula, you are probable the last civilian to ride in a fully armed B-26"

After exiting the plane, Bill turned in the log book to Lou. Lou asked, "How was the trip?"

Paula answered the question with, "Great, but the starboard engine is slightly out of sync."

"It's what?"

"She's pulling your leg, Lou. She runs beautiful." They loaded the box in Bill's Lincoln and headed home.

When they got to the bike shop, Jacky had coffee and Danish waiting for them. After all the greetings and a couple of cups of coffee, Paula said, "Well, Jacky, before I forget it, I just want to tell you that I brought something for you. It's in the box that Bill laid on the dining room floor." Bill lifted the box up on the dining table.

Bill started to open the box and Paula said, "Back off, Bill, you might be a General in the RAF, but today and tomorrow you've got to follow the rules. Go downstairs and play with your bikes until we tell you that you can come up."

He said, "Your wish is my command."

Bill went downstairs to the bike shop. The two women went over to the table and Jacky started to open the box, but then she backed off, saying, "Paula, you open it, I'm just starting to get too nervous. I think I'm starting to feel like a bride."

"Well, Jacky, it's about time. Your friend Kelly called me in Hannibal, I talked to her and your friend Sandra and they were both worried about you. They said that even within a few days of the wedding, you didn't show any sign of being the least bit nervous, which would be typical of any bride at even a week or two before the wedding. It looks like you finally made it, welcome to the club."

"Now, let's open the box." Paula opened it. It had tissue paper over the gown. When Jacky lifted the tissue, what she saw was a beautiful bright white. It was snow white satin, over-laid with fine gossamer Irish Lace, threaded with gold.

"Paula you're a genius, it's beautiful."

"Well, Jacky, it's like they say, you ain't seen nothing yet." Paula lifted the gown out and laid it on a bed. Then she opened another section of the box. In that section was the Tiara. It was beautifully hand sewn and crocheted with white, silver and gold and trimmed beautifully with pearlescent beads. Attached to the tiara was a blusher veil down to the shoulders. Attached underneath was a 15 foot veil trimmed with Irish Lace threaded with gold.

"Paula, it's absolutely beautiful. You are a genius. You know that eight of the top bridal salons showed their gowns at the Drake Hotel here in Chicago, six of them from Chicago and New York and two from Paris. I turned them all down in favor of one of your gowns sight unseen. I was right. Also, most of them had rip off prices. They have all been auctioned off. Some of the salons that had the highest prices, went for the lowest prices in the auction.

"Speaking of money, Jacky, you told me to do my thing and not to worry about money. I wanted to do it right. I used the best of materials."

"I can see that, you sure did."

"Everything was first class."

"I can see that too. So what are you trying to tell me?"

"I'm trying to justify a price of $1,600.00."

"Would you mind if I dicker price with you?"

"No problem, Jacky. What kind of price did you have in mind?"

"How about $4,800.00 and that's firm."

"I can't accept that Jacky."

"Yes you can, you beat out some of the best who had much higher pieces than

that."

"Okay, if you insist, but let's try it on and see if it fits."

"One other thing I have to tell you, but you have to keep it quiet. Princess Elizabeth has had gowns made by Pierre of Paris and George Girard of Paris and when she heard that I turned them down in favor of a gown made in Hannibal, Missouri, she said that she had to get invited to the wedding, mostly to see your gown. So, you wouldn't want it to be known that I paid only $1,600.00 for this beautiful gown, especially when a Princess wants to come and see it. You are now top dog, Paula."

They went into the bedroom where the gown lay on the bed. Jacky slipped off her outer garments. Then with Paula's help, she put on the gown. It fit like a glove. No alterations. She put on the Tiara. It was a perfect fit also. Jacky looked in the mirror and almost started to cry.

Paula said, "No tears, Jacky, until you get out of the gown."

She took off the gown and Tiara and put them back in the box. Then she hugged Paula and said, "You really are a wonderful genius. Now with it back in the box, Bill can come back upstairs." Jacky called Bill on the intercom and he was upstairs in a flash.

He asked if it fit. Both Jacky and Paula said, "Perfectly."

"How does it look?"

Paula said, "Bill, it is the most beautiful gown I have ever made and it was made for the most wonderful person I've ever known. Bill, you are marrying an Angel."

Bill said, "That's no big secret, Paula, believe it or not, all these people who are over-flowing the cathedral and from what I've been told, will be lined up outside of the church, these people will not have come to see just a wedding, they want to see Jacky in person."

Bill, Jacky and Paula did nothing important for the rest of the day until it was time to go to the church for the rehearsal. It was a little after five when they arrived at the church. Bill and Jacky didn't think the rehearsal was a necessary thing to do, but they followed protocol and did the rehearsal. Everyone was there who was in the wedding party except Jimbo. Paula said that she had talked to him a few days ago. He said that he might be running a little late, but he would be on time for the wedding. Jacky said, "If Jimbo said that he would be on time for the wedding, he will be on time."

The rehearsal went smoothly and Jacky said that, no she would not sing at the rehearsal. They all met at a Dixieland bar on N. Rush St. Sandra said that she and Kelly used to sing at this place a couple years ago. The place has probably changed and no one would remember them now. But, remember them they did. It was the same band and the same owner and bartender. After the bartender greeted them, the owner came over and told the waitress to treat these people good. Sandy and Kelly are good friends. The waitress, Lilly, told Jim, the owner, that she remembered Kelly and Sandra, not Sandy. I also recognize the famous Jacky Sax.

Bill said, "Okay keep it quiet."

Jim introduced them as Sandy and Kelly's good friends from England. They sang the Tennessee Waltz and a few other songs.

Someone finally said, "That's Jacky Sax."

Chapter 37

Wedding Reception, Greetings from German Soldiers

People started coming forward. Jacky and the rest of their group got up and headed for the door. Sandra looked straight at the man and said, "Thanks, Big Mouth, enjoy the silence." They all headed back home or to their hotel and agreed to meet at the church at 11:00 A.M. The ceremony is to be held at 1:00 P.M.

At 11:00 A.M., everyone in the wedding party was at the church except the Bride, but she was not expected until 1:00 P.M. Jimbo was the only one who was missing that should have been at the church. Everyone wondered where he was. He was supposed to arrive yesterday afternoon.

Jimbo left Hannibal at 9:00 A.M. on Friday. It was about three hundred miles to Chicago. Jimbo planned on a leisurely five to six hour ride. He took Rt. 36 to Springfield and Rt. 72 to Decatur. Then stopped in Decatur at around noon with approximately one hundred and fifty miles to go. If he left Decatur at about 1:00 P.M., he would be at his destination by 3:30 or 4:00. No problem. That's what he thought. At 1:00 he looked out of the restaurant window. This was November 14, it looked like Christmas. It was snowing pretty wet and heavy. If he had his own 74 Harley, he would keep on riding, but he was riding Jacky's immaculate Black Lightning and he did not want to chance a spill with her perfectly clean bike. He talked to one of the local police officer. He said the snow would be ending in the morning. At what time he did not know.

Jimbo decided to get a room, leave a wakeup call for 7:00 A.M. have breakfast and if the snow was letting up, he would leave by 9:00 A.M. It was 7:30 and he talked to a truck driver who told him that there was no snow in Urbana. Jimbo decided that he had better move on as the snow was moving in the same direction that he was going, best to get on the bike and ride out the snow. One big advantage was there were very few cars on the road.

He started to pull out of the restaurant parking lot. Jimbo looked up the road and here comes a real neat 34 Ford Coupe, neat paint job, 41 Ford wheels, the whole bit, but the kid driving it was having a little too much fun doing spins in the snow. He lost control, went sliding right for Jimbo. Jimbo pushed the bike backward about two feet. It slid by missing Jacky's bike by six inches. It then slammed broadside into a telephone pole, so much for a nice neat 34 Ford coupe. The sad kid got out and walked around to see the damage.

Jimbo then took off into the snow. The Vincent handled real good, but he didn't dare ride at over forty mph until the snow lightened up. The snow stopped as he got close to Urbana. It was about 9A.M.. He had 135 miles to go and the last 30 miles was through city traffic on a busy Saturday morning.

He should be at the church no later than 11:30. He has to take a shower and change into his tuxedo. The priest, knowing the situation, said that he could shower, shave and change clothes in his apartment in the back of the church. Jimbo had called Jacky and asked her to bring his tuxedo to the church, which she did the night of the rehearsal.

When he got on Rt.57, a straight shot North to Chicago, he realized that he did not have a lot of time to spare, so he kicked it up to 100 mph. He was cruising along pretty smooth and making good time. Jimbo got to the Kankakee bypass when he hit a snag. A State Cop was parked on the side of the road giving someone a ticket.

He passed at 100 mph and said to himself, "Oh, Shit". He decided that he had no choice and cranked on the throttle. It settled out at 145 mph and he left the cop in the dust. It was 30 miles to Rt. 80. He crossed Rt. 80 in 12 minutes, in another 5 minutes, he was within a couple of miles of the Dan Ryan Expressway, which headed straight north to downtown Chicago and the Holy Name Cathedral. Jimbo was only 12 to 13 miles from his final destination.

This is where he came to a screeching halt. State police and Cook County police were blockading the road. They let the cars through, but were waiting for Jimbo at 103rd and the expressway. Jimbo pulled up to the line of cars. The State Police and the Cook County Sheriffs Police were at the scene. The Sheriffs Police showed up when they heard on their radio that State couldn't catch some guy who was heading to Chicago at 150 mph. They had to see this.

They now had Jimbo stopped. The first officer, a Lieutenant, walked up to Jimbo. "You were doing 150 mph."

Jimbo said, "145, sir."

"Don't be a smart ass, we have been chasing you for 70 miles. Now, where were you going that you had to be doing 150 mph?" "I was going to a church, sir and it's getting late." The Lieutenant says, "Bullshit, it will be much later when you get your ass out of jail." "Sir, I've got to go. I'm the head groomsman at a wedding."

The Lieutenant started to spout off another wise remark when a captain came over and said, "Back off Lieutenant or I'll have your ass.

He said, "Son, I've got a couple of questions. Number one, what church and number two, what kind of bike is that?"

Jimbo said, "First, it's the Holy Name Cathedral and second, this is a Vincent Black Lightning and it belongs to Jacky Sax."

"What's your name, Son?"

"Jimbo Scott."

"Okay, Jimbo, you said that you had to be at the Cathedral by 11:30. We have a lot of traffic right now, but we will get you there by 11:30 – 11:45."

"That will be good Captain."

"One thing, Jimbo, tell Jacky that Captain Tom Atkins said hello. I was a Lieutenant the last time I saw her and I watched her kick the shit out of three muscle bound rapists while I was handcuff to a tree. I would love to go to that wedding."

"Get me to the church on time and I'll get you and your wife into the church and the reception. Jacky told me about you and she would like to see you again."

Captain Tom told Jimbo to follow him and he would get him to the church on time, just like in the play "My Fair Lady". The Captain called in to Headquarters and ordered a series of Chicago squad cars to block off streets all the way to the Holy Name Cathedral. As soon as they heard the name of the church, everyone knew that was important. They flew through the city at 80 mph, not stopping at any lights. Word got to the church that Jimbo was on his way and that Jimbo requested some seating for two people, Captain Tom Atkin of the Sheriff's Police and his wife.

"Daley heard about the request, and said make it happen."

Then Daley called Jacky, who was home getting dressed for the event. He told her about Jimbo and Captain Tom Atkin. She said, "Great, I would really like to see him again."

Jacky was now starting to get a little nervous. She had put on her gown and taken it off twice. She was going to try it on again when Paula stopped her by saying, "It fits, Jacky and you look beautiful. You are going to wear it out just trying it on. Let's just sit down and have a glass of wine. We have a whole hour before the limo picks us up." After two glasses of wine, they both fell asleep.

When they woke up, it was 12:15. "Okay, Jacky, we have 15 minutes to get ready. I think that with all the practice putting the gown on and taking it off, it should be no problem."

At 12:30, they were both ready and the limo arrived. "This is it, Jacky, are you nervous now?"

"Not anymore, Paula, I am now terrified." Paula carried Jacky's tiara and veil, which was carefully rolled. It was 15 feet long.

When they got to the cathedral, it was about 1:00 pm. There were at least 500 people standing outside, waiting to get a glimpse of Jacky. The big white stretch limo worked its way through the crowd and parked in front of the church. General Arthur Hobson stood at the rear door of the limo. Resplendent in his dress uniform and a chest full of medals, he stood at attention as the driver opened the rear door of the limo.

Inside the church was an amazing sight, Army, Navy, Marine, Air Force and Coast Guard officers in their dress uniforms. Then there were the Chicago, Illinois State and the Cook County Top Officers, also in their dress uniforms. They all brought their wives with them, also dressed in their best finery. Many of the women wore large hats which the ushers told them to remove and put in their lap. They did not like this until they were informed that it was Jacky's suggestion.

Jimbo Scott had arrived on time. Captain Atkins said that he would find a place to secure Jacky's bike. Before he went to get cleaned up and get tuxedoed, he went into the church and found Dick Daley. Jimbo explained how Captain Atkins got him to the church on time and that he as a Lieutenant was assigned to be Jacky's escort. Daley said, "I remember. I was the one that assigned him." Then he pulled out one of his business cards, and wrote a pass for Jacky's wedding for Mr. and Mrs. Captain Atkins. Jimbo gave this pass to the Captain, then, went to take a shower.

By 12:55 pm, the whole bridal party was at their designated positions. The Maid of Honor and four Bridesmaids on one side, the Best Man and four Groomsman on the other side.

The driver opened the door of the limousine and Jacky stepped out onto the sidewalk. Paula got out holding the Tiara with the veils attached. Jacky stooped down as Paula put it on her head. All the people were quiet while Paula was adjusting Jacky's headpiece. When she stood up, they could see the beautiful snow white satin gown, with an over-lay of fine gossamer Irish lace threaded with gold. The Tiara was crocheted in white threaded with silver and gold, all handmade by Paula. Both of the veils were trimmed in Irish lace threaded with gold.

It was a sunny day so the white and gold showed up magnificently. There were cheers and sounds of appreciation for the beautiful Bride wearing a magnificent gown. As Jacky moved away from the limo, Paula unrolled the long veil. Two 7 and 8 year old boys in miniature tuxedos picked up the ends of the veil. These kids were Mario's nephews.

Jacky just stood there for a moment, looked over and waved to the crowd. A British Brigadier General in his full dress uniform and chest full of medals, General Arthur Hobson, took Jacky by the arm and they walked up the stairs and through gigantic open bronze doors.

Just then the music started. It was the giant organ with 72 stops. The music was loud and beautiful. The organist was masterful at working that big pipe organ. He was playing Mendelssohn's "Wedding March" which was written in 1842 and was first used in a wedding in 1847. It was the wedding of Dorothy Carew and Tom Daniel at St. Peters in Tiverton, UK.

General Arthur Hobson led Jacky into the church it was immense. It even looked more so with the 150 foot ceiling with rows of beautiful stained glass windows on each side of the church. The sun was shining very brightly through these windows, it seemed that some of these panels were shinning their rays directly on Jacky and her magnificent wedding gown. When they started down the aisle, all heads turned. They stared in amazement at the beautiful Bride walking slowly toward the front of the church where the Bridesmaids and the Groomsmen were standing. Also standing there was a three star Admiral in his immaculate dress whites and chest full of medals. Next to Admiral Robert (Doc) Hunter was a two star Major General, also with a chest full of medals. It was Major General Bill Turner of the RAF Reserves.

Jacky and Art walked right up to where Bill and Doc were standing. She lifted her veil and acknowledged Bill, then put it down. At this time, the priest had everyone standing. Art walked Jacky up the three steps, right in front of the altar. Her two young veil handlers sorted out the veil behind and to the side of her. Art and the veil handlers stepped down from the altar. Art stood with Kelly, the Maid of Honor.

Jacky stood in front of the altar with the sun shining down on her. It reflected off her snow white gown and gold trimmed lace. It made her look like the angel that many people thought she was. When Jacky lifted her veil, the priest motioned for the people to sit. The organ started to play the beautiful *Ave Maria*. People wondered why the bride was standing at the altar while the organist played. Jacky started to sing *Ave Maria*, gradually the volume of the organ diminished and Jacky sang louder. Then the organ was silent, Jacky was singing acappella. There was not a sound in the church other than Jacky singing. It was a beautiful rendition of an angel singing *Ave Maria*. Everyone would have liked to applaud, but not in church.

By now, the police gave up on trying to keep people out. They allowed people to stand in the rear and down the side aisles. Jacky and Bill had agreed to allow one television crew into the church. They agreed to this because so many people had requested a seat in the church. They felt that these people could at least watch it on television.

Now Jacky lowered her veil and Art came up to the altar and led Jacky down to stand by General Turner. The Priest came over and did what priests do best. He married them. They were now Mr. and Mrs. Bill Turner.

With the ceremony over, the Priest congratulated them and then said, almost in a whisper, "See you at the reception. I could use a martini!"

Bill said, "So could I!"

Jacky said, "A double for me!"

The Priest said a very loud "Amen" and they turned and walked back down the aisle and out the door. The crowd was waving and throwing rice. Bill and Jacky got into the stretch limo, then Art and Doc and finally, Jimbo and Kelly. The limo pulled out and another limo pulled into its place. The rest of the wedding party got into the second limo.

Both limos took off and dropped everyone off at the Merchandise Mart. Bill and Jacky got back into the limo. Bill told the driver to head for Lake Shore Drive and pull over in the Buckingham Fountain area. It was a beautiful sunny day. When they got there, they got out on the lake side and took a walk along the lake front to get some fresh air before they faced all the people at the reception.

After walking about ten minutes, Jacky asked Bill, "Do you feel refreshed enough to head back."

"I guess they will be wondering where we are, so I think maybe we should head back and face the music. Speaking of music, we have three bands that will be playing."

When they got to the Merchandise Mart, they could follow the sound of music right to the reception hall. It was Bob Crosby's Dixieland Band playing and the Andrews Sisters singing. As they walked through the door, the guard said loudly, "Mr. and Mrs. Turner have arrived." Jimbo led them to their place of honor. The band temporarily quit playing, the dancers sat down.

The room quieted down as Dick Daley banged on his glass. He said that he was not going to make a speech, "I just want to congratulate Mr. and Mrs. Turner.

I would like to thank them for having their celebration in Chicago. I'm also glad to see that Jacky is now a beautiful redhead again. We have celebrities from the entertainment world. There are famous people from the military field, some politicians were welcomed, some were not. The Mayor of Chicago is here."

"Also here, is the, Designer and maker of Jacky's wedding gown." There was loud applause.

We have been honored with the presence of Princess Elisabeth. "She wishes to congratulate Paula Jensen on the beautiful gown she designed and made for Jacky."

Paula and Jacky were talking when the Princess came over. The Princess congratulated Jacky on her marriage to an RAF General. She said, "Mrs. Turner, or may I call you Jacky?"

"Why not, everyone else does."

"Jacky, you have led a fantastic life. You were a hero as a commando. You are a hero in your adopted City of Chicago, the people here love you. You and your friends have captured some of the most notorious traitors that operated during the second war, who have since been hung. Then you and your friends rescued the daughter of the American Ambassador to Ireland. Heather Quinn is here at your reception with her mother today, which would not have happened if not for you and your friends. After all of that, our Scotland Yard requested your help to rescue four daughters of members of our Parliament. You saved the four daughters, then you rescued forty five other girls that were about to be sold into Asian prostitution rings. On top of that, you and your friends captured the people in the drug and prostitution ring, including the leaders. They are now all in prison thanks to you and your friends. Jacky, you are a hero in the USA, Canada, England and Ireland."

"Jacky, I am a Princess, I was born into it, but you did it yourself. I can honestly say that you are the only person I was ever jealous of, but I do have a job to do and you have given me the inspiration to do my job as well as I can. Jacky, you are one fantastic person, it's nice that you just happen to be English."

Elisabeth then said, "That's enough of the small talk. I would really like a closer look at your gown and to talk to Paula Jensen."

"I'm right here Princess."

"Call me Elisabeth, I get tired of all this royalty stuff."

"Do you have a staff of designers?"

"No, just myself."

"I heard that you made this beautiful gown in less than a month. Twenty one days from conception to finish. I also heard that there were no alterations."

"No, I knew Jacky's size."

"It must be difficult to get all your seamstresses working together so there are no mistakes to repair."

"Not really, I do it all myself."

"That is fantastic, I must attend many royal functions and I need many gowns. I have most of my gowns made in Paris by Pierre of Paris or George's Girrard of Paris. I have seen pictures of the Paris gowns that were prepared for Jacky which she rejected. I can see why. Paula, would you have the time to make some gowns for me? I will need about ten gowns for the next year. I have to get back to London on a flight out tonight. If you would be willing, I will have one of my people send you a first class ticket and when you have the time, come to the palace and take the measurements you will need. While you are there, I will have you escorted to fine entertainment and fine dining. Would you be interested?"

"Of course I would!"

The Princess then said, "I seem to have taken up much of your time, Jacky."

Jacky said, "It was an honor to speak with you, Princess." The Princess waved and walked back to her table.

Jacky turned to Paula and said, "Remember what I said about your prices. The $4,800.00 is not out of line for a gown like this. Paula, I think you have just gone high class."

"Jacky, I just can hardly believe what you have done for me."

"What are friends for?"

Guy Lombardo's Band started playing and a lot of people got up to dance. Theresa Brewer, The Andrews Sisters and Perry Como came over and talked to Jacky. They all thanked Jacky for being invited. She told them that Dick Daley was in charge of invitations, "But I'm sure glad you are here."

Theresa said, "As long as we are here, we might as well sing a song and earn our keep."

Patty Andrews said, "We have already earned our appetizers, but I think we should do some more." She said to Theresa that she heard that Jacky was going to sing again at the reception.

"Yes, the four of us, Sandra, Kelly, Patti Page and I got recruited to sing *The*

Tennessee Waltz".

Perry Como said, "He and Tony Bennett were going to sing *Because Of You*. It is because of Jacky, that we are all here, but I don't think anything would compare to the beautiful angel that sang *Ave Maria* in the cathedral!"

Dinner was now being served. You could order steak, chicken or seafood, or you could elect to go through the buffet line, featuring Southwestern BBQ Pork or Beef, Cajun Shrimp, many kinds of seafood, Italian food of all kinds, New England Oysters and Clam Chowder. No one was going to go away hungry.

After dinner, Artie Shaw played and Nat King Cole sang *Mona Lisa*. After Nat finished, he said, "There are some great singers in this crowd."

He called Patti Page up on the stage and she in turn rousted up Sandra and Kelly. Kelly said into the microphone, "This is not a proper quartet without the blushing bride in it."

Jacky went up on stage. The four of them sang *The Tennessee Waltz* and received a standing ovation. Everybody kept standing, waiting for an encore. Jacky held up her hands and it became silent.

She said, "Folks, we have something special for you, a singing politician. I would like to introduce the lady in the emerald green gown to you. This lady is the American Ambassador to Ireland and a pretty damned good singer. The lady I'm talking about is Crystall Quinn."

Crystall came up on the stage, took the mike and said, "As per previous agreement, this will be a duet."

"I guess she is right, I did agree to sing *Amazing Grace* with her." They sang a beautiful version of a great song. They sang it acappella, but they did it differently from most versions, they sang the whole song, every verse. It was beautiful and received another standing ovation.

After that, the party went like a good party should. Bob Crosby started playing again and Tony Bennett and Perry Como sang their duet of *Because of You.* After much applause, they did an encore.

Jacky went back to her table and sat down next to Bill and said, "Miss me?"

"No, not a bit. Sandra has been keeping me company. She has been telling me all about Nashville and the recording business. Sounds like Sandy's doing pretty good."

"I'm glad to hear that Sandra."

Just then, Dick Daley walked up to their table. He was leading two men. Daley said, "Jacky, these are two men out of your past, who have been looking for you for quite a few years." The taller one, who seemed to be the leader, spoke first.

He said, "First, I must congratulate you on your most beautiful wedding."

Jacky said, "Thank you very much Lieutenant, I am very glad to see that you and the Corporal were rescued from the woods."

"It was your kindness that saved our lives."

"Kindness works both ways. We thought that we could make it to our pickup point in ten minutes, it took us almost thirty because of our wounded. The flare that I asked you not to fire for fifteen minutes was not fired for forty minutes, which gave us enough time to reach our boat. You must have known that we could not make it in fifteen minutes. I'm glad to see the extra time did not cause you to bleed to death."

"It was close, but thanks to you, we survived and it looks very much like you survived also. We came to the U.S. for two reasons, one to say hello and to thank you for saving our lives. Our doctors told us that without your British Army first aid kit, we would have bled to death, so thank you again. The second reason is we wish to return your watch. We thought you would not mind that we had a jeweler in Berlin add our names to the back of the case so you would not forget us. The jeweler also added six small diamonds on the bezel." He handed her the watch. She looked at the names that were engraved.

She said, "It's beautiful." As she put it on, she had tears in her eyes and said, "Thank you Joseph and Hans, I can now feel that I did one good thing in that war."

Bill said, "Jacky, you did more than one good thing in that war, you pulled a banged up pilot out of a cracked up spitfire and he appreciates that very much." He leaned over and gave her a kiss on the cheek.

She grabbed him around the neck and said, "That's not the way to show appreciation." She kissed him hard on the mouth. Bill reciprocated and kissed her on the mouth, which showed Jacky how much he really appreciated her.

Mario was walking by and said out loud, "Hey look folks, I think the honeymoon has started."

Bill said, "Just practice, Mario."

Frankie Laine got up on the stage and said, "Hi folks, just in case one or two of you people in the crowd do not recognize me, I'm Frankie Laine. I think that I had better sing a couple of songs for you. The first one will wake you up and get your blood moving and the second song may put you back to sleep. I don't know about you, but it's past my bed time." He really did wake up the crowd with his trademark song *Mule Train*. Then he put them back to sleep with *That Lucky Old Sun*.

It was now getting kind of late. It was 2:00 am, time to go. It was a good party.

Dick Daley and his wife came over and wished the new Mr. and Mrs. Turner the best and headed for home. One after the other, all the guests did the same, until they were all gone, except the original crew. There was Doc, Art and Linda, Charlie and his wife, Mario and Kelly, Sandra, Jimbo, Peter, Arch and Eric.

"Mario said, "It looks like everybody except for two people are going to be doing a lot of sleeping tomorrow, but Monday night everyone is invited to a world famous pizza and Reuben bash at the "Home Port." After that, I guess everyone is going their separate ways. The time will be 7:00 pm. The new Turners are also invited, unless they will be off on their honeymoon."

"Not until Wednesday, Mario."

"Do you have any idea where you are going?"

Bill said, "We have a few places in mind , but we don't know exactly where we end will up, Mario, but we know how we are going. On Wednesday morning, a four engine Boeing 314 Clipper Flying Boat is going to pick us up in Monroe Harbor. We don't know who our benefactor is other than his first name is Howard. He has chartered this aircraft to fly us anywhere for a whole month. It's a flying penthouse with a fully equipped staff. We will even have a top chef aboard, an old friend of yours, Mario. Sergio has taken a month off of his executive chef job to cruise around the world with us."

Mario said, "With Sergio cooking, you ain't going to starve. See you Monday night and congratulations again." Mario grabbed Kelly and said, "Let's go home, Honey."

"I'm with you Mario." And they left.

The bands had quit and the celebrities came over and wished them well and left. Bill then said, "Jacky, what say we roust up our limousine and head for Bill and Jacky's Bike Shop . By the time we get back from our honeymoon, our new house should be ready."

"Well, Bill, that was some hell of a party and I agree that it's time to go home. I can hardly wait to get into the sack, next to my new husband."

Chapter 38

Jacky's Black Lightning

The next day, which was Sunday, Jimbo rode up to the bike shop on Jacky's Black Lightning. He had called at about noon and they invited him over for brunch. It was now 1:00 pm and everyone was hungry.

In the limo the day before, on the way to the Merchandise Mart, they had talked to the driver about food. He said that he loved ribs. Bill told him to come back about 9:00 pm and go back to the kitchen and tell them that Jacky wants you to pick up some ribs. Jimmy, the driver, said he did that and two guys carried a cooler out and put it in his trunk. The cooler was well insulated and they were still hot as hell. He said that there were about twelve big slabs of ribs and he and his wife could not eat all of them. So Jacky and Bill agreed to take half of the ribs to eat on Sunday.

When Jimbo arrived at 1:00 pm, they told him that they had six full slabs of ribs. He thought that he had found heaven. Jacky had put the ribs in the oven and they sat down to eat. Jacky ate a whole slab. Bill had called down to the bike shop and invited Benny to have some too. "I'll be right up, Boss." Bill and Benny split three slabs and Jimbo polished off two slabs by himself.

While they were eating, Benny had his guys clean up the road dirt and do a super job of polishing Jacky's bike.

Jimbo asked Benny if the guys downstairs would be through polishing Jacky's bike? Jimbo said, "Let's go down and take a look at the bike. I made a few minor changes."

When they saw the bike, they were amazed at the looks of this powerful machine. Jimbo said that he had the Duralumin fenders and anything else that was bright aluminum, all anodized black. Then he had these parts painted gloss black and baked. The bike was now really black. It was a "Black Lightning".

Jacky said, "It's beautiful, Jimbo."

"I have one more thing to show you." He pointed to the gas tank, on each side in gold it said, "Jacky Sax" and on top of the tank it said, "Jacky's Lightning".

Jacky said, "I'm going to take this beast for a ride." She started it up and it startled everyone. Jimbo had replaced the stock muffler with a hardened brass megaphone.

"It sounds beautiful, Jimbo, but I don't think the cops will like it."

Benny opened the front rollup door and she rolled out onto the street. It was Sunday, so the street was pretty empty. She turned it on and was up to 90 mph in nothing flat. She shut it down to 35 mph. A red flashing light came up behind her. Jacky pulled over and put the center stand down and leaned against the seat. A cop got out of the passenger seat and came over to Jacky. He pulled out his ticket book and said, "Buddy, this is going to cost you, excessive noise and excessive speed. You must have been doing 70 mph."

"No, 90." And she pulled off her helmet. He gulped when he saw this beautiful redhead looking at him.

"Sorry, Miss, but I've got to give you a ticket, my Sergeant is with me." He looked to his side and his Sergeant was standing there. The Sergeant said, "Put your book away, Officer, you were ready to give a ticket to Jacky Sax."

The officer said, "Sorry, Miss."

The Sergeant then asked, "If this was the bike that Lieutenant Atkins escorted to the Cathedral yesterday? They said that the State Police just plain couldn't catch him. No wonder, "Bob, take a look at that speedometer, 250 mph."

Jacky said, "That's kilometers. She only does 150."

"Never seen a bike like this before."

"You will be seeing more of them, we will be selling them at "Bill and Jacky's Bike's" a mile down this street."

The officers said, "Nice meeting you." And they left. Jacky headed back to the bike shop. She pulled up to the door and it opened. Jacky ran the bike into the shop. Bill, Jimbo and Benny were still standing there. Bill said, "Well, Doll face, how did you get out of that one?"

"No problem, Bill. Jimbo got me out of that one. He had my name painted on the tank and after they saw that, the cops were very nice."

Benny said, "I don't think there is a cop in Chicago who would give Jacky a ticket."

"I think you are right, Benny. She can do no wrong in Chicago," said Bill.

Bill and Jacky took Jimbo to the airport for his flight back to Hannibal. They stopped at Berghoff's Restaurant on the way. When they got there, the valet service took Bill's car. Just as they walked in, Jimbo asked if they had been there before. She started to answer when the headwaiter walked up and said, "Good evening, Miss Sax. Excuse me, I mean Mrs. Turner. We have a nice table all ready for you."

"But, your man at the door said that there would be a 30 minute wait."

"Not for the Sweetheart of Chicago, your table is ready."

Jimbo said, "Believe it or not, you are just as popular in Hannibal." They had a good dinner, dropped Jimbo off at Midway Airport and headed back home.

They did what any newlywed couple would do and then relaxed watching a TV show.

The next morning which was Monday, Bill called Eric and asked him to get ahold of Arch. "No problem, Bill, Arch is right here. He is staying at our house."

"I would like to have you both come over to the bike shop this morning."

"What time?"

"How about 10:00 am?"

"I'll borrow my dad's truck."

"Be ready at 9:30 and I'll ask Jacky to pick you up."

"Why? I can drive over."

"But you want to be able to ride your bikes back."

"Have you got them all finished and ready to ride?"

"They are finished and you will hardly recognize them."

"Why? Did you repaint them?"

"They have been repainted. Just wait until you see them."

Jacky took Bill's Lincoln and went to pick up Eric and Arch.

When they got to the bike shop, Eric said, "Wow, this place sure has changed and I like the new sign."

Arch looked around and saw all the neat bikes on the original side. Then Jacky took them over and showed them the English and Italian bikes.

Benny was just completing a deal with a customer on a brand new Triumph Trophy. Bill walked in and said, "Come to the workshop and I'll show you your bikes."

As they walked through the shop, they saw six bikes mounted up on work stands. Eric poked Arch and said, "Isn't that your 1947 Indian?"

"Yeah, I think so and there is your 1946 Harley. I thought you said they were finished, Bill."

"They are, but you are looking at the wrong bikes." Bill led them to another room where there was about six custom bikes. Bill pointed to two bikes that were set apart. One was a beautiful 1950 Indian "80" Chief, painted a metallic gold. The other bike was a 1950 Harley Hydra-glide. It was a bright candy apple red. Both bikes had large sets of saddlebags and each had almost legal megaphone exhausts. "There are your bikes, Guys."

"They are beautiful," Eric said to Bill, "But what happened to our old bikes?"

Benny said that your bikes had too many mechanical problems. "I took these two 1950 models in trade. Benny's mechanics went through these 1950 bikes. They are like new. We had them painted like your old bikes."

Arch said, "They are beautiful, but how much do we owe you?"

"Nothing, Guys. It's Jacky's gift to you for all your help."

Eric said that he could hardly wait to ride. They rolled the bikes to the front door, got on and rode down the street. They rode side by side, then cracked on the throttles. They were up to 60 mph in nothing flat as they went by the squad car parked on the side street. They were the same two cops that stopped Jacky.

Bob, the driver started to pull out. The Sergeant said, "No way, Bob, these two guys are part of Jacky's crew. I was talking to Benny the other day and he showed me these two bikes. If we book these two guys, the Chief will hang us out to dry." So Arch and Eric just kept on riding. It was a nice day for a ride.

Chapter 39

Party at the Home Port

At 7:00 pm, the whole crew showed up at the Home Port Restaurant. Mario had explained that they were normally closed on Sundays and Mondays. Doc was back in Washington, Crystall Quinn and her daughter went back home, but Dick Daley and his wife were there. Dick did not want to miss Kelly's Reubens. Sandra was there, this would be her last dinner with the crew for a while as she was heading back down to Nashville to make records. Art and Linda were heading back to Beaver Island with Charlie. Eric and Arch parked their new bikes on the sidewalk, right in front of Mario's picture window. Everyone looked out to admire the bikes.

Jacky and Bill showed up, they all congratulated them again on their marriage. Kelly asked them where they were going on their honeymoon. Bill and Jacky both agreed that they did not know exactly where they were going to end up, but they did have a few places in mind. Bill said, "Wednesday morning, a four engine Boeing 314 Flying Boat is going to land outside of Monroe Harbor and taxi in. This plane has been chartered by someone unknown to us. The only thing we know is that his first name is Howard. It has been chartered for a whole month. It has been converted from a 74 passenger flying boat to a Luxury Flying Yacht. Mario's friend, Sergio, will be our Chef. We will also have maids and stewardesses, a First Class private yacht will be ours for a month!"

"Our First stop will be to Beaver Island to see Art and Linda. Next we will go to Washington. We will land on the Potomac and go to see Doc. Next, we will go to Bermuda to get a little sun."

"Have you got reservations at hotels?" asked Kelly.

"We don't need a reservation. The plane is a flying and floating hotel, but if we decide to stay at a resort or hotel, the pilot will radio ahead. From Bermuda we will go to Lisbon, Spain and from there to London to see some of our old friends. After that we go to Monte Carlo. I have been told that we have a $50,000.00 credit line in the Casino."

Mario said, "You can't pass that up."

Kelly asked Sandra when she was going back to Nashville. She said her flight was at 1:00 pm tomorrow. Kelly then said, "Maybe we can get the group together to see you off. I'm going to miss you all."

Mario said, "Chow, let's eat." They did just that after Mario brought out four beautiful pizzas. He cut them up and put them on the buffet table. Next, Kelly came out with two trays full of Reubens.

After Mrs. Daley had eaten a slice of pizza and was eating a Reuben sandwich, she said, "Dick, this sure beats going to a canasta party. None of my canasta friends can cook anything worth eating. Do you think that we might have our next canasta party here?"

"Maybe, but you will have to ask Mario, also there is no menu. You take what the house cooks and it's strictly by reservation. With food this good, it's nice to have someone knowledgeable make the choice. I think Mario and Kelly will be glad to have you, but you have to call, he will tell you what's cooking."

It was now about 11:45 pm and Arch and Eric got up and thanked Mario and Kelly for a great meal. "It's almost midnight and it's time for us to get moving on down to Phoenix . Good times are waiting for us in Arizona."

Peter said, "Are you sure about that?"

Arch said, "I'm sure, Pete, we got the gals waiting for us. Why don't you come with us? You will have a ball."

"I don't have a bike."

"No problem, Bill and I will get you one tomorrow. We will wait for you."

"I don't know how to ride a bike."

"We will teach you on the way down to Arizona."

"Thanks, but no way, Guys. I told my girlfriend that I would be home tomorrow."

"Okay, Pete, have fun in Kansas City."

"You guys have fun in Phoenix too."

"We will."

Chapter 40

Concert at Midway Airport

They got on their bikes, fired them up and the sound of the four megaphones was beautiful music to anyone that liked to hear a well-tuned engine. They both cranked up the RPMs, engaged the clutch and they peeled off down the street. They turned west on Route 290, went south on Route 294 and were on their way to Phoenix.

Everybody went back inside. Mario said, "There go two guys off to the big party. I think we should toast those two guys." He came up with a bottle of Cognac. "I did not want to do it while they were here because I knew they were going to ride tonight." They toasted Eric and Arch.

Peter said, "I don't think I'll drink tonight either, I am going to drive to Kansas City." He said goodbye and they all reciprocated. Peter got into his new Ford convertible and headed for Kansas City.

Mario poured Cognac for seven people. They now toasted Peter. "Mario, we have no one else to toast."

At this time, Sandra was feeling pretty good, she said, "How about a toast for me?" They did.

"Well, there are seven of us left, do we all agree to see Sandra off at 1:00 pm tomorrow?" They all agreed. Bill said, "If we all meet here at 11:00 am in the morning, I will get Jimmy, the limousine driver, to bring his stretch limousine to haul us to Midway."

Jimmy was at the Home Port Restaurant at 10:45 am the next day. Everybody showed up by 10:50, they climbed aboard and got an early start.

They arrived at Midway and were in the boarding area by 11:45. Sandra already had her ticket, so she was all set to go.

They sat down for a short while when Kelly stood up and said, "We may not see each other for quite a while, what say we sing a little song as a trio."

Jacky, Kelly and Sandra stood up with the runway as a back drop and the three of them started singing *The Tennessee Waltz.* Sandra's ticket and boarding pass said Gate 6, but people wandered over from gates 5 and 7. They just intended to sing one song, but with all the applause, they just couldn't quit. Stewardesses who were on their way to another plane, stopped to listen. By now the whole boarding and gate area was packed with people.

It was now fifteen minutes to boarding time. The Pilot and Co-Pilot worked their way through the crowd. They asked if the people there were on flight 714 to Nashville. Most of them said they were. The Pilot said that 714 was their flight. It was now twenty minutes past boarding time and the gals just kept singing requests.

The Pilot said, "We can't go anyplace without passengers."

A couple of the people said, "And we can't go anyplace without Pilots." It was now forty minutes late and the airport manager showed up.

He was steaming hot when he went over to the Pilots and started complaining and making a lot of noise. Some of the people told him that if he couldn't be quiet, then he should get out of the area. He started to tell them that he was the airport manager when Jacky started to sing *Ave Maria.* He shut up and listened to Jacky sing. He then walked away from the crowd.

He pulled his walkie-talkie out of its holster and called the Tower. He said, "Flight 714 has been unavoidably detained for one and a half to two hours." He went back to listen to the singing.

The people didn't seem to care about boarding as long as the Pilots stayed. The Pilot didn't care as long as the manager stayed and the manager knew that they could not take off without passengers. It ended up being a two hour delay and none of the passengers complained. One of the passengers just happened to be a Chicago Tribune columnist. There was an article in the Tribune the next day. In big letters it said "JACKY'S CREW HOLDS UP AIRLINER", then it went on to explain what happened. None of the people who were supposedly in charge were admonished for their actions.

Chapter 41

Jacky and Bill Off in the Big Clipper

Everyone had agreed that it would have been a sin to stop those three beautiful girls from singing and even worse to stop Jacky from singing *Ave Maria*.

Sandy went to Nashville and everyone else went home. The next morning at 7:00 am, Jimmy picked up Bill and Jacky at the bike shop. Benny was there to say goodbye. Bill said, "See you in a month, Benny." They were off, they arrived at the Chicago Yacht Club at 7:45 am. They looked out over the harbor and there it was, that giant Boeing Flying Clipper. It looked beautiful out there with the launch circling the plane, probably to keep curious people from tying up and climbing on the Sponsons (wing like floats on each side of the hull). It was a beautiful sight and shortly they would be taking off, spending a month on that plane.

They decided they had better go into the club if they wanted breakfast. When Bill and Jacky come into the dining room, everyone got up and applauded. Jacky and Bill were wondering why. At that time, Richard J. Daley came over and handed Jacky the morning Tribune. She burst out laughing after reading the article. Bill read it and laughed. Jacky said, "We had better get on that plane before something else happens."

The Captain introduced himself as Tom Walsh, the Copilot was Bob Hansen and the most important man aboard, Sergio. "Mario said that we won't starve," said Bill to Sergio.

Sergio said, "You are right there!" He then asked if Mario still remembered how to cook.

Bill said, "Yeah, he still remembers and now he and his future wife have their own restaurant. It's high class and by reservation only. Mario asked me to give you this." It was an ivory colored card with raised gold letters. It said, "The Home Port"- Mario and Kelly, Proprietors – One Free Pass For Chef Sergio And Friends."

The Captain then introduced the two stewardesses, a maid and a maintenance mechanic. Bill asked, "Why a mechanic?" Tom said, "We don't want to rely on local people. We have four big 1600 horsepower, R2600 14 cylinder engines. We don't want anyone but experts touching those engines."

Bill said, "Sounds like good thinking."

Captain said, "Maybe we should get under way so that you will have a nice afternoon up in Beaver Island. I'm told that your friend, Art, does a hell of a fish boil."

"Who told you that?"

"He did."

"You talked to him?"

"I did, just before we got on the plane. I called him because I like to know the weather and wave conditions. Landings in heavy wave conditions are rough on the hull, so I like to know. Art told me that it's pretty flat this morning, so it's best to get there this morning."

Bill said, "Then let's go."

Bill and Jacky thanked Daley for coming to see them off. Dick said, "It was a pleasure to be here and that he didn't see the Clipper come in, but he really wants to see it take off."

The launch came back in to pick them up. All nine of them got into the launch and they headed to the plane.

The future Mayor Richard J. Daley stood on the dock waving goodbye and wishing them luck. They entered the side door of the plane. Daley watched as one after the other of the four big 1600 horsepower engines started. Then a door opened in the bow and the mechanic disconnected the anchor pennant and anchor.

The Pilot let her drift free of the can and then pushed all four throttles forward. There were no boats coming in or out of the mouth of the harbor. The big bird just skipped across the water like a flat stone. It finally broke free and climbed out. It was a beautiful sight. Daley said to himself, "This will be a fantastic trip and it couldn't happen to nicer people."